"This story is as sweet and spunky as the title. Melody is gifted at creating characters and settings right out of a Hallmark movie. Enter this charming world and you'll find yourself believing in fresh starts right along with Dillon."

Robin Jones Gunn, bestselling author of *Becoming Us*

Praise for *Courting Mr. Emerson*

"Carlson illustrates how love can come at any age in her heartfelt latest."

Publishers Weekly

"Carlson has created a refreshing inspirational romance focusing on mature characters who don't have every aspect of their lives figured out."

Booklist

"Clean, light, and full of second chances."

Foreword Reviews

Books by Melody Carlson

Courting Mr. Emerson

The Happy Camper

Follow Your Heart Series

Once Upon a Summertime

All Summer Long

Under a Summer Sky

Holiday Novellas

Christmas at Harrington's

The Christmas Shoppe

The Joy of Christmas

The Treasure of Christmas

The Christmas Pony

A Simple Christmas Wish

The Christmas Cat

The Christmas Joy Ride

The Christmas Angel Project

The Christmas Blessing

A Christmas by the Sea

Christmas in Winter Hill

The Happy Camper

MELODY CARLSON

Revell

a division of Baker Publishing Group
Grand Rapids, Michigan

© 2020 by Carlson Management, Inc.

Published by Revell
a division of Baker Publishing Group
PO Box 6287, Grand Rapids, MI 49516-6287
www.revellbooks.com

Printed in the United States of America

Library of Congress Cataloging-in-Publication Data
Names: Carlson, Melody, author.
Title: The happy camper / Melody Carlson.
Description: Grand Rapids, Michigan : Revell, a division of Baker Publishing Group, [2020]
Identifiers: LCCN 2019027434 | ISBN 9780800737238 (paperback)
Subjects: GSAFD: Love stories.
Classification: LCC PS3553.A73257 H37 2020 | DDC 813/.54—dc23
LC record available at https://lccn.loc.gov/2019027434

ISBN 978-0-8007-3786-3 (casebound)

20 21 22 23 24 25 26   7 6 5 4 3 2 1

CHAPTER
1

*D*illon Michaels was fed up—but it wasn't with dinner. In fact, she was ravenous. And Brandon was late. Again. Dillon hadn't eaten since breakfast, but her appetite wasn't simply a desire for food. Despite the tantalizing aroma of mussels and garlic from her favorite house special, *cozze in padella*, Dillon realized she longed for something more . . . something intangible.

"Will your date be here soon?" the waiter asked—for the third time.

"I hope so." Dillon forced a smile while she reached for her phone. As the waiter refilled her water glass, Dillon grimaced to see the time. "I'll text him again," she muttered. Too embarrassed to look up, she shot Brandon her fifth message.

WHERE R U?

But what she really wanted to say was, *Why are you ALWAYS late?*

Of course, that raised another question: *Why do I always put up with it?* She set her phone down, trying to relax as she sipped her water. She was well aware that Brandon was a pro at concocting plausible excuses. But why did she automatically accept them? Why didn't she believe she deserved better than this? Dillon glanced around the restaurant's crowded patio. Other couples and families visited congenially, enjoying this unexpectedly warm evening in Colorado Springs. And seated among cheery flower boxes and merry strings of lights at De-Marco's was the perfect place to celebrate the start of summer. Such a happy scene . . . but Dillon's frustration was quickly turning to fury, bubbling straight to the surface.

She'd had enough. Snatching up her things, she stood and laid a small tip on the table, signaling the waiter that she was leaving. And seeing relief in his eyes, she ducked her head and hurried out of the popular Italian restaurant. She was nearly to the parking lot when she heard Brandon call her name. With her cheeks still warm from embarrassment, she turned to face him.

"Where are you going?" He frowned. "I thought you made the reservation for—"

"I made the reservation for 6:45," she shot back. "It is now 7:35 and I am going home—thank you very much."

"But what about our table, Dillon?" He gave her his feel-sorry-for-me look. "What about dinner? What about me?"

"What about you?" She glared back at him, bracing herself for a showdown. "I've had it, Brandon. I'm done waiting on you and—"

"But I couldn't help it. I was—"

"Save your breath, Brandon. You know this happens *all the time*. Do you have any idea what it feels like to be the one waiting and waiting and waiting? Why is it that you are *never* on time? *Never!*"

"I'm really sorry, Dillon. But I was tied up with a client and we had to get the deal wrapped up before the weekend and it—"

"Yes, that's what I thought you'd say." She took a deep calming breath. "And I'm sorry for sounding so angry right now. But I just can't do this anymore—"

"Do what?" he demanded.

"*This.*" She wildly waved her arms as if that explained everything. "I'm done, Brandon. I'm not going to keep waiting for you. I'm moving on. I'm finished with you."

"Oh, Dillon." His tone turned placating. "You're hungry and tired. It's been a long, hard week at work and you just need a nice evening of—"

"No!" She held her palms toward him. "I'm finished, Brandon. I mean it. Don't try to talk me out of—"

"Fine," he snapped. "If that's how you want it. *Fine!*" He turned, and she could tell by the way he clomped the heels of his good calfskin loafers, he was vexed. But she really didn't care. She'd meant what she said. She was done with him— finito!

But as she got into her car, she felt a mix of conflicting emotions. On one hand and to her surprise, she was relieved— how incredibly freeing to put an end to a two-year relationship that appeared to be destined for nowhere. On the other hand, she felt a shaky sense of uneasiness. What had she just done? What if she woke up tomorrow morning and regretted this? What if she had to eat her words? To beg his forgiveness . . .

As she drove home, Dillon had no doubts that multitudes of women would consider Brandon a great catch. And maybe he was—if anyone could actually catch him. Good luck! Sure, he was good-looking, had a decent job, was responsible, owned his condo unit, drove a nice car, and even went to church. But Mr. Perfect was afraid of commitment. How many times had he told her that very thing—acting as if she were the key to unlock that door? But she didn't want to wait ten years for it!

Dillon would turn thirty-four this summer. And although she'd never confess it, she could hear her biological clock ticking faster and faster each year. She knew this was a by-product of being an only child with a single mom. Since girlhood, Dillon had dreamed of becoming a wife and mother . . . someday. But someday just got farther and farther away. And even if she couldn't admit her outdated fantasy out loud, she couldn't deny it either. Not to herself.

As Dillon parked in her apartment complex lot, she couldn't help but notice how many spaces were vacant tonight. Tenants were probably relishing the beginning of a summery weekend. Maybe her roommates would be out too. Dillon hoped so. Right now she just wanted to be alone—a pity party of one. As she headed for the apartment, she realized Brandon had been right about a couple things. She was worn out from a long, hard week—and she was hungry too. Microwaved lasagna wasn't the same as mussels and pesto pasta, but it would do in a pinch. Fortunately, she'd stocked up on Lean Cuisine a few days ago.

Dillon heard music as she unlocked the apartment door. That probably meant that Reba was home tonight. Hopefully her boyfriend wasn't here too. Dillon never knew what to expect from her roommates. They were best friends and she was always the odd one out. It was a good setup a few years ago when she'd gotten a job with the software company. Cheap rent and close to work. But she'd never planned to stay this long.

"You're home." Reba sounded disappointed. "I thought you were on your standard Friday night date with Brandon Kranze."

"I thought so too." Dillon dumped her bags into a chair then quickly explained about the impromptu breakup.

"You're kidding!" Reba's eyes grew wide. "I thought you guys were about to get engaged."

Dillon shrugged. "I guess I thought so too . . . or I used to. But I gave myself a serious reality check tonight. Brandon has no interest in marriage."

Reba's brows arched. "Well, I'm hoping that Jarrod does." She pointed to the clock on the stove. "And he'll be here in a few minutes. He's bringing pizza and we planned to watch a movie."

"Oh . . . nice." Dillon opened the freezer part of the fridge. "I'll just nuke some dinner and lay low in my room." She poked around, looking for her frozen meals, but only saw a half-empty carton of licorice ice cream, a crusty bag of mixed vegetables, and a frost-covered guinea hen that had been there since Christmas. "Hey, what happened to my Lean Cuisine meals?" she asked Reba.

"Val started her swimsuit diet this week." Reba chuckled. "She probably ate them."

Dillon removed the ice cream and firmly shut the freezer door. "Figures!" Grabbing a spoon, she took the carton to her room and changed into her "comfort jammies" before pulling her auburn hair back into a ponytail. Then, even though she disliked licorice, she plopped down on her bed and proceeded to consume every last drop of the gooey, sweet, charcoal-colored ice cream. As she plunked the soggy container into her wastebasket, she caught a shocking glimpse of herself in the closet door mirror. Her licorice-blackened lips and grayed teeth looked strangely stark against her pale skin, which hadn't seen sunshine due to long work hours. And with her hair pulled tightly back, her dark blue eyes looked even larger than usual—resulting in an image that could easily land her a zombie role in a horror flick. *Attractive.* Hearing Reba and Jarrod out in the living room, Dillon didn't want to frighten them by going to the hall bath to brush her teeth and wash her face, so she simply crawled into bed and turned out the light. Feeling pathetic and hopeless and lonely, she cried herself to sleep.

The sound of her phone's jingle dragged her back into consciousness. Assuming it was the wee hours of the morning, she felt a jolt of concern as she grabbed up her phone—was it Brandon? Was he sorry? But seeing Margot's name on caller ID, Dillon braced herself for bad news. The last time her mother had called late at night was to inform her that Grandma had passed away.

"Who died?" Dillon demanded without even saying hello.

"No one died, silly Dilly." Margot's tone was light. "Why would you even say such a thing?"

"Well, it's the middle of the night and—"

"Middle of the night? Good grief, it's not even nine o'clock yet."

"Oh? Well, uh, I thought it was, uh, later." Dillon turned on her bedside light.

"Don't tell me you were already in bed. What are you—like, eighty?"

"Funny." Dillon didn't hide her irritation. "So why are you calling me? What's up, Margot?" She'd called her mother *Margot* for as long as she could remember. She couldn't even imagine calling her *Mother*. That would be just plain weird.

"Maybe I simply want to hear my little girl's voice."

"Right . . ." Dillon rolled her eyes. Margot rarely called for any reason—certainly not to hear Dillon's voice. "How's Grandpa doing?"

"As a matter of fact, that's partly why I'm calling."

Dillon sat up in bed, concerned. "Is he okay?"

"Well, I don't know—"

"What's wrong?"

"Nothing's wrong exactly, Dilly. But I think he misses your grandma."

"I'm sure he does. It's only been about eight months. But I'd hoped he was getting over it."

"I'm not so sure . . . I think he's depressed and I'm worried about his health. His diet is atrocious, he's letting the farm go and staying in bed too long."

"That doesn't sound like him."

"Well, he is getting old. Do you realize he'll be seventy-seven soon?"

"I know—I already got a birthday card for him. But he's always been so active and energetic and young for his age. I can't imagine him sleeping in when the sun is up."

13

"You haven't seen him lately, Dilly. Don't forget, you didn't even come home for Christmas."

"That's because I'd taken that time off for Grandma's funeral in the fall. And I couldn't get more time for Christmas—"

"I know, I know. I also know you're a hopeless workaholic, Dillon. I just don't understand how it happened, though. I certainly didn't raise you that way."

"That's for sure." Dillon was assaulted by an unwanted flashback from her childhood—a sad snapshot of herself and Margot living on child support, food stamps, and government handouts. It wasn't until Dillon moved to her grandparents' farm as a teen that she eventually quit worrying about her next meal.

"Well, there are things more important than work, Dilly. Like having a life. Do you ever think about *that*?"

"Yeah . . . right." Dillon wanted an excuse to end this conversation.

"So how are things with Brandon? Any wedding bells yet?" Margot's voice tinkled with sarcasm.

"For your information, we broke up." Dillon instantly regretted disclosing her personal news.

"Broke up? But I thought he was your Mr. Right."

"More like Mr. Not-Right-Now."

"Well, I'm sorry to hear that, Dilly."

Unwilling to continue down this path, Dillon inquired about her mother's boyfriend. "Are you and Don still together?"

"Just getting ready to celebrate seven years."

"Congratulations. And I can probably assume you're not hearing any wedding bells either." Dillon knew that Margot and Don had no intention of marrying—ever. Just one more irritating element of her mother's nontraditional lifestyle.

"Don and I don't need a piece of paper to prove our love for each other, Dilly. You know that."

Dillon rolled her eyes again, but she'd asked for it, so why cringe over Margot's worn-out answer? "Back to Grandpa—do you really think he's depressed? Should he see a professional or something?"

"You mean like a shrink?" Margot laughed. "Can you imagine your stubborn grandfather talking to a shrink? Or taking antidepressants?"

"No . . . not really. But I hate hearing that he's unhappy. I wish I could come out there to see him. Maybe for his birthday." Even as she said this, Dillon knew it was unlikely. It wasn't that she couldn't afford the airfare, but after recent layoffs and cutbacks, getting a few days off work was a major challenge.

"Oh, that'd be sweet, Dilly. He'd love to see you. He was just saying how much he misses you."

"Tell him I miss him too. Give him my love." Dillon felt close to tears again. So much for thinking she'd been cried out.

"I'll be sure to tell him. And I hope you're not feeling too miserable over Brandon. I never wanted to say anything, but based on what you've told me, he sounded too good to be true. I'm glad you found it out before it was too late."

Even though Margot was partially right, Dillon wasn't ready to hear those words just yet—especially from a woman who had never committed to a marital relationship. So Dillon told her goodbye and shut off the light. Lying there in the darkness with only the muffled noise of an action movie for company, she longed for an escape. But what exactly did she hope to escape? After all, she'd already jumped ship from a two-year relationship with Brandon. Shouldn't that be enough for one day?

But she still longed for something more. Or maybe it was for something less. She wasn't quite sure. Maybe she simply wanted to escape from herself and her dreary little life for a while. Thankfully it was the weekend, but even the thought of some time off brought no comfort. As she lay there, listening to the thumpity-thump of the film's explosives in the living room, she realized she was stiff as a board, clenching her fists, and probably would be grinding her teeth before long. Her dentist had warned her this was problematic and had recommended a bite guard for sleeping. Although she promised to think about it, she'd also started to practice calming exercises before bedtime.

But deep breathing and happy thoughts were not working tonight. So she turned to prayer, begging God for some serious help. It was the first time in a long time that she'd asked God to direct her path—but that's exactly what she said. Because Dillon had no idea where her life was headed—for all she knew it was about to go over a cliff. Admittedly, it wasn't much of a prayer, but it was heartfelt, and when Dillon whispered amen, she felt slightly more at ease. Like Scarlett O'Hara said, tomorrow was another day.

CHAPTER
2

*O*nce again, Dillon woke to the sound of her phone jingling. But judging by the light sneaking beneath the blinds, at least it was morning. She reached for her phone, thinking it might be Brandon calling to apologize, but seeing it was her boss, she ignored it. Of course, she knew this would only result in more calls, usually about three minutes apart until Dillon finally answered. LeeAnn was relentless.

On the second call, Dillon answered. "Hey, LeeAnn." She said in a flat tone. "What's up?"

"I need you to work today."

"It's *Saturday*." Dillon knew this excuse never worked with LeeAnn, but it was worth a try.

"I know it's Saturday, Dillon." Her voice dripped of exasperation. "It's Saturday for me too and I'm already here at work."

Dillon wanted to point out that LeeAnn was paid more than

Dillon, and that she got paid double-time for weekend work. "I'm exhausted, LeeAnn, and I need a—"

"Who isn't exhausted? But if I have to work, you do too. I expect you here by—"

"What if I can't come in today?" Dillon held her breath, knowing she'd just shoved her big toe over the proverbial line.

"Are you dying?"

"No, but I—"

"Then you get in here or else."

"Or else what?" She felt another toe sliding across the line.

"Or else, get yourself to the unemployment office."

"Seriously?" Dillon jumped out of bed. "You'd fire me for not working on a Saturday? Seriously?"

"You bet I would. And I'd have every right to dismiss you . . ." LeeAnn's tone softened. "But I know you won't put me in that position, Dillon. You're always such a trooper. I can always count on you. Besides, I just sent out for breakfast bagels and lattes."

Although the thought of food was tempting, Dillon decided to stand her ground. "I'm sorry, LeeAnn, but I cannot come in today. You'll just have to get by without—"

"Then consider yourself unemployed, Ms. Michaels. I'll send a memo about this to Reggie."

"Honestly?" Dillon didn't believe it. "You'd do that after all I've done for—"

"You can clear out your cubicle on Monday." Her tone was firm.

Too stunned to respond, Dillon simply hung up and began pacing back and forth in her tiny bedroom. Within twenty-four hours she had lost her boyfriend and her job? How was that even possible? As she paced, two things became very clear. She was ravenous . . . and homesick.

By one o'clock, after a hearty brunch at a nearby café, Dillon had carelessly crammed all her belongings into her small car, surprised that they actually fit. Then, standing in the apartment parking lot, she handed her apartment keys over to her stunned roommates who'd just pulled up.

"Are you leaving because of the Lean Cuisine incident last night?" Reba poked Val in her padded midsection. "Told you she was mad at you."

"I'm really sorry," Val said. "It's just that I started that dumb diet, and I got so hungry, well, I totally meant to replace your food."

"It's okay." Dillon sighed.

"Was it because our movie was too loud last night?" Reba asked.

"It's because I'm going home to Oregon," Dillon admitted.

"Because of your breakup?" Reba sounded sympathetic.

"No, not really. It's a combination of things. I think my grandfather needs me right now." Dillon jotted down his address on the back of a now-defunct business card. "I just need to go home . . . it's been too long."

"But what about your job?" Val's eyes grew wide. She worked at the same company. "What about your boss—the Dragon Lady? She'll fire you for sure if you're not there on Monday."

"That ship has sailed." Dillon forced a sheepish smile. "Lee-Ann fired me this morning, for not working today."

"Oh wow, but maybe it's for the best." Val patted her shoulder. "It could've gotten awkward with Brandon still working there—remember how it went down with Cassie and Tom after they broke up? What a mess."

"Yeah, I hadn't really considered that." Dillon handed Val the business card. "This is to forward my mail. And would you mind boxing up my personal stuff at my workstation and sending it on?" She reached for her wallet. "I'll give you postage to—"

"I'll mail it, but you keep your money. I owe you for the Lean Cuisines."

The three of them hugged and, feeling surprised that her roommates looked genuinely sad to see her go, Dillon got into her jam-packed car, waved goodbye, and drove away. As she headed westward on the interstate, she felt strangely free. Almost like a bird that had just been released from its cage. It was a gorgeous day with clear blue skies and a beautiful landscape. Perfect for driving. What could be better? She put on a mix of her favorite songs and even sang along.

But as the day wore on and the flat Wyoming landscape made her sleepy, she began to feel worried. What on earth was she doing out here like this? It was one thing to give up on Brandon . . . but her job as well? Had she lost her mind? Throughout high school and college, Dillon had always worked hard. Some had labeled her an "overachiever," which she felt was a compliment. She'd taken the first decent-paying job offered after graduation, relocated to the Colorado Springs software company, and continued with her hard work ethic. For more than a decade, she'd lived frugally, whittling away her college loans, which she'd paid off last year. She'd always been careful and responsible and reliable—something Margot had never understood or even appreciated.

Dillon had never done anything that could've been considered spontaneous or impetuous or risky. Even the Subaru she was driving right now, her first and only car, had been carefully researched for gas mileage, safety, and dependability. But today she was taking a long trip in it, and she hadn't even checked to see if her oil needed changing. Had she gone completely mad?

Suddenly Dillon remembered last night's prayer . . . how she'd asked God to direct her path. And here she was on the outskirts of Wyoming, heading for Silverdale, Oregon. Was this really the path she was supposed to take? If so, why? Nothing made much sense right now. Well, except for the fact that she was not going to make it to Salt Lake before sundown. And she was hungry. But she'd made no plans on where to stop for the night.

Up ahead was an old-fashioned-looking camp trailer. One of those cutie-pies that someone must've lovingly restored. It was white and Pepto-Bismol pink, shaped like a teardrop—and adorable. As she passed the trailer, she tried not to stare at the driver in the white pickup that was pulling it, but she felt curious. What kind of people did that sort of thing? To her surprise, there was another vintage trailer up ahead. This one was white and turquoise and even cuter than the one she'd just passed. Was it a coincidence, or were they friends traveling together? She wasn't sure, but noticing an exit sign for Evanston, she decided it was time to find food and lodging.

To her surprise, the trailer in front of her exited too, and as she followed it off the freeway, she realized she was now between the two trailers. As if mesmerized or hypnotized, she continued to follow the turquoise trailer until she realized she'd just entered the Stay Awhile Trailer Park and was now stuck on a one-way lane with the pink-and-white trailer behind her. Embarrassed, she had no choice but to continue on, driving up to the gate of the trailer park.

"Can I help you?" a middle-aged woman asked pleasantly.

"I, uh, made a wrong turn," Dillon said quickly. "I was, uh, looking for food and lodging and I—"

"We have food and lodging." The woman smiled.

"But I don't have a trailer." Dillon gestured behind her.

"You don't need a trailer to stay here." The woman explained that most of the park was for campers with trailers. "But the trailers in that section over there"—she pointed to where a row of cute trailers were situated—"are nightly rentals."

"Really?" Dillon blinked in surprise. "You mean I can stay overnight in one—you have a vacancy?"

"You're in luck. I just had a cancellation." The woman introduced herself as Susan and told Dillon where to park her car. "After I take care of these folks, I'll meet you in the office."

Before long, Susan registered Dillon as a guest, handed her a map of the park, and gave her the key to the *Lemon Drop* trailer. "It's the one closest to us." She pointed it out. "And our restaurant is in that Airstream down on the end. They close at nine. Enjoy your stay."

Dillon felt a childlike excitement as she entered the tiny abode. It reminded her of a child's playhouse. Everything was small and sweet—and yellow and white—from the checked curtains in the tiny kitchenette to the quilted bedspread on the full-sized bed in back. Perfectly charming!

Dillon decided to take a quick stroll through the trailer park since she wanted to get a peek at the other campsites before it got too dark. Then she stopped at the restaurant trailer, which had a few small tables inside and outdoor dining as well. She ordered from the limited menu and, sitting outside in the dusky light, consumed the most delicious blue cheese buffalo burger ever.

By the time she was tucked into the surprisingly comfortable sunny yellow bed, she felt almost completely happy . . . and before she drifted off to sleep, she said a little prayer, gratefully thanking God for directing her path today.

○ ○ ○

With more than ten hours of driving ahead of her, Dillon got up with the sun the next morning. Her hope was to reach Grandpa's farm before dinnertime. She had purposely not called—in the hopes of giving Grandpa a pleasant surprise. But she didn't want to arrive after he'd gone to bed and scare him to death.

It was a long drive, but after her good night's rest, she felt refreshed. And the scenery through Utah, Idaho, and into Oregon was beautiful. But with dark clouds ahead, she could tell she was heading for bad weather, and about an hour from Silverdale, in the middle of nowhere, it began to pour. Fortunately, there weren't many cars on the road, but to her dismay, after half an hour of vigorous swiping, her windshield wiper blades appeared to be disintegrating—right before her eyes.

By the time she reached Silverdale, it was still pouring and she could barely see the car in front of her. But if her memory was correct, the old hardware store was on this end of town. Hopefully it was still open. When she found the hardware store, now called Atwood's Feed and Seed and Hardware, she could see the OPEN sign still on. Parking in front, she made a fast dash through the rain, reaching the door just as the sign turned off. But when she tried the door, it was still unlocked. "Hello?" she called out hopefully.

"Sorry, ma'am, we're closed," the man briskly told her. "I'm just locking up."

"But I really need some windshield wiper blades." Dillon remained inside the door, ready to plead her case.

He pointed to the clock over the door. "Sorry, but we close at six on Sundays. We open tomorrow at—"

"But I can barely see out my windshield—and it's raining cats and dogs out there. I'm desperate."

His expression softened. "Okay, what kind of blades do you need? Our automotive section is kind of limited."

"I, uh, I don't know. Are there different kinds?"

"What kind of car do you drive?" His tone sounded impatient.

She quickly told him the make and the year, and he disappeared for a couple of minutes. When he returned, he had a package in hand. "I think these will work—at least for now. But you should replace them with the ones specifically recommended for your vehicle. We have an auto parts store in town, but they're closed now."

"Thanks, I'll do that." As he rang up the purchase, she realized this guy was rather nice looking. She took in his hazel eyes and wavy brown hair, and as he ran her debit card, she noticed his name tag read *Jordan*. "I really appreciate your help. I've been driving all day, but the last hour—in all that rain—well, it was torturous." She paused to sign the receipt. "I don't have far to drive, but it's a narrow gravel farm road. And I'd rather not drive into the ditch."

He handed her the receipt with a crooked smile. "So . . . do you know how to install new blades?"

"Not really . . . Is it difficult?"

"It can be tricky. If you want to wait a minute, I'll lock up and give you a hand."

"That'd be great. Thanks." He walked her to the door, locking it after she went outside. She stood under the awning, trying to avoid the rain still pouring down in sheets. One by one, the lights in the store went out until it was dark inside. Wishing she'd put on a jacket, which was probably buried in the back of her car, she continued to wait. Then, wondering if Jordan had forgotten her, she decided to open the box of blades. Perhaps she was on her own now. How hard could it be to put on wiper blades? She was just giving up on ever getting the plastic box open when Jordan came around the side of the building.

"Sorry to take so long." He shook the rain from his head. "The security system can be finicky." He produced a large pocketknife. "Let me get that box open for you."

"It might need the jaws of life."

He chuckled as he slit it open. "Packaging is a pain." He dropped the waste into a nearby trash barrel, then nodded to her Subaru. "That your car?"

"Yep." She followed him out into the pouring rain, noticing that he, like her, didn't have on a coat. "Can I help?" She reached out to hold the new blades while he proceeded to use his pocketknife tool to remove the old blades.

"You're right, these are shot." He handed them to her.

"Colorado had a long, hard winter."

"That where you're coming from?" He already had one blade installed and moved to the passenger side.

25

"Yes. Colorado Springs."

He handed her the second worn-out blade and she threw them both into the trash barrel, taking a moment to stand under the awning, even though she was already soaked. Jordan fiddled a bit with the blades, then joined her under the awning. "Well, hopefully that will keep you from driving into the ditch."

"I don't have far to go. My grandpa's farm is about six miles out of town."

"Well, drive safely."

"Thanks. And I'm sorry you had to get so wet." She looked up at him. "Can I pay you for your time?"

He held up his hands. "Nope. That was my good deed for the day." He pushed the trash barrel closer to the building so the rain couldn't go into it, then smiled at her. "Now, you be safe out there, ma'am."

She returned the smile. "The name's Dillon."

"Dillon?" He nodded with a thoughtful look. "Interesting."

"It's Celtic. A boy's name, really. It has something to do with the sea."

"Well, it's nice to meet you, Dillon." He stuck out his hand. "I'm Jordan."

The warmth of his hand soaked into hers, and perhaps she held on a bit too long. Then, her face flushed with embarrassment, she hurriedly thanked him once more and dashed through the pouring rain to her car. As she slowly drove through town, relieved to be able to see out of her windshield, she wondered about this Jordan fellow. Was he simply an attractive former Boy Scout employed by the local hardware store? Or was there more to him than met the eye?

CHAPTER

3

*D*illon felt a rush of excitement as she drove down the familiar farm road. And, as if to reassure her, the rain began to let up and the sun peeked out from behind a bank of clouds in the western sky. Then, just as the farm buildings came into sight, a rainbow began to appear, suspended over Grandpa's white clapboard farmhouse like a sweet promise of better things ahead. It was so pretty that Dillon was tempted to stop and snap a photo on her phone, but shivering from the damp and cold, she couldn't wait to get inside the house.

As she parked in front, she considered her tactic—should she knock on the door or slip inside and surprise him? Either way might startle him since he didn't usually get many visitors out here. As she went up the porch steps she decided to simply let herself in and quietly call out. She paused in the living room, taking in the old plaid sofa, Grandma's gold velveteen rocker, and Grandpa's worn brown recliner. Nothing much had changed since she'd lived here during high school. But the dust-covered end tables, old newspapers, stained coffee mugs, and clutter spread about was a stark reminder that Grandma was gone. The room looked depressed. Grandpa probably was too. Dillon hadn't come a moment too soon. She couldn't wait to hug him.

"Grandpa?" Dillon said. "Are you home?" Hearing noise in the kitchen, she imagined him in there. Probably still wearing his dirty overalls and a plaid flannel shirt . . . maybe heating up some canned soup. "Hello?" she called out as she pushed open the swinging door.

"Dillon!" Margot dropped a frying pan with a loud clang. "What on earth?"

Dillon tried to hide her disappointment. "Hi, Margot," she said with a fixed smile. "Is everything okay? Is Grandpa here?"

"Grandpa's just coming in." She nodded to the back door, just opening. "Does he know you're coming?" she whispered.

"No, I wanted to surprise him." Dillon waited as Grandpa came into the kitchen, hanging his barn coat and John Deere cap by the door without spotting her.

"Hello, Grandpa," Dillon said cheerfully.

He turned to face her, breaking into a wide grin. "Well, if it's not my favorite granddaughter." He spread his arms and she ran into them.

"Yes, look what the cat dragged in," Margot said.

"You're a sight for sore eyes." Grandpa held Dillon at arm's length, looking her over carefully. "Still my pretty girl."

"Looks like a drowned rat to me." Margot tweaked a soggy strand of Dillon's hair.

"Thanks a lot." Dillon wrinkled her nose at Margot.

"But Margot's right. You're all wet, Dillon." He rubbed his bristled chin. "What happened?"

She explained about her windshield wipers and Grandpa encouraged her to go put on dry clothes. "Don't need you getting sick on us." He patted her cheek. "And then we'll have supper and catch up on everything."

Dillon grabbed a bag from her car and hurried back into the house, heading straight up the stairs for her old bedroom. But when she opened the door, it looked as if someone else was staying here. Clothes were spread on the bed and over the chair with various personal items littered over the bureau. Had Grandpa taken in a roommate? Perhaps a live-in housekeeper?

Feeling disgruntled over losing her old bedroom, she went to the spare room that her grandmother had used for sewing and crafts. But it was packed even more than she recalled, with barely room to stand. Finally, she decided to just change clothes in the bathroom. As she towel-dried her shoulder-length hair, which had gone from wavy to frizzy, she wondered about the items in her old room. What was going on here? Did Grandpa have a girlfriend? No, Margot would've mentioned this.

Feeling warmer and dryer, she hurried downstairs to find Margot still in the kitchen. "Where's Grandpa?" Dillon asked.

"He went to clean up for dinner. He even said he was going to shave."

"Good for him." Dillon watched with concern as Margot

attempted to peel an onion with an oversized knife. Hopefully she wouldn't need stitches tonight. "So . . . are you really cooking dinner?"

"What's that supposed to mean?" Margot held up the knife with a furrowed brow.

"Well, I didn't think you knew how to cook." Dillon attempted a weak smile.

"That just shows how much you don't know, silly Dilly."

"Uh-huh . . . Do you want some help?"

"Yes." Margot handed her the onion. "Chop this for me. It'll just make me cry, anyway."

Dillon cut the onion in half. "It looks like someone's been staying in my room. Has Grandpa taken in a—"

"That would be me." Margot filled a large pan with water.

"You're staying here—at the house?"

"That's right."

"You mean for just tonight?"

"I've been here since Friday."

"But I talked to you on Friday. You never mentioned—"

"Yeah . . ." She put the pan on the stove with a clunk.

"So did you come to help with Grandpa . . . because you were worried?"

"That's part of it." She turned on the gas stove.

"Well, since I'm here, I can help with him. You won't have to stay any longer now." Feeling relieved, she started to dice the onion.

"Thanks, but I'm not going anywhere." Margot put her hands on her hips, glaring at Dillon with defiance.

"Huh?" Dillon paused from chopping. "But what about Don? Won't he miss—"

"Don is history." Margot tore open a box of pasta.

"What do you mean? I thought you were just celebrating seven—"

"I thought so too." Margot pointed at Dillon. "But thanks to *you*, we're not."

"What?" Dillon frowned. "Thanks to *me*?"

"Yeah. After I talked to you on Friday night, I told Don about your breakup with Mr. Right. I was worried that you might be taking it hard. I told Don about how you'd always wanted to get married and how marriage was such a big deal to you. White lace and promises and all that. So then Don got all gooey and mushy, and he said it was a big deal to him too." She rolled her eyes. "So, yeah, thanks to you, Don proposed on Friday." She shook the pasta box at Dillon. "Can you believe it?"

"Why don't you marry him, Margot?"

"Because I don't believe in all that till-death-do-we-part nonsense. And Don knows it. I think he proposed just to make me mad. Anyway, we got into a huge fight and I walked out the same night. Dad was a little surprised to see me, but I think he's glad for the company. And that I can be of help. And I'm sorry, but I've taken your old room. It's the only other room with a bed."

Dillon felt sick. "So you plan to live here . . . *indefinitely*?"

"Well, I can't say indefinitely. Who knows? But I'm here now. And yesterday morning when I was walking around the property, I got my big idea."

"Big idea."

"Yeah, and because of that, I definitely plan to be here all summer."

"Huh?"

"I ordered a bunch of lavender plants yesterday."

"What?"

"Yeah. Dad gave me permission to start a lavender farm in the south field. He didn't have any plans for it anyway. And the rest of the property is leased out."

"*You* are going to farm lavender?" Dillon felt incredulous. Margot had always hated hard work of any kind. She probably wouldn't last two days as a farmer.

"Yes. I'll grow lavender. Then I'll use it to make soap and oil and candles and all sorts of delicious lavender things. I ordered ten dozen plants. They'll be here by the end of the week."

"You are going to plant a *hundred and twenty* plants?" Dillon couldn't keep the disbelief out of her voice.

"Still good at math." Margot dumped the pasta into the still-cold water, then turned to Dillon. "And that's just for starters. I'll probably order more varieties in the fall. The nursery guy was telling me all about it."

"Wow . . . that's, uh, interesting." Dillon checked the pasta clumped together in the now-lukewarm water, then grabbed the pasta spoon from the utensil pot.

"Now, tell me, Dilly, what exactly are you doing here?"

"I'm stirring the pasta before it glues itself together." She started to pick it apart. "Since you didn't let the water boil."

"Still telling me what to do?" Margot's tone was sharp. "But that's not what I meant. What are you doing here? You know Dad's birthday isn't until July, and you didn't even let us know you were coming. What's up?"

"I think we should focus on dinner." She pointed to a jar of canned tomatoes. "Do you plan to make marinara sauce?"

"Dad requested spaghetti like Mom used to make." Margot struggled to open the jar. "He claims all the preserves are still good. But Mom put them up before she died."

Dillon sniffed the jar. "Smells good to me." She felt a wave of sadness, missing Grandma . . . thinking how hard she'd work to can the produce from her big garden.

"Well, Dad's bent on meat sauce, but I told him it's not good for him. So I got some ground free-range turkey breast. I doubt he'll notice."

"Don't be so sure." Dillon returned to chopping the onion. "He likes his beef. And I'll guess he's got a freezer full of it."

"Maybe so, but he's been eating all the wrong things. It's no wonder he's been feeling low. I plan to get him into healthier eating habits."

"Uh-huh." Dillon didn't even want to think about that.

"Anyway, quit beating about the bush, Dilly. What are you doing here? And why didn't you call?"

"I wanted to surprise Grandpa." Dillon felt her eyes fill with tears but wasn't sure if it was the onion or thinking of Grandma or something else. "I, uh, sort of quit my job. Then I packed up all my stuff and I just . . . well, I wanted to come home." She sniffed, then reached for a paper towel to wipe her wet cheeks.

"Oh, Dilly-Dilly." Margot came over to hug her. "Are you crying?"

Dillon blew her nose. "It's the onions."

"Oh." Margot handed her a garlic clove. "Can you chop this too?"

"Sure." Dillon focused on this task, using the side of her knife to smash the clove like Grandma had taught her, then peeling it.

"Well, I suppose you can bunk with me, but it might be crowded. It's the smallest room in the house." Margot didn't sound pleased with this idea. And Dillon felt like throwing something. Maybe the knife.

"Or else you could move into Grandma's craft room," Dillon suggested. "It's bigger anyway. Then I could have my old room back."

"Are you kidding? That sewing room looks like a scene from *Hoarders*. It'd take me all summer to clear it all out. And then where would I put that junk? The attic is already full. Besides that, I'm going to be busy with my lavender farm."

"Right . . ."

"Maybe you could turn Dad's den into your bedroom," Margot suggested.

"No thanks. Grandpa loves that room. I'm not taking it from him." Dillon pursed her lips as she minced the garlic. None of this was turning out how she'd hoped. "I'll just sleep on the sofa tonight," she finally said.

"Good idea." Margot set the cast-iron frying pan on the stove with a frown. "Hey, maybe you'd like to take it from here, Dilly? Your grandma used to brag about what a good cook you were."

"Only because she taught me everything I know. But I haven't done much cooking of late." Dillon knew exactly what was happening. Margot would start something . . . and Dillon would finish it. That was how it always used to go. Back when she was a girl Margot would say, "Let's clean the house," and then Margot would disappear and Dillon would be stuck with the actual cleaning. Or it'd be, "Let's make a vegetable garden," and Dillon would be the only one outside digging in the dirt.

"Well, if you handle this, I can set the table in the dining room. And I'll make it look pretty. Don't you think Grandpa would like that for a change?"

"Yes . . . I'm sure he would." Dillon forced a smile. "I'll take it from here."

"I'm sure you know your way around this kitchen better than I do anyway."

"Probably." Dillon was actually relieved to have the kitchen to herself. She hadn't wanted to tell Margot, but she'd been doing it all wrong. Grandma always started the marinara sauce *before* the pasta. Hopefully, she could rescue the spaghetti that was about to boil. As far as rescuing her plan to live here on the farm and help her grandfather . . . that felt hopeless.

CHAPTER

4

illon was pleasantly surprised to see that Margot had actually put some energy and creativity into setting the dinner table. Not only had she put out a small bouquet of flowers, which must've come from Grandma's garden, she'd lit some candles too.

"The table looks pretty," she told Margot after Grandpa said the blessing.

"Thank you." Margot smiled. "I thought we should celebrate this reunion."

"This looks good." Grandpa forked into his pasta, which Dillon had plated in the kitchen—just like Grandma used to do.

"We used Grandma's recipe," Margot said a bit smugly.

Dillon considered mentioning the turkey substitution, but she didn't want to spoil it for Grandpa. Instead, she told him about losing her job and breaking up with Brandon. She just wanted to get it out of the way and move on. "It all happened pretty fast," she admitted. "I decided it was a good excuse to come home. But maybe I should've thought it through better. Taken more time to figure things out. I guess it's too late now."

"Well, you've always been a planner, that's for sure, but can't say I'm disappointed—since it brought you back home." He grinned. "And you know you're welcome to stay here as long as you like." He turned to Margot. "You both are. Here I'd been feeling lonely and sorry for myself—and suddenly my house is full. I guess it's true what they say: when it rains it pours."

"I hope we don't overwhelm you." Dillon poured dressing over the green salad she'd hastily thrown together while the sauce had simmered.

"Not at all." He held up a fork of spaghetti. "And I must say your cooking skills have improved, Margot. This is a little different than what your mother used to make, but it's not half bad."

"Well, thank you, Dad. Dilly helped a little."

Dillon grimaced, but said nothing to claim the credit. Besides, the ground turkey was Margot's idea. Dillon still felt beef would've been better. Maybe she'd let Margot cook the next meal unassisted. See how that turned out.

After Dillon brought him a second helping, Grandpa patted her hand with a sympathetic smile. "You've been awfully quiet. I hope you're not feeling bad about that boy. If you ask me, he was a fool to let you go."

"Thanks." She forced a smile as she sat down. "To be honest, I haven't really given him much thought tonight."

"That's good. Sounds like he wasn't the right one anyway. And it pays to get the right one, Dilly. Marie was my proof of that." He sighed.

"I know." Dillon forced a smile. "Your marriage to Grandma was an inspiration."

"Well, I could be wrong, but I think Dilly was more in love with the idea of marriage than she was in love with her groom-to-be." Margot winked at Grandpa as she reached for the salt. "Otherwise you wouldn't have broken up with him, Dilly. I think you missed a bullet."

As much as Dillon hated to agree with Margot on this, she suspected it was probably true. Even so, it felt insensitive. But why be surprised by that?

"Give yourself time," Grandpa told Dillon. "You'll get over it." And now, in typical Grandpa style, he began to go over the upcoming weather forecast. "We really needed that rain, but it's supposed to be sunny throughout the week. My tractor's running good again. I think I'll start tilling the south field first thing in the morning." He turned to Dillon. "Did you hear your mom wants to grow lavender?"

"She mentioned that." Dillon frowned. "Sounds like hard work."

"Yep." He nodded. "But hard work's like medicine. Good for what ails you."

"Well, maybe I can help out in the house," Dillon offered. "Looks like you could use a good housekeeper."

"I'm sure you're right about that." He slowly shook his head. "I've let things go . . . since Marie passed on."

"Well, with the three of us working together, I'm sure we can get this place back into great shape in no time." Margot held up her water glass for a toast. "Here's to us being the Three Musketeers—able to conquer whatever comes our way."

Dillon lifted her glass, but her heart wasn't into the toast.

Perhaps the best plan would be for her to start doing an online job search tomorrow, and move on and out as quickly as possible. Leave Margot and Grandpa to lavender farming . . . and housekeeping . . . without her.

Grandpa excused himself to bed early, which wasn't so unusual, and Margot, claiming she needed to read up on lavender plants, made herself scarce as well. But Dillon didn't mind being left with the cleanup. She was glad to be alone in Grandma's kitchen. Losing her grandmother so suddenly last fall—hearing the news of the brain aneurism after it was too late—Dillon had felt robbed. With no warning, she'd never had the chance to say her goodbye. But being in Grandma's kitchen helped some. It was almost like being with her.

While cooking dinner, Dillon had observed what must've been six month's accumulation of grease and grime—understandable since Grandpa wasn't accustomed to being a bachelor, but something Grandma never would've tolerated. It felt good to scrub things down now. Unlike her previous job, it was rewarding to see the fruit of her labors right in front of her. And by the time she finished, the kitchen was gleaming and orderly. But it was past eleven and she was worn out and ready for bed . . . and hopefully ready for that sofa.

○ ○ ○

By morning, Dillon's back ached from a restless night on the saggy sofa. After a few stretches, she heard noises from the kitchen and, knowing Grandpa had always been an early riser, she suspected it was him.

"I'm making us oatmeal," he said when she joined him. "Not as good as bacon and eggs. I put them on my shopping list—as well as some other food that never made it home. Stuff that Margot claims isn't good for me."

"Oh, that's too bad. I like bacon and eggs too. But if Margot doesn't get up too early, maybe we can sneak some tomorrow."

"Sounds good to me." He winked. "I'm almost sorry I gave Marie's laying hens to the neighbor last winter. But I kept forgetting to feed them. Now I sort of miss those eggs."

"Maybe you should get some more chickens."

He nodded. "I'll be thinking on that."

"In the meantime, I'll make a store run later today," she told him.

"Margot's really into this health-food nonsense. Tried to get me to drink some awful green stuff for lunch yesterday." He made a face. "I poured it down the sink when she wasn't looking."

"She's worried you aren't eating right."

"Well, drinking green slime doesn't sound like eating right to me."

Dillon laughed. "I agree."

"Anyway, oatmeal's quick and easy." He paused to stir it. "And I wanted to get out there and get my tractor running while the soil is still damp from yesterday's rain. It'll dry up fast on this warm day."

"Well, oatmeal sounds just fine to me." She got out bowls and spoons and a few other things, setting them on the old maple kitchen table.

He dished hearty portions of oatmeal into their bowls, and she followed his lead in dousing hers with milk and dollops of butter and brown sugar. "Margot wouldn't approve of this." He chuckled. "But we won't worry about that."

"Looks like the coffee's done." Dillon got up to pour them each a mug. She added two spoonfuls of sugar into Grandpa's like she'd always done before she sat back down, bowing her head as he said his usual blessing.

"Good oatmeal," she said after taking a bite. "I've gotten used to the instant microwave kind, but it's not nearly this good."

"I added cinnamon just like Marie used to do."

"Well, it's perfect." She smiled. "Grandma would be proud."

He nodded. "So what do you really think of your mom's plan to grow lavender?"

"Sounds like an enterprising challenge." Dillon was starting to look forward to Margot out there digging in the dirt.

"Don't know that she's cut out to be a clod-buster."

"Like you said, hard work is good medicine."

He chuckled. "Well, I suppose I can always hire some young fellers from town to take over if it proves too much for her."

"I wouldn't be in too big of a hurry to do that." She sipped her coffee.

"Don't worry. I'm not." He grinned.

"Besides housecleaning, I was thinking about Grandma's garden. Does it need any work? I'm a good weeder."

He nodded. "I started to do some weeding a few weeks back, but it just made me miss her more. I knew she'd have had it all cleaned up and partly planted by now. Peas and beans would be sprouting. She'd be moving plants from the greenhouse. I hope they're not all dead by now. I don't even go in there." He sighed. "The garden and greenhouse . . . well, they were like her sanctuary."

"I know. But it's sad to just let them go. How about if I spend some time out there? I could try to bring some order to it. I used to help her out there sometimes."

"I think your grandma would like that." His eyes lit up. "You know, Marie always kept her garden diary in the greenhouse. She listed exactly when to plant what and then she'd record how various plants did when she planted them a bit early or late."

"Yes, I remember that."

"And she stored a lot of leftover seeds in the freezer chest. Kept 'em in a big zipper baggie. I saw them the other day. I'm sure they're still good . . . in case you feel like planting."

"You wouldn't mind?"

"Not at all. I'm sure it would make your grandma happy too."

"Great." She picked up their now-empty bowls. "Looks like we both have our work cut out for us today."

"And I'm ready to get to it too." He smiled. "I'm sure glad you came home, Dillon. It's been lonely."

She nodded. "I know."

After Grandpa left, Dillon did a quick cleanup in the kitchen. She was about to dump the last of the coffee when Margot came in. "There's still coffee if you want." Dillon pointed to the carafe.

"You can toss that poison. I drink ginger tea and lemon water for breakfast."

"Oh . . . okay." Dillon poured the coffee into the sink, carefully rinsing the dark brown streaks from the recently scrubbed white enamel. She rinsed the carafe, then forced a smile for Margot. "Then I'll leave you to it." She picked up the bucket of cleaning things she'd gathered to use in the rest of the house. "I've got work to do."

"Uh-huh." Margot walked like a zombie over to the fridge. Naturally, she was oblivious to how much cleaner the kitchen was. Big surprise.

Eager to escape her mother, Dillon hurried out to the living room and, after a thorough de-cluttering, started in on "deep cleaning," as her grandma called it. Grandma had taught Dillon the "proper way" to do these chores twenty years ago. During the school year, Grandma managed on her own. But in the summertime, when school was out and Grandma's time was devoted to her garden, it became Dillon's job to manage the housekeeping. She well remembered the routine—almost as if Grandma were talking to her now.

First, open the windows and give the curtains a good shake. Next, haul all the throw rugs out to the front porch and vigorously shake them *away* from the house, then drape them over the railing for some sunshine. Grandma called sunshine "God's free cleaning service." After that, sweep the hard floors and vacuum the carpet.

Since she'd also spent a night on the dusty sofa, Dillon decided to vacuum the upholstered furniture and lampshades too. Next she dusted the wood furnishings, followed by a good rubdown with lemon oil. Finally, she ran a damp mop over the hard floor surfaces and returned the throw rugs to their places. Despite the worn furnishings, the room looked much happier now.

Dillon performed similar services in the downstairs bath room and the master bedroom, which needed a thorough airing and cleaning. The gray, grungy sheets looked like they hadn't been changed in months . . . maybe not since Grandma had done it. Dillon was tempted to throw them away, but instead she decided to run them and some equally filthy towels through the washer with bleach. If nothing else, they'd make good rags.

It was almost one o'clock as she loaded the washing machine, and it looked like Grandpa was coming in for lunch. "I put some ground beef in the fridge yesterday," he told her. "I know Margot didn't use it in the spaghetti sauce last night, but I thought you and me might like burgers for lunch. What d'ya think?"

"Cheeseburgers?"

He smacked his lips and nodded.

She pointed to his dirty hands and shirt. "Why don't you go clean up? Put your feet up while I fix us some lunch."

"Don't worry about your mom. I just noticed her car leaving."

She grinned. "Good timing too."

Something about being in this kitchen, systematically fixing food for Grandpa, was so comforting. Like really good therapy. As Dillon served up their lunch, she could hardly believe that she'd felt hopeless and broken up only a few days ago. It felt like a month had passed since then.

As they sat down to lunch together, Grandpa talked about how he'd given his old tractor a tune-up yesterday. "And she's running like a top today. I'll have the south field all tilled up by tomorrow."

"Is Margot going to use that whole field for lavender?"

"No. It's far too big for that." His blue eyes twinkled. "I got some plans of my own."

"Really? What?"

"Pumpkins. It's a little late, but if I get 'em in soon, they should be ready in time. I just called Atwood's and asked them to order me a bag of seeds. Supposed to be here in a week or less."

"Growing pumpkins? Now that's different. What about Paulson's Pumpkin Patch? Won't they resent the competition?"

"George Paulson leased all his land for hay last year. No more pumpkin patch. I remember how disappointed Marie was to hear about it . . . so concerned the school kids wouldn't have anyplace to get their pumpkins for Halloween. Of course, she passed away in early October . . . so she never found out she was right. Everyone in town was upset."

"So you'll have a pumpkin patch." Dillon smiled to imagine this. "And will you invite school kids out here before Halloween?"

"I hope so."

"That's a great plan. And if Margot's lavender is a success, it should all look pretty. Pumpkins and lavender. I hope I'm still around to see it in the fall."

His brow creased. "Well, sure you'll be around, Dillon. You said you'd come home. You're not going to take off again, are you?"

She forced a smile as she began to clear the table. "Well, it's hard to say. But I guess time will tell." She didn't want to admit to him that sleeping in the living room was already getting old. And even though it was barely two in the afternoon, she was starting to dread that old sofa again. But another more careful check on Grandma's sewing room had been too overwhelming to even think about. Besides being packed full, she could tell that many of the things in there couldn't be simply given away or disposed of. There were boxes of old photos and mementoes from family and all sorts of things. Margot had been right about one thing. It would take more than a month to sort through it. Dillon's best hope of getting her old room back was that Margot would tire of digging in the dirt and go back to Don. Not that it appeared to be happening anytime soon.

CHAPTER

5

For the next couple of days, most of Dillon's time was spent in Grandma's garden and greenhouse. Although it was clearly neglected—no one had cleaned it last fall and weeds had started to grow this spring—it wasn't quite as hopeless as Grandpa had painted it. Thanks to good vents and a drip watering system in the greenhouse, a lot of the sturdier perennial plants were still alive but in need of TLC. And some hardy plants, like kale, were already coming up as volunteers in the garden beds.

Still, it was a challenging project. Probably not as challenging as what Margot had taken on. And it gave Dillon a good excuse not to help her.

"Hello there." Grandpa opened the gate and looked around. "Well, Dillon, I'm impressed. You've made good progress."

She stood up straight, rubbing her back. "Thanks." She

looked over the garden, which looked remarkably better. "I didn't realize I liked gardening so much."

"Must be in your blood." He pointed to his watch. "It's past six."

"And I'll bet you're hungry." Seeing another unweeded section, she was almost reluctant to stop but knew it was quitting time.

"I used to work late this time of year—when the sun stays up so late—but I'm worn out." He patted her shoulder. "You probably are too."

"And I never made it into town." She frowned. "I was going to get bacon and eggs."

"Don't worry about that now. But if we don't get into the kitchen, Margot might start concocting some sort of health food. I don't know about you, but I'm not eating grass and beans tonight."

"Let's beat her to it." Dillon dropped her spade and hurried out behind him, securely closing the gate since she knew deer could wreak havoc in a garden.

"I got a couple of thick sirloin steaks out of the freezer last night," he said in a hushed tone as they walked to the house, almost as if they were planning some kind of heist. "They're in the bottom of the fridge right now, in the meat drawer and out of sight."

"Hiding them from Margot in case she wanted to throw them out?"

His eyes flashed. "She wouldn't dare."

Dillon wasn't so sure, but just the same she hurried to the kitchen and set to work getting dinner ready. Although she knew Margot wouldn't touch red meat, she did make extra salad. And hopefully Margot had no reason to ban Grandma's home-canned green beans and peaches.

"Look at you," Margot said as she entered the kitchen through the back door. "Making dinner again." She sniffed. "But what's that I smell?"

"Grandpa and I are having steak." She checked the broiler to see they were almost done. "There's leftover spaghetti if you want to warm it up."

"You're letting him eat red meat?" Margot scowled. "If he rolls over from a heart attack, you'll only have yourself to blame."

Dillon considered this. "Grandpa's a grown man, Margot. He has a right to make his own choices. And he's the one who wanted steak tonight."

"Humph." Margot turned toward the sink and washed her hands.

"How's the lavender project coming?" Dillon asked lightly.

"Well, I thought I got all the sprinkler parts I needed yesterday, but it seems I missed some pieces." She dried her hands. "It's aggravating to have to make another trip to town."

"Maybe I can get them for you to—"

"Oh, would you? Can you get them this evening?"

"I was about to say tomorrow." She turned off the broiler, leaving the door open.

"But I need the parts first thing tomorrow. I'd be so grateful, Dillon. I'm exhausted."

"I'm worn out too." Dillon used the mitt to pull out the broiler pan.

"I'll clean the kitchen for you." Margot's brows lifted. "You can leave right after dinner. The hardware store is open late in the summertime. But only until eight."

As Dillon loaded two plates with steaks and green beans, she remembered the man who'd helped her with windshield wipers last weekend. Would he be at the hardware store? "Okay." She nodded. "I guess I can go for you." Now she called for Grandpa. "We're eating in here tonight," she told Margot. "Less work than using the dining room."

"That's fine with me." Margot busied herself at the sink.

"Something smells mighty tasty." Grandpa rubbed his hands as he came in—then stopped. "What on earth?" he demanded.

"Dinnertime?" Dillon pointed at the table with confusion. "Sirloin steaks, just like you—"

"Not you." He pointed beyond her with a horrified look. "Your mother." He marched over and grabbed Margot's free arm. "What in heaven's name are you doing?"

Margot held up a colander full of peaches. "Just washing the peaches."

"Grandma's canned peaches?" Dillon frowned.

"I'm getting the sugar off." Margot shook the colander. "Do you have any idea how much sugar Mom used to make—"

"I do not care how much sugar she put into it!" Grandpa declared. "Those are *my* peaches and that is *my* sugar and you are not allowed to wash it off!"

"But sugar is like cocaine, Dad, it'll kill you."

"And what a way to go," he growled. "You can eat those washed-off peaches, Margot, but from now on you keep your hands off your mother's preserves." He turned to Dillon. "Please, go fetch us a fresh jar, Dilly."

She just nodded, trying not to chuckle as she hurried to the pantry. Dinner was quiet and somewhat awkward, but Grandpa eventually calmed down. He appreciated his steak—

and his peaches as well. When they finished, Dillon reminded Margot of her agreement to clean the kitchen, then excused herself. If she was going to the hardware store—and possibly crossing paths with that Jordan fellow—she didn't want to look like a grungy old farmhand. And she didn't want to get there just minutes before closing either.

Before long, she was crossing the threshold to enter Atwood's. With Margot's list in hand, Dillon attempted to locate the right section, taking her time in the hopes that Jordan might appear. Instead, it was a young man who knew as much about irrigation systems as Dillon. "I better get Mr. Atwood," he told her.

"The owner?" She hid her disappointment, wondering if it would be weird to request Jordan's help. "I hate to bother him."

"It's okay. He really likes helping customers."

She nodded, immediately deciding to tell the owner how helpful Jordan had been with her wiper blades, how he'd gone the extra mile. Maybe they would make him employee of the month or give him a raise.

"Can I help you, ma'am?"

She turned to see Jordan behind her. "Oh, it's you." She smiled brightly. "I thought your boss was coming to help."

His brow creased slightly, but then he grinned. "Nope, just me. So what are you looking for?"

She handed him Margot's list. "Sprinkler parts."

He took a moment to study it. "Hmm . . . that's a lot of sprinkler heads. What's this for?"

"One hundred twenty lavender plants."

"Wow. That's a big garden." He led her down the row, pointing to a bin. "Hopefully, we have enough." He bent down and gathered them up, counting as he went. "Well, you're in luck." He loaded them into the small shopping basket she'd looped over her arm. "But if you want the other things on that list, we should get you a cart."

As he walked her to the front of the store, he inquired about the lavender project, but before she had a chance to answer, he was distracted by another customer. Instead of waiting, she put the sprinkler heads in the cart and rolled it back to the irrigation aisle, attempting to prove she wasn't a helpless female by locating the next item on the list. She thought she had almost figured it out when Jordan came back.

"Sorry to take so long." He looked at her cart. "Looks like you're finding your items, but . . ."

"But?"

"Well, my mom's quite a gardener. In fact she's president of the garden club. And she grows lavender. Not 120 plants, but she's got a fair amount of it. Anyway, I just gave her a quick call to ask about watering. And she recommends a drip system laid over landscaping fabric."

"A drip system?" Dillon tried to appear smarter than she felt. "And why does she recommend that?"

"She said in the long run, it's better for the plants plus it conserves water. She said you could install sprinkler irrigation—and for sure the lavender plants will require a lot of water in the first year. Especially since we live in such an arid climate. But after the plants are established, a drip system would be preferable. Besides saving you water, it's less expensive too."

"Oh?"

"But it's your call."

"I guess that's what I should do." Dillon pulled out her phone. "Call."

"While you do that, I'll help another customer load something. Let me know what you decide."

She nodded, and after Margot answered the phone she quickly explained what she'd just been told. Margot let out a long sigh. "But the website I read says to use a sprinkler system."

"Well, the guy helping me says his mom is an expert gardener."

"And she uses a drip line?"

"Yes. And he said it'd be cheaper plus conserve water." She thought Margot should appreciate that. "He mentioned our arid climate, Margot. Is it possible you researched lavender grown on the west side of the mountains? I'm guessing they do things differently over there since it's so much wetter."

"You're right. I've been researching a farm I visited last summer and it's on the western side. Rats! Okay, Dilly, see if my parts can be returned and get the pieces for the system he's talking about. And don't forget to put it on the farm account."

Dillon glanced at her watch. "But it's almost closing, Margot. I doubt they can get it figured out that quickly."

"They have to, Dilly. The irrigation has to be installed before the plants come."

Dillon wanted to point out that "haste makes waste," but remembered who she was talking to. How many other half-hatched plans had Margot leaped into? "Okay, I'll do my best," she told her. "But I'm not a miracle worker."

Margot thanked her, and as Dillon was putting the sprinkler parts back in their bins, Jordan returned. "Change your mind?" he asked.

53

"What you said makes sense." As she replaced the last piece, she asked about their exchange policy.

"No problem." He smiled.

"Well, there's still a problem. We need the system installed ASAP because 120 plants will be here on Friday."

"And you're doing this work yourself?" He ran his fingers through his wavy hair. "Wow, that's cutting it close."

"I know." She pointed to her watch. "And I realize it's almost closing time."

He nodded. "Well, how about I help you with this? You have a calculator on your phone?"

"Sure." She got it out, and suddenly he was giving her figures. As she calculated, he made notes on his phone until he finally told her they were done. "These are sort of ballpark figures," he explained. "I don't know how many rows you'll plant or about any corners you'll need to turn. But I'll put enough together so that you'll have more than you need. And you can just return the unused parts when you're done. Along with the sprinkler system parts."

"You're a lifesaver."

"I assume no one's going to be working on your irrigation system tonight, so how about if we deliver the pieces to you first thing in the morning—will that work?"

"That would be fabulous." She told him Grandpa's address and he put it into his phone.

"The Michaelses' farm?" he asked. "Does that mean you're related to Alex?"

"He's my grandfather."

Jordan smiled. "Well, he's a good man, that's for sure. And I hear he's going to grow pumpkins this year."

"That's right."

He held up his phone. "I better get this ordered up."

"Thank you." She beamed at him. "You've been so helpful, Jordan. You really should tell your boss to give you a raise."

He chuckled. "Yeah, I might just do that. And the delivery should arrive about seven tomorrow? That okay?"

"That's great." Dillon actually liked the idea of waking up Margot that early. It was about time she started keeping a farmer's hours. And since the grocery store was still open, Dillon stopped in to get the items on Grandpa's list. She could just imagine Margot's face when she saw bacon and eggs sizzling on the stove tomorrow morning.

CHAPTER
6

By the time Dillon got home, the house was quiet. As she put the groceries away, she was dismayed to see the kitchen was not very clean. But at least Margot had loaded and run the dishwasher. Dillon still remembered when Grandpa had given Grandma the portable dishwasher for Christmas. Grandma hadn't wanted it at first, saying that the bulky appliance was in the way. But before long, she got used to it and even used its butcher-block top as a cutting board. As Dillon wiped down the counters and stove and table, scrubbed the sink, and swept the floor, she could almost feel her grandmother's presence . . . and instead of feeling weary of the housework, she felt strangely soothed.

But as she gathered bed things from the linen closet, she felt resentful of Margot, who was upstairs sleeping in Dillon's bed. Why was she doing this? Being so stubborn, and acting like her lavender project was some sort of a spiritual calling? And what would happen when she tired of the hard work and gave up? Would Grandpa be stuck with the mess? And who was paying for everything?

As Dillon settled into the sagging sofa, she wondered if it would be wrong to pray for Don to show up and beg Margot to return to him and continue living together in less-than-holy-matrimony so that Dillon could have her old bed back. Probably. Fortunately she was so worn out, she hardly noticed the sofa's shortcomings. She realized she could probably sleep anywhere tonight.

When she woke the next morning, she wasn't sure whether she was relieved to get up or not. Although her back begged to escape the sofa, she was still sleepy. But the aroma of coffee wafting in from the kitchen was enticing.

Grandpa greeted her as he spooned sugar into a mug.

"Bacon and eggs?" she asked as she poured herself some coffee.

"Count me in." He nodded eagerly.

As Dillon laid bacon strips in the big cast-iron frying pan, she told Grandpa about her visit to the hardware store and the change in irrigation plans.

"A drip line makes sense," he agreed. "I didn't question Margot because she told me she was researching everything."

"Right. Which brings me to another question. Are you pay ing for all this? Or is Margot investing in it herself?"

He sighed. "Margot doesn't really have anything to invest."

"Well, it doesn't seem fair to put the expense on you. I mean, it could be profitable." She actually questioned this. "But what if it all falls apart? Can you afford it?"

"Your grandmother got life insurance policies on both of us a long time ago. I'd assumed they'd lapsed, but it turned out she kept up the payments all these years. So, anyway, I can afford to help your mother with her lavender project."

"Speaking of Margot, I wanted to wake her up early. The parts for the watering system will be here by seven and I think she should be up when the delivery comes, don't you?"

He grinned. "You bet, I do. I've been telling her that farmers can't afford to sleep the morning away. Gotta make hay while the sun shines."

Dillon turned the flame down under the bacon, then ran upstairs and banged on the bedroom door, calling out that Margot's delivery would be here in about fifteen minutes. "So get up—*now!*" Margot mumbled something unintelligible but, worried about the bacon, Dillon didn't stick around.

It was almost seven when Dillon started dishing up breakfast, but Margot still hadn't come down. "There's the Atwood truck." Grandpa pointed to the window over the sink. "I'll go out and see to it."

Dillon would've preferred to drag Margot out of bed kicking and screaming but knew it was pointless. Instead, she poured the orange juice and suppressed her desire to phone Don and beg or bribe him to come get Margot.

"I invited Jordan to breakfast," Grandpa announced as he came in through the back door. "I hope you have enough."

Dillon blinked then nodded. "Sure, there's plenty." She smiled at Jordan. He looked bright and shiny in a plaid Western shirt and blue jeans. She resisted the urge to smooth her bed-head curls, wishing she'd taken some time with her own rumpled appearance. "Have a seat." She set down the two loaded plates, then turned back to the stove to scramble a couple more eggs. Fortunately she'd made lots of bacon.

"Want coffee?" she asked Jordan as she poured an extra glass of orange juice.

"Sounds great. I'm not used to such accommodating customers. Guess I'll have to start making more morning deliveries. Say, Alex, your pumpkin seed should be here by Monday. Want it delivered?" He winked as Dillon set his coffee down.

"Why not?" Grandpa laughed.

"But we could be having oatmeal then." Dillon sat down with her plate.

"So you're growing pumpkins and lavender now?" Jordan asked Grandpa.

"Looks that way." Grandpa glumly shook his head. "If anyone told me that a year ago, I'd have called 'em crazy. But . . . well, things change."

"I sort of know how you feel."

Grandpa nodded. "Yeah, I suppose you never planned to be running the family business." He turned to Dillon. "Jordan's dad passed away about a month after your grandma."

"But we had more warning," Jordan told Dillon. "My dad battled cancer for a couple of years."

"Dale Atwood was a good man," Grandpa said with respect.

"Atwood?" Dillon frowned. "Isn't that the name of the hardware store?"

"Of course," Grandpa told her. "Atwood's Feed and Seed and Hardware."

"Oh?" She looked at Jordan. "So *you're* Mr. Atwood?"

He laughed. "Most people just call me Jordan."

"Jordan's been in charge of the store for about a year now," Grandpa told her. "And doing a good job too."

"We thought it was just to help out when Dad got sick. No one expected I'd stick it out this long. But the town sort of grows on you. Such a great family place. And, as it turns out, I like running the store."

"Good morning," Margot said crisply as she entered the kitchen. "Are we having a party?"

"No, just breakfast." Grandpa introduced her to Jordan, then lifted his coffee mug with a twinkle in his eye. "Feel free to join us."

"You don't expect me to eat *that*." Margot turned her nose up. "Looks like a heart attack on a plate."

"You go ahead and drink green slime if you like," Grandpa teased, "and leave the bacon and eggs to us. We need some fortitude to help us work."

"Speaking of work, I better get going." Jordan pushed back his chair. "But I do appreciate the breakfast. Compliments to the cook."

"Don't sue us if your cholesterol count is sky-high," Margot said lightly.

Jordan just laughed, but Dillon felt annoyed—and as if she were ten years old again . . . trying to make sense of her peculiar parent. As an excuse to escape Margot, Dillon walked Jordan outside, thanking him again for all his help. "I should've guessed you were more than just an employee at the hardware store."

He grinned. "That's okay. It took a while for the town to adjust when I stepped in for Dad. They're barely used to me now."

"I'm sorry for your loss," she said. "But I'm sure your dad would be proud of how well you're managing the hardware store."

"Well, it's a family business. We do our best." He thanked her again for breakfast, then hopped in his pickup and took off. As she watched the trail of dust behind the dark green hardware-store truck, she thought Jordan Atwood was a man of many layers. Not the kind of enigma Brandon had been, always keeping her slightly off guard. But Jordan was definitely a bit mysterious. He'd sounded amused by her assumption that he was an employee at the hardware store. As if he'd enjoyed the joke. And yet he wasn't malicious.

Instead of returning to the kitchen, where she knew she'd only exchange more snipes with Margot, she headed for Grandma's garden. It wasn't long until she found peace there. Systematically weeding, hoeing the beds, emptying pots, getting everything all nice and neat and ready for planting. Even though it was physical labor, it didn't feel like real work. Not like the stressful job she'd been doing since college. And the clean, cool morning air was like a tonic.

She continued puttering about the garden. Taking a sort of inventory. Some of the hardy herbs, including lots of mint, were growing. The well-established berry vines looked healthy, the strawberry plants had blossoms, and the fruit trees looked strong and healthy. Despite the neglect, Dillon thought Grandma would be pleased. And perhaps it wasn't too late to plant a few things. Unless her memory was wrong, Grandma used to plant lettuce and several salad veggies into the summer.

Dillon returned to the house for seeds. She was relieved that Margot wasn't around and snuck into the kitchen to refill her water bottle. Dismayed to see messy countertops and the sink full of dirty dishes, Dillon suspected this was Margot's way of showing her dietary disapproval. But the kitchen would have to wait.

With her bag of seeds in hand, Dillon spotted Margot just standing in the south field. Her irrigation equipment was spread all about, but nothing was happening. Not wanting to know more, Dillon hurried back to the comfort of the garden.

Nestled into Grandma's favorite lawn swing, situated in a shady corner, Dillon studied the planting schedule in the garden diary and tried to decide which seeds to plant. It was too late for most, and since no seedlings had been started in the green-house, Dillon knew the vegetable part of the garden might be on the sparse side this year. But at least it wouldn't be full of weeds.

"Dilly-Dilly," Margot called out in a sugary tone. "Where are you, girlfriend?"

Dillon tried to disappear into the shadows, pretending not to hear.

"Dilly-Dilly. I need your help."

Dillon considered ducking behind the row of raspberries but knew that was childish. "Over here," she called without enthusiasm.

"Well, well . . . just look at how nice Mom's garden looks now." Margot nodded approval. "I came out here last week, thinking I could grow lavender here, but it looked like too much work to clean it up. But you've made progress. And in such a short time too. Nice work, Dilly."

"Just rolled up my sleeves." She held up her dirty hands.

"Ugh. You should get yourself some good gloves." She pulled a brand-new pair from her back pocket.

"Grandma never used gloves to garden." Dillon closed the diary. "She said she needed to feel the plants with her fingers."

"I suppose that's okay if you don't mind having farmer's hands. But you're going to need a manicure now."

"Is that what you came here for? To lecture me about hand care?"

"No, of course not." Margot's smile looked desperate. "I really need your help, Dilly."

Everything in Dillon wanted to scream in protest, but instead she set aside the diary and slowly stood. "I assume it's with your irrigation project."

"Yes. It's more complicated than I realized."

"Uh-huh." Dillon followed her out, latching the gate securely behind her.

"I get the landscaping cloth spread out, and then a breeze comes and messes it up. But what I really need is help with those confounded tubes. It's a two-person job." As they walked to the field, Margot explained her basic layout plan. "I drew it all out—I want six rows with twenty plants in each. I need room for paths in between, you know, to walk through. It's all pretty straightforward and simple."

"But you still need my help?"

"It will make it go faster." Margot's irritation started to show. "And don't forget, the plants are coming tomorrow."

"I suppose you'll need more help with that?"

"Well . . . there are a lot of holes to dig, Dillon."

"Right . . ." Dillon knew by Margot's tone that it wouldn't help to poke at her. Still, it irked her to think how half-hatched this plan really was. But why was that surprising? Dillon went right to work, knowing that the best way to get through this was to simply get it done. Of course, the more she worked with Margot, the more convinced she became that her mother would never be able to finish this. Before long, Dillon was making suggestions . . . and then she began to call the shots, and finally she created a plan that would save both time and energy.

After one o'clock, the sun was hot and Dillon was hungry, but when she suggested they break for lunch, Margot balked. "We're not even half done."

"Obviously." Dillon dropped the hammer she'd been using to drive the U-shaped stakes over the tubing. "But it's not worth killing ourselves." She marched back into the house, splashed herself with cool water, and quickly devoured a peanut butter sandwich, an apple, and two glasses of milk. Then, refilling her water bottle and putting on Grandma's old straw hat, she returned to the south field.

Surprised that Margot was still doggedly securing the tubes, Dillon went straight to work installing emitters into the tubes. Before long, she'd figured a quicker way to accomplish this and felt hopeful they'd actually finish the system before dark. She had just finished her second row when she heard Margot groaning.

"What's wrong?" She turned to see that Margot's face was flushed—and she was staggering.

"Margot!" Dillon ran to check her. "You've probably got heatstroke. Let's get you inside fast." Putting an arm around her mother's waist, she escorted her into the house and sat her down in the recliner. Then she hurried to dampen a hand towel, laying it over Margot's head. Trying to remember her high school first-aid training, Dillon pulled out her phone and googled "heatstroke." "It says call 911," she said with alarm.

"No, no, don't do that," Margot muttered. "I—I'll be okay."

"But it says it's dangerous to people over fifty and—"

"I'm young . . . for my age." Margot sat up straighter. "I just got tired."

"And overheated." Dillon stared down at her. "Your face is beet red."

"I used sunscreen."

"Not that kind of red." Dillon read the first-aid treatment. "Okay, if I can't call 911, let's get you into a cool shower." She helped Margot to her feet and into the downstairs bathroom, and with her clothes still on, she put her mother in the shower and turned the tap on to cool. Ignoring Margot's shrieks, Dillon kept her there in the cool water, getting herself soaked in the process.

Finally, with Margot sitting on the side of the tub in a soggy heap, Dillon dashed to the kitchen, returning with a can of Grandpa's favorite root beer and a glass of water. "Drink this first." She held out the soda.

Margot scowled. "That's loaded with sugar!"

"You probably have low blood sugar. Drink some and then you can have water." Dillon watched with amusement as Margot polished off the whole can. Then Dillon handed her the water.

Margot sighed. "Thanks, Dillon. I feel better."

Convinced that Margot was out of danger, Dillon wrapped a bath towel around her shoulders. "Better not go back outside again today."

"What about the irrigation—"

"Never mind about that." Dillon shook her head. "It's not worth dying for, Margot."

"You mean you'd care if I perished?"

Dillon couldn't help but roll her eyes. "Well, as long as you don't plan to kick the bucket right now, I'm going to go back out to work on it."

"Thank you, Dilly-Dilly."

Dillon felt both rattled and relieved, but she refilled her water bottle and, with sun hat on, returned to the south field. After an hour or so, she came back to check on Margot. Then, reassured she was just fine, Dillon returned again to the irrigation project. *It figures*, she thought as she worked through the afternoon. *Once again, Margot started something she can't finish.* And even though Dillon didn't think Margot got heatstroke on purpose, it was hard not to feel vexed.

As the afternoon shadows grew longer and the air cooled significantly, Grandpa came out to check on the progress. "I hear Margot got too much sun."

"Yeah." Dillon stood, rubbing her sore back.

"Nice of you to help her." He looked over the rows. "Looks like you're doing a good job too. I laid the sprinkler system in Marie's garden. It was similar to this. I can connect the lines to the water and set up the timer."

"Great." She pointed to the row she was working on. "This is the last of the emitters. Then it should be ready to go."

He nodded. "We'll run a test." While she finished the last row, he went to work hooking it up to water, and they both finished about the same time.

"I'll turn 'er on," Grandpa said. "Then, unless we spring a leak, we'll go get ourselves some supper and check it later. Won't hurt to give the soil a good soak since the lavender's coming tomorrow."

Dillon watched him set the timer, then looked over the field with trepidation, hoping that it wasn't going to explode or turn into a water park. But other than a few misdirected emitters, nothing spectacular happened. She and Grandpa adjusted the emitters and agreed it was a success.

As they walked to the house, Dillon asked what they should do about the plants coming tomorrow. "I don't think Margot should be out in the sun too much. But now I don't see how she's going to get that lavender planted."

"Yep. I think you're right."

"I'll help as much as I can, but that's a lot of plants." She did the mental math. "I guess if I planted one every five minutes, that'd be twelve in an hour—I'd be done in ten hours or so."

Grandpa laughed. "And then we'd be treating you for exhaustion or heatstroke."

"Not if I paced myself."

"Well, rest assured, Dilly. When I saw your mom was beat, I called in some help. Got a team of teenage boys coming first thing tomorrow morning. They're from the church youth group and need to earn money for summer camp. I'm guessing they'll finish up by noon. All you need to do is cook 'em up a good lunch. I promised the youth pastor we'd feed 'em."

"I'll gladly do that." Relief washed over her as they went inside. Grandpa was no fool. He'd probably known all along that this project was too much for his somewhat unmotivated daughter. But, seriously, did he really plan to spend the latter part of his farming life growing pumpkins and lavender?

CHAPTER

7

So Dillon's surprise, Grandpa already had breakfast going the next morning. "Thought we could use hotcakes today." He expertly flipped a golden disk.

"Sounds great." She went to the coffeepot, hoping it would wake her up after another uncomfortable night's sleep.

"Believe it or not, your mother is already up." Grandpa handed her a plate of hotcakes.

"Seriously?" She sat down. "She did this on her own?"

He chuckled. "With a little help. Anyway, she's out there with her nasty-smelling green drink, waiting for her work crew."

"Well, I'm impressed." She reached for the maple syrup.

"Hopefully the boys will get here before the lavender plants. That way they can help unload the truck."

"And hopefully Margot will avoid the sun today."

As they ate breakfast, Grandpa talked about his pumpkin patch plans, and it was plain to see his enthusiasm was growing. "I've been thinking about this fall. Might be fun to set out hay bales and some fun and games for the kids when they come out."

"Wouldn't Grandma love that?" Dillon knew most of his motivation was out of respect for his wife.

"Speaking of your grandma, I took a peek at Marie's garden yesterday afternoon. Nice work, Dillon."

"Thanks, but after reading her garden diary, I can see it's a little late for a lot of the vegetables Grandma used to plant."

"Well, being that she's not here to can and freeze 'em this fall, might be just as well. That garden can really produce."

"Yeah, I remember. But I did transplant the tomatoes—the ones that survived—and I planted some lettuce and radish seeds . . . and a few others. So at least we can have salad—in a while. For the time being, there's not much else to do out there."

As Dillon got up to refill her coffee mug, she questioned herself . . . What was she doing here? She appreciated her time with Grandpa, but it didn't really take both her and Margot to help him out of his slump. He seemed to be doing just fine now. And although she'd enjoyed the garden work and helping around the house, it wasn't as if she were really needed here. Thankfully, the hardest part of the lavender project would be done by the end of the day. She rubbed her aching back, grateful that the teen boys were coming to help.

"I'll bet you're sore from yesterday."

She simply nodded as she sat back down.

"How've you been sleeping? Is the sofa comfortable enough?"

"It's okay." That wasn't exactly true, but she didn't want him to feel bad.

"I was thinking we could set you up a bedroom in my den. It used to be my bedroom back when I was a boy and I'd—"

"No, Grandpa, I don't want to take your den. All your agricultural books and farm records and everything are in there." She tried to think of a different conversation topic. "You know, the best night of sleep I've had in ages was in a pretty unconventional place."

"Where was that?" He swiped a forkful of hotcakes through the syrup.

"Strangely enough, it was this little trailer park in Wyoming. Just last weekend." She explained about getting trapped between the two vehicles hauling vintage trailers. "Well, it turned out that this place rented trailers by the night too. And I got to stay in this darling little yellow trailer. And it had the most comfortable bed ever. With fine linens that smelled like sunshine. So peaceful and quiet. It was truly magical."

"Fine linens in a camp trailer?" He shook his head with disbelief. "Last time I slept in a camp trailer, we were elk hunting and all I had was a smelly sleeping bag and a couple of snoring hunting buddies."

She laughed. "That sounds terrible."

He sighed. "Maybe to you. But it's a good memory to me."

"I took pictures of the trailer park. It was really something. All these charming old trailers that had been so carefully restored. Really quaint and sweet. I'd never seen anything like it before."

"You don't say . . ." His eyes twinkled.

After breakfast, Dillon automatically started to rinse the dishes.

"Why don't you let that go for now?" Grandpa pulled on his John Deere ball cap and work coat. "Come on outside with me first." He held out Grandma's old green barn jacket. "Still cool out there. Better wear this."

"Okay." She peered at him with curiosity. Something about this felt mysterious.

Outside, three teenage boys were energetically unloading lavender plants from the nursery delivery truck, with Margot shouting orders like a Marine sergeant. "Over there! No, I mean there. Line them up by the rows."

"Looks like Margot's found her calling," Dillon observed.

"She always did like to give the orders." Grandpa chuckled.

"Believe me, I know."

"Something I want to show you." Grandpa tugged Dillon's arm, directing her toward the barn. "Hearing you talking about those old trailers reminded me of something I'd nearly forgotten." He took her past the barn and over to the attached loafing shed where, to her surprise, an old camp trailer sat.

"What in the world?" Her eyes grew wide as she looked at the rounded shape of the trailer—like something out of a cartoon. "Where did you get this?"

"Remember my buddy Jack Martin?"

She nodded, walking around to see the other side of the trailer, taking in the dry, flaking paint and grime-encrusted windows, running her hand over the dirty aluminum door. What a treasure!

"Well, Jack passed on and left this to me last summer. As well as his old pickup truck. I didn't know what to do with them. Almost sold 'em last fall, but then Marie got sick . . . and I sort of forgot about the whole works."

"Jack left this to you?" Dillon stood on tiptoe, trying to see in a grimy side window. "He must've really liked you."

Grandpa snickered. "Or else Rose just made that up as an excuse to get it off her property. She went off to California to live with her sister after Jack passed. I'm sure she didn't want to be bothered." He grew more serious. "But Jack and my hunting buddies did have some awfully good times in this trailer. I guess Jack thought I'd appreciate it."

"I think it's wonderful, Grandpa." She peered curiously at him. "Why are you showing it to me?"

"Well, you mentioned that trailer park in Wyoming. And I knew it was something you could appreciate."

"Can I see inside?"

"Sure. But I'll warn you, it was infested with mice when I brought it home. Although I'm sure my barn cats have taken care of that since then. I left it open all last summer. Only closed it up after I realized that Curly and Mo had taken up permanent residence inside."

"You still have the three stooges?" she asked. "I haven't seen them around all week."

"Well, Larry was the friendly one. Unfortunately, he disappeared a couple years ago. Probably by coyote. Curly and Mo are still around. The females were never too sociable, but good mousers. If you hang around the barn long enough, they'll probably show up. Especially if you rattle their food bag." Grandpa extracted a brass key from beneath a well-worn welcome mat and handed it to her. "Here you go, have a look."

She unlocked and opened the metal door and then an old-fashioned screen door before going inside. "It does smell a little mousy." She looked around with fascination. "But it seems solid."

"It's solid, alright. Jack always kept it under cover."

"Oh, look at those adorable little appliances." She traced her finger through the dust on top of the bright orange stove. "I wonder if this works."

"Don't know why it shouldn't. This Aloha trailer was top of the line back in 1964, when Jack and Rose got it brand new. Last time we took it hunting—not so very long ago—it all worked."

She opened the fridge and, although it smelled musty, it was spotless inside. Even a tiny set of ice cube trays was in the freezer section. "Looks like someone kept this clean." She closed the door and hooked the latch pin into place.

"Rose probably."

She opened a cabinet door. "It all seems very well built."

"They built everything better back in those days."

She checked out what appeared to be a couch in the back.

"That pulls out into a full-size bed." Grandpa demonstrated how it worked, pulling down the pads. "Jack always slept here." He pointed to the bunk overhead. "That was mine. But last time we took it out, I had a hard time getting my old bones up there."

"This is so cool, Grandpa. What do you plan to do with it?"

"I don't plan to do anything with it, Dilly. But it's yours if you want it."

"Are you serious?" Dillon could hardly believe it.

"Yep. It's not much. But I'd like you to have it. Consider it my thank-you for all the work you've done around here this week. Rescuing Marie's garden . . . and the housework too. You've been a trooper."

"Thanks." She felt slightly teary to think he'd really noticed these things. "So that means I can fix it up—however I like? I mean, with paint and fabrics and everything?"

His blue eyes twinkled. "It's all yours, Dilly. See what you can make of it."

"Is there anything I should know about it?" She tried to turn on the light, disappointed to see it didn't work.

"It's not hooked up. But I'll show you how that works." He led her outside, showing her a door where a long electrical cord was stored. After unwinding it he plugged it into the exterior outlet. Next, he showed her a place where she could fill a holding tank with water. "As I recall the water from this tank was mostly for washing and the bathroom. We always carried our own drinking water."

"So water and electricity," she said cheerfully. "Modern living."

"At its finest." He glanced upward. "Now I better get busy before the sun gets any higher."

She thanked him again, feeling like she'd just won the lottery. Dillon filled the water tank, then continued to explore every nook and cranny of the compact trailer. Although it was small, it wasn't as tiny as the yellow trailer she'd slept so well in just a week ago. It even had a tiny bathroom in the back corner across from the rear sleeping area. And up in the front, just over a sweet little dining table, was what appeared to be a second bunk with a railing that doubled as a ladder. Clever! Not that she planned to climb up there, but it would make a good storage area.

Dillon went back outside to look at the trailer again—with the full realization that it was truly hers. It was almost unbelievable. Glad that no one could see her, she actually did a Snoopy happy dance all around it. This was a dream come true!

She wasn't blind. She could see the spiders' webs and mouse droppings, and although Rose had probably taken good care of it back in the day, the whole thing needed a deep and thorough cleaning. Probably thanks to the hunters. She went back inside and opened all the windows to air it out. Then she began to take down the curtains, which looked original but were deteriorated beyond rescuing. That alone made it look better.

Thrilled over the potential of this unexpected but delightful project, Dillon hurried to the house. She retrieved a broom, mop, and a bucket of cleaning supplies, and was just stepping outside when Margot stopped her on the back porch.

"What on earth are you doing with *that*?" Margot frowned at the bucket and its contents.

"Cleaning." Dillon paused on the back porch, impatient to get back to her trailer but curious as to why Margot even cared.

"But you've already cleaned everything in the house. What's next? The barn?" She laughed.

"No, no . . . just an old trailer."

"Why are you cleaning a trailer?"

"Because I *am*." Dillon grimaced.

"But this is a farm, Dilly. Won't the trailer just get dirty again?"

Dillon could tell Margot assumed she was cleaning Grandpa's flatbed hay bale trailer, and that was just fine. For some reason she wanted to keep her camp trailer project private for the time being. Probably because she figured Margot would make fun of the dusty, dirty "rattrap." "I'm sure it'll get dirty again," Dillon said tersely. "But that's what I'm working on today."

"But I need help with the lavender planting."

"You have help."

"I know. And the boys are full of energy, but they need lots and lots of direction and I don't think I should be out in the sun today."

Dillon set down her bucket, carefully considering her answer. If she agreed to "help" she would very likely get stuck until every last lavender was planted. "Sorry," she firmly told Margot. "But I've already got a lot to do today." She pointed to the patio table that Grandma had used for outdoor meals. "Why don't you dig out the sun umbrella and set that table up over near the planting area. You could even bring out some cold drinks for your workers."

Margot blinked. "That's not a bad idea. How about you give me a hand with it?"

Dillon set her tools on the porch. Knowing this would be the quickest way to resolve the situation, she helped Margot carry and set up the table and umbrella. "Are you able to handle the cold drinks yourself?" Dillon asked in a patronizing tone.

"I'm not helpless," Margot declared.

"No, I wasn't suggesting that. But you probably won't want to fix your workers lunch." Dillon knew she was attempting reverse psychology, and she didn't expect it to work. "Grandpa promised them food. I suppose I'll have to do that too."

"I'm perfectly capable of fixing them food."

"But they won't want green smoothies. I thawed out hamburger and thought I'd fire up the grill. Plus, I planned to make macaroni salad. You know, like Grandma used to—"

"I'll make their lunch," Margot declared. "After all, this is *my* project."

"Well, okay then." Dillon nodded, trying not to look overly pleased as she gathered up her cleaning supplies and hurried back to her wonderful little trailer. Was it possible that Margot really did want to step up? Or was it simply the reverse psychology?

Dillon felt a rush of happiness as she came around the corner of the barn—just seeing her little trailer there waiting for her. She was glad that it was parked in the shade—and out of view of the house. About to open the door, she paused to read the manufacturer's metal plate fastened next to the door.

"Oasis," she said with amusement. "Well, you might not exactly look like an oasis yet, but you will." She patted the side of the trailer, then took out her phone and began to photograph the full exterior and interior. "These are your *before* pics," she said as she put her phone in her pocket. "With a little elbow grease and TLC, we'll have you looking like a million bucks in no time." Was it weird to talk to an old trailer like this? If so, she didn't really care.

Dillon set to work removing all the old upholstery, which was falling apart anyway, and tossing it into the trash can she'd set outside for her debris. Then she swept up mouse droppings from every nook and cranny, marveling at how much storage potential this small space contained. She scrubbed and cleaned and wiped and, after a couple of hours, the sturdy little trailer looked and smelled much better.

Dillon sat down at the dinette, gazing around the compact space, imagining what it might look like and wondering how she should bring out the trailer's personality. She remembered all the colorful trailers she'd seen in Wyoming. Each one looked unique. Perhaps they were a reflection of their owners. She wanted hers to be special too.

The only thing she knew she wouldn't change was the appliance color—that bright orange tone was cheerful and fun. But what color would look good with it?

Dillon pulled out her phone, thinking she might google some ideas. Instead, she was staring at the turquoise case cover. She'd gotten it last year, probably an inspiration from the Navajo jewelry she'd inherited from Grandma. Suddenly she held her phone case next to the stove—and it looked perfect. Decision made. She would paint the cabinets a cheery turquoise blue. Now she went to the note section of her phone and began to list the things she would need to make her trailer not only livable but beautiful too. As her list grew, she realized this would call for a trip to town . . . and that was a good excuse to see Jordan at the hardware store. Perfect!

CHAPTER

8

For the past week, other than a quick shower before bedtime, Dillon had seriously neglected her appearance. But knowing she was going to town today—more specifically to the hardware store—she wanted to look presentable. Or better.

It was past one by the time Dillon got to town. Although she hadn't eaten since breakfast, she didn't feel the least bit hungry. Mostly she was excited about her new vintage trailer and eager to acquire the items on her list. And she hoped to cross paths with Jordan again.

She could hardly believe it'd been only a week since she and Brandon had parted ways. And the way she'd felt that night—like she'd blown up her future and her world was unraveling—seemed far away now. Brandon Kranze hadn't been worth the emotion. And it wasn't as if he cared. He'd never called or even texted . . . never apologized. And for that, she was glad. It was a relief to be done with it.

According to Val's text informing Dillon her personal office items had been mailed, Brandon acted unaffected by the breakup. In fact, Val had spied him lunching with Bethany Myers—the Kate Hudson "twinny" from finance. Although initially disturbing, it was reassuring now—confirming that Brandon Kranze was not Mr. Right after all. He was simply Mr. Kranze. Thank goodness she'd had the sense to move on.

With her list on her phone, Dillon walked into Atwood's Feed and Seed and Hardware—on a mission. Granted, it was a twofold mission. She did hope to see Jordan Atwood. But even more than that, she was eager to gather what she needed to continue the restoration of her beloved Oasis. Just thinking of her little vintage trailer truly warmed her heart!

Not seeing Jordan in the front of the store, Dillon got a cart and began her shopping expedition. As was her habit, she made selections with frugality in mind. Even though her savings account had grown since paying off her school loans, old habits died hard. Plus, she needed to remember her current unemployed status. And unlike her mother's lavender project expenses, Dillon would not charge any trailer purchases to Grandpa's account. That was just wrong.

After gathering various pieces of hardware, some window screen, and items for the bathroom, she discovered the paint department. To her delight, the man working there assured her that he could mix any color she wanted. She explained what she was working on and her relative inexperience with painting.

"Don't worry, I can help with everything. Just pick your

colors." He waved to a display full of paint sample swatches. Eventually, she found a turquoise blue, an exact match to her grandmother's ring, which she'd purposely worn. And she was just selecting a nice creamy white color for the walls and ceilings when Jordan came over to say hello.

"Painting?" he asked.

"I am," she told him.

"How's the lavender project coming?"

She told him how the drip line was in place and working. "I'm sorry we haven't returned the unused pieces yet. I'll bring them on my next trip to town."

"I'm surprised you have time to paint. I assumed you'd be up to your ears planting lavender right now."

She was about to explain the teen helpers and that the lavender project was actually her mother's responsibility when a feminine voice called out her name. Dillon was pleasantly surprised to see her old school friend. "Chelsea Willets!" Dillon declared. "Is that really you?"

"It is." Chelsea hugged her. "Oh, it's so good to see you, Dillon. You look fabulous!"

"You too!" Dillon felt dismayed to see Jordan waving goodbye to her as he went to assist a customer. "What are you doing in Silverdale, Chelsea?"

"Good question." Chelsea laughed. "Blame my sister Kellie. She took a management job at the parks and recreation and begged me to come help her out. To be honest, I was getting disenchanted with big city life. So here I am, back on my home turf again. Have you moved back too?"

"I'm not sure." She handed the young paint guy her color samples, explaining the uses for each one. She read the name tag on his shirt. "So, Ryan, can you figure out what I need and how much?"

"No problem." Ryan's smile was congenial. "But it'll take a while to get it done. I've got a real big order to mix that's already in the works."

"Have you had lunch?" Chelsea asked. Dillon admitted she hadn't, and Chelsea insisted on going to Lucianna's. "It's not as swanky as it used to be, but the food is good."

Dillon smiled. "I haven't been to Lucianna's in ages. Not since my grandma took me there on my eighteenth birthday." She looked at her cart. "Just let me pay for these, and I'll meet you there."

Before long, the two old friends were having lunch at what used to be the fanciest restaurant in Silverdale. Dillon couldn't help but notice it had grown a bit shabby around the edges. Still, it felt nostalgic to be there.

"So what are you doing back in town?" Chelsea asked after their iced tea was served.

"I'm not really sure." Dillon explained she'd left her job and boyfriend, and that she'd hoped to be of some help with her grandpa. "I've been doing some housekeeping, working in my grandma's garden, helping with an irrigation system, and—"

"Sounds like you've been uber-busy." Chelsea laughed. "But isn't that the way you always were—no one could ever keep up with your achievements."

"Or overachievements."

"But what about a job? Will you be looking for employment?" Chelsea sounded hopeful.

"Well, I don't know. I haven't had time to even consider—"

"Because I have a job for you—if you want it." Now Chelsea explained how her sister had put her in charge of the aquatics program. "Just because I used to be on swim team." She pointed to Dillon. "Remember those days?"

Dillon smiled. "Yeah, that was a good time."

"Well, unfortunately the swimming classes have been severely mismanaged. As it is, I've barely got the summer program in place and we're getting a late start, but registration is full, and I plan to start classes next week."

"That must be fun for you to manage the old pool."

"Frustrating fun. Anyway, here's the deal, I'm still short a couple of teachers. And you'd be such a godsend, Dillon. Remember the summers we both taught together? You were so good at it. All the kids loved you."

"That was a long time ago."

"Yes, but you were a great instructor. And what kid didn't want to be taught by the star of our high school swim team?"

"Flattery will get you—"

"*Please*, Dillon. Even if you only agree to one session, it would help me immensely."

"How's the pay?" Dillon's expectations were low.

"Oh, you know, it's not great. But for you, well, I'll talk Kellie into top wages."

Dillon considered the expenses of restoring her little trailer. Perhaps this would be a way to preserve her savings. "Okay," she agreed. "I'll do it. But just part-time."

"Fantastic." Chelsea reached into an oversized bag. "As fate would have it, I just happen to have a schedule on me." She grabbed a pen, using it to circle the sessions she really hoped Dillon would teach. "Your first class will be Monday at eight.

Your last class will end at one. Does that work for you? Or do you want more hours?"

"That's perfect. Then I can have afternoons to work on my trailer."

"Your trailer?"

"Yes. That's what I was getting paint for." As they ate, Dillon described her plans to restore her vintage trailer. "I know it's silly to be so excited about an old trailer. But I just love it. And I want everything in it to be absolutely perfect."

"Well, then you need to go to see Vivian Porter ASAP."

"Why?"

"She owns the Silver Slipper."

"Huh?"

"It's this sort of funky home décor shop just a couple blocks down. Vivian has a real knack. And listen to this—she loves old trailers too. She has a section in her store dedicated to old trailers. I'll be honest—I don't get it. But Vivian is a fanatic."

Dillon could hardly wait to finish lunch now, and as soon as they were done, after Chelsea insisted on picking up the check, Dillon excused herself and hurried on down to the Silver Slipper. She was barely in the door, but aware she'd come to the right place, when a tall brunette offered assistance. Dillon quickly explained how Chelsea had recommended the shop, and the woman introduced herself as Vivian.

Still slightly breathless, Dillon explained her mission to restore an old trailer. "It's an Aloha Oasis and it's a real mess right now, but she's going to be a beauty."

"She?" Vivian grinned. "Sounds like you're hooked."

"It was love at first sight."

Vivian chuckled as she took Dillon to the back of the shop.

"I know exactly what you mean. This shop is named after my trailer. I bought and restored a 1960 Airstream on the heels of a bad breakup several years ago. I actually kept my trailer at my parents' house and lived in it for a couple years. I named her *The Silver Slipper*."

"So you really do understand." Dillon felt her eyes grow wide as she surveyed the vintage trailer section. It was filled with all sorts of retro items—some new and some not—as well as a tempting selection of books on vintage trailers, and she wasn't sure where to begin.

"I feel like I'm in trailer heaven." Dillon selected a book with a pink teardrop trailer on the cover.

"Well, you've come to the right place. Not just my shop, but Silverdale. We have a number of people who've restored vintage trailers. We've even created a trailer club."

"How exciting." Dillon told Vivian more about her trailer, even showing her the photos on her phone.

"That's definitely a keeper." Vivian nodded. "Those orange appliances are to die for."

"I absolutely love them."

"So are you planning to do the restoration yourself? Or do you want to hire—"

"Oh, I definitely want to do it all myself," Dillon said. "I think it'll be good therapy. Already, it's been fun cleaning it out, and I can't wait to start painting." She showed Vivian the paint sample colors that she'd stuck in her purse, explaining her plan to paint the cabinets turquoise. "Do you think that's too bright? Will it look okay?"

Vivian studied the colors and photos. "Kind of a Southwest look—but sixties style?"

"I guess so." Dillon explained about living in Colorado. "I suppose that's influenced me some."

"Well, I love the color palette you've chosen. Admittedly, pink, blue, and yellow are mid-century colors, but not everyone wants a pastel-toned trailer. I believe you should do whatever makes you happiest. One guy did his in lime-green, black, and white. And it was gorgeous."

"Well, these colors do make me happy." Dillon picked up a turquoise teakettle. "See! This would be perfect in my Oasis." She noticed some striped kitchen towels and pot holders with orange and turquoise shades. "These too."

"Tell you what," Vivian said. "I'll give you a one-day first-time-buyer discount. Everything and anything you get will be 20 percent off for today only."

"Thank you so much!" Dillon felt like a kid in a candy store.

"And I'll show you some things that might work with your color scheme and Southwest theme."

It didn't take long for Dillon, assisted by Vivian, to accumulate quite a pile of kitchen items and charming knickknacks that she knew would be perfect for her trailer. But her favorite thing, besides the teakettle, was a set of unbreakable dishes in the perfect shade of turquoise. And there were plastic tumblers that looked like glass to go with it. She couldn't wait to try them on her little dinette table.

"Do you know how to sew?" Vivian asked as she set a box on the counter. "If you don't, I have a good seamstress that I use for my projects."

"My grandma taught me when I was a teen, but I haven't sewn in years."

"Well, you'll save money if you do it yourself." Vivian led

her to a fabric section. "My selection is somewhat limited, but I keep it like this on purpose. Too many choices just confuse people. And I'm certain we can find something to work with your colors."

"Great." Dillon wondered how hard it would be to dig Grandma's sewing machine out from her craft room—and if she could remember how to run it.

Vivian picked out a number of fabrics that could work for curtains, and Dillon fell in love with a print that resembled a Navajo blanket in Southwest tones.

"And I always recommend keeping your upholstery color neutral. That's another reason I carry a limited selection. Sturdy fabrics in basic colors." She pulled out a tweedy fabric in earth tones. "I think this would be perfect."

"It looks kind of boring to me," Dillon admitted.

"Maybe it does now. But think of it like a backdrop. You just have to spice it up." She spread the tweed fabric out on the cutting table, then laid the curtain fabric nearby. Then she perused her shop, bringing back several pretty throw pillows and a colorful knitted throw with hues of turquoise and orange. "Imagine it all together, Dillon."

"Yes—I get it now. I think you're absolutely right. I want these too." She gathered the soft goods into her arms. "I feel like a bird who's feathering her nest."

Vivian laughed. "Yes, you're definitely hooked." Now she called her assistant over, telling her which fabrics to cut and how much was needed. Then she told Dillon about a website with a good tutorial on upholstering dinette benches. "It's much easier than you think. All you need is a good pair of scissors and a sturdy staple gun."

Dillon added those items to the list on her phone. More things to hunt down at the hardware store. "I hate to think of how much this will all cost," Dillon admitted. "I mean, I think it's totally worth it. But I'm preparing myself for sticker shock."

"Restoring a trailer is definitely an investment. But I don't think you should scrimp unless you have to. The payoff is a beautiful tiny home that you can take anywhere. It's like freedom on wheels. And if you live in it, you'll save a bundle in rent money. Really, it's a win-win."

Seeing a pretty display of fine bed linens, Dillon remembered her last good night of sleep in the tiny yellow trailer. "I'm not sure about the bed." She showed Vivian a photo of her pull-out sofa/bed. "I want it to be really comfortable." She didn't want to admit she'd been sleeping on her grandpa's couch because her mom had taken her old room. That sounded too pathetic.

"Well, if I were you, I'd convert that pull-out sofa into a regular bed with a good full-sized mattress. You could make it double as a daybed with some big comfy pillows in back. Then you could just toss the pillows onto the bunk above and sleep comfortably."

"Yes, I can just see that. I love that idea."

"There's a great online mattress company I can recommend. The mattress comes packed in this relatively small box, then you open it up and—presto chango—you've got a deliciously comfortable bed." She showed Dillon the website on her phone. "Look, they even do rush orders." With a little help, Dillon soon had a mattress ordered with guaranteed delivery by Monday.

"Fabulous." Dillon put her phone away, imagining the wonders of sleeping in a comfy bed in her own little trailer as soon as next week. Was that even possible?

"If you really want luxury, you should check out these sheets." Vivian picked up a thick package tied with a blue satin ribbon. "They're top-of-the-line and unbelievably soft. A little pricey, but with your one-day discount . . ."

Dillon knew she was being extravagant—something she'd never been before—but she didn't care. In the same way she was giving her trailer a makeover, she was making over her way of thinking. She had entered a new era of life—a time for reinvention, taking risks, spontaneity, and fun!

By the time Dillon saw the grand total, she was glad for three things. First, she was getting a 20 percent discount today. Second, she had enough in her bank account to cover this "investment." And third, she would be gainfully employed by Monday.

CHAPTER

9

*A*fter she'd loaded her car with what Vivian said was "trailer treasure," Dillon drove back to the hardware store to pick up her paint and the other items on her list. Of course, she was hoping to bump into Jordan, but although she perused almost every corner of the store in search of her needed odds and ends, he was MIA. Unfortunately, she was unable to think of any good reason to inquire as to his whereabouts, so she went ahead and checked out. More than anything, she was eager to get back to her trailer. It was getting late in the day, and she really wanted to work on it some more.

After parking out by the trailer, Dillon decided to leave her lovely purchases from the Silver Slipper in her car. Her vehicle could double as a temporary storage unit, and she would simply unload the tools and supplies she needed for now. She took each item out of its packaging, lining up tools and hardware in happy anticipation of their use.

She was eager to see her turquoise paint on the cabinets but knew it was late in the day to start that task. And Ryan had warned her not to rush it. He'd even written down preparation tips about sanding and such, suggesting she remove the cabinet doors and hardware. "And be sure to number everything so you can get it back into the right spots." He'd even suggested she get a rechargeable screwdriver to make it easier. "It's a handywoman's best friend," he'd assured her.

It was past six by the time she'd removed all the doors and hardware and, hoping that Margot wasn't already concocting some sort of health meal, she decided to call it quits. She knew Grandpa would prefer some real food. Plus, she didn't want him to think she was too distracted with her little Oasis to help him anymore. That would be a sorry sort of thank-you.

Before going into the house, Dillon stopped to survey the lavender field. The young plants were set into neat rows and evenly spaced apart. Even though it wasn't really her project, she felt a sense of pleasure to know she'd helped. And it was reassuring to see the soil still moist from the drip lines.

Grandpa called out a greeting as he strolled over from the barn. "Looks pretty good, don't it?" He squatted down to pinch the damp soil.

"Yeah, I was just thinking that." Dillon glanced over to the section where Grandpa had been working today. "How's your pumpkin patch coming?"

"Well, I just finished tilling a bunch of old steer manure in. To *beef* up the soil." He chuckled as he slapped dirt off his hands. "Steer . . . beef. Get it?"

"Uh-huh." She smiled. "Very funny."

"Tomorrow I'll make planting mounds. Pumpkins like to be a little elevated so they can grow downward. After that's done, I'll move irrigation pipes into place. And hopefully my seed will be here by Monday. Not a moment too soon."

"I'll bet you're hungry."

"I put some T-bones in the fridge to thaw last night. Thought we could throw them on the barbecue. How's that sound?"

"Delicious. I'll get the rest of supper going if you want to grill the steaks." She glanced toward the house. "Hopefully Margot won't freak over the smell of charred meat."

"Well, she did complain about cooking those hamburgers for the boys today." Grandpa chuckled. "But when she saw how appreciative they were, I think she got over it."

It wasn't long before the steaks were done. And since Margot did voice her opinion against the "carnivores," Dillon and Grandpa opted to eat outside, leaving the kitchen to Margot. As they ate, Dillon told Grandpa about all her plans for her trailer, and he made some suggestions and offered the use of some tools and things in the barn. "Sounds like you got your work cut out for you." He picked up the bone from his steak and chewed on it.

Dillon laughed. "You might call it work, but I call it fun. I can hardly wait to get back at it."

"Well, you've got electricity hooked up, so you've got lights. I suppose you can fuss with it this evening if you like." He set down the bone and slapped his midsection. "That was just what the doctor ordered."

Dillon grinned as she gathered the plates. "Don't let Margot hear you saying that."

"I know. She'll lecture me on my cholesterol again."

As Dillon carried the dishes into the kitchen, she smiled at Margot. "I didn't say anything before, but your lavender field looks spectacular. You must be proud."

Margot's face lit up. "You think so?"

"Absolutely. Those boys did a great job. And it'll be fun to see those plants in bloom." She rinsed the dishes, loading them into the dishwasher. "It really was a great idea to grow lavender."

"Well, thank you." Margot sighed. "It's nice to hear some appreciation."

Dillon made a bit more pleasant small talk while cleaning the kitchen, then headed for the back door.

"Where you going?" Margot asked.

"Just outside."

"To look at my lavender field?"

"Uh, no . . . well, I guess."

"Then I'll come with you."

Dillon wanted to make an excuse—find some way to ditch her mother. "I, uh, I thought I'd take a little walk too . . ."

"Oh, good. I could use a walk. And it's such a lovely evening."

And so with Margot by her side, Dillon walked around the farm, making more pleasant small talk and trying to think of a way to part from Margot and go work on her trailer, but as they came around the back of the barn, Margot noticed Dillon's car.

"Why's your car parked way over here?" Margot asked.

"I, uh, I just thought it was a good spot."

"What is that by your car?" Margot continued walking toward the loafing shed, and now the vintage trailer was in full view.

"Just an old trailer." Dillon grimaced.

"I didn't know Dad had a camp trailer."

"His buddy Jack left it to him," Dillon said.

"That was real nice," Margot said with sarcasm. "Probably cheaper than taking it to a wrecking yard."

"It's actually a *vintage* trailer," Dillon said defensively.

"Nowadays anything old is vintage." Margot picked off a piece of flaking paint. "What a mess."

"Well, it happens to be *my* mess." With hands on hips, Dillon faced her mother. "And I happen to like her."

"Her?"

"Whatever." Dillon stood protectively in front of the trailer. "I didn't expect you to understand."

"You're right. I don't understand. Why are you saying this is *your* mess?" Margot peeked inside Dillon's packed car. "And what is all that? Looks like you went on some huge shopping spree."

Dillon really did not want to explain, but knew she had no choice. And so she quickly told about how Grandpa had given her the trailer and her plans to restore it.

"Why?"

"Because I want to." Dillon sighed.

"What's it look like inside?" Margot tried to peer in the window. "Hopefully better than the outside."

Dillon unlocked the door, stepping aside. "Go ahead and look around." She waited while Margot went in, trying not to listen to all the negative comments.

"Well, it's interesting," Margot said as she stepped out. "But it's a mess."

"I know it's a mess . . . now. But it's going to be fabulous when I'm done restoring it."

Margot laughed. "What on earth do you know about re-storing trailers?"

"I'll learn as I go." Dillon held up her phone. "And I can always google how-to videos."

"Well, you've got your work cut out for you." Margot looked amused.

"Yes, I know." Dillon nodded. "And I'm going to work on it right now."

"Can't say I envy you," Margot teased. "But whatever floats your boat."

"Uh-huh." Dillon forced a cheesy smile. "See you later, al-ligator." And then she firmly closed the door. "Don't take it personally," she patted the dinette table. "Margot doesn't un-derstand your potential, but I do." And then she tuned her phone to some lively music and set to work sanding the wood surfaces that she planned to paint tomorrow.

◖◖◖

Dillon got up extra early on Saturday. Partly because the sofa was so uncomfortable, but mostly because she couldn't wait to get to her trailer. Seeing that coffee was already made and dishes were in the sink, she guessed that Grandpa had gotten up even earlier. When she went outside, she spotted him out on his small tractor making his pumpkin mounds.

She went straight to work on the trailer. Using sawhorses from the barn, she laid out all the cabinet doors and drawers and began to paint. After that, she set to work painting the inside of the trailer. Barely breaking for lunch, Dillon had all the painting completed by the end of the day. And, although she was an exhausted, paint-speckled mess, she couldn't have been happier with the results as she locked the trailer's door and headed for the house.

The next day, after going to early church with Grandpa, Dillon was back in her trailer. After touching up the paint from yesterday, putting the cabinet doors and drawers back into place, and giving it another cleaning, she stood back to admire her work. The trailer was so much improved! Having the turquoise cabinets next to the orange appliances was bright and fun and cheerful. Now if she could just unearth her grandma's old Singer sewing machine.

Up in the old craft room, Dillon pretended she was on a treasure hunt. And after finding a few items she could use for the trailer, she realized it really was a treasure hunt. It started when she discovered some old paint-by-number pictures that she and Grandma had painted one Christmas. They were outdoor scenes, and the colors were perfect for her trailer. She found a few other charming items and eventually spotted the olive-green case of the old Singer machine, as well as Grandma's old sewing basket. Perfect.

Realizing this room was too crowded to set up the machine, Dillon decided to take it back to the trailer and sew down there. Hopefully, she would remember how to operate it. And hopefully she wouldn't cross paths with Margot on her way out there. She just did not want to be questioned—or mocked—again.

She gathered everything she needed to start sewing, then locked herself in the trailer. She wasn't able to recall how to thread the old sewing machine, so she googled it on her phone. Not only did she find instructions, she found some helpful sewing tips and even watched a few tutorials for making curtains. And then she set to work, measuring and marking and cutting and pinning . . . and finally sewing. By noon, she had one window outfitted with its new curtain. And, okay, maybe the hem was a tad uneven, but all in all it was beautiful.

By the end of the day she'd finished most of the curtains and could hardly believe how charming the trailer was starting to look. The one thing she was unsure about was how to refinish the floor. At first she thought she'd just leave it as is, but the old linoleum tiles were loose, and after poking around with a screwdriver, she discovered that they popped off easily.

She got out the cute trailer book she'd found at the Silver Slipper and looked at the clever photos for some inspiration, but she still wasn't sure. With the colorful cabinets, appliances, and curtains, she thought maybe she needed something less busy than the checkerboards she was looking at in the book. Finally, she remembered what Vivian had told her about neutral tones. Perhaps that was what her floor needed.

As much as she would've liked to continue working out here, it was getting dusky outside, which meant it was late. And tomorrow morning, she was expected at the pool to teach swimming lessons. Of course, this meant she needed to don a swimsuit—not a task she was looking forward to. Hopefully she'd be able to dig one out of the bags of clothing she'd stashed in a storage closet. But first she wanted to unload her car. She carefully took load after load into the trailer, piling things onto the bunks and on the dinette . . . and controlling herself from opening up the items and "playing house" like she wanted to do. That would come in due time. Tomorrow—after swim lessons.

When Dillon finally went to bed—on the sagging sofa—she

was not looking forward to morning. And if she hadn't promised to work at the pool, she would've gladly bailed. But, she reminded herself, Chelsea was her friend. Besides that, Dillon needed the income. She had a trailer to support! And for all she knew, baby needed new shoes—tires. At least that was something she'd read today in her trailer book. Most vintage trailers required new tires and bearings and a number of other mechanical things that she knew nothing about but sounded costly. But her trailer project was an investment—an investment in happiness.

CHAPTER

10

On Monday morning, Dillon tried to look bright and cheery as she reported to Chelsea for work, but the idea of getting into the water with a bunch of wily kids was not enticing.

"Your first class is probably in the dressing room right now," Chelsea said as Dillon filled out the paperwork. "And I think I mentioned your last class will end at one."

"And then I get the whole afternoon to myself." Dillon wanted to add "with my sweet trailer," but she knew that sounded fanatical.

"And here's your roster." Chelsea handed her a clipboard. "Good luck." She grinned. "Not that you'll need it." She glanced down at Dillon's swimsuit, partially covered by an oversized denim shirt. "Is that your old team suit?"

Dillon shrugged. "It was the only one I could find. Does it matter?"

"Not at all. I just can't believe you still fit into it."

Dillon laughed. "I just wish I had a little tan to go with it."

"Well, your classes are with the little ones. I remember how good you were with them. So you'll be outside in the shallow pool. Maybe you can work on your tan out there."

Dillon picked up her duffel bag and, bracing herself for a lot of squealing and splashing, she headed for the shallow pool. It wasn't that she didn't like preschoolers. In fact, she did. But they did take a lot of patience and energy. Pulling her hair into a ponytail, she greeted the mothers and children already waiting on the deck. She briefly introduced herself, explaining the expectations of the class, and then, getting the children to hold hands "like a long dragon," she led them down the steps and into the shallow water.

It was amazing how it all came back to her. Getting the kids comfortable in the water. Playing ring-around-the-rosy, blowing bubbles, imitating ducklings, and so on, until it was finally her last class. By now the sun was high in the sky and the air was warm. She greeted her last set of parents, went over the routine, and was about to take the kids into the water when a nicely dressed and attractive mother pulled her aside. She introduced herself as Janelle and the mother of the twin blonde girls. "I don't like to be a helicopter mommy, but I need to warn you that Emma and Chloe have a slight phobia of water. I realize they're older than the other kids in this class, but this is their first swimming lesson experience and I'm—"

"Don't worry." Dillon smiled. "I'm sure they'll be just fine," she assured Janelle.

"I would like to stay and watch, you know, to encourage the girls to cooperate with you, but I'm a Realtor and I have a showing in ten minutes."

"Some children do better without their parents observing," Dillon said. "Really, don't worry."

"Okay. I won't." Janelle held up her phone. "And you have my number . . . just in case."

Dillon nodded, waving to the worried mom as she led the line of children toward the water. The twins were the tail of the dragon, and based on their expressions, were not looking forward to this. "Our dragon is not your ordinary dragon," Dillon said like she usually did. "Our dragon loves the water. He's the best swimmer ever." They were all in the pool—except Emma and Chloe, who were clinging to each other on the top step.

Dillon trailed the "dragon" back over to the twins. "Come on, girls, you don't want to miss out on the fun." She held out her hand.

"We don't want to learn to swim," the girl in the pink-and-white-striped suit declared with a frown.

"But we're going to play games." Dillon smiled. "Which are you? Emma or Chloe?"

"She's Chloe," the other girl said with a nervous smile. She had on an identical swimsuit, but with lavender-and-white stripes. "I'm Emma."

"Emma," Dillon said as she reached for her hand, "you look like a brave girl. Are you ready to come play games with us?"

Emma glanced at Chloe, who firmly shook her head, then looked back at Dillon. "I don't know."

"Come on." Dillon took Emma's hand. "I'll help you. And you'll see how much fun it is." She nodded toward the sky where the sun was shining brightly. "And it's a great way to cool off." She led Emma down one step, keeping her eyes on Chloe. "See how easy this is," she told Chloe. "Your sister can do it."

Somehow, with a lot of coaxing and waiting, she got the twins into the water. But when it was time to play games, they clung to the side of the pool, unwilling to participate. Dillon made numerous attempts to get them to interact and finally decided that if Chloe could relax a bit, Emma would probably engage. Finally, it was one o'clock and Dillon was relieved to dismiss her class. But not seeing Janelle anywhere, she decided to capitalize on this time to work with the girls individually. "You sit here." She lifted Chloe up, setting her on the edge of the pool. "And watch what Emma can do." Now she took Emma's hand and did a few bobbles and jumps with her and even got her to blow some bubbles with her face in the water. "Very good," she told Emma, keeping her eyes on Chloe. "You're going to be a natural."

She led Emma back to the pool's edge, and after setting her on the deck, she reached for Chloe. "Now, it's your turn." But as she lifted Chloe into the water, the little girl began to scream. "It's okay," Dillon reassured her, trying to be heard over the wailing. "I'm right here with you. Remember how Emma did this. You just need to hold onto my hands and—"

"I want my momma!" Chloe howled, kicking wildly. "I hate you! I hate you!"

"But we're just going to—"

"That's enough," a male voice said loudly from behind Dillon.

She turned around to see Jordan Atwood wrapping a towel around Emma and scowling darkly. "Oh?" He blinked. "It's you."

"And it's you," she said as she helped Chloe to the edge of the pool. Jordan wrapped her in a towel and she clung to him.

"Janelle asked me to get the girls," he told her. "She got way-laid."

"I was trying to use the time to help—"

"I wanna go home," Chloe cried pitifully. "I want my momma. I hate swimming lessons."

"Emma made some progress," Dillon said meekly as Jordan quickly gathered up the girls' things.

"The twins have a fear of water." He looped a strap of their pink beach bag over his shoulder, keeping a girl on each side. "I warned Janelle that this could be a mistake. But she insisted it was the right thing." He shook his head. "I'm not sure if they'll be back again tomorrow or not."

Dillon just nodded. She actually hoped that they wouldn't be back. She didn't need that kind of stress in her life. And to see that Jordan Atwood was obviously a father with children and Janelle's husband did not help matters either. Dillon emerged from the pool feeling waterlogged and defeated and wondering if the meager salary of swim instructor was worth it. But a deal was a deal. She'd made Chelsea a promise, and she intended to keep it.

Dillon stopped at a taco cart before going home. As she sat at a shady table to eat, she processed the fact that Jordan Atwood was not a bachelor. Then, as she drove home, she wondered why on earth she'd jumped to that conclusion in the first place. Yes, she'd noticed his bare left-hand ring finger, but that wasn't real proof. Lots of men didn't like wearing rings. Especially guys who worked with their hands. But besides the missing ring, what about the way he'd spoken to her . . . the way he'd looked at her? The feeling she'd gotten when their eyes had met? He had not acted like a married man. Perhaps he was divorced. That would make sense.

Except that, in her opinion, it made no difference. Dillon had no desire to be involved with a divorced guy. Especially with children involved. And Janelle seemed like a genuinely nice person. No, that was not for Dillon. And why was she still thinking about it?

Whatever it was, it was not her problem. "Not my monkey, not my circus," she said aloud as she turned onto the farm road. Of course, it was irritating to remember that was one of Brandon's favorite sayings—his way of backing off from responsibilities he didn't want. And thinking of Brandon was just another reminder of how Dillon had never ever been a good judge of men. Not as a teen, not in college, not in Colorado. What made her think she'd magically gotten better at it here in Silverdale?

Well, at least she had her trailer. That was enough to occupy her thoughts and energies. Who needed a man anyway? Certainly not her. As she parked her car by the trailer, she suddenly remembered all the treasures she'd unloaded last night. Maybe it was time to play house. That would certainly distract her from moping over Jordan.

Once inside the trailer, after admiring the first stages of transformation, Dillon knew she needed to finish her sewing and upholstery projects before she unpacked her trailer treasures. Otherwise, she might never go back to the old Singer.

So with fresh motivation, she studied another online tutorial. A "simple" how-to on upholstering dinette benches. She watched it several times. Then, feeling relatively confident, she started to measure—and re-measure—the foam seat. Next she marked the measurements on the tweedy upholstery fabric, and praying she'd done it right, she held her breath and cut. Hoping it would fit, she laid the fabric piece on the dinette table, setting the foam bench on top, and like the tutorial showed, she folded the corners of the fabric. Then she refolded—again and again.

Finally, convinced that the corner looked right, she pulled out the staple gun and secured the fabric to the wooden board underneath. It felt empowering to hear the staple going into the wood. She continued with the rest of the stapling, unsure what she'd discover when she flipped it over. But to her surprise, the results were amazing. It was smooth and neat. Just like in the tutorial. As Dillon surveyed her work, she wondered if she'd just found her calling. And did upholsterers get paid more than swimming instructors?

Of course, thinking about this morning's swim lessons only reminded her of Jordan again . . . and those fractious twin girls, Emma and Chloe. She still felt aggravated at how their dad had flown off the handle at Dillon's attempts to get Chloe more comfortable in the water. Well, hopefully Jordan would stick to his guns and take his girls out of her class. Good riddance to all of them!

Grateful for the distraction of her trailer, she blocked the Atwood family from her mind, focusing all her energy and effort back on the upholstery project. She was just finishing it up when she heard someone knocking on the trailer door.

She opened it to see Grandpa and his wheelbarrow, which had a large square box in it. "Special delivery for Dillon Michaels," he told her.

She stared at the large box then suddenly remembered. "My bed!"

"Bed?" He frowned at the box. "Must not be very big."

"It gets bigger." She went out, picking up the bulky box and hoping it would fit through the door.

"This I gotta see." He followed her inside, then, pulling out his pocketknife, he helped her open the box. She removed a square plastic-covered thing from the box. "Is that your bed?" he asked.

"It says to open it carefully." She read the directions. "And to stand back."

Grandpa chuckled as she followed the instructions to free the mattress. Then they both jumped back as it magically grew before their eyes.

"Well, I'll be." Grandpa just shook his head. "Never saw anything like that before."

She wrestled the mattress into place on the bed, then flopped down on it and grinned. "It's really comfortable."

"Better than my old sofa?"

She sighed. "Way better. In fact, I might just move myself out here now."

"Not a bad idea." Grandpa looked around the trailer, letting out a low whistle. "You've really transformed this thing, Dillon." He ran a hand over a freshly painted cabinet door, then examined the upholstery she'd just finished. "Nice work. I had no idea this old thing could look this great."

She stood up and smiled. "Thank you. I love doing this. In fact, I was just wishing I could do this kind of thing for a living."

He shrugged. "Maybe you can." He knelt down to look at the floor. "What're you going to put down here?"

"I'd like to get some stick-down vinyl tiles. Nothing fancy. Just clean and light."

"The hardware store probably has some."

She grimaced, unsure she wanted to go back there and risk running into Jordan Atwood again. Now Grandpa inquired about swimming lessons and, not wanting to mention Jordan and the twins, she told him a sweetened-condensed version of her morning. "But it's just a summer job," she said. "And I didn't commit for more than the first session, which ends in mid-July."

Grandpa touched her bare shoulder. "Looks like you got a little sunburn."

She frowned. "Yeah, guess I'll have to be more careful."

"Fortunately you've got your grandmother's coloring." He tweaked her auburn hair. "You'll be tan by the end of the week." He reached for the door. "I better get back to my pumpkin patch."

"How's it coming?"

"Got it about half planted. Want to finish before sundown and get the irrigation going on it. And, oh yeah, Margot told me to tell you she's fixing dinner tonight—and she doesn't want to hear us whining for red meat."

"Oh, delightful." Dillon rolled her eyes, then thanked him for delivering her wonderful bed. Suddenly excited over the prospect of sleeping out here, she went to work sewing the last two sets of curtains. When she was finally hanging the last curtains on the window next to her new bed, she wondered why it felt so satisfying to get these little tasks completed. Just a few weeks ago, she would've had absolutely no interest in something like this. She probably would've laughed if someone had told her she'd be rehabbing an old trailer and thrilled about the prospect of inhabiting it. Was she losing it? If she was, she wasn't sure she cared.

CHAPTER

11

*A*lthough her first classes had gone well, Dillon was not looking forward to her last class of little swimmers. And although she felt guilty for it, she hoped and prayed those blonde twins would be a no-show. It wasn't that she didn't want them to learn to swim. She felt everyone should learn to swim. She just wanted them to learn from someone else.

But apparently Jordan's disapproval hadn't discouraged his wife, because Janelle, once again looking stylishly chic, showed up with the two girls. "I hear they gave you a bad time yesterday," she told Dillon. "I gave them a stern talk." She bent down to help her girls get their sandals off. "You two are going to do your best, right?" Janelle pointed at who Dillon assumed was Chloe since she had on the pink-striped suit again. "And you need to go into the water with Emma. Understand?"

Chloe nodded. "Okay, Mommy."

"And if I don't get a good report, there'll be no ice cream treat afterward."

Dillon forced a smile, then organizing the water dragon, she led the kids into the pool. Emma was trying a bit more, but Chloe was holding back, unwilling to go down the steps. "Go ahead and sit down here," Dillon told Chloe. "You can watch the others." Chloe sat down and Dillon, hoping to use some reverse psychology, tried to make their water games look as fun as possible. Even though Emma was dragging her heels, she was trying. Meanwhile, Chloe glowered from her position on the top step. Janelle came down to the pool and Dillon thought she was about to intervene, but instead she held up her phone. "I'm sorry, I've got to go do another showing again. A client is certain they've found a great house." She shook her finger at Chloe. "You better get in there with your sister."

Chloe inched down to the next step, sitting waist deep in the water, but as soon as her mother left, she returned to the top step. After a few more games, where the other children were making nice progress of holding their breath and blowing bubbles, Dillon had the class move to the edge and practice kicking. Determined to get Chloe into the water, she went over and took the girl's hands. "Come and play a game with me."

"I don't wanna." Chloe leaned back, but Dillon continued to pull her into the water.

"I won't let go of you," Dillon assured her. "See how nice it is in the water."

"I don't wanna!" Chloe shouted. "Lemme go—lemme go."

"You'll be okay." Dillon continued talking quietly. "We're just going over to Emma. Don't you want to be with your sister?"

"No! I don't wanna swim. I want out." Chloe's screams grew louder and Dillon could see the other children, including Emma, getting worried. So she took Chloe back to the steps.

"See, that wasn't so bad." She patted her head. "Next time I want you to do that with no screaming, okay?"

Chloe said nothing, but her face was flushed and her arms were tightly folded in front of her. Dillon just smiled. "Someday you're going to love the water, Chloe. You'll be like a real mermaid."

"I won't," she seethed.

As Dillon returned to the other children, she wondered if there was a reason Chloe hated the water so much, or if she was just a thoroughly unpleasant child. Instead of trying to figure it out, Dillon focused on the other children, trying harder than ever to make swimming look like the most fun in the world.

Once again, when the class ended, Janelle was not back from her showing. "Let's keep playing," Dillon told Emma. "You've been doing so well." She glanced over at Chloe. "Too bad your sister doesn't want to play in the water with us." She got a beach ball. "Let's play catch."

"Okay." Emma held up her hands, bouncing in the waist-high water.

"I want Emma with me," Chloe yelled. "She's *my* sister."

Emma looked uneasy, but Dillon tossed her the ball anyway and they went back and forth a bit, laughing and jumping. "Now I'll throw the ball to Chloe." Dillon threw the ball, making sure it was just short of the steps. "Get it, Chloe," she called out.

"No! I don't wanna. I hate you! I want my momma!" She stood up. "I wanna go home!"

Naturally, now that Chloe was throwing another full-blown fit, Jordan walked in again. "Let's get out," Dillon told Emma. "Time to go home."

Jordan was already wrapping Chloe in a towel and looking perplexed. "What happened?" he asked Dillon with concern. "Why is she so upset again?"

"Chloe has a serious aversion to the pool. Emma is making wonderful progress. But Chloe refuses to try." Dillon reached for her bag, tugging out her beach towel.

"Maybe she just needs encouragement."

"I've been trying to encourage her." She wrapped her towel around her waist like a sarong. "To be honest, I'm not sure that it's worthwhile for her to continue with lessons. And it's possible Emma would do better if Chloe wasn't—"

"Janelle is determined that both girls will learn to swim this summer. She seems to think that a qualified instructor can handle it. But if you can't . . ."

"I can't force a child to like the water." Dillon didn't conceal her frustration.

"No, I'm not suggesting that. But can't you do something to entice her?"

"I've been trying, but I do have other children to teach. And I don't want to traumatize Chloe." She wanted to add she'd taught obstinate children before, but nothing like this one.

"So you think it's useless then?"

Dillon glanced up at the clock with aggravation. What was

wrong with this family? They were determined to torture her. "If you'll excuse me." She smiled stiffly. "That was my last class for the day."

"Yes, yes. I'm sorry for being late again," he said quickly. "Janelle didn't know her clients were going to write up an offer, and I got busy at the store."

"Please, tell Janelle I'm sorry that I can't give a good report on Chloe. But Emma did her best." Dillon grabbed up her bag, pulled on her swimsuit cover-up, and, feeling more than a little irritated, walked away. She didn't want to be rude, but wasn't her time as valuable as anyone's?

As she got into her car, she realized this might be a good opportunity to make a quick trip to the hardware store and check out their flooring options. Jordan would have his hands full with the twins. Probably getting them both ice cream despite Janelle's ultimatum.

Thanks to the limited flooring options, it didn't take long to make a decision. She opted for squares the color of oatmeal. Hoping her math was right, she purchased three boxes of self-adhering tiles, which she thought was more than enough, as well as a couple of tools the salesperson recommended. To her relief, she paid for her purchases and was on her way home without having crossed paths with Mr. Atwood. Funny how just a few days ago, she'd tried to casually bump into him. Now she cringed to even think about him.

After a quick lunch, Dillon went to work laying the floor tiles. As with everything in the trailer, she studied a couple of tutorials first. But really, it was relatively easy. And before dinnertime, her clean new floor was securely laid. Dillon was so pleased with herself that she did a stocking-foot happy dance.

That evening, determined to take full occupancy of her trailer, Dillon began to open and unpack her treasures. With music playing on her phone, she began to put all her lovely things into place. It truly felt like Christmas in June. The kitchen, other than a few missing items, was set. The bathroom was mostly set. And after making her comfy bed up with the smooth, luxurious sheets, Dillon could hardly wait to try it out. She made several trips to the house, carrying back her clothes and personal items and neatly stowing them away.

The only thing missing was a shower. But since she'd spent the whole morning in the pool, she wasn't too concerned. And before long, feeling happy as a clam in her sweet little shell, she had on her summer PJs and was about to get into bed when she heard a knock on the door.

"Are you still out here?" Margot called through the open window.

Dillon cracked open the door. "Yes. This is where I live now."

"What?" Margot frowned. "You're staying in this nasty little trailer?"

"It's not nasty." She opened the door wider. "Take a look if you don't believe me." She looked at Margot's feet. "But please remove your shoes."

"Why?" Margot came up the steps and glanced inside. "Oh, wow." She kicked off her sandals and came in. "What happened?"

Dillon couldn't help but laugh. "I renovated it."

"Dilly-Dilly." Margot walked around with wide eyes. "This is gorgeous."

"Really?" Dillon felt hopeful. "You like it?"

"It's fabulous." Margot opened a kitchen cabinet. "And you've got dishes and everything."

"Go ahead and look around." Dillon nodded. "It's like a tiny home."

Margot examined everything, exclaiming about how nice it all was. "I had no idea my daughter was so talented. This is really nice."

Dillon thanked her. "It was a lot of work, but it's worth it." She pointed to the bed. "That is so comfortable. My back will be grateful in the morning."

"And Dad gave you this trailer?" Margot asked her. "Yours to keep?"

"Yes. Remember, I told you."

"Well, I wasn't sure if it was for keeps . . . or just to use for now."

Dillon felt a rush of concern. Had she misunderstood? "I'm pretty sure he said it was all mine."

Margot frowned. "Well, then I'm jealous."

"But you hated this trailer. You made fun of it. Remember?"

"I don't hate it now. I could actually imagine living here. For someone my age, jobless and virtually homeless, well, something like this makes a lot of sense. Maybe you'd like your own bedroom back."

Dillon was perplexed. Did her mom plan to swap? To move in and take over? "Tell you what, Margot, you find yourself an old trailer and I'll help you fix it up."

Margot wrinkled her nose. "Thanks a lot, but I've got my hands full with the lavender."

"Really? Why's that? I thought it just needed water and sunshine."

"According to Dad, it needs weeding too. And then I've got to plan for what I'll do once I start harvesting. It'll be quite a job."

"Oh." Dillon suppressed a yawn. "Well, it's kinda late. I have to get up—"

"Yeah, I don't want to keep you up. I know you have work tomorrow. I was just curious." She looked around one more time. "This really is nice, Dillon."

"Thanks." She watched as Margot tugged her sandals back on, and then told her mother good night. But as Dillon closed the door, she felt worried. Did Margot feel she had some right to this trailer? Hadn't Grandpa given it to Dillon—free and clear? Surely, she hadn't misheard him. She was tempted to run into the house and ask him to set her straight, but knowing he went to bed with the chickens, she knew he'd be asleep. Still, as she climbed into her delightfully comfortable bed, some of her earlier joy was diminished a bit. What if Margot really wanted this trailer now? What if she felt it was unfair that Grandpa had given it to Dillon? What then?

CHAPTER
12

She next day at the pool went more smoothly for Dillon. Her first classes were much the same, and then to her relief, her last class went better. Chloe appeared to be actually trying. Reluctantly perhaps, but at least she was willing to go waist deep in the water. Perhaps it was because Janelle remained at the pool for the entire lesson. Whatever, it was an improvement.

"You did great today," Dillon told Chloe as class ended. She clasped the little girl's hand. "I'm really proud of you."

"You are?" Chloe blinked.

"Yes. You were very brave." Dillon waited for the other children to clamber out of the water, then slowly led Chloe toward the steps where Emma waited. "I really do think you're going to be a mermaid someday."

"Like Ariel?" Chloe's eyes lit up.

"Yes. Do you know that *The Little Mermaid* used to be my favorite movie," Dillon told both girls as they stood on the bottom step. "Do you like it too?"

They both nodded eagerly.

"Do you remember how eager Ariel was to live outside of the water?" Dillon asked. "That's how I used to feel too."

"You wanted to live out of the water?" Emma looked confused.

"No. In the water. I wanted to be a mermaid. That was the first time I took swimming lessons. Right here in this pool. And I've been swimming ever since."

"I'd like to be a mermaid," Emma said.

"Do you think I could ever really swim?" Chloe asked Dillon. "For real."

"I know you could swim. You just have to learn."

"Like me," Emma said. "Did you see me floating today, Chloe? Just like a real mermaid."

Chloe frowned. "I can't do that."

"Not now," Dillon said. "But you can learn."

Janelle held up their bag. "Come on, girls. Don't make Dillon stay late."

"It's okay." Dillon took both girls by the hand, leading them onto the deck. "And both girls did their best today," she told Janelle. "They get a good report."

"Wonderful." Janelle smiled brightly. "Thank you."

Dillon was relieved that Jordan wasn't the one picking up the girls today. She hurried over to the locker room to grab a shower. Her plan was to pay the Silver Slipper a visit. She wanted to show Vivian the "after" photos of her little trailer and ask for some advice.

Fortunately, Grandpa had confirmed to Dillon that the Oasis trailer truly was hers. Over breakfast, he assured her that had been his intention. "And I'll dig up the title and sign it over to you," he promised. "I know both Jack and Rose would be pleased to see how you've rescued it."

"At least the inside of it." She frowned. "I'm not sure what to do about the exterior."

"Paint it."

"But how?"

"With paint." He grinned. "I'm always painting my farm equipment. Sometimes I use spray paint. Sometimes I just get a heavy-duty metal paint. It's not hard to do. As long as you do the prep work first."

"Do you really think I could paint it myself?"

"Don't know why you couldn't. You sure did a nice job on the inside."

"Thanks to online tutorials."

"Well, I'm sure you can find some tips on exterior painting too."

"Okay," she told him. "I guess I'll look into it."

But first she wanted to visit the Silver Slipper. And, according to Vivian, there were various schools of thought on the subject. "Some people insist that only a professional paint job is good enough. But I know others who've done it themselves with great results. You just need to do it right."

"I'm sure I can find some online help for that. I found it for everything else so far." Dillon paused to show her pictures of the renovated interior.

"You're a whiz!" Vivian declared. "I can't believe how quickly you turned it around. Impressive."

"I suppose I was sort of desperate." Dillon confessed about her less-than-ideal sleeping quarters in the living room. "But I slept like a baby last night." She asked Vivian a few more questions and showed her a list of items she thought her trailer might still need. Vivian recommended various products and websites. "But you can get some of those things at the hardware store. Jordan carries a lot of standard trailer and RV stuff. That section is clear in the back of the store."

"Oh, yeah . . . right." Dillon had no desire to visit the hardware store, but since a couple was asking Vivian for help, she thanked her and headed down the street, hoping that Jordan might be on a lunch break just now.

Since she didn't see Jordan as she entered Atwood's, she went straight to the back of the store. There, sure enough, was a fairly large RV section. Before long, she'd gathered up several items from her list. She was just picking out a fresh water pressure relief valve when Jordan walked up. "Can I help you?" he asked with a surprisingly warm smile.

"I think I found what I'm looking for." She held up the package.

He looked confused . . . or maybe amused. "Is that for your irrigation system?"

"No," she said curtly. "This is for my camp trailer." She dropped it into her cart.

"Oh." He nodded. "You have a camp trailer?"

"Yes." She pointed to the package of RV toilet paper in her cart as if proof. Then immediately felt embarrassed.

"Well, that's great. What kind of trailer is it?"

"An old one." She started to roll her cart—as in, hint, hint.

"How old is it?"

She thought about that. "Well, it's older than me. That's for sure." She attempted to do the mental math, then gave up. "It's well over fifty years old."

His brows arched. "Really, that old?"

She nodded, trying to think of a way to curtail this pointless conversation and escape.

"Vintage?" He set a hand on her cart, as if to detain her.

"Yes, I guess you could say that."

"What make?"

She wondered why it mattered, but told him it was an Aloha.

"Aloha?" He frowned. "What model?"

She told him it was an Oasis, thinking he'd probably assume it might look like an Arabian tent, at home in the desert.

"What year Oasis?"

She tipped her head to one side. "I, uh, I think it's 1964."

"With a cab-over?" he asked.

"Cab-over?" She made a confused frown.

He made a high wavy motion with his hand. "You know, it would hang over the pickup bed. Just slightly. But it'd have a bunk inside it. Right over the dinette."

She blinked. "Yeah, it's exactly like that."

"Cool." He nodded. "And does it have a tiny bathroom in the back corner? Barely big enough to stand in?"

"Yes. But how can you possibly know so much about a 1964 Oasis?"

"Because my uncle used to have one like that."

"Oh." She nodded.

"Yeah, I used to go hunting with him. I slept in the cab-over bunk. Pretty cool since it had its own windows. Always loved Uncle Jack's old trailer."

"Uncle Jack?"

"Yeah. Jack Martin. He passed away last year."

"Jack and Rose Martin?"

"That's right." He nodded. "Aunt Rose moved to the coast and—"

"Jack left his old trailer to my grandpa," she said somberly. "They used to be hunting buddies."

"Oh, that's right. I remember now—your grandpa went hunting with my uncle sometimes. Man, those were good ol' days. Just the guys out in the woods, hunting elk or deer. Or if no game showed up, just shooting the bull and eating great food." He rubbed his chin with a wistful look. "Seriously, you have Uncle Jack's old trailer?"

She bit her lip, suddenly worried that Jordan, like her mom, might feel he had some sort of ancestral right to *her* trailer. What if he thought his uncle should've left it to him—or he wanted to contest the will? "Yeah, well, my grandfather gave it to me last week," she said quickly. "I've been fixing it up."

"Well, good for you." His smile looked genuine. "I'm sure it needed some serious TLC."

She felt slight relief. "Yeah, it's been great working on it. Kind of therapeutic."

"Therapeutic?" He peered closely at her.

She felt her cheeks warm. "Well, cathartic or something. I just left a job and everything behind in Colorado. I guess I needed something to occupy myself."

"You mean besides teaching swimming lessons?" His brows arched with obvious amusement.

"Yeah, that's not really my career choice. Just filling my time."

121

She stood up straighter. "By the way, Chloe made impressive improvements today. I was very pleased with her."

His eyes lit up. "That's great news. I meant to tell you this, but I didn't want to say it in front of her. Chloe had a real scare last summer. She fell into the deep end of the pool and, thanks to one of those floating alarm devices, she was rescued. But ever since then, she's been totally paranoid of pools. And it was starting to affect Emma too. That's why Janelle insisted on lessons this summer. But it's a challenge for Janelle because of work demands. And the nanny doesn't drive. Which is why I've been picking up the slack some."

Dillon nodded. "I wondered if something had happened to make her so fearful. It actually helps to know this. Thanks." She pointed to her cart. "Well, if I'm going to get any work done on my trailer today, I better get going."

"And if you need any pointers or any—"

"Jordan?" a guy called out from the other end of the aisle. "Delivery question—we need you in back."

Dillon thanked him and rolled her cart away. It rattled her that Jordan was being so nice and friendly. A bit too friendly. Or else was she just being overly sensitive . . . because of her earlier assumptions? Whatever the case, she was glad to get away from him.

CHAPTER

13

*B*y Friday morning, after much online research, Dillon's mind was made up. She was going DIY. She would paint her own trailer—and save thousands of dollars. At least that's what she hoped. She'd already spent several hours sanding the metal siding, masking the windows, and removing hardware and lights, until she finally felt like this was a task she could handle. And after looking at her bank balance, she knew it was belt-tightening time.

Her plan was to take each step slowly and carefully—and she would get the recommended paint products. To this end, she found herself at the hardware store on Friday afternoon. Relatively sure that Jordan wouldn't be there since he'd just picked up the twins at the pool—on time for a change—she'd hurried to Atwood's. Now with paint samples of a nice milky white and a medium-toned turquoise picked out, she was explaining her DIY plan to Ryan the paint guy.

"You're seriously going to do it all by yourself?" he asked.

She nodded. "That's my plan. It'll probably take my whole weekend, or longer, but I don't care. It's worth the savings. And I've seen great photos of trailers that were painted this same way."

"Well, I'd like to see your photos when you're done." Ryan put the first gallon of paint in the shaking machine.

"Then you will." She glanced over her shoulder, still worried that Jordan might pop in and start offering his opinions . . . and really, she didn't want any more advice. And she didn't want to see him. She just wanted to get her little trailer looking as sweet on the outside as it was on the inside. And her plan was to start painting first thing tomorrow morning.

"Well, hello." Jordan, with the twins still wearing their swimsuits and cover-ups, noisily entered the store. "Didn't expect to see you here, Dillon. Painting something?" He leaned on the paint counter with a curious expression.

Before she could answer him, the twins yelled out happy greetings, running over to hug and greet her, treating her like their long-lost best friend, and giving Dillon an excuse to momentarily ignore their dad. "Did you girls get your ice cream treat for doing so well in class today?" she asked them. "Because you were both fabulous."

"Nope." Emma firmly shook her head. "Not yet!"

"Silly Uncle Jordan said we had to come here *first*," Chloe explained with equal exasperation. "He's s'posed to check something."

"*Uncle* Jordan?" Dillon couldn't help but repeat this.

"Yeah." Chloe nodded. "He said no ice cream till we're done here."

"Hurry up, Uncle Jordan." Emma poked him in the back. "We need ice cream."

"Patience, please." He turned around, kneeling to look at the girls. "Tell you what, ladies, I'll let you pick one thing from over there." He pointed to the snack rack beside the register. "As long as you promise not to tell your mother."

They gave their word and were immediately distracted with the colorful assortment in the snack section, instantly arguing about which was the best choice.

Now Jordan smiled at Dillon. "So Ryan tells me you're painting your Oasis."

Too flustered to answer, she simply nodded. Was Jordan really the uncle—not the dad? Not Janelle's husband? Had Dillon simply jumped to the wrong conclusion?

"By hand?" he persisted.

"Well, I was planning to use brushes and rollers," she said dryly.

He chuckled. "Yeah, I figured that much." He pointed to the can already mixed. "Well, you've got the right product for it. As long as you follow the manufacturers' recommendations, you should be okay."

"What recommendations do you mean?"

"For instance, you need the right temperature. Not too hot. Not too cold."

"Right." She nodded. "Well, I plan to start painting tomorrow. And I think the temperature is supposed to be fairly moderate this weekend."

"Need any help?"

125

"Help?" She still felt off-kilter. "What kind of help?"

"Well, to be honest, I'd like an excuse to see the old Aloha Oasis. But I can be a pretty hard worker too. Two of us painting would make it go a lot faster. Might even wrap most of it up in a day. A long day."

"Really? You'd do that for me?"

He nodded. "Sure. It'd be fun."

She still felt uncertain about his relationship with Emma and Chloe. Sometimes divorced moms would call their boyfriends "uncles." What if that was the case here? She glanced to where the girls were still making their selections. "So Emma and Chloe are your nieces." She tried to sound casual. "I kind of assumed you were their dad."

He grinned. "Well, I've probably stepped in like a dad at times. Especially after Janelle's husband stepped out a couple years ago. I try to make myself available."

"So Janelle's last name is Atwood too?" Dillon hoped she didn't sound nosy, but she'd double-checked the roster the day after Jordan had picked the twins up. "Does that mean she was married to your brother then?"

"No. My baby sister was married to a jerk. She took back her maiden name after an unhappy divorce. Can't say I blame her either."

"I see." Dillon felt a rush of pure joy. So Janelle was Jordan's sister. Of course, it all made sense now.

"Paint's ready," Ryan announced.

"Great!" Although Dillon no longer felt the need to hurry, she turned to pick up the cardboard box of paint cans, but Jordan beat her to it, carrying it over to the register. "Have someone help her out with this," he instructed the cashier.

"Thanks," Dillon told him.

"So what time then?" He waited.

"What time . . . ?" She still felt dazed.

"*When* do you plan to get started tomorrow?" His eyes brightened. "Or maybe I should ask, when's breakfast?"

"Breakfast." She nodded. "How does seven sound?"

"Perfect. I'll see you then." He went to check on his nieces, and still feeling stunned, Dillon paid for her purchase. But as Ryan carried her paint out to her car, she wondered . . . This news still didn't guarantee that Jordan wasn't married. What if she'd simply jumped from one wrong conclusion to another? She opened the hatchback, waiting as Ryan set the box in. "Thanks." She smiled nervously. "Uh, can I ask you a question?"

"You bet." He nodded.

"Is Jordan Atwood married?"

"Nope." Ryan laughed. "He's not. Some people claim he's the most available bachelor in Silverdale, but if you ask me, the dude's *unavailable*." He closed her hatchback.

"Unavailable?"

He nodded. "No girl's been able to catch him. And, trust me, plenty are trying. Including my older sister—until she gave up. Now, instead of calling him an eligible bachelor, she calls him an *eternal* bachelor."

"Oh, well . . ." She smiled stiffly, trying to think of something else to say.

"Yep. We see it all the time in the store. Females coming in here for random items that we doubt they really need." He laughed. "One lady will buy something one day then return it the next. She really gets some bang for her buck."

"Well, you don't need to mention that I asked." She attempted to appear nonchalant. "I was just curious. You know, because his nieces are in my swim class, and I'd mistaken him for their dad. Anyway, have a nice day, Ryan. Thanks."

By the time she got behind the wheel, her cheeks felt overly warm and flushed. And it wasn't from the sun either. In fact, her sunburn had settled into a nice golden tan. But as she drove through town, she could imagine Ryan informing Jordan of her inquiry. And why not? They could share a good laugh over it.

Well, at least she knew the whole truth now. Jordan Atwood was not married, and according to Ryan, he was not available. As she turned down the farm road, she wondered if Jordan was simply another Brandon—emotionally unavailable and afraid of commitment. The eternal bachelor. Leave it to her to be attracted to another guy like that! When would she learn?

CHAPTER
14

Since Dillon had renovated and taken up occupancy of her little Oasis, she hadn't spent much time inside Grandpa's house lately. And to be honest, she didn't want to. She still helped with meals and KP, but assuming that Margot had moved to the farm in order to "help out," it was only right to let Margot take responsibility for running the household. Besides, Dillon figured Margot was probably glad to have her out of her hair.

Despite her trailer focus, Dillon still maintained her grandma's garden, which was coming along nicely. And with the trailer in good shape, she'd decided to spend the rest of her Friday afternoon catching up on some garden chores. After the weeding and a few other things, she sat down on the lawn swing, determined to leisurely enjoy the rest of the pleasant summer afternoon. She was overdue for a break—and trailer painting tomorrow might be a long day. Stretched out on the lawn swing, she was just dozing off when she heard the slow creak of the garden-gate hinge.

"Well, *here* you are," Margot announced, coming into the garden. "I've been looking all over for you, lazybones."

"Lazybones?" Dillon was about to point out how hard she'd been working ever since coming home to the farm but realized it would probably just start an argument. She sat up and stared at her mom. "Is something wrong? Is Grandpa okay?"

"No, nothing is wrong. Your grandfather is fit as a fiddle— his words, not mine. But during lunch, he mentioned dinner plans. He's under the impression you're cooking tonight."

"That's fine." Dillon stood and stretched. "I don't mind."

"Maybe *I* mind." Margot placed her hands on her hips and narrowed her eyes, almost like she was looking for a standoff.

"Why's that?"

"Because I'm trying to get Dad—and *all* of us—to eat more healthfully, Dillon. Haven't I made that perfectly clear?"

"Yes. We're well aware of your nutrition goals. But unfortunately, Grandpa and I don't care for your kind of health foods."

"I know." Margot looked defeated. "And it's pretty frustrating. After all, I try my best and all I get is complaints and mocking."

Dillon felt a tinge of guilt.

"I'm only trying to help Dad get healthy so that he can live a good long life. After losing Mom like that . . . well, it was a wake-up call for me. I've been committed to a healthier lifestyle ever since."

"Right . . ."

"But you and Dad—well, you make it impossible."

Dillon thought hard for a solution. "Maybe if there were a way we could compromise . . . if we could incorporate your health foods with the foods that Grandpa loves . . . maybe we'd all be happier."

"Right. Like serve my chickpea-kale salad with a big, fat steak?" Her tone was laced with sarcasm.

"That actually sounds good to me. Especially if you slathered your salad with blue cheese dressing."

Margot rolled her eyes. "What's the point?"

"The point is you're never going to get Grandpa to eat your kind of food if you keep shoving it at him. You know how stubborn he can be. You weren't around when Grandma tried to cut back on Grandpa's salt intake because she was worried about his blood pressure. He just started sneaking salt on the sly, probably consuming more than he would've if she'd just left him alone."

Margot sighed. "Yeah. You're probably right."

"So why not compromise?"

"You really think I can teach an old dog new tricks?"

"It doesn't have to be *new* tricks, Margot. I remember how Grandma fixed healthy food and he never complained." Dillon waved her hand at the bed of salad veggies just sprouting. "They always had fresh produce in the summer. And home-preserved fruits and veggies after that. Isn't that healthy enough?"

"I guess so. But after Mom died, Dad got into some pretty sloppy eating habits. You weren't around to see it, Dillon. I walked in once to find him eating a TV dinner that he hadn't even bothered to heat."

"That's not surprising. He was depressed and grieving. He's doing better now. But how about my suggestion, Margot, why not try a compromise?"

"Okay." She nodded. "I'm willing to try it. But only if you promise to show some enthusiasm for the foods I bring to the table."

"Fine. Well, as long as it's not some slimy green drink with undisclosed ingredients."

"Yeah, yeah, I know how you and Dad simply *adore* my smoothies." Margot's mouth twisted to one side. "Anyway, there's something else I want to discuss with you, young lady." She sat down on the swing, patting the spot beside her with a grim expression.

"What's that?" Dillon suddenly felt like she was ten years old again.

"Housework."

Dillon sat down. "Yeah?"

"We've noticed that you've been neglecting it lately."

"Well, I've been pretty busy with my trailer." Dillon frowned. "Besides that, I'm not living in the house anymore so why should—"

"You've completely moved out?" Margot looked doubtful. "You're living in that trailer 24/7? Never coming into the house at all?"

"Well, I may have to grab a shower here and there on the weekends, but during the week, I'm at the pool so showers aren't a problem. And I'll probably use the laundry room here from time to time. And the kitchen. But I always clean up after myself." She wanted to add "unlike my mother," but didn't.

"Right. So are you suggesting I'm in charge of housekeeping now?"

Dillon shrugged. "Well, you said you moved back here to help with Grandpa. Isn't that part of the deal? You do live in the house. And since I have my own tiny home now . . ." She tipped her head toward the barn. "Well, yeah, I think you should be in charge of housekeeping. It's fair."

"What about grocery shopping? Am I in charge of that too? You eat here."

"I don't mind picking up a few things when I'm in town. I've brought home eggs and milk and bacon and whatever Grandpa asks—"

"Yeah, more foods that aren't good for him."

"Are we going there again?" Dillon slowly stood. "Because I've got other things—"

"Isn't it great to have your own little hideaway?" Margot scowled as she stood.

Dillon smiled, perhaps a bit smugly. "Yeah, it is pretty great. Very comfy and cozy. But it still needs work. So if you'll excuse me, I'll—"

"Didn't look like it needed much work to me the other night. What's left to do? Or is this just your excuse to—?"

"I'm painting the exterior tomorrow. And I still have some prep work to do." Dillon headed for the gate, which Margot had left open.

"You're painting that whole trailer? All by yourself?" Margot followed her. "Do you even know how to do something like that?"

"I've done the research. I think I can handle it. And I've got someone coming to help tomorrow." Dillon was tempted to keep the news about Jordan to herself, but since it would be obvious by tomorrow, she decided to get it over with. What difference did it make anyway?

"Who's coming to help?"

"Jordan Atwood." Dillon waited.

Margot's brows arched. "Is this some new kind of customer service from the hardware store?"

"No, it's just a friend helping a friend."

"Jordan Atwood is your friend?" Margot looked skeptical.

"Sure. He's a nice guy. I have his nieces in swimming lessons. I've gotten to know him and his family a little."

"And you do know that he's single, don't you?" She waved a finger at her. "Are you sure this isn't something more than just friendship, Dilly-Dilly?"

She let out a long sigh. "He's just a friend. And it seems that his uncle used to own my trailer so he was curious to see—"

"Oh, that's right. I forgot the Atwood family's related to Jack and Rose."

"So anyway, Jordan wanted to help out. Probably just wants to make sure I don't mess it up." Dillon waited for Margot to go through the gate before securely latching it behind them. "Don't forget to keep this closed at all times, Margot. Otherwise the deer will invade and devour everything. Grandma would threaten to skin anyone alive who ever dared leave this gate open."

"Yes, yes, but back to Jordan Atwood. This is very interesting."

"Really, it's not that interesting." Dillon wished she'd kept her mouth shut now.

"Well, Jordan Atwood would be quite a catch, Dilly. And it's no wonder he's interested in you." Margot tweaked an auburn curl. "You're a very pretty girl. Especially if you took a little better care of yourself."

"Thanks." Dillon frowned. "I think."

"So, anyway, if Jordan's coming out here to help tomorrow, maybe we should make him a nice lunch."

"Actually, I'm making him breakfast at seven, but I hadn't planned on—"

"How about if *I* make you guys lunch?" Margot smiled sweetly.

"Really?" Dillon felt worried. "Some kind of health food—"

"No, no . . . like I said . . . I'm willing to try your compromise plan. I'm sure I could make you guys a very palatable lunch. Remember when I made macaroni salad and burgers for my planter boys? They didn't even complain."

"Probably because they were ravenous."

Margot gave Dillon a playful punch in the arm. "Anyway, I could serve you guys lunch outside. Make it sort of festive. Maybe under the aspen grove. It should be cool and comfortable there."

"Why are you being so nice?" Dillon suddenly felt suspicious.

"What? Are you saying I'm *not* nice? *Moi?*" Margot touched her chest like she was deeply offended.

Dillon pursed her lips . . . and bit her tongue.

"You might not realize it, Dilly, but I'm actually a very good cook. Don used to adore my cooking until . . ."

"Until?"

"Well, to be honest, he wasn't a fan of the healthy changes I made. You know, after Mom died."

"Oh." Dillon nodded. "How's old Don doing anyway?"

"I wouldn't know." Margot scowled. "But back to your question. Why would I be willing to make a special lunch for you and your handsome painting buddy tomorrow?"

"Yes. Why?"

"Well, I was just thinking . . . if you wanted to help with some housecleaning in exchange, I wouldn't complain." Margot's smile looked sheepish. "You know, I've never been too great at housekeeping. Not like you, Dilly-Dilly."

Dillon considered this. Of course, that was absolutely true. Margot had always been useless at the simplest household chores. Or else just plain lazy. "Fine," Dillon agreed. "I'll clean the house if you promise to make a really nice lunch for us tomorrow. And that means something on the barbecue too. And I don't mean tofu."

Margot nodded. "Fine. It's a deal. Do you think you could attack the house today? Dad mentioned it was looking a little shabby this morning. I was actually surprised he even noticed. But he did."

"Okay. I'll go do it right now." Dillon turned to look at Margot. "But one more thing about tomorrow's lunch. I don't want it to be just for Jordan and me. That would be weird. I'd like you and Grandpa to join us too. Just a regular casual sort of midday meal, you know? No big deal."

"Oh, yeah. I know." Margot winked like she knew better and planned to do exactly as she pleased.

Instead of reacting to Margot's game, Dillon just headed into the house and went straight into housecleaning mode. As she performed the relatively simple chores—just like her grandma had taught her—she knew she was getting the easy end of this deal. She would have the place looking shipshape in no time. Margot would probably be stuck in the kitchen for several hours tomorrow. And that was fine. It would keep her from meddling. Because the idea of Margot hovering around, making her comments and insinuations that Jordan was there for something more than just plain friendship . . . well, that would be maddening.

CHAPTER

15

*D*illon got up early the next morning. Knowing that Jordan would probably want a peek inside of her trailer, she spent a few minutes getting everything perfect. Of course, it didn't take long to straighten up such a small space. Such a small adorable space! She even took a few minutes to cut some fresh flowers and put them in an old mason jar vase on the dinette. Perfect.

Then she went into the house to start breakfast. She'd already told Grandpa they were having a guest this morning. To her relief, he'd taken the news in stride. No insinuations about romance. And since it was early, she had no worries that Margot would be up.

When Jordan arrived, Grandpa acted perfectly normal, making small talk about the farm and weather and whatnot. And before long, Dillon was dishing up their breakfast.

"It's nothing special," she said as she set a generous plate in front of Jordan.

"Not special?" He shook his head. "Bacon and eggs and hotcakes? That is as special as it gets in my book."

As they ate, Dillon outlined her plan for painting the trailer. "Of course, that's all based on what I found online," she finally said. "But it made sense to me."

"Sounds like a good plan to me." He forked another hotcake. "To be honest, I took the lazy way out with my trailer. Had it professionally painted."

"*Your* trailer?" She got up to refill their coffee cups.

"Yeah, didn't I mention that I own a vintage trailer too?"

"No." Dillon stared at him in wonder. "When did you get it?"

"A few years ago, but I never had time to work on it until I moved back here. I've been restoring it this past year."

"What's your trailer like?"

"It's an Aloha too. A little older than yours. And not as big or nice."

"Sounds like trailer envy," she teased with a good-natured smile.

He grinned. "Yeah, maybe a little. I can't wait to see the old Oasis."

"Dillon's really fixed it up," Grandpa told him. "I never dreamed it could be that nice."

"Last time I saw that trailer was on an elk hunting trip," Jordan said.

"Oh, yeah, I remember those hunting trips. That trailer looked and smelled a whole lot different back in those days." Grandpa laughed. And suddenly they were rehashing old hunting memories.

"Well, as much as I'd like to keep going down memory lane, Dillon and I probably better get to it." Jordan pushed out his chair and Dillon started to clear the table.

"You leave that," Grandpa told her. "You two got your work cut out for you today. I can manage this."

She thanked him, then led Jordan outside. "My trailer's parked on the other side of the barn. Under a loafing shed roof."

"I brought some painting things with me." He pointed to an old red pickup that looked like it had been carefully restored. "How about if we park it by your trailer?"

"Great." She followed him, climbing into the cab of the pickup. "This is a really cute truck."

"Cute, eh?" He patted the dash. "Don't take it personally, *Harvey*."

"*Harvey*?"

"Yep. *Harvey*." The sides of his eyes crinkled when he smiled. "*Harvey's* a 1960 Chevy and his favorite job is to pull *Helen*."

"*Helen*?"

"*Helen's* my trailer. She's a 1960 too. I named them after my grandparents, Harvey and Helen."

"I can't believe you actually have a vintage trailer."

"Why not? I got *Harvey* first. Back in high school. But I'd wanted a trailer for quite a while. I guess I was inspired by Uncle Jack. Anyway, I found *Helen* shortly before I moved back home. She was a wreck. In need of TLC. It's been fun fixing her up. I'm sure she was in worse shape than your Oasis. Lots of stuff had to be replaced."

"Yeah, other than being dirty and old and neglected, the

Oasis seemed pretty solid." She wondered if she should name her trailer too. "So I mostly just painted and cleaned."

"Well, my aunt and uncle took pretty good care of it. I remember as a kid, before Uncle Jack turned it into his hunting trailer, Aunt Rose kept everything in the Oasis in apple-pie order. It was like her little playhouse. Sometimes if she and my uncle got into a spat, she'd go sit in her trailer until he came out and apologized."

Dillon laughed. "I can just imagine that." She waved to where the Oasis was parked. "It's kind of like a she shed. But way better than a shed. It feels like my tiny hideaway."

"And thar she blows." Jordan sighed deeply as they got out of the pickup. "Uncle Jack and Aunt Rose's trailer. I can hardly believe it. It's like meeting an old friend." He patted the side of it.

"Well, the exterior, as you can see, is in need of serious help."

"And help is here." He ran his hand over the sanded metal. "Looks like you've been busy, Dillon. So, can I see inside first?"

"Of course." She opened the door and then the screen, which she'd painted burnt orange to match the cheerful appliances.

"Wow!" he exclaimed as he climbed the steps. "This place looks better than ever. I can't believe it's the same trailer. I love the colors you picked out. My aunt would love them too. Rose's kitchen had colors similar to this. She loved the Southwest."

Dillon followed him inside, savoring his comments and compliments as he examined almost every inch of the small space. "So how long did it take for you to do all this?" he asked with an impressed expression that warmed her heart.

"Not that long really. Although I worked practically night and day on it at first. But I wasn't teaching lessons at the pool yet. And, to be fair, I was very motivated." She described her previous sleeping arrangement. "So it was well worth my efforts." She patted the bed. "And I've slept like a baby ever since I moved in. I can't believe how comfortable and quiet it is out here."

"Have you tried out the appliances or the furnace?" He opened the propane oven and looked inside.

"Not yet. But it's next on my to-do list. After the exterior painting. But I figured I'd probably need to get an expert to look at it."

"Maybe not. I just happen to have a spare propane tank in the back of my pickup. Maybe later on, we can hook it up and give it a try. But we'll have to blow out the gas lines first. They tend to fill up with tiny spider webs."

"Really? But how do you blow them out?"

"Air compressor. I'll bet your grandpa has one."

"So, you know a lot about vintage trailers?"

"I doubt I know too much more than you do. Well, maybe mechanically. But it sounds like you've been doing your research. It's a good way to learn . . . as you go." He closed and fastened the fridge door. "What about towing? Ever done that before?"

"Towing?" She considered this. "You mean like on the road?"

His smile looked amused. "Yeah. Like camping."

She cringed. "No, I've never towed . . . or camped." She didn't want to admit that her small car probably couldn't pull anything bigger than a bicycle trailer. "Mostly I just wanted the trailer to live in . . . well, until I figure things out."

"What kind of things?" He tilted his head to one side.

"You know, life . . . job . . . where I'm going to live."

"I thought you were living here."

"Yeah, well, I am . . . for now."

He pointed upward. "Speaking of *now*, we're burning daylight. Want to get started?"

"Absolutely." She nodded. "I've got all the paint stuff outside, but I'll warn you again, this is new to me. Other than painting the interior, I've never done anything like this before."

"Well, I painted my mom's house last year. I doubt this is too different."

"Just smaller."

He nodded, surveying the trailer's exterior. "Looks like you've got it good and ready to go. I watched a couple howto tutorials last night." He turned to her with a confident smile. "I'm sure we can do this, Dillon."

Before long, he'd unloaded some drop cloths and a few other things he thought would be helpful from his pickup. Soon they were making good progress applying the first coat of paint. Like the tutorials recommended, they applied a thin coat that dried quickly. "It's looking nice and smooth," Jordan said as he stepped back to admire their work. "It might turn out to be almost as good as a professional job."

"Almost?"

"Well, it's hard to beat a pro spray job." Using a paint rag, he gently wiped a fresh spot of paint off her chin. "For a beginner painter, you've managed to keep yourself fairly tidy."

"That's probably because I'm so much slower than you." She pointed to the large section he'd just finished. "You got twice as much done as me."

142

"Well, you were being more careful. And you had to use the stepladder." He stretched his arm to show his height advantage. "I didn't." He checked his watch. "At this rate, we should have the first coat finished in a couple of hours. And with the sun hitting this side, it might even be ready for a second coat later today."

"That reminds me." Dillon pulled her phone out of her jeans pocket. "I promised to let Margot know when to serve lunch."

"Serve lunch?" His eyes lit up.

"Well, don't expect too much. My mom is kind of a whacky cook. I begged her to spare us from her health food obsession. Made her promise to grill some real meat. No tofu burgers."

He grimaced. "Good for you." He dipped his brush in the bucket and went back to work.

Dillon texted Margot that they would be ready for lunch at one, then joined Jordan, painting with a bit of conversation here and there. Dillon thought this was the most pleasant work she'd ever done. But she knew that had something to do with her painting partner.

"You say you're trying to figure out your life," he said as he turned a corner on the trailer. "What is it you think you want to do?"

"I'm not sure." She briefly explained about her previous job. "I never liked my job. I just stuck with it because it seemed the responsible thing to do. And because I had college debt to pay off. Fortunately, I got that taken care of last year."

"So you enjoy techie work then?"

"To be honest, I only got a computer degree because everyone said that was the surest way to get hired. And, sure, I got a fairly decent job. But I didn't like it. And despite long hours,

I couldn't move upward in the corporation." She sighed. "I'm so glad to have it behind me."

"But now you don't know where you're going?"

"Yeah. I don't really see a career in teaching swim lessons."

He laughed. "Well, you're good at it. You have completely won my nieces over. I can't believe the progress they're making. I really thought Chloe was a lost cause."

"We definitely had our moments." Dillon remembered hoping Chloe wouldn't return to class. Now she enjoyed both the girls.

"I suppose I sort of felt like that about running the store after my dad got sick." He paused from painting to adjust a drop cloth. "At first it felt like an unwanted interruption to my life. But then I started to settle in. And now I like it. I feel like I'm where I should be. I really do enjoy small-town life."

"I do too."

"Speaking of small-town life, when was the last time you were here for a Fourth of July celebration?" he asked. "That's one of my favorite Silverdale events, and next week's celebration promises to be a good one."

"It's been ages. Probably not since graduating college. I used to come home during the summers, to help on the farm. I always looked forward to seeing my friends on the Fourth."

"You were smarter than me. Once I went off to college, I hardly ever came back home. I thought I was a big city boy then. And Silverdale was just a Podunk, one-horse town." He paused to dip his paintbrush. "Took me quite a while to figure it all out."

"What did you do after college, before you moved back home?"

"I worked in marketing." He chuckled. "Which is just a fancy name for selling and advertising. I guess I thought I was pretty clever back then and the salary and benefits were motivating, but I wouldn't go back to that now if they paid me millions."

"Kind of like my old job," she said. "Not that anyone would've paid me millions. But I was upset when I left it, worried I'd made a huge mistake. Now I don't regret it at all."

"Sometimes a life needs to get shaken up . . . in order to put the pieces together right."

She paused from painting. "Are you quoting someone, or did you just make that up?"

He laughed. "I guess my old smart-aleck marketing man is still in there somewhere."

"That didn't sound like marketing talk to me." She shook her head. "It sounded like plain old wisdom."

"Well, I suppose if life kicks you around enough, you better get smarter. Get smarter or get beat up."

She laughed now. "There you go again. Maybe you should write these things down, Jordan. You could make little plaques and sell them at the Silver Slipper."

"For folks to hang in their vintage trailers?" he teased back.

"I could probably use some of that wisdom on my walls," she confessed.

They continued to visit and exchange friendly banter . . . and before they knew it, they'd finished the first coat and it was almost one.

"Time for lunch break." Dillon pulled off the old bandana she'd used to tie her hair away from her face and shook her head.

"Wow." Jordan's eyes grew wide. "You should see your hair

in the sunlight. It's like, well, I'm not sure. But kind of like fire or autumn leaves or something."

"Like burning leaves?" she joked.

"Sort of." He smiled. "It's pretty."

She felt her cheeks warm with the compliment. "Thanks," she murmured as she opened the trailer door. "I'm going to clean up for lunch. Feel free to go into the house if you want to clean up too."

"Sure." He nodded, but remained in front of the trailer, just looking at her.

Unable to think of anything to say, and feeling very self-conscious, she turned and hurried inside. Unless she was mistaken, Jordan Atwood was into her . . . maybe not as much as she was into him . . . but something was definitely happening. And it filled her with such a great degree of hope that she felt like singing and dancing as she scrubbed the white paint speckles off her hands. She didn't even mind the cold water coming out of the bathroom tap. And maybe Jordan would help her figure out the hot water heater too. Yes, as her grandma used to say, this was going to be a red-letter day.

Since it was getting warmer outside, she changed into cooler clothes. Not exactly painting clothes, since it was a good pair of khaki shorts and her favorite T-shirt. Hopefully, she'd keep them free of paint—if not, it would be worth it. She even paused to rub some lotion into her arms and legs, admiring the golden tan she'd acquired at the pool recently. She knew that some people would lecture her about sunscreen and all that, but according to her research, the jury was still out—and sunshine's vitamin D was a good cure-all for many things.

As Dillon finished up with a bit of lip gloss and a touch

of mascara, she heard a knocking at the door. Thinking it was Jordan, she opened it, smiling in anticipation. But to her complete and horrified shock, it was not. She was literally speechless and tempted to shut the door and pretend this was just a bad dream.

Instead, she just stared at Brandon Kranze, dressed in a navy blue suit like he was on his way to meet an important client or pose for GQ. He had a bouquet of red roses in his hand and a huge smile on his face. "Dillon, darling!" he exclaimed. "I'm here!"

CHAPTER
16

Although everything in Dillon wanted to slam the door and crawl under her bed, which was impossible since there were cabinets beneath it, she managed to utter a mechanical-sounding greeting. "Hello?"

"It's so good to see you!" Brandon beamed up at her.

"What are you doing here?" she stammered.

"I'm here for you." Brandon came up the step, trying to look over her shoulder and peer into her trailer. "Is this where you're really living?"

"Yes." She nodded firmly, not budging from her hold on the front door. "This is my home."

"Oh, Dillon." His tone was patronizing. "That is so incredibly sad. I'm sorry. I feel like this is all my fault."

"What's your fault?"

"That you're living in poverty like this."

She glanced behind her. "But I love living here."

"You always were a glass-half-full sort of girl, weren't you? I like that."

She frowned. "I still don't understand why you've come."

"I told you, Dillon. I came for you. I want to repair our broken bridge and—"

She held out a bare foot. "Uh, excuse me, I need to put on some shoes." She nudged him off the step, pulled the door closed and even locked it. Then with rubbery knees, she sat on the edge of her bed and picked up her sandals. As she struggled to put them on, her brain was whirling. What on earth was she supposed to do about this? Of all the people she did not want to see! And today of all days! Why was he really here? And how was she going to get rid of him?

Knowing she could delay the inevitable no longer, she took in several deep, calming breaths and, hoping to appear more poised, stepped out of the trailer. "I still don't quite understand why you're here," she told him in a level tone. "How did you even find me?"

"I got your Grandpa's address from your old roommate, Val. She refused at first, but I assured her I only wanted a chance to make things right with you, Dillon." He held out the roses again. "Forgive me?"

"Of course. All is forgiven." She wanted to add that changed nothing, but instead, she took the roses. Brandon obviously had forgotten that of all rose colors, red was her least favorite. And she had no intention of putting them in her trailer. Besides disliking that harsh color, the roses would look ridiculous in there. Just like Brandon looked ridiculous in his fancy suit on her grandpa's farm. But, standing there, speechlessly holding the detested roses, she didn't know what to do next.

"Margot invited me to lunch," he said lightly, as if this were just another day. "In fact, she said to tell you to hurry. She's already putting it on the table."

"Uh, right." Dillon looked at the roses. "Let's take these into the house."

As they walked toward the house, Brandon made small talk, acting like there was nothing the least bit strange about this unexpected visit. Dillon said nothing.

"There you are," Margot called out as she carried a jug of tea down the back-porch steps. "I told Brandon where to find you, Dilly. Isn't it nice he could pop in like this?"

Dillon tossed her mother a sharp glance, as if she were somehow responsible for this debacle. "Here." She held out the roses to Margot. "You take these inside and I'll take the tea. We're under the aspens, right?"

"That's right. Ooh, these are so pretty. I'll put them in a vase for you."

"And do you need any more help bringing things out?" Dillon asked hopefully. "I'm sure Brandon wouldn't mind giving you a hand."

"That's okay. I only have one more thing. You guys go out and join Jordan and Grandpa, and I'll grab the burgers. I was keeping them warm in the oven."

"I didn't know I was coming to a party," Brandon said cheerfully as Dillon led him to where the old picnic table was draped with an old-fashioned tablecloth and nicely set. Even with flowers from the garden. Margot had outdone herself. Not that any of this mattered, because Dillon knew that lunch was ruined now. At least for her.

She set the jug of tea on the table and introduced Brandon to Jordan. "And you remember my grandpa," she said to Brandon.

"Yes." Brandon shook both their hands, lingering with Grandpa. "From two Christmases ago. Before Dillon's grandmother passed. I'm so sorry for your loss, sir."

Grandpa just nodded, then exchanged concerned glances with Dillon.

"I'm as surprised as anyone," Dillon said lightly as she sat next to Jordan. "I had no idea Brandon was paying us a visit. No warning whatsoever."

"That's because I wanted to surprise you." Brandon sat beside Grandpa. "You see, I had to meet with a new client in Bend yesterday." He unfolded a cloth napkin, another reminder that Margot had really pulled out all the stops. "It was such a short drive over here, I thought why not make a weekend of it?" He grinned at Dillon. "I suppose I was thinking about all the times I'd let you down by not showing up when you expected me. I thought you deserved to be surprised by my arrival today."

"Well, you certainly did that." Dillon turned to smile at Jordan, but his expression was hard to read. "Although you didn't pick the best day for an unexpected visit. You see, we're painting my trailer today. Jordan's been helping me. And we really need to continue working on it after lunch. So I'm sorry to say I won't be able to spend any time with—"

"I'll help you paint," Brandon offered, and before Dillon could respond, Margot appeared, setting a big platter of burgers in the center of the table.

"I realize it's nothing fancy," she said as she sat down. "But at least it's not tofu burgers."

"Everything looks really nice," Dillon told her.

"I'll say grace." Grandpa bowed his head.

As Grandpa asked a blessing, Dillon prayed too. She prayed that Brandon would take the hint and disappear after lunch. But as they began to eat, it was clear that he was trying to ingratiate himself to everyone at the table. Even Jordan. He talked and acted as if he and Dillon had never broken up. As if she hadn't left him and anything to do with him behind in Colorado. For good.

Then, acting like the center attraction, Brandon talked about himself and his job, bragging about how successful yesterday's business meeting had gone, and saying how much he liked Oregon, although Colorado had better mountains.

"Yes, but we have the ocean," Dillon countered.

"I know. And I remember our plan to see the Oregon Coast together," he said without missing a beat. "Hopefully we can do that someday. Maybe we can drive from Colorado. I've heard it's a beautiful drive through Utah and—"

"I'm sorry," she interrupted. "But you seem to be under the impression that I didn't leave Colorado for good, Brandon. I have no plans to go back there."

"Well, I'm sure you felt that way when you left. But you made such a rash decision about that. Really out of character for you. And you took off so quickly that you never gave anyone time to talk you out of it."

"It was simply time to go," she said in her defense. "I wanted to come home."

"I agree you were probably overdue for a visit, Dillon. And it's nice you've had this time. But I'm sure you don't know how much you've been missed at work. By LeeAnn more than anyone." He redirected his conversation to the rest of the table. "LeeAnn was Dillon's boss. She told me that Dillon was her right-hand girl."

"More like her slave," Dillon said sullenly.

"LeeAnn admits she may have taken you for granted. But she assured me that if you come back, she'll not only give you a promotion, but a substantial raise as well."

"I don't care about that anymore," Dillon declared. "I'm done with that job."

"Maybe you're being too hasty," Margot said with concern. "You really should give yourself time to consider that offer, Dilly."

"Dilly." Brandon chuckled. "I forgot about that nickname. So cute. So fitting."

Dillon wanted to throw her iced tea in his face but controlled herself. To her relief, Grandpa redirected the conversation by talking to Jordan about his pumpkin patch. And then Margot told Brandon about her lavender project, describing the kinds of products she planned to make after the first harvest. Somehow, they managed to work through a very awkward lunch. Despite Margot's best efforts, Dillon barely touched her food. While everyone else was finishing up, Dillon's stomach felt like she'd swallowed a brick.

"Well, thank you for stopping by," she told Brandon. "And I hate to cut our visit short, but I have a lot of work to do on my trailer."

"That's right." Jordan stood, thanking Margot for their lunch.

"Yes," Dillon said quickly. "You really outdid yourself today, Margot. Thanks."

"But I told you I want to help," Brandon protested.

"Oh." Dillon nodded. "I'm sure Margot would love some help putting all these things away." She smiled at Margot. "What a lot of work it must've been to bring all this out here for us. But it really was lovely to eat outside. Such a pretty day too." She noticed her uneaten burger still on her plate. "In fact, I think I'll take this with me for my afternoon snack." She snatched it up, then grabbed Jordan's arm. "Daylight's burning, right?"

He chuckled as she tugged him away from the picnic site.

"Sorry about that." As they hurried away, she released his arm.

"Sorry?"

"About Brandon." She looked down at her partially eaten burger as they walked. Maybe her appetite was returning now that Brandon was behind them. Hopefully he was helping Margot to clear and carry.

"He appears to be a nice enough guy." Jordan tossed her a sideways glance. "And he really seems to like you."

"Well, appearances are deceiving. Trust me, Brandon is—"

"Hey, wait up!"

They both turned to see Brandon jogging toward them, waving with enthusiasm, his suit jacket flapping behind him.

"Oh, great," she muttered.

"Margot gave me a reprieve on helping her," Brandon announced. "So I'm free to help you guys with the trailer."

Dillon pointed at him. "In *that* suit? Did you not hear that we're *painting*?"

"That's okay." Brandon pulled off his jacket as they walked, and then removed his tie. "I'm not concerned."

"What about your fancy shoes?" She pointed to his favorite Italian loafers. "They're sure to be ruined."

"Then I'll take them off. It's warm enough to go barefoot."

"But you'll—"

"Oh, you worry too much." Brandon patted her on the head in a condescending way. "Lighten up, Dilly."

She felt rage rising within her. "Do you even know *how* to paint?"

"How hard can it be?"

"Not that hard," Jordan told him. "As long as you do it right."

"It's just an old trailer," Brandon said lightly. "Does it even matter?"

"It matters to me," Dillon said curtly. "And unless you can follow our directions and paint it right, I suggest you don't bother to—"

"I'm not an idiot, Dilly. I can follow directions. Remember when you helped me build those IKEA cabinets for my condo? They turned out just fine. I can be handy when it's necessary."

Instead of challenging him, like she wanted, Dillon strode toward the barn. Knowing Brandon, he'd tire of painting before long. And, even though she hadn't mentioned it, she was the one who'd finished putting those IKEA cabinets together. Because Brandon had gotten distracted by a new video game, claiming the cabinet project was boring. Hopefully, he'd get bored of trying to win her over as well. Her plan was to simply chill him out. But she would do it politely. Not for Brandon's sake so much . . . but because she wasn't eager for Jordan to perceive her as an angry old fishwife. Although that was exactly how she felt!

"Jordan, since you're a more experienced painter, perhaps you could instruct Brandon on the basics." She opened the door to her trailer. "I'm going to change into my paint-speckled tennis shoes."

Inside the trailer, she looked down at her leftover hamburger. Closing the dinette curtains for privacy, she sat down and proceeded to slowly eat it. She had no desire to go back outside and risk losing her temper with Brandon. But finally, her burger was gone. Not wanting to look like a slacker, she put on her old shoes and, with no more excuses to remain inside, went out to discover that the guys were working on the door side of the trailer.

Wanting to distance herself from Brandon, she went to work on the rear end. Far enough to be out of sight, but close enough to eavesdrop on their conversation. To her surprise, it sounded as if Brandon was questioning Jordan's credentials, asking about his college and career goals. Like it was any of Brandon's business!

Jordan, not surprisingly, played himself down, acting as if he were merely a store clerk. Not unlike the way he'd portrayed his role to her when they'd first met. She'd been confused then, but now she found it amusing . . . and endearing. Jordan, unlike Brandon, was not full of himself.

"It's been a good way to learn about tools and agriculture and all sorts of helpful things," Jordan said. "And the people are great."

"So is that your life goal?" Brandon asked. "To live in a small town and work in a hardware store?"

"It is for now. And maybe forever. Hard to say."

"What about family?"

"Well, family is what brought me back here. My dad got sick and passed away, so I've been helping my mom. And my sister and her twins."

"But no wife and kids of your own?"

Dillon stopped painting, trying to hear every word.

"Nope. Not yet."

"But maybe someday?"

"God willing . . . and the creek don't rise." Jordan chuckled.

"Well, I used to think I'd never settle down," Brandon said. "But I'm having second thoughts now."

"So, is that why you're here?" Jordan asked pointedly.

"Might be . . . guess we'll see . . ."

For a long moment, neither guy said anything, but Dillon knew she couldn't just bite her tongue on this. "Excuse me." She stepped around the corner, waving a paintbrush at Brandon. "I couldn't help but overhear what you just said. And if you think that there's any hope for us, well, I'm sorry, but you might as well forget it."

Brandon paused from painting. "I thought you'd act like this. At first, anyway. And I don't even blame you for being mad at me. I deserve that. But I also know how you really feel about me. Deep down. Underneath your recent cover-up . . . pretending not to care. I know that you—"

"I *don't care* and I wish you'd—"

"I honestly didn't expect you to fall into my arms, Dilly." His smile remained fixed and persistent. "The only reason I came here today was to make you understand my feelings for you haven't changed. It's just that I was pretty bad at sharing them before. But I've changed."

"You've changed?" she studied him, trying to grasp this concept. If a skunk changed its stripes, wasn't it still a stinker?

"I can see now that you were right about a lot of things. And I know that I took you for granted."

"That's for sure." She wasn't sure which was more irritating

. . . that he had taken her for granted or that he was admitting it now. Now that it was too late.

Jordan laid his brush down. "Maybe I should excuse myself from this—"

"No." Dillon firmly shook her head. "I am not going to let Brandon stop me from painting my trailer today."

"Well, it sounds like you two have old business to attend to." Jordan smiled apologetically at her. "I don't want to get in the middle of it."

"Thanks, buddy. Really appreciate that. Because you're right, we need to deal with this privately." Brandon's tone was dismissive and Jordan started to leave.

"No way!" Dillon held her brush inches from Brandon's face. "There's *nothing* I need to deal with as far as you're concerned. I just want to paint my trailer. If you guys don't want to help me—fine." She turned abruptly, hoping to stop Jordan from going.

"Hey, careful, Dilly!" Brandon exclaimed.

Dillon turned back to see that she'd accidentally knocked the shoulder of Brandon's sky-blue shirt with a swath of white paint. "Oops." She smiled sheepishly. "I really didn't mean to do that. Sorry."

"Oh, no?" Brandon swiped his brush right across the bustline of her T-shirt. "I didn't mean to do *that* either." He laughed like this was hilarious fun, holding his brush like a weapon, challenging her to a duel.

Dillon stared down at her favorite T-shirt, trying to control her temper and feeling uncomfortably close to tears. Not because of the ruined shirt, but because of what was feeling like a ruined day. Why had he come? Why wouldn't he leave?

"Hey, that wasn't necessary, Brandon." Jordan's tone was gentle but firm, reminding her of how he spoke to his nieces at times.

"She started it," Brandon responded—like a juvenile.

"Hers was accidental." Jordan looked at Dillon. "Right?"

"Yes." Then, seeing the satisfied smirk on Brandon's face, she lost it. "But *this* isn't." Now she wiped her brush right across his smug face. She knew it was a stupid move, and that Jordan would probably think she was childish, but she no longer cared. Prepared to call it quits and abandon her hopes of painting her trailer today, she was caught totally off guard by Jordan's uncontrolled laughter.

Feeling somewhat relieved, she turned to him, holding up her hands in a helpless gesture. "I know that was wrong and I should be—" Her words were stopped by a swat from behind. She whipped around to see that Brandon had swiped his loaded paintbrush right across the seat of her shorts. Her favorite shorts! "Brandon Kranze!" She glared at him. "You are no gentleman!"

"Just tit for tat." In one hand, he wielded his paintbrush like a weapon while using the other hand to wipe his paint-smeared face with a rag. "Care to go at it?"

She held her brush defensively, resisting the temptation to let him have it full force. "No, no. I think that's enough." She watched in amusement as his paint-smeared face only grew worse with his wiping. "You look like a mime!" She couldn't help but giggle at his pasty white face.

"Maybe you'd like to become a mime too." He dipped his brush into the paint and aiming it at her face, approached with a menacing expression.

"No," she yelled. "Leave me—"

"Back off, Brandon." Jordan grabbed his paintbrush and stepped between them. And just like that, it turned into a full-blown paint fight—like they were ten-year-olds. Although there was some laughter and joking as paint splattered and splashed, there was also some underlying seriousness. At least with Brandon. By the time they quit, all three of them were covered in white paint. And Dillon was angry.

"Look at this mess," she told Brandon.

"Hey, don't blame me." He looked down at his ruined pants and shirt. "I took the worst of it."

Dillon turned to Jordan, instantly filling with guilt and shame. "I'm sorry you got dragged into this. I can't believe how childish we were."

"It's okay." He grinned. "To be honest, I kind of enjoyed it. Good thing this paint's water soluble." He pointed to the nearby pump and water trough. "Maybe we should go clean up some."

As they attempted to wash off the paint, Jordan tried to smooth things over. "I guess that was some kind of paint therapy." He removed his T-shirt, rinsing it in the trough. "Maybe not as effective as real couple's therapy, but probably more fun, eh?"

Dillon nodded, trying not to stare at his firm torso as he wrung out his shirt.

"See what happens when you don't take care of old business," Brandon said to Dillon. Then, as if to compete with Jordan, he unbuttoned and removed his dress shirt, washing it in the trough as well. But Brandon's physique didn't compare with Jordan's. And not wanting to get caught gaping, Dillon excused herself to the house, where she planned to take a good, long shower.

"What on earth happened to you?" Margot demanded when Dillon came in through the kitchen.

"Don't ask. I'm going to take a shower, but I didn't bring any dry clothes. Can I borrow a bathrobe or sweats or something?"

"Sure. Go use the second-floor bath and I'll find something." Margot laughed as she followed her up the stairs. "You're a mess, girlfriend. What did the other guy look like?"

"They both look a lot like me."

"So was it fun?"

"Not particularly." Dillon went into the bathroom. "I wish Brandon would take a hint and make himself scarce."

"But I thought you were in love with him and broken-hearted. And now it looks like he's in love with you, Dilly."

"That was then. This is now." Dillon closed the door and peeled off her clothes, putting them in the bathroom sink to soak, hoping she might be able to rescue them later. As she got into the shower, she wondered. Did she really want Brandon to leave her alone? Or did a small part of her enjoy this sudden and unexpected attention? Sure, he was aggravating. But was she aggravated about today . . . or still holding a grudge about the way he'd treated her before? She might've claimed she'd forgiven him, but maybe she hadn't . . . completely.

As she shampooed her hair, her thoughts migrated to Jordan. The more she knew him, the more she liked him. And he hadn't seemed like the eternal bachelor this morning. In fact, things had been going so well that she really believed they were stepping into a new sort of relationship. Something beyond "just friends." She didn't think she'd imagined

161

it. But then Brandon had appeared and literally messed up everything.

What would've happened if Brandon hadn't made his unexpected appearance? Where would she and Jordan be right now? Happily painting together like mature adults, conversing, getting more acquainted . . . maybe something more . . . She blew out a sigh as she rinsed her hair. There was no denying she liked Jordan a lot. Apparently most of the single women in town did as well. But unless she'd imagined it, the attraction was mutual.

As Dillon reached for a towel, she remembered that only a few weeks ago, she'd felt similar sentiments for Brandon. And when he hurt her—and never called—she'd been brokenhearted and disappointed and hopeless. But then she'd come home . . . and recovered so quickly. So maybe her heartache hadn't really been about Brandon at all. Maybe it had simply been about her—and her whole messed-up life.

She was happy with her life now. At least she had been until Brandon showed up today. She felt like her life, for the first time in her adulthood, was finally on track. She felt strong and resilient in her ability to put Brandon firmly behind her. But now she questioned herself. How could she spend years hoping to marry a man . . . and just a few weeks later wish he would vanish into thin air? Wasn't that just plain flaky?

CHAPTER
17

With her hair turbaned in one towel and the other wrapped around like a sarong, Dillon opened the bathroom door to her mother.

"Here you go, Dilly-Dilly." Margot came in with what looked like a short dress or a long top, setting underthings on the countertop.

"Don't you have some sweats or something more casual?" Dillon asked.

"It's enough to get you back to your trailer." Margot dropped a pair of green flip-flops on the floor. "Then you can change into something else if you want."

"Thanks a lot." Dillon held up the summery mint-green dress, which was definitely on the short side. "Seriously?"

"Beggars can't be choosers." Margot laughed as she shut the door.

As Dillon pulled on the dress, she suspected that Margot had picked this feminine garment for a specific reason. She'd never seemed overly pleased that Dillon had come home to roost, and she probably hoped her daughter would hook herself a man—either Brandon or Jordan, move away from the farm . . . and get out of her hair. This dress was probably meant to be bachelor bait. Well, whatever. And to be fair, it looked better than expected.

The house was quiet when Dillon went downstairs. Her plan was to slip out to her trailer and quickly change into casual clothes. And then, even if she had to do it by herself— she planned to continue working on her trailer. Hoping that Brandon had the good sense to make his exit, she went outside and peered off the porch, disappointed to see that his sporty rental car was still parked in front of the house.

But as she headed toward the barn, she felt encouraged to see that *Harvey*, the old red pickup, was still here too. Hopefully no white paint had splashed onto it. Going around the corner of the barn, she was about to enter her trailer when she spotted Jordan squatted down and fiddling with something up front. She called out a cautious hello.

He looked up and smiled. "Well, you sure clean up good." He stood, wiping his hands on an oily rag. "That was quite a paint fight."

She glumly shook her head. "I'm sorry you got caught in the middle of it, Jordan. You didn't deserve that." She touched his damp shirt. "And you're still wearing wet clothes too."

"Keeps me nice and cool." He grinned, then looked more somber. "Seemed like there was more going on than just paint throwing."

"Yeah . . . maybe so." She sighed. "What a mess we made." She looked around the trailer to see the drop cloths and all the painting things were gone. "But looks like you cleaned up. Thanks."

"Well, it was a good time to call it quits. While smoothing out some of the splashes on the trailer, I realized the first coat could use some more time to cure and dry anyway." He tipped his head toward her. "Besides that, you look too pretty to paint now."

"Thanks." She pointed to the front of the trailer. "What are you doing up there?"

"I just hooked up your propane tank. I already used your grandpa's air compressor to blow out the lines, and I was getting ready to check your stove. Want to help?"

"Of course."

"Do you have matches in there?"

"I have a lighter. I use it for candles at night. And I have this cute little kerosene lamp too, in case I lose electricity, but I like lighting it just for the fun of it."

"Nice. Go ahead and put your lighter by the stove. And open all the windows in there."

She did what he said and came back out. "Now you can stay out here." He showed her how to operate the propane tank. "And I'll go inside and experiment with the stove and other appliances. Hopefully, they're all in good shape."

"Maybe I should be the one in there," she suggested.

"No. It might be, uh, hazardous—and I know what I'm doing. You just stay here by the tank and if I yell turn it off, don't hesitate."

"And if it looks dangerous, you get out of there—pronto."

He smiled. "Don't worry."

As they tested the appliances, yelling back and forth, Dillon wondered what had become of Brandon. Not that she cared, particularly. Or maybe she did. Now that she was clean and dry, she felt guilty for the way she'd taken pleasure while slapping white paint all over his fancy shirt and pants. She knew it was part of an expensive suit . . . and what if he got paint on the upholstery of his rental car?

"Looks like everything in there runs just fine," Jordan said as he came out of the trailer. "Do you want me to show you how they all work today? Or are you worn out from all our activities?"

"No, I'd love to learn how to use everything." She still felt bad for his damp and paint-stained clothes. "But what about you? Maybe you'd like to call it a day."

"I'm fine. Might as well figure this out now."

"Great. I'll get my little notebook. I want to write it all down so I don't forget."

They went inside and Jordan took her through all the steps. She asked questions and took careful notes. "This is so exciting. This means I can use the fridge and the stove and have hot water." She looked around in wonder. "I could really live out here?"

"Well, we're still assuming they all work. The stove works perfectly fine, and the fridge sounds like it's running, but it'll take time to tell if it's cold. The hot water heater seems to be okay. And I'm guessing you'll want to wait for cold weather before testing the furnace." Jordan replaced the padded bench seat on the dinette, then checked his pants for paint and sat down. "Although I'm not sure you'd want to live out here when it's really cold. These old trailers don't have much insulation, Dillon. And as you know, winter can be harsh in these parts."

Dillon set her turquoise teakettle back on the stove burner, imagining it whistling . . . making hot tea. "You know what I think I'll name her, Jordan?"

"Huh?" Jordan looked confused.

"My Oasis. I don't think I should call her an Oasis since that's not very personal." She sat across from him. "I think I'll name her *Rose*. After your aunt. Since this was her trailer."

He grinned. "I think Aunt Rose would like that. And with your Southwest color scheme, you could even call her *Desert Rose*." He chuckled. "An appropriate name for an Oasis."

"Yes," she agreed. "I love that. She will be called *Desert Rose*."

He looked around again. "My aunt Rose would really like what you've done in here. It's so cozy and homey and welcoming. Much more so than my trailer." His eyes lit up. "In fact, maybe I should hire you to give *Helen* more personality."

"Really? You'd trust me with your trailer?"

"Well, I suppose I'd want to have sign-off for approval."

"Of course. But you don't have to hire me, Jordan. I'd gladly do it for free. Or think of it as an exchange for all your help with my trailer. I love fixing up—"

"Hello?" Brandon called from outside, knocking loudly on the door. "Anybody home? I hear voices in there."

Jordan, closer to the door, reached over to open it.

"Is this a private party?" Brandon asked. "Or can anybody come?"

Dillon sighed. "Sure, come on in," she called out halfheartedly. "We were just working in here."

Brandon stepped in and, positioned by the door, glanced

around with a doubtful expression. "Doesn't look like you're working to me."

"We were testing the appliances," Jordan explained. "We're done."

"Hey, you changed your clothes." Dillon pointed at his neat khakis and white polo shirt. "How'd you accomplish that?"

"I just happened to have my suitcase in the rental car. And your mom let me use the bathroom to clean up." He smoothed his hair. "I feel like a new man." He frowned at Jordan. "You look a little worse for wear, old man." He turned to Dillon with raised brows. "But you, Dilly, look like a million bucks."

"Thanks a lot," she said without enthusiasm.

"Well, now that we got the appliances working, I should be shoving off." Jordan stood.

"Yeah." Brandon nodded. "You better get into some dry clothes, buddy."

Jordan shrugged. "It's a good cooling system."

Dillon got up too, following him outside with Brandon on her heels. "Thank you so much for your help, Jordan. And my offer's genuine. I'd love to help with your trailer. I mean, if you trust me."

"We can talk later." He nodded. "Nice to meet you, Brandon." His brow creased. "Well, anyway, it was interesting."

Brandon just laughed and Dillon watched with dismay as Jordan climbed into his old red pickup and slowly drove away. She hoped that he hadn't misunderstood anything about Brandon and her. Surely, she'd made it crystal clear that she didn't want her ex-boyfriend around. Good grief, hadn't she attacked him with paint? That should make it obvious enough.

"So what's going on with you and this Jordan dude?" Brandon asked. Ignoring his inquisition, she strolled toward the house. There was nothing she wanted inside. But she did not want to remain out in her trailer with Brandon nosing around. He clearly disapproved of *Rose*, and she had no intention of listening to him pass judgment. Besides, Brandon's car was parked over here. Maybe he'd take the hint and vamoose.

No big surprise, Brandon did not take the hint. In fact, when Margot invited him, he gladly stayed for dinner. And as if to make up for his bad behavior while painting, he was sweeter than sugar to everyone. But Dillon continued to keep him at arm's length, almost to the point of rudeness. And when he finally left, shortly after sunset and only after Dillon made it very clear they had no room for a guest, Margot took her to task for her bad manners.

"I don't see why you're so mean to him," Margot said as she and Dillon stood on the front porch, watching the rental car's taillights disappearing into the dusky twilight along the farm road.

"Because he was an uninvited guest." Dillon sat in a rocker.

"But Brandon really seems to have changed." Margot sat down too.

"*Seems* is the operative word." Dillon let out a long, frustrated sigh. "This is all just an act. I know it."

"Why would it be an act? What's the point?"

"To win me back." Dillon leaned back in the rocker. "But I just don't get why. What does he possibly hope to gain?"

"It's because he's realized he loves you, Dilly. Anyway, that's what he told me. He's missed you a lot. And he really wants you back."

"It makes no sense. I honestly wonder if this is all related to work. Maybe he promised to drag me back to Colorado so that LeeAnn could enslave me again."

Margot laughed. "Don't be ridiculous. There are laws against human trafficking."

"Then why is he so insistent? What's his motivation?"

"I already told you, Dilly. He loves you. Absence has made his heart grow fonder. I happen to think it's all very sweet. I can even hear wedding bells."

"Then you should get your hearing checked. I think the only reason Brandon's trying so hard is because I'm pushing him away. He's a salesman at heart. He loves the challenge. It's how he's wired. It's all about winning. I resist him and he tries harder."

"Maybe you should've played hard-to-get back in Colorado. You might've been married by now. After all, that was always your dream, Dilly."

"For starters, I'm not *playing*, Margot. I mean it. And sure, maybe I always did want to get married, but I do not want to marry Brandon Kranze."

"I think you're still mad at him, Dilly, for hurting you. You never got over it and now you're punishing him. Underneath all that angst, you probably still love him. Remember what they say: 'True love never runs smooth.'"

"Right. And since when did you become the expert on true love and romantic relationships?" Dillon demanded. "What about you and Don? Aren't you punishing him? For wanting to get married?"

Margot laughed. "I guess we have more in common than I realized."

"Maybe so. But I'm tired." Dillon stood. "It's been a long day."

"For me too." Margot stretched. "Dad already hit the hay. Can't say that I blame him either. The older I get the more I start to appreciate early bedtimes." She poked her in the arm. "But you're young, Dilly. You shouldn't be going to bed with the chickens."

Dillon told her good night. While taking her time to walk to the barn, she paused to look up at the starry sky. This could've been such a fabulous day. It had started so well. This morning had been perfect, and she'd imagined them working together for the whole day. She'd even hoped to invite Jordan for dinner after they finished the trailer—as a thank-you and an excuse to spend more time together. By now they could've been sitting out here under the stars together . . . and then who knew what might happen?

But instead, it had all gone sideways. Her trailer was only half painted—if that—plus she'd had to endure Brandon for the duration of the night. So much for her red-letter day.

CHAPTER
18

After going to church with Grandpa, Dillon spent the rest of Sunday afternoon painting her trailer. By herself. She'd just finished when Grandpa came out to check on her. "Looks good," he said. "Nice and neat and clean. Are you going to leave it all white like that?"

"No. I've got a contrast color for a nice wide stripe." She used her hands to motion how she wanted it to look. "I won't try to reproduce the shape of the original stripes. They were so wavy it'd be hard to make it look right. And even though the paint was faded, I could see the stripe was a yellow-orange shade." She pulled a paint swatch from the top of the paint can. "This is the turquoise color I plan to use."

"Turquoise?" Grandpa nodded. "That's interesting."

"Well, it goes with the cabinets. And it has personality."

"That's true." He smiled. "I think Jack and Rose would like it."

Now she told him about naming the trailer. "Do you think that's okay? Jordan said his aunt would like it."

"I think Rose would be honored." He gave her a sideways hug. "I'm real proud of the way you've worked on this old trailer, Dillon. I knew I gave it to the right person."

As she thanked him, Margot rang the dinner bell at the house. "Did Margot cook tonight?" Dillon asked. "I thought you were barbecuing ribs."

"Well, Margot wanted to make some salad and things. But the ribs are about done. That's what I came to tell you."

As they walked to the house, Grandpa asked about Brandon. "Do you know where your young man is staying?"

"First of all, he's *not* my young man."

"Yeah, sorry. My bad."

"And as far as staying anywhere, I assume he's back in Colorado by now."

"Maybe not. Margot said he dropped by this morning . . . when we were at church."

"Oh?" Dillon didn't like the sound of this.

"I'll give him one thing, he's persistent." Grandpa stopped in his tracks, pointing down the driveway. "Speak of the devil—doesn't that look a lot like the car he drove over here yesterday?"

Dillon shaded her eyes to see better. "Oh no."

"So you didn't know he was coming?"

"No." She felt her stomach tying into a knot.

"Looks like he's already in the house too." Grandpa nodded toward the kitchen window, where he was talking to Margot.

"Probably inviting himself to dinner." Dillon groaned. "And I was really looking forward to those ribs too."

"No reason for you to miss out on them."

"I'd rather starve than—"

"Hello!" Brandon came bounding down the back porch steps, hurrying toward them. Today, he was dressed casually and, as much as she hated to admit it, he looked handsome in his jeans and plaid shirt. Very un-Brandon-like. And, unless she was mistaken, he was wearing cowboy boots. Seriously?

"What are you doing here?" Dillon asked him as Grandpa went to check on the barbecue.

"Didn't Margot mention I'd stopped by this morning?"

"Not exactly." She remained in the driveway, arms folded across her front.

"Well, I was sorry to miss you. I had a golf date with one of the clients I'd met with on Friday. So Margot suggested I come by for dinner." He held out his arms. "So here I am. Aren't you just a teeny-tiny bit glad to see me?"

It felt mean to say how she really felt, so she just shrugged. "Interesting outfit."

He grinned. "I was hoping you'd like it. I got it in town after my golf game. Looks like what the guys around here are wearing."

"Uh-huh." She frowned.

"Oh, Dillon. I wish I could turn back the clock on all the stupid things I did. You don't know how much I miss your old sweet smile."

She forced a smile. "It's not that it's completely gone. It's just that—"

"I know, I know. You're still mad at me. I was a jerk. I'm trying to own that now. All I want is for you to give me a second chance. Is that too much to ask? Can't we try again?"

She blew out a sigh. "Brandon, you don't get it. We're through. You and I are a thing of the past."

He shrugged. "I know that's how you feel right now. Margot explained a few things to me this morning. She says it'll take time for you to get over our breakup. I understand that. Like I said yesterday, I deserve some of your angst. But I'm willing to wait for you to cool off. Because I know deep down you want to be with me, Dilly. I know we can make this work again."

Why did he not get it? Dillon was speechless. But she was also hungry and, despite her unwanted guest, was determined to indulge in Grandpa's ribs. The smell alone made her stomach rumble. Deciding Brandon wasn't worth missing dinner, she headed for the house.

"Oh, there you are." Margot smiled at them. "We're eating in the dining room tonight. Easier than hauling everything outside again. Dillon, can you take this—"

"I need to go wash up." Dillon held out paint-speckled hands. "Maybe Brandon can help you." Then she hurried to the upstairs bathroom, where she planned to leisurely wash her hands and while away the minutes until she heard Grandpa come in with the ribs. After that, well, she would just have to grin and bear it.

A few minutes later, Dillon sat down at the table with her focus on food, trying to pretend Brandon wasn't sitting across from her. As usual, Brandon took control of the conversation. His charisma and charm were apparently winning not only Margot but Grandpa too. Especially when he asked them more questions about their farming projects, making enthused comments and offering some of his own ideas. For a brief moment, Dillon fell under his spell, thinking he wasn't so bad. She even wondered why it was she had absolutely no interest in him. Except that she didn't. But was that only because of Jordan? What if she'd never met Jordan? Would she be making plans right now to return to Colorado with Brandon?

Brandon shared with them that he planned to remain in town through the Fourth of July. "I'm overdue for some time off." He explained how he'd taken a hotel room at the Best Western. "And I'm enjoying your small town." He winked at Dillon. "I can see why you like it so much."

Despite her confusion—and even if there were no Jordan Atwood—Dillon didn't think her old feelings for Brandon would ever reawaken. And she was determined to set him straight on this—before the sun went down. So after dinner, Dillon took him outside. Her goal was to make her position clear—but with a softer approach this time.

"Brandon," she began as they sat on the front porch together. "I've been thinking about what you've said and it seems possible that you really have changed. That's great. I'm truly happy for you. And you need to know that I *do* forgive you. I don't hold anything from the past against you anymore. Maybe I used to, but I'm done with that now."

"I knew it was just a matter of time." He sounded triumphant.

"But that's not all, Brandon. You also need to understand that it is over between us. What we used to have was good . . . in its own way. But I'm done with that. I have moved on."

"I don't think you really mean that." He reached for her hand, but she pulled it away. "You used to have deep feelings for me, Dillon. You told me that you loved me. You can't take that back—"

"I *thought* I loved you, Brandon. But now I realize that wasn't love. And I seriously doubt that you ever loved me. Not really."

"That's not true. I did love you. I still love you. More than ever. But I used to suppress my feelings, Dilly. I know it sounds cliché, but I was afraid of commitment. Then after you left me, I had time to think about it. Time to realize what you meant to me. And, you're right, I have changed. I can see us together now. And I'm even willing to consider a wedding date—as soon as next summer if—"

"That's not going to happen. I'll admit that marriage was definitely on my mind before. To be perfectly honest, and I'm not proud to admit this, that's probably what made me stick with you so long. But whatever we had before, I've gotten over. I've outgrown it, Brandon. And I've outgrown my old job too. I have no intention of returning to Colorado. Or going back with you."

He stood up with clenched fists and a firm jaw. "I don't think you really mean that, Dillon. I think you just want to see me crawling back to you."

"No, I don't." She stood to face him. "I just want you to go back to Colorado. Find yourself another girl. What about Bethany Myers? I heard that—"

"Is that it?" he demanded loudly. "You're jealous of Bethany? Because that was nothing. Just a little fling. If that's what this is all about—"

"That's not it, Brandon," she said loudly. "Honestly, it's not. I just want you to leave! Please, leave me alone." The screen door squeaked open behind them and Dillon turned to see Grandpa's silhouette in the doorway.

"You need to listen to my granddaughter," he said in a firm

voice. "She's asking you to go, young man. And I think it's high time you did."

"Fine." Brandon went down the steps. "But this doesn't mean I'm giving up." Before Dillon or Grandpa could respond, he stomped off to his car.

"Thanks, Grandpa," she said quietly, choking back tears of frustration. "For some reason he just won't listen to me."

Grandpa came out to the porch, putting his arm around her. "It's because he's finally realized what he's lost, Dillon. He knows what a fool he was to let you go."

"Meanwhile I feel like I dodged a bullet."

"Still, I can't blame him for trying." He lowered his voice. "Margot is certainly impressed with him."

"Because Brandon's won her over." Dillon sighed. "Thanks for standing up for me just now. I really appreciate it."

"I can't deny that I'm impressed with his persistence. Seems bound and determined to win you back. Some young women would appreciate a man with that kind of devotion."

"I'll admit he's stubborn." She bit her lip. "But so am I."

"Are you certain you don't still have feelings for him? Margot thinks you're just punishing him for what happened before."

"Margot is wrong."

"Well, unless I'm mistaken, you haven't seen the last of that young man."

"Do you think he'll really stick around until the Fourth of July? Even after what I said to him?"

"You're the one who said he's stubborn. But you could have worse problems, Dillon." Grandpa chuckled.

"Meaning?"

"Well, I sort of suspected you might have some, uh, feelings for Jordan Atwood. But maybe I'm wrong about that?"

Dillon let out a long sigh. "I actually thought, for a moment there yesterday, that Jordan might have feelings for me too."

Grandpa sat down in a rocker. "Care for a bit of advice?"

"Sure." She sat down.

"Well, when I was a young man, I had an interest in your grandma. But I suppose I was a little like Brandon. I took her for granted."

"You took Grandma for granted?"

"Sadly, I did." He nodded glumly. "But when I saw a buddy of mine going out with Marie, I was livid. I guess it was my wake-up call. I got off my hindquarters and made hasty work of winning her over." He grinned. "And that was that."

"That's a good story, and I'm glad it turned out alright, but I'm not sure what it has to do with me."

"Well, in this town, I suspect that Jordan Atwood is considered quite a catch. I spend a fair amount of time at Atwood's and I've observed local women trying to win him over."

"Yes, I've heard he's one of Silverdale's most eligible bachelors. Or as some say, he's the town's eternal bachelor."

Grandpa chuckled. "That doesn't surprise me."

"So what's your point?"

"Well, Brandon's persistence might just be what it takes to get Jordan's attention. Sort of like my buddy and Marie. A wake-up call."

Dillon didn't like the sound of this but didn't want to hurt Grandpa's feelings. "Interesting theory."

"Just saying."

"Well, I'll think about it," she said.

"Good. Because if you ask me, Jordan Atwood is a good man."

"Yeah, I think so too." Dillon didn't want to mention the fact that Jordan hadn't stopped by the farm today. Or her disappointment that he hadn't. While painting her trailer, she'd imagined him showing up unexpected in his old red truck. *Harvey.* She'd imagined his bright, easy smile and a kind offer to help. At first, she'd been almost certain that he'd show. But as the day wore on, she could think of a dozen reasons why he wouldn't. And, of course, he didn't.

She wished Jordan was as persistent as Brandon, but she knew it wasn't Jordan's style. He was a lot more laid-back. And sometimes a bit difficult to read. Not to mention the possible "unavailable" factor. Maybe he really was an eternal bachelor.

As she walked back to her trailer, she paused to watch a nearly full moon creeping up over the barn. How romantic. She could imagine a summer night like this with Jordan. She wondered if he might even be looking at the glowing moon right now. If somehow the luminous light could be connecting them. "Don't be silly," she told herself as she continued on to her trailer.

Inside her trailer, Dillon turned on the lights and smiled at the welcoming space. It really was sweet. Small perhaps, but everything she needed. Especially now that the appliances worked. Thanks to Jordan. Now she wondered about his invitation to give his trailer more personality. The thought definitely had intrigued her, but dismayed that he'd never stopped by today, she wondered if he was having second thoughts about her. Or perhaps she'd misread him completely. Maybe he simply wanted to engage her in a business relationship.

In that case, it might be smart to simply step away . . . not give her heart any more opportunity to wander down another dead-end street.

As she climbed into her comfy bed, she considered Grandpa's suggestion. Was it possible that Jordan really did need a little nudge? A wake-up call, like the one that pried Grandpa off his bachelor fence? That felt like game-playing . . . or even worse, manipulation. She hated the idea of toying with someone who appeared to be as genuine as Jordan Atwood. Especially if it meant involving Brandon to do it. She knew Grandpa meant well, but she also knew it was better to let life and love take its course.

CHAPTER
19

On Monday, after Janelle dropped the twins off at the pool and hurried off to a meeting, Dillon hoped that Uncle Jordan would pick them up. But to her disappointment, it was Janelle who came. She was as friendly and warm as ever. But she wasn't Jordan.

Dillon tried not to show her dismay as she chatted with Jordan's sister while the twins toweled off. She described the progress the girls were making. "It's turned into a healthy competition," she said quietly. "Chloe doesn't want Emma to show her up, and that pushes Emma even harder. I expect they'll both be swimming unassisted soon."

"That's wonderful." Janelle smiled. "I'm so glad they had you for their instructor. Anyone else might've given up after Chloe's first tantrum."

"Well, I'm glad I didn't. Their enthusiasm has become the inspiration for the others. Don't tell, but it's become my favorite class of the day."

Janelle laughed. "Isn't it your last class?"

Dillon nodded. "Yeah, that helps too."

Janelle chatted a bit more as the twins pulled on their swim-suit covers. And, despite her curiosity, Dillon resisted the urge to ask about Jordan's whereabouts yesterday . . . or anything else that would surely be considered overly inquisitive. After all, Janelle was not her brother's keeper.

After grabbing a quick bite of lunch at one of the food trail-ers situated at the city park, Dillon went by the hardware store for a special brand of painting tape she'd read about online. Of course, she hoped to see Jordan there as well, but it was Ryan the paint guy who assisted her.

"What's this for?" he asked as he directed her to the tape.

"For the accent stripe on my trailer."

"Cool." He nodded. "So did you get the main body all painted already?"

"Yes. Your boss actually came by to lend me a hand."

Ryan's brows arched. "He did?"

"Yes. And he was very helpful." She glanced around, hoping to spy Jordan coming down the main aisle.

"Well, he's a trailer guy." Ryan handed her a roll of tape. "Don't forget to bring photos when you're done. I want to see the final results."

She thanked him and, with no sign of Jordan, paid for her purchase and headed home, telling herself not to think about it. Just because Jordan had been helpful didn't mean anything. After all, it was his uncle's old trailer. He probably just wanted to make sure she wasn't ruining it. Besides, she had better things to do than pine over Jordan. Her trailer was calling!

By the time she finished the first coat on the stripe, she was more than a little excited. "*Rose*, you are turning into a real head-turner," she declared. She stepped back to admire her work, knowing it would look even better when she removed the painter's tape.

"Looking good." Grandpa came over to her.

"And that's just the first coat. It'll be even better when I finish it. I think I'll wait until after the Fourth. Give it a few days to cure."

"Sounds like a good plan." Grandpa rubbed his chin. "I still think it's interesting that you used turquoise for the stripe."

"You mean because it's different from the original color?" She wondered if he was disappointed. "I hope that doesn't bother you. I did consider keeping it the way it was, but it just didn't feel that cheerful and—"

"No, no, that's not it. I like it a lot. But I'm still curious as to why you picked that color, Dillon. You could've painted it pink or red or orange, and it would've been okay. It's your trailer."

"Well, I think *Rose* looks sweet and cheerful like this."

"I do too." He nodded with approval.

She knelt down to put a lid on the paint can. "And I plan to paint the propane tanks turquoise too. I saw that in one of my vintage trailer books and it looked cute."

"There's a reason I asked you about the turquoise color you picked . . ." Grandpa's grin looked a little sly.

"Uh-huh?" She stood up, trying to figure out what he was getting at. "And, oh yeah, I forgot. The real inspiration originally came from some of the vintage jewelry that Grandma left to me. Her turquoise and silver. It's so pretty."

"Well, that's nice." He adjusted the brim of his hat. "Wanna see something, Dillon?"

"Sure—what?"

"Come with me." He led her around the back of the barn and over to the metal storage building that he used to store his tractor and oversized farm tools. "Seems to me that someone's having a birthday this month."

Dillon grinned. "You mean me?"

"Yep." He rolled open a door.

"I know, I'm finally getting that pony!" she teased.

"You never wanted a pony," he said. "Not that I ever heard tell of."

She sighed. "Actually, I did want a pony. When I was a little girl and still living with Margot. But she said our apartment was too small."

"Oh?" He frowned.

"By the time I came here to live with you and Grandma, I was too old for a pony." She didn't want to admit that she had wanted a horse by then, but she'd known moving in with her grandparents had been an imposition—Margot had made that clear—so she hadn't wanted to press her luck.

"Well, this isn't a pony, but it's better suited to get your trailer around." As the sunlight poured into the building, she caught a glimpse of what looked like vehicle wheels beneath a large brown tarp.

"What is it?" she asked.

"Jack's old Chevy pickup. Remember, I said that he left it to me along with the trailer."

"I guess I sort of forgot."

He pulled off the tarp to reveal an old-fashioned turquoise-blue pickup. "Well, they were never a matched set . . . before. But sort of looks like they might be now."

"What a cool truck." She went closer to see it.

"Well, as you know, I don't need another truck. My old Ford is as good as ever."

"Yeah?" It seemed like too much to hope for . . . Dillon held her breath.

"Seeing how you have a birthday and you restored Jack's old trailer, well, I think you should have this pickup to pull it with."

"Oh, Grandpa." She turned to look at him. "You mean it?"

"You bet I do. Happy birthday, Dillon."

She threw her arms around him. "This is the best birthday present ever!"

He chuckled. "Never expected anyone to get that excited over Jack's old truck, but I'm glad you like it."

She was already opening the door, looking inside. It was pretty well worn, but charming. "This is perfect, Grandpa. Absolutely perfect."

"I'm not sure how well it runs. Not that there's anything wrong with it—and Jack was a mechanical fellow, always kept all his rigs in good working order, but it's old and it's been sitting out here for more'n a year. You should get it thoroughly checked out before you try to pull your trailer."

"Of course." She slid into the driver's seat. "Not that I'm planning on taking *Rose* anywhere, not anytime soon. But if and when the day comes, it'll be fantastic to pull her with this." She looked at Grandpa. "I think I'll name the pickup *Jack*."

Grandpa's laugh was hearty. "Well, that's just about right. Because those two were a great pair. Kind of like Marie and me. But in real life it was usually Rose who was leading Jack around by the nose. Anyway, I think they'd both have a good chuckle over this. Rose over at the coast . . . and Jack up in heaven."

"Well, it really is the best birthday present ever."

"I kept it in here to protect it, but you can move it out anytime you want. Wouldn't mind getting some more space in here. Keys are in the jockey box."

"You mean the glove compartment?" she teased as she reached for the keys.

"Guess that's what you gals call it. So do you know how to drive three-on-the-tree?"

"What?" She held up the keys.

"It's how you shift gears. All on the steering column. Pretty simple, as long as you know how."

"I don't know how," she confessed.

"Well, let me drive it out for you. Don't want you to wreck my good tractor. Then I'll give you some lessons."

She got out of the driver's seat, watching as he attempted to start the engine, but when it wouldn't turn over, he explained it was probably a dead battery. "It'll take a while to get it charged up good. And seeing it's almost dinnertime, you'll have to wait to try it out. How about we plan on tomorrow afternoon, when you're done at the pool? Or if you want, we can wait until after the Fourth."

"Whatever's best for you," she agreed. "Although I'm dying to drive it around. And I'd love to clean it up. Maybe even wax it."

"I'm sure that's not been done in the past few decades."

"I'd like to get used to driving a pickup again. I haven't driven one since back when I used to drive yours, Grandpa. And that was always fun."

"Yeah, but mine's an automatic. You'll have to get used to this one."

As they walked back to the house, Dillon could just imagine that cool vintage turquoise truck pulling her cool vintage trailer. They would be cuter than cute! But as far as the how-to part of towing a trailer . . . that was still pretty intimidating. Would she really be up to the task? Well, there should be plenty of time to figure that out.

○○○

Another day passed without Dillon seeing Jordan. Not that she had expected to see him since Janelle had remained to watch the girls' lesson. But since she planned to stop by the hardware store before going home, she wasn't giving up hope . . . yet. Dillon told her students goodbye, reminding them there were no lessons until Monday due to the Fourth. She was just telling them to have a fun holiday when she noticed Brandon striding toward her. A slight shock wave ran through her. Why was he still here? She remembered his plan to stay in town until the Fourth, but she assumed his plans would change after she'd sent him packing on Sunday. Apparently not.

"Hey, Dilly." He approached her with a broad smile. "How's it going?"

"Fine." She wrapped the towel around her like a sarong. "What're you doing here?"

"Came to see you." His smile grew uneasy. Very un-Brandon-like. "I hope you don't mind."

She glanced around at the moms and kids. They were obviously watching her with open curiosity. "I don't mind," she said stiffly. "It's a free country."

He frowned. "That's not very friendly."

"Sorry." She reached for her bag. "I need to go shower and dress if you'll ex—"

"Nothing wrong with the outfit you're wearing." His brows

arched. "Small town living agrees with you, Dilly. I never saw you look prettier—ever."

"Well, uh, thanks."

"But go ahead and change. I'll wait for you."

"You'll wait?"

"Yeah. I just wanted to talk to you. You know, one last time. How about if we talk over lunch? And I promise to be perfectly civilized."

"Well, I—"

"Come on, you gotta be hungry."

Feeling all the kids' and moms' eyes on them, she just nodded, then scurried over to the shower room. As she showered and dressed, she reminded herself that he had said "one last time." That was encouraging. Besides, he was right, she was hungry.

"Who's that good-looking guy waiting for you in the lobby?" Chelsea asked as Dillon pulled on her sandals.

"He told you he was waiting for me?" Dillon frowned.

"Well, I asked if he needed help. He explained he was with you." Chelsea winked. "He's a looker alright."

"I suppose." She stuffed her wet things into her bag.

"You don't sound very enthused."

Dillon gave a quick explanation of her relationship with Brandon and how he'd come out here to win her back. "But I told him it was pointless."

"Why?" Chelsea looked shocked. "What's wrong with him?"

As Dillon touched up some makeup, wondering why she bothered, she briefly explained Brandon's history of "unavailability."

"He doesn't seem unavailable now, Dillon. Maybe you should give him a second chance."

Dillon shoved her lip gloss back into her bag. "But I feel like we're through, Chelsea. Like, been there—done that. Not again."

"Nice that you can be so choosy." Chelsea glumly shook her head. "At our age, I find it refreshing to have any interested and available male pursuing me."

"Our age?" Dillon frowned. "We're in our early thirties, girlfriend."

"Early maybe—but pushing mid," Chelsea teased.

"Whatever." Dillon rolled her eyes. "Excuse me for not feeling that desperate for a guy. Not at the moment anyway. And I plan to let Brandon know."

"Hey, speaking of desperate." Chelsea grabbed her arm before she exited the locker room. "I wanted to ask if you were going to the Fourth of July dance tomorrow night."

"Well, I wanted to go to the usual festivities during the day. It'd be fun to go to the dance too." Dillon didn't want to admit that she'd been hoping Jordan would ask her. Especially since he'd raised the subject on Saturday. But now it seemed hopeless.

"Then let's go together," Chelsea said. "That way we won't look quite so desperate. We'll just be two single girls having a good time. Okay?"

Dillon gave her a thumbs-up. "Sounds great." And as she went out to the lobby, she couldn't help but smile with amusement at this irony. Brandon was waiting on her for a change. "Hope I didn't take too long." Her tone was teasing.

"Not at all." His eyes twinkled. "I'm sure there were plenty of times I made you wait lots longer."

"So you really do remember that?" she asked as they went out to the parking lot.

"I'm embarrassed to admit I do remember." He paused to look into her eyes. "And I really am sorry. I hope you believe me, Dillon."

She felt uncomfortable. Her brain felt impaired by Brandon acting so nice. But was it sincere? "I, uh, need to put my swim bag in my car," she told him. "Where did you plan to have lunch? Maybe we should just meet there?"

"I made a lunch reservation at a place called McLaughlin's. A woman at the hotel highly recommended it. She said the food's fabulous, and they only serve lunch in the summertime."

"Yes, I've heard of McLaughlin's before. But I've never been there."

"Great. Let's take my car. Because according to my GPS, it's a little bit of a drive."

Before long they were going down the highway and Brandon was still being disturbingly polite. "The hotel lady told me the restaurant's next to Silver Lake. And that it looks like an old log cabin lodge."

"Sounds charming."

"She said they have a patio that overlooks the lake. And I know how you always liked to eat outside in the summer."

"It's a nice day for it too." Despite herself, she was getting into this. It was nice to be treated like a lady for a change. Still, she planned to keep up her guard. Initially she'd imagined them grabbing a bit of lunch at a food cart. She'd have a quick meal and listen to Brandon's farewell speech. But this was feeling like a date. Well, whatever. At least there'd be good food involved. And if this is what it took to cut her ties with him, so be it.

CHAPTER

20

*D*illon could hardly believe how charming McLaughlin's was—not just the natural beauty of snow-capped mountains behind a clear blue lake, but the lodge and restaurant were rustic perfection. "I feel like I just stepped into another world," she told Brandon as they waited outside for their table.

"I'm sorry that took so long." The hostess led them to the patio. "But the Silverdale Chamber of Commerce is having lunch upstairs. They always meet here this time of the month. And that keeps us hopping."

"No problem," Dillon told her. "I can't think of a more beautiful place to wait."

"Here you go." She stopped by a lakeside table set for two. "Enjoy."

"This place is gorgeous." Brandon slowly sat down, staring

at the shimmering lake. "I hate to say it, Dillon, but I'm starting to imagine how Oregon could win me over from Colorado."

"Really?" She wasn't sure if that was good or bad news.

Brandon chuckled. "Just don't tell my mom I said that."

"How's your mom?" She laid her napkin in her lap.

"She's fine, which reminds me, she really misses you, Dillon."

She felt a stab of guilt to think of his mother. Brenda Kranze would've made a wonderful mother-in-law. They'd immediately hit it off and, after a year of dating Brandon, Brenda had begun discussing wedding plans with Dillon. Like Dillon, she'd assumed a marriage was inevitable. Of course, Brandon's dad was a different story. He was domineering and chauvinistic, and Dillon had never felt comfortable with him.

"Be sure and give your mom my best," she told Brandon.

"She was pretty upset that you never told her goodbye, Dillon. You know how much she likes you."

"Please, tell her I'm sorry about that . . . maybe you can explain how upset I was at the time. You know, losing my job and everything." She sighed as she gazed over the pine-tree fringed lake, wishing she could put those memories to rest. "This is so lovely, Brandon. Thanks for bringing me here."

"It really is special. Isn't it?"

She waited as the hostess filled their water glasses. "Can I ask you a favor?"

"Sure. Anything," he agreed.

"How about if we don't talk about what went on in Colorado while we have lunch? Let's not try to figure things out, or replay the past, or even try to predict the future. Let's just be here and now. Okay?"

"Okay." He lifted his water goblet to toast. "I'm totally down with that."

She clinked her glass against his. "Thanks. It's such a gorgeous day and a pretty place . . . I'd love to just enjoy it."

"And the company is gorgeous too." His brows arched. "I know you dislike compliments, Dillon, but I'm not kidding when I say you've never looked prettier. I don't know what it is . . . Oregon, or being home with your family, or what, but you look more beautiful than ever."

She felt her cheeks warm and quickly changed the subject by telling him about her swim classes. Even describing Chloe and Emma and how badly it started out with the troubled twins. "But then everything smoothed out. And now I just love those two little girls."

"That's just one more thing I admire about you, Dillon. You have such a gracious heart toward everyone."

"Thank you." Once again, she changed the topic. She told him all about her vintage trailer and how therapeutic it had been to restore it. She described how it had looked before and some of the tasks she'd performed to renovate it. She knew she was probably boring him, but he hid it well.

"I still can't believe you're so talented at restorations."

"Thanks to all the DIY videos on the internet."

As they ate, she told him about the pickup Grandpa was giving her and how she couldn't wait to clean it up and make it shine. Of course, she didn't mention it was an early birthday present. She didn't want to remind him of that . . . didn't want to give him any incentive to stick around longer than necessary. Already, she felt concerned he'd stayed too long. But at least he'd be back in the Springs by the end of the week.

To Dillon's pleased surprise, their lunch date passed quickly and painlessly . . . and rather enjoyably. And the food was fabulous. By the end of the meal, she was almost having second thoughts about Brandon . . . almost. The drive back to town was quiet, but it didn't feel like a strained silence. Finally, they were standing by her car in the swimming pool parking lot. "Thanks so much for a really enjoyable lunch," she told him as she unlocked her car.

"Thank *you*," he said brightly. "You made it that way." His smile faded. "You've also made it harder than ever to tell you goodbye like I'd planned to do."

"I'm sorry, Brandon." She really did feel bad for hurting him. And her antagonism toward him had evaporated. "You know," she said slowly, "I hope we'll always be friends."

He frowned. "I wish we could be more than that . . ."

"I know." She nodded. "Don't take it wrong, but I'm relieved not to hate you anymore."

"You hated me?"

She shrugged. "Yeah, sort of. I mean I tried to forgive you. I told myself I'd forgiven you. But it didn't happen all at once. I think I'm over it now."

His smile returned. "Well, that's a relief."

"So what are your plans? When do you go back to the Springs?"

"Friday." His eyes lit up. "Which means I'm here all day tomorrow for the Fourth festivities. I assume you'll be around for it too. Right?"

"Of course." She nodded. "Wouldn't miss it."

"I heard there's a really great dance in the evening. Any chance I can talk you into going with me?"

"Sorry." She firmly shook her head. "I already have a date."

His lower lip jutted out. "Let me guess. That hardware store dude who tried to give me painting lessons?"

She laughed. "Nope. I'm going with my old BFF. Chelsea Willits and I plan to go stag together."

He brightened. "So maybe I can snag a dance or two with you? If I promise to mind my manners?"

"I think that could be arranged." She glanced at her watch. "But I really need to go. Grandpa promised to get my pickup running this afternoon. And he wants to teach me how to drive three-on-the-tree."

"What's that?"

She laughed and explained how the gear shifting worked in the pickup. Then, promising to see him tomorrow, she hopped in her car. But before going home, she made a quick stop at the hardware store. This was not an excuse to see Jordan either. At least that's what she told herself as she parked in front. She'd gotten tired of using a dirty old barn broom in her trailer. She felt that *Rose* deserved a daintier broom and dustpan, as well as a nice welcome mat to put outside the front door. Of course, if she bumped into Jordan, she wouldn't complain. But by the time she checked out, she knew that wasn't happening. She didn't like being paranoid, but she did wonder if he was avoiding her.

As she drove home, she told herself it didn't matter. She did not care. Mostly she wanted to find out how her "new" vintage pickup was doing. Had Grandpa managed to charge the battery, or was there more to be fixed? She hoped and prayed that *Jack* wouldn't turn into a money pit. But seeing the pickup parked in front of the house, her spirits lifted. And

196

right next to it was Grandpa's truck and some jumper cables already connected.

"Ready to try it out?" Grandpa asked as Dillon got out.

"You bet."

Grandpa told her to get into his truck and what to do. "Hope this works." He carried the other ends of the cables to her truck. "Fire it up as soon as I give you the signal." Before long, he was in the cab, yelling at her to start it up, and after a few tries, *Jack* was running.

"Let's let 'er idle awhile," Grandpa said as he revved up *Jack*'s engine. He disconnected the jumper cables. "You go park my truck by the barn, and in about ten minutes, I'll give you your first driving lesson."

She parked his truck, then, feeling the afternoon heat baking into her, ducked into her trailer to change into cutoffs, a T-shirt, and tennis shoes. Within a few minutes she'd gone out to see Grandpa dropping the hood of her pickup. "*Jack*'s rip-roaring to go now." He went to the passenger side, telling Dillon to take the wheel.

Next he explained how three-on-the-tree worked, taking her through each step. After a lot of trips around the farm—which included some loud grinding of gears—she was finally able to go up and down the farm road without too much trouble.

"You drop me at the house," Grandpa told her, "but keep that engine running to get that battery good and charged."

"How long?"

"Just take 'er for a nice long spin—" he paused—"I mean *him*. I put some gas in, so you won't have any problem there. Why not drive *Jack* to town? Get yourself some ice cream or something, then drive around some more and come back."

"Okay." She nodded, glad that her phone was in her back pocket—just in case she needed a tow truck. "Here I go." Thinking through the positions for shifting, and when and how to change gears, she cautiously continued down the driveway. Really, it wasn't that hard. In fact, it was fairly easy. And then she realized it was fun. Driving her old pickup with the windows open, hair flying in the breeze, she didn't feel midthirties like Chelsea had suggested. She felt sixteen again. And it was awesome! Like this was what life was meant to be—and she planned to embrace it.

By the time she was rolling into town, she'd gotten three-on-the-tree down pat. And although she knew she shouldn't be hungry after that fantastic lunch, Grandpa's suggestion of ice cream sounded like a good reward. Especially since it was a hot afternoon and the old pickup didn't have AC. She didn't really mind that. But ice cream did sound cool. She parked on the street in front of the Cream Cup, Silverdale's oldest and best ice cream and burger shop, then got in line at the window—along with the Fourth of July tourists. It took a few minutes, but when she saw her soft-swirled vanilla cone, she knew it was worth it.

Feeling pleased with herself, she carried her ice cream back to the pickup. But since she was not confident enough to eat and drive, she opened the tailgate and sat down on it, watching the holiday traffic and remembering how she used to do this very thing as a teenager. Kicking the heels of her tennis shoes, she felt so right. Like she was exactly where she needed to be at the moment. And she didn't need a guy by her side. Not Brandon. Not even Jordan. This was more than good enough, and she planned to savor it.

Finally her ice cream was gone and it was time to restart the pickup. But it only gave out a strange little growl . . . and then nothing. She tried again. Nothing. "Oh, *Jack,*" she said. "What's wrong?" As she got out of the pickup, wondering what to do, she noticed a familiar pickup coming down the street toward her. An old red pickup, with Jordan Atwood at the wheel. She made a halfhearted wave, and he stopped on the opposite side of the street and hopped out. To her dismay, Vivian Porter was sitting in the passenger seat, peering curiously at Dillon.

As Jordan crossed the street toward her, she almost didn't recognize him. She'd never seen him in a tie and jacket—and wondered why he was so dressed up. She also wondered about Vivian. She looked dressed up too. But Dillon didn't want to ask.

"Is this Uncle Jack's old Chevy?" Jordan's brow creased.

"Yep." She nodded glumly. "But it's not running."

"Then how did it get *here*?" He tilted his head to one side.

She quickly explained about Grandpa charging the battery and telling her to take it for a drive. "I got an ice cream, and now the pickup won't start."

"You didn't shut down the engine, did you?" His expression suggested that would be an idiotic thing to do.

"Yeah," she confessed.

He shook his head with a grim expression. "Well, that's not how you recharge a battery, Dillon. Didn't you know that?"

"If I had *known* it, do you think I would've done it?" She wasn't quite sure why she felt so exasperated at him, but she did. It felt like he was criticizing her . . . or maybe he just resented her having his uncle's pickup. Whatever it was, it didn't feel good . . . or right. And for the first time since meeting Jordan, she didn't like him quite so much. Not only that, but she felt funny standing next to him in her shorts and T-shirt—with him looking like a city slicker.

"Well, if you don't know much about an old pickup, why are you driving it around?" He removed his sports coat and loosened his tie with an aggravated expression.

It didn't help that Vivian was now getting out and coming over. "What's up?" she asked as Jordan headed back to his pickup.

"Broken down," Jordan tossed back at her.

"I, uh, think it's the battery," Dillon told Vivian.

"Good thing we came along." Vivian frowned in a way that suggested she didn't approve of Dillon's ultra-casual attire. Or maybe it was just Dillon's imagination, since Vivian looked even more chic than usual.

Jordan put his coat and tie in his pickup cab. Then, after rolling up the sleeves of his light blue shirt, he began to rummage through the big chrome toolbox in the back. Finally, pulling out what looked like jumper cables, he headed back.

"Jordan is always prepared for anything," Vivian told Dillon.

"Lucky for me."

"I'm going to pull my pickup over there," he called out as he got back into his cab. Before long, he was parked alongside her—but still in the street. He jumped out and lifted her hood.

"You're blocking traffic," Dillon pointed out.

"Then you get out there and direct them," he told her. "Hopefully, this will be quick." But it took a few minutes for him to get everything hooked up, and although traffic wasn't too busy on this side street, there were still a couple of cars waiting to pass when he yelled at her to get back in her truck. "Hurry," he yelled. "You know what to do?"

"Yes," she shouted back.

"Vivian, you get into my truck and start it up for me, okay?"

"You got it." Vivian hurried around to the driver's side.

And with Jordan directing them, Dillon's truck was running again a few moments later. Without turning it off, she got out and watched as Jordan removed the cables. As she thanked him, she noticed he'd gotten grease on his shirt. But before she could apologize, he was looping the cables over his arm and waving at the cars still waiting to pass.

"Thanks for your patience!" he called out. Jordan hopped back into his pickup and, with Vivian by his side, took off.

She watched as his pickup went down the street and the clogged traffic moved along. Thinking he might circle the block and return to check on her, she waited a few minutes. But after a while, she realized he was gone. He'd done his good deed, and obviously he and Vivian had more important things to attend to. Well, fine. Whatever. She didn't need to sit around moping about it. And why shouldn't he be involved with Vivian? After all, they had much in common. Like him, she had her own business and owned a vintage trailer, and they were connected to the same people . . . Why shouldn't they go out together? Still, Dillon felt keenly disappointed as she drove home. She also felt slightly irritated at Jordan . . . as if he'd been stringing her along.

She chided herself for her bad feelings. She should be grateful for his assistance, not irritated. But it was unsettling to see him with Vivian like that. Had she completely misread

Jordan last weekend? If he had no feelings for her, why had he been so warm and friendly and helpful? Why had he wanted to know so much about her and tried to draw her out? Had she imagined he'd wanted something more than just casual friendship? Was she really that naïve? That was the obvious answer. Based on his chilly treatment in front of the Cream Cup, not to mention his date, he had zero interest now. And she should just get over it.

But it was still disturbing. Oddly enough, it made Brandon appear that much better. Especially after he'd been the perfect gentleman today. Not that Dillon had any intentions of getting back with him. She did not. Despite Chelsea's insinuation that they couldn't be choosy when it came to potential male attention, Dillon didn't feel that desperate. But she did feel confused.

CHAPTER
21

*A*fter spending the evening and following morning cleaning, waxing, and polishing her old pickup, Dillon couldn't wait to drive it. Fortunately, the battery was working just fine now, and Dillon had agreed to meet Chelsea in town.

First on their agenda today was the Fourth of July parade. Dillon couldn't help but smile at the small-town charm of marching bands, dance teams, old cars, homemade floats, and the exact same things she remembered from her youth.

"You should be driving your pickup in this," Chelsea told Dillon as several old-timer trucks rolled by. "You could've represented the swimming program with a bunch of pool kids in the back."

"Maybe next year," Dillon said.

"Seriously? You think you'll still be around by then?"

Dillon shrugged. "I kinda hope so." She pointed to a pickup with Boy Scouts dressed like forest animals.

"Maybe we could have the pool kids dress up like fish or mermaids or something aquatic."

"Fabulous idea." Chelsea nodded. "I hope you're still here next year. I'll put you in charge."

"Hey, there's the twins." Dillon waved at Emma and Chloe as they marched with a group of little majorettes, attempting to spin mini-batons and chasing them as they spun out of control. "This is all adorable."

"Nothing has changed," Chelsea said after she snapped several pictures of her sister on the Parks and Recreation float. "It's like a time warp."

As usual, the parade ended with the small fleet of fire engines sounding loud horns and sirens. "That was fun," Dillon told Chelsea. "I'm glad you talked me into coming." She glanced through the crowd lining both sides of Main Street. "I'm just glad I didn't run into Brandon. And, if you don't mind, I think I'll take off before that happens."

"So how did it go yesterday?" Chelsea asked as they went to the parking lot where they'd met earlier.

"Brandon took me to McLaughlin's."

"I'm jealous. I've been dying to go there ever since I moved back to town. How was it?"

"The place is absolutely gorgeous and the food is great. The whole thing went surprisingly well."

"So, maybe you want to rethink your plans for dumping the poor guy?"

"I wouldn't go that far, but I have to admit, he was very decent yesterday." Dillon controlled herself from adding that he'd been much more congenial than Jordan Atwood. "But, while we're on the topic, I'll warn you that he plans to go to the dance tonight. So we'll probably cross paths. Hey, maybe we can take turns dancing with him. He's not a bad dancer actually."

"You won't have to twist my arm," Chelsea said as they paused by the parking lot next to Atwood's. "I don't know about you, but I plan to dress up a little. Nothing fancy, but I feel like wearing a summery dress. More fun for dancing." She nudged Dillon. "How about you?"

Dillon thought. "I'm storing most of my clothes in the barn. You know, my trailer space is pretty limited. To be honest, I don't even own a summer dress."

"How's that possible?"

Dillon shrugged. "I had mostly business clothes for during the week, and jeans and casual clothes for the weekends."

"Well, we're still about the same size. How about if I bring you a dress?"

"Oh, I don't want you to go to any trouble."

"No trouble. I'll bring it by around seven, and then we can go to town together and make a big splash. That'll be fun."

Dillon still wasn't sure about the borrowed dress—was it too much for her? But Chelsea looked so hopeful. "Okay. I guess that'll work."

"Great. And how about the picnic today? Are you going?"

"It might be fun. How about you?"

"Yeah, I promised my sister I'd manage the dessert table. Parks and Rec is the main sponsor. Hey, you want to help?"

Dillon gladly agreed, then nodded over to Atwood's. "Looks like the hardware store is open today. I think I'll go take a look at those outdoor chairs out in front," she said. "I could use some outside my trailer."

"Then I'll see you at one," Chelsea told her.

As Dillon walked to Atwood's she knew that she was looking for more than just a cute lawn chair or two. Maybe she was a glutton for punishment, but she hoped to see Jordan. And she was determined not to act overly friendly this time. She would simply thank him for his help yesterday—and be on her way. That is, if he were here.

As she examined the outdoor furniture more closely, she was pleasantly surprised to see they were having a one-day-only Fourth of July sale. When she saw their selection of all-weather chairs in the color she wanted, a bright coral orange that would look perfect outside of her trailer, she decided to get them. She found a few other outdoor things as well—feeling really glad she'd stopped by.

"Can I help you?"

She looked up from a side table she was considering to see Jordan looking at her with an amused expression. She smiled politely. "No, I think I've decided on the pieces I want to get. Do I just go inside and tell the cashier?"

"Or I can write them up for you out here." He pulled out a little pad.

"Thank you." She pointed out the coral chairs and a few other things she wanted, and as he wrote it all down, she thanked him for helping with her pickup yesterday. "I really appreciated it. And I was sorry you got your good clothes dirty. You looked like you were going somewhere special too. I hope that didn't make a problem—"

"Actually, I'd just come from a chamber meeting."

"Chamber?"

"Chamber of Commerce. I don't usually get that dressed up, but they'd elected me as the new president, so I thought I should try to look the part."

"Oh." She nodded. "Was that meeting out at McLaughlin's?"

"Yep. In fact, I saw you and Brandon out on the deck. Looked like you were having a pretty good time."

She studied his expression, trying to discern whether she was imagining it, or if he was actually jealous. "Brandon only asked me to lunch in order to tell me goodbye," she said in an even and hopefully disinterested tone.

"Looked more like he was saying hello." Jordan's smile looked fixed.

"Well, I'm sure he was hoping for something more, but I tried to make it clear that the past was the past . . . and that I want to move on." She looked down at the sidewalk, hoping she wasn't being too obvious.

"So, is this all you want?" He held up the slip of paper.

"I, uh, I guess so." She glanced around. "I plan to put these outside my trailer. You know, to create an outdoor living space."

"Nice." He pointed to another section out front. "All our outdoor lighting and grills and everything are on sale today too. Good time to pick up some bargains."

"Oh?" She went over to look at a rack. "These are cool." She picked up a box of outdoor lights. "I could string them outside my trailer."

"Do you have an awning?" he asked. "They'd look great hanging from that."

"No. But I hope to get one. I've seen some pretty cute ones in my vintage trailer books."

"You should check out this website." He wrote something down on a card and handed it to her. "They're well-made and affordable."

"Thanks." She had several items in her hands now.

"How about if I take these inside for you," he said in a friendlier tone. Had her words about cutting ties with Brandon made a difference? Or was he just helping a customer?

Once her selections were made, Dillon was paying for her purchase at the cash register when Jordan reappeared. "Need any help getting these things loaded up?"

"I was hoping I could pull the pickup up to the store, but looks like there's no room out there." She explained where she was parked.

"I'll help you get it over there," he offered.

After two trips, everything was loaded in the pickup bed. "Looks like you cleaned up the old truck."

"Yes, I wanted to get *Jack* looking good. Couldn't let *Rose* show him up."

Jordan grinned. "So you named him *Jack*. That's nice." He ran his hand over the recently polished hood. "This original paint job is holding up alright. But then Uncle Jack usually parked it under cover."

Dillon jumped at the sound of a loud bang nearby. "Oh— that must be a firecracker," she said with relief. "I forgot it's the Fourth."

"Did you see the parade?" he asked, obviously in no hurry to get back to the store.

"Yes. And I saw your nieces too. I'd forgotten how sweet a small-town parade could be. Did you see it?"

"Yep. From in front of the store. Wouldn't miss it. Are you going to any of the other festivities?"

She told him she was planning to help Chelsea with the picnic. "And she and I are going to the dance together. Stag." Hopefully that didn't sound like a hint . . . or like she was desperate.

"I thought I might check it out too. I hear the band's supposed to be good."

"Cool." She nodded, trying to think of something else to say.

"Well, I better get back to work. We're only open until four today. But campers always appreciate being able to pick up whatever it was they forgot at home." He tipped his head. "See you later."

She smiled and thanked him again for helping her. And she continued to smile all the way back to the farm. Maybe she had given up too soon on Jordan Atwood. Maybe he had simply been scared off by Brandon. And really, who could blame him?

By the time she got her hardware store purchases unloaded, she was sorely tempted to get them all set up—and play "outdoor house." But it was almost time to return to town and she wanted to put on something cooler. With the hope of seeing Jordan again, she decided to freshen up some. And since the day was growing hot, she decided to pamper herself by taking her car—and turning up the AC.

As she drove back to town, she hoped she wasn't setting herself up for heartache again, but Jordan appeared to be back to his old self. She wasn't sure if it was explained by her grandpa's theory about jealousy—and she hoped not—but she did feel that Jordan had needed some reassurance. And she planned to give it to him.

Dillon was just entering the city park, which was already getting crowded, when Brandon came over to join her. Like the other day, he was dressed in casual Western wear again. But it still looked totally out of character for a guy like Brandon. "Hey, Dillon. Are you here for the picnic? I hear the barbecued chicken is killer."

She explained that she wasn't here to eat. "I'm volunteering with Chelsea. But I hope you enjoy it."

He frowned. "So they don't let the volunteers eat?"

Her smile was polite. "I really don't know." She pointed to the food tables. "But I see Chelsea. I better go help her."

"Guess I'll see you later," he said, looking disappointed.

"Sure. Later." She nodded then hurried away. She really didn't want to be rude, but she wished he'd take her rejection more seriously. As she helped set up and organize the dessert table, Chelsea questioned her about Brandon.

"I saw him trailing you over here." Chelsea set a piece of chocolate cake on a paper plate. "And, don't look now, but he seems to be keeping a close eye on you."

"I don't know why he doesn't give up. I've made it perfectly clear."

"Apparently he's smitten."

"Or he just wants what he can't have." Dillon cut into a pie. "I'm pretty sure that's what it is. He's very competitive. I'm guessing if I'd played hard-to-get a year ago, we'd have been married by now."

"Maybe you need to try some reverse psychology." Chelsea chuckled. "Act like you're really into him and can't wait to tie the knot—maybe he'll take off running."

Dillon actually considered this. "Interesting idea. But I don't know . . ." She handed a piece of apple pie to an elderly gentleman. "Enjoy," she told him. "Sure smells good."

As they continued serving dessert, Dillon considered Chelsea's suggestion. Perhaps it would work, but Dillon did not want to play games. Not with Brandon any more than she wanted to with Jordan.

"Looks like most people have been served," Chelsea told her. "Feel free to go grab some food—if there's anything left."

"How about if I get us both some," Dillon offered. "We can take turns eating."

"Great."

Dillon headed for the chicken first, but trying to balance two plates and get food and drinks for two was tricky. And that's when Brandon appeared. "Could you use a spare hand?" He reached for a plate. "Looks like you're hungry."

She smirked at him. "One of these is for Chelsea."

"That's a relief. I'd hate to think you've turned into such a porker." He chuckled like this was clever.

"No worries." She scooped some potato salad onto both plates. "But, as you know, I've always had a healthy appetite."

"Something I've always admired."

"Right." She set a roll on both plates. "I can remember you teasing me before, Brandon. Don't pretend you didn't."

His lower lip jutted out. "That was then, Dillon. This is now."

She was just putting green salad on her plate when she felt someone watching her. She looked up to see Jordan less than twenty feet away. Smiling, she wanted to wave, but her hands were full. And then, just like that, he turned and walked away. *Great.* Had she managed to alienate him again? Or maybe Brandon had sent him a signal. Although Brandon was so focused on salad dressing, he appeared oblivious. Maybe that was a good thing. She didn't want him to think he was winning.

Brandon carried the plate for Chelsea back to the dessert tent. But instead of going on his merry way while they ate, he continued to hang around. And when people came for desserts, seeing that Chelsea and Dillon were eating, he stepped in to help. Naturally, Chelsea thought that was charming and didn't mind saying so.

"I hear you're going to meet us at the dance tonight," she told Brandon as they were cleaning up. "And that you're a good dancer."

"Now who said that?" Brandon winked at Dillon.

"I promised Chelsea that we'd share you," Dillon told him. "I hope you don't mind."

He looked uncertain, but nodded. "That sounds like fun."

Dillon turned to Chelsea. "Looks like things are under control here. Especially with Brandon to help. Do you mind if I take off? I have some things I need to take care of on the farm."

"No problem. Take off. I'll see you later tonight." Chelsea grinned at Dillon. "And I'll keep Brandon busy packing this stuff up."

Dillon patted Brandon on the back. "So glad you offered to help." And not giving him a chance to back out of his forced volunteerism, she hurried away. But instead of feeling pleased with herself, she felt discouraged. Jordan probably thought she was totally flaky. One moment she was telling him that Brandon was history, the next moment she appeared to be sharing lunch with him—again. Would she ever get this right?

CHAPTER 22

*B*ack at the farm, with several hours to kill before to-night's dance and fireworks show, Dillon decided to set up her outdoor space. She put her bargain purchases into place, arranging the chairs and table just so. But somehow it just didn't look quite right—the concrete pad and metal building wasn't a very pretty backdrop. She looked over to what used to be one of her favorite spots. Not far from the barn, a grove of aspen trees and the irrigation pond looked temptingly perfect. She wondered if Grandpa would mind if she moved her "camp" over there.

Spotting Grandpa's pickup just pulling up to the farm, she went over to meet him. "So how'd you like that picnic?" she asked as they went into the kitchen.

"Not bad. But I think the chicken was a little overdone this year."

"Better than underdone."

"That's true," he agreed. As he filled a glass with water, she told him about her idea to relocate her trailer. "Can't see any problem with that." He swigged the water. "I think we can even stretch an extension cord and hose that far."

"That'd be fantastic."

"Need any help moving it over there?" Grandpa's expression suggested he knew she would.

"Well, being that I don't have a clue as to how to hook the trailer to the pickup . . . although I could probably go online and find a tutorial—"

"I think you could use a human for this. And I'm happy to help."

As they walked to the barn, Grandpa mentioned Brandon. "I noticed he was hovering pretty close to the dessert table, but I'll bet he wasn't just there for the apple pie."

She sighed. "Yeah, he hasn't given up yet. The weird thing is that he's being awfully nice. It almost makes me wonder if he's really turned over a new leaf."

"Stranger things happen."

"Fortunately he should be on his way back to Colorado soon."

"Uh-huh." Grandpa nodded. "Think you'll still feel the same once he's gone? You know what they say, absence makes the heart grow fonder."

She shrugged. "I'm pretty sure of my feelings."

"I saw Jordan at the picnic . . . We chatted a bit."

"Yeah. I saw him too. But I was with Brandon." She shook her head. "I think Jordan got the wrong message."

Grandpa chuckled. "Or maybe he got the right message, Dillon. Maybe he's getting the jealous bug after all."

Before Dillon could think of a response, Grandpa told her

to get the pickup. "Back it up to the hitch, but keep your eyes on me." He explained how he'd use his hands to show her how far to back up when it got down to inches. And before long, she was backing up, stepping on the brakes as his hands clapped together. She hopped out and went to watch as he showed her how to adjust the hitch height and then drop it onto the trailer ball. "This is how you clamp it," he explained.

"And that's all it takes to hold the trailer secure?" She hated the idea of her beautiful trailer breaking free of the pickup and careening over a cliff.

"Well, if you were towing a distance you'd want to use these safety chains." He pointed to a couple of rusty chains draped beneath the trailer. Then he showed her how to connect the lights to the pickup. "You obviously don't need them now, but if you were on a road, you have to hook 'em up."

"And what do they do exactly?"

"They're synchronized with your pickup. You use your turn signal and the trailer does too."

"Cool." She nodded.

"I'll check 'em out for you when you pull out. Test the signals and brake lights."

"So that's it? Ready to roll?"

"Not yet." Grandpa knelt down, pointing beneath the trailer. "First you gotta take out those stabilizing jacks."

"Huh?"

Grandpa pointed out some metal things beneath the trailer. "You gotta get a little dirty."

"That's okay."

"Get down there, lay on your side, then crank those handles counterclockwise to lower them."

215

"Okay." She got down and tried. "I can't seem to move them."

"You probably need a little WD-40. I'll be right back."

As she lay on the ground beneath her trailer, she wondered if she'd bitten off more than she could chew. It was one thing to make the trailer all cute and cozy, but would she ever be able to remember—or do—all this stuff and take it on the road? By herself?

"Here you go." Grandpa bent down to hand her a spray can. "Just give 'em a good squirt."

After a few squirts, she was finally able to get the jacks lowered. "What do I do with them?"

"For now just put 'em in the back of your pickup. There's a hold that Jack would keep 'em in." He pointed to a small exterior door. "That's what the little brass key on your trailer key ring is for."

"Oh." She nodded. "Good to know. So, are we ready to do this?"

"As soon as we check your lights." He nodded to the cab. "Go ahead."

"Anything I should know before I start the engine?"

"Nah. Just crank 'er up. We'll check the lights and then I'll ride over to the pond with you."

"Okay." She felt a little uneasy as she started the engine, but she followed Grandpa's instructions. He confirmed the lights worked fine, then got into the passenger's seat.

"So far so good." Grandpa nodded, pointing to the dirt road. "Now just head that way. Circle around and then we'll back her up so that your door will open out toward the pond."

"Sounds good." Dillon tried to look more confident as she drove over the bumpy road.

"I hope you battened down the hatches in your trailer."

"Huh?" She slowed down.

"Well, everything that's loose inside will bounce around and—"

"Oh no." She stepped on the brakes. "I didn't batten down anything."

"Oh . . . well, you might want to check."

She put the pickup into park and raced around to see that the interior of her sweet, tidy trailer was now a mess. "Oh no." She started to pick up the pieces, relieved to see that nothing appeared broken. She carefully stowed the loose things here and there, hoping they would stay put until she parked it again.

"How was it?" Grandpa asked as she got back in.

"Not great, but nothing broke. And I suppose it was a good lesson. Before I tow the trailer, I must batten down the hatches." She put the pickup into gear, wondering how she'd manage to remember all these things. Of course, she would write them in her handy notebook, but would that be enough?

She finally looped around and, after a couple of tries, got the pickup and trailer positioned the way Grandpa had recommended. "Now I'll get out and direct you," he told her. "Just keep your eyes on me and back 'er up. It's pretty tight in there, but I'm sure the trailer will fit."

She waited for Grandpa to get into place and motion her. Then she began to back it up. When he pointed to turn right, she did as told, but he held up his hands, yelling to stop. "Not like that," he explained. "The steering wheel is opposite of the trailer."

"Oh." She nodded, like she understood. "Okay."

But when she tried again, it quickly happened again. And Grandpa explained again, telling her to put her hand on the bottom of the steering wheel to help. But it didn't help and this time she actually bumped her trailer into an aspen tree.

Grandpa gave her another quick lesson and pep talk, but something in her brain just refused to listen. When he said turn right, she wanted to turn the pickup right. And he kept yelling "No!"

Finally, on the verge of tears, she got out, begging him to back it up for her. And he climbed in and managed to do it— just like that. "See, it's easy," he said as he hopped out. "You just need to remember that left is right and right is left when you're backing up a trailer."

"Right." She went around to check where she'd bumped the aspen. The paint was slightly scuffed, but she figured she could touch it up.

"So, what d'ya think?" Grandpa gazed over the pond. "These aspens should keep you shady in the afternoon and you can watch the sun rise over the pond in the morning."

She looked around and smiled. "It's a beautiful place to camp, Grandpa. Thanks." She wanted to add that she might never move her trailer from this spot—because of her concerns about backing up—but didn't want to sound pathetic. "And thanks for helping me to get it over here. I couldn't have done it without you."

"We're not done yet," he told her. "We still need to put the jacks in place or you'll be bouncing around in there. But we'll have to get some boards to put under the jacks, then round up hoses and extension cords."

By the time they got the trailer all set up, Dillon was worn out—and filthy. In less than two hours, Chelsea would be here with a sundress to loan her, with the hope they were going to town to make a "splash." But the only splash Dillon needed right now was a shower.

After getting cleaned up, Dillon returned to her new campsite in the aspens. Feeling refreshed and energetic, she decided to set up her outdoor room. She set out the chairs and tables and lanterns and other cute campy things. And even though the sun was still out, she hung her string of camp lights. She even picked a fresh bouquet of flowers and, after putting them in an old mason jar, set them on the table. Finally, she sat down. Perfect. Absolutely perfect!

As she sat there soaking in the sweet ambiance of her new digs and imagining how charming it would look in the evening with the lights and lanterns lit, she was tempted to back out on the dance and just stay put. After all, she knew how tonight would go. Brandon would monopolize her time at the dance and, if Jordan was there, he would probably keep a distance. And because Dillon had agreed to ride with Chelsea, there'd be no sneaking out early. She was tempted to call Chelsea and make an excuse. She could claim she was worn out . . . and on some levels she was tired. But, as badly as she wanted to remain home, she didn't want to let her friend down.

She considered the word *home*. Is that what this truly was? A funky old trailer parked by an irrigation pond? As weird as it was, it sure seemed like it. It felt good to know that her tiny home was all hers—with no one to tell her what to do or how to do it. Dillon suddenly realized she hadn't felt this much at home in her entire adulthood. As she leaned back in her new Adirondack chair, she was grateful to God . . . and happy. She was truly a happy camper! Maybe it was just her imagination, but she thought she could live like this forever. And that felt good.

For so many years, she'd been striving . . . working hard . . .
performing . . . And for what? Where did it get her? In this
moment, she realized that her efforts had been symptomatic
of something much bigger. Something eternal. Dillon remembered when she'd made a commitment to God as a freshman in
high school. During the following years, while living with her
grandparents, she faithfully attended youth group and church.
She lived the best life she thought possible. Far more orderly
and disciplined than her chaotic childhood years spent with
her mother. And she probably took some pride in that.

Although she'd never backed away from that spiritual commitment, college had slowly eroded it. Not that she abandoned
her faith, but she definitely placed God on the back burner.
Then as she entered the workplace, she relied less and less on
God . . . and more on herself. Her old resolve to trust God with
every part of her life had been set aside. Now she wanted it
back. A Scripture she'd tried to live by as a teen came to her,
and surprised she could even remember it, she said it aloud.

"Trust the Lord with your whole heart, don't depend on
your own knowledge and experience, include God in all you
do, and he will direct you through life." She paused, listening
to the breeze rustling through the aspens. "That's what I want
now." She took in a deep breath of fresh, clean air, then slowly
exhaled. "Please, God, help me get back there."

She'd barely finished her short but heartfelt prayer when she
heard a car coming down the driveway. She went beyond the
aspen grove to spot Chelsea parking by the house. "I'm over
here," she called out, waving Chelsea's car toward the barn
and explaining about her new trailer location.

"I want to see that trailer." Chelsea opened the back of her SUV.

"You look pretty," Dillon said. She had on a blue-and-white sundress with a little flair in the skirt.

Chelsea held up a garment. "And here's your gown, Cinderella."

Dillon frowned at the creamy white sundress.

"You don't like it?" Chelsea sounded disappointed. "I thought it would look great against your tan."

Dillon didn't want to rain on Chelsea's parade, but she also didn't want to show up at the dance in a white sundress trimmed in lace. It could probably serve as a bridal gown in certain circles. This just wasn't her style. "I, uh, don't know."

"Don't make up your mind until you try it on," Chelsea told her. "Where's the dressing room?"

"My trailer."

As they walked to the irrigation pond, Dillon was already planning a different outfit for the dance. She'd humor Chelsea by trying it on. But then she'd explain that she usually wore no-nonsense clothes and just wasn't comfortable.

"Oh, Dillon!" Chelsea exclaimed. "Your trailer is adorable. And the way it's all set up—it's fabulous."

"Thanks! Wait until you see it inside." Dillon felt encouraged as she opened the door, smiling as Chelsea oohed and aahed over Dillon's renovations.

"No wonder you love it so much. I wish I had one of my own." Chelsea held out the dress. "Now you slip this on and see if you hate it as much as you think you will."

As Dillon put on the dress, Chelsea continued to examine the trailer, commenting on every small detail. "Hey, you should wear some of this turquoise with the dress. It will look perfect. Where'd you get these pieces anyway? They look like vintage."

"My grandma," Dillon said as she pulled up the zipper.

Chelsea brought over a squash blossom necklace and looped it over Dillon's head. "Very nice." Now she added a turquoise and silver bracelet. "Even better."

Dillon felt uncertain. As much as she loved her grandma's jewelry, she rarely wore it. And never two pieces at once. "I, uh, I don't—"

"And these too." Chelsea picked up the cowboy boots Dillon had been wearing around the farm. Like the jewelry, they'd been her grandma's too.

"Seriously?"

"Yes. That will look perfect."

Dillon slipped on the boots, then stood in front of the full-length mirror on the closet door. To her surprise, the ensemble didn't look half bad. In fact, it looked pretty good. She turned to Chelsea. "What are you—a stylist?"

Chelsea laughed. "Well, not exactly, but I do pay attention to trends. And since you're sort of a farm girl at heart, I think this suits you." She reached for Dillon's old denim jacket. "And when it gets cooler tonight, you can wear this."

"Really?" Dillon took the jacket, experimenting with it over the dress. "Hey, that actually looks pretty cool. Thanks, Chels."

"Ready to rock and roll?"

Feeling a little strange—but good—Dillon nodded. She knew this evening could go totally sideways on her. Between Brandon's obsessive attentions and Jordan's casual disdain, this dance could be destined for disaster. But she patted her trailer as she closed the door—at least home sweet home would be waiting for her afterward. That was a comfort.

CHAPTER
23

*T*he park looked even more festive than it had earlier. The tennis court area, now doubling as the dance floor, was decorated with strings of red-white-and-blue lights. The band was already playing, and a few couples were dancing.

"Let's get something to drink and nab a table," Chelsea suggested. "Then we can just wait and see how it goes."

"You mean, like whether we'll be wallflowers or not?" Dillon teased as they went over to a food kiosk.

Before long, they were seated on the sidelines, attempting to act nonchalant and taking in their surroundings. Dillon wondered if her prediction was right—maybe they really were destined to be wallflowers.

"Where's Brandon?" Chelsea asked.

"I don't know. He said he's coming." Dillon glanced toward

the street, but she wasn't really watching for Brandon. It was a certain vintage red pickup that she hoped to spot.

"Speaking of your not-so-secret admirer . . ." Chelsea nudged her, and Dillon followed her gaze to see Brandon approaching. Once again, he was wearing his Western duds and not looking much like the buttoned-up Brandon she remembered from work.

"Hello, ladies." He actually tipped his cowboy hat to them. "Nice night for a dance. Mind if I join you?"

"Please do." Chelsea smiled up at him. "I think we were just starting to get bored with each other's company."

Brandon chuckled as he sat down. "I can assure you ladies, I won't get bored with either of you." He nodded in appreciation as he set his drink on the table. "And, if you don't mind me saying, you two are the prettiest girls here tonight."

"Oh, do go on, sir," Chelsea teased.

"And I hope you girls wore your dancing shoes." He glanced at Dillon's feet. "Or should I say boots?"

She shrugged. "I think these boots should be able to dance."

He reached for her hand. "Then why not give it a try?"

Before she could protest, he pulled her to her feet and was leading her out to the dance floor, where a lively song was playing. "You really do look great," he told her. "I never saw you looking prettier."

"Thanks." She forced a smile. "But flattery will get you nowhere."

He grinned. "I didn't expect it would."

Dillon hated to admit it, even to herself, but it was fun dancing with Brandon. And his open admiration did feel surprisingly nice. Did that mean she'd had a change of heart where he was concerned? Not even close. But what was the harm of spending some time with him? Still, when the song ended, she reminded him of the agreement they'd made.

"I told Chelsea we were sharing you." Now Dillon grabbed him by the hand and led him back to the table. "He's all yours," she told Chelsea. Then, as Brandon took a sip of his drink, she whispered into Chelsea's ear, "And feel free to keep him out there as long as you like. If you can."

"Is that a challenge?" Chelsea's eyes twinkled.

"Maybe so." Dillon winked and then sat down. Even if she ended up looking like a wallflower tonight, she thought that was preferable to being stuck with Brandon all night. As she sipped her drink, she gazed over the crowd that was steadily growing in the dusky evening light. People of all ages had come out tonight. She felt sad to think that Grandpa had insisted on hitting the hay early as usual, and that Margot had voiced she had no intention of coming.

"Hello, Dillon."

She blinked to see an older man looking down at her, then realized it was Margot's ex. "Hey, Don." She smiled. "Fancy seeing you here tonight."

He shrugged. "Yeah, I almost didn't come. Is, uh, is your mom here?"

She shook her head. "No, she didn't want to come."

"Oh. So are you here by yourself then?"

"No. I'm with friends. They're dancing."

"Mind if I join you for a bit?"

"Not at all."

His brow creased as he sat down. "So . . . well, how is Margot doing?"

Dillon gave him a lowdown on the lavender project, not going into detail about how much she and Grandpa had helped Margot to get it going. "The little plants are doing well. Getting bigger every day."

"Oh, that's nice." He nodded. "That should make her happy."

Dillon frowned as she pulled on her denim jacket.

He leaned forward. "So, is she happy?"

"To be honest, I don't think so."

"Mind if I ask why?"

"I'm not really sure why. But she's been in a mood this past week."

"Well, she can be moody."

"Believe me, I know. But she seems more down than normal." She peered closely at Don, taking in his long gray hair which, as usual, was pulled back in a ponytail. He'd always reminded her of Willie Nelson. "I think she secretly misses you."

He brightened. "Really?"

"It's just a suspicion. But she acts kind of lost to me."

"Do you think there's a chance she'll come back to me?"

Dillon sighed. "I honestly don't know. She can be pretty stubborn."

"Yeah, I know."

"But I think living on the farm's getting old for her."

"She's never struck me as the get-your-hands-dirty kind of girl."

Dillon laughed. "You got that right."

"So, do you have any suggestions? Any thoughts on how I might win her back? I know I won't make any points by getting down on one knee."

"That's for sure. I still don't know why she's so opposed to marriage."

"It's too conventional for her. She thinks she's a free spirit. You know."

"Yeah . . . but sometimes I wonder. I mean, it could be an act."

"So, seriously, is there anything you can think of that I could do? You probably know Margot as well as anyone."

"I'm not so sure about that." Just the same, Dillon thought hard. "I know she likes feeling needed. And if you happened to like her health food concoctions, well, that could go a long way." She explained about how she and Grandpa had been rebelling in the kitchen.

Don grinned. "I know how that goes. You can only take so much kale."

"But if you acted like you missed her cooking and if perhaps your health was in some sort of peril . . . that might get her attention. I think she wants to be appreciated."

"Yeah. That makes sense."

"What about just asking her out on a date? Her life looks pretty bleak to me. She might enjoy getting off the farm."

"Good idea." He nodded. "I didn't even think of that."

"The worst she can do is say no." Dillon noticed Don watching something behind her.

"Hey, Jordan." Don stood and was now shaking Jordan's hand. "How's it going, bud?"

"Okay." Jordan politely greeted both of them.

"Dillon's just giving me some romantic advice."

Jordan's brows arched. "Romantic advice?"

Don chuckled. "You know, for her mother."

Jordan nodded. "Of course."

"But if you came over to ask Dillon to dance, don't let me stand in your way." Don beamed at Dillon. "I assume you two know each other, but if you don't, I can give a hearty recommendation for Mr. Jordan Atwood here. He's one of the good guys."

"We've met," Dillon told him.

"Then you kids should get out there and dance," Don urged.

"How about it?" Jordan asked Dillon.

"Sure." She tried not to sound nervous. "Sounds good."

Dillon began to relax some as they began to dance. Like Brandon, Jordan was a pretty good dancer. Before long, she was actually having fun—and when Jordan asked her for a second dance, she gladly said yes. But as they were dancing, she noticed that Brandon, still dancing with Chelsea, had his eyes fixed on her. And when the second dance ended, he swept in, suggesting they trade partners.

Before Dillon could protest, Brandon had her by the hand and was leading her to the center of the floor. And so it went for the next hour. Dancing with Brandon . . . and then with Jordan. But Jordan wasn't only dancing with Chelsea. He also danced with the owner of the Silver Slipper. And, unless Dillon was imagining it, Vivian and Jordan were thoroughly enjoying themselves. Although Dillon had liked Vivian . . . at first . . . she wasn't sure how she felt about her now. Not after seeing her with Jordan again. But, she reminded herself, Jordan had every right to be with whomever he wished. After all, she'd been warned he was a confirmed bachelor.

Adding to Dillon's dismay, Chelsea had also managed to find new dance partners as well. And this meant Dillon was stuck with Brandon—for dance after dance. "I think I need a break," she finally told him. And without waiting for him to concede, she headed back to their table.

It wasn't long before Chelsea and several others, including Jordan, joined them. Apparently Vivian was dancing with someone else. And, hoping to keep Jordan from bolting like she expected he might—probably to dance with Vivian again—Dillon attempted to engage him in conversation by telling him about her towing lessons with Grandpa and how she was now "camping" in the aspens by the irrigation pond. "It's really pretty there."

"So you think you can hitch and pull your own trailer now?" Jordan asked with a skeptical expression.

"Sure," she said with more confidence than she really felt. "Grandpa taught me all the steps and I even wrote them down just in case."

"Impressive."

"Hey, that's one of my favorite songs." She grabbed Jordan's hand. "How about it?"

He nodded. "Sure."

Before Brandon could protest, they hurried out to the dance floor again. "I really like this song too," Jordan said as they began to dance.

"So when do they start the fireworks?" Dillon asked him. "It's pretty dark now."

He checked his watch. "Should be anytime now."

"Oh, good."

"I know a good spot to watch from," he said. "If you want, we could get over there and get a spot before the fireworks start."

"Sure." She nodded.

As he led her through a back exit from the tennis court, she asked if they still used the Preston Ranch to shoot the fireworks from.

"Yep. But now they keep a bunch of fire trucks nearby. I guess they had a grass fire that nearly got to the trees a few years ago."

"I always wondered if that could happen." They were at the edge of town now, where the ranch was in open view.

"I parked my pickup here so I could get a good seat." He opened the tailgate, helping her to get into it. "And I just happened to bring a spare camp chair with me." He unfolded two chairs. "As well as some popcorn and sodas."

"Wow." She sat down. "I'm impressed. It's almost like you were expecting company."

"Maybe hoping." And then, just like clockwork, the amplified sound of the national anthem began to boom from the park area, and then the first of the fireworks were shot off.

As they sat there, watching and commenting over the bright and colorful display, Dillon wondered if she'd ever experienced such a perfectly romantic evening. But she also wondered, had Jordan planned it to be like this—specifically with her? Or did she just happen to be at the right place at the right time? What if he'd been dancing with Vivian right before the fireworks show? Would she be sitting here now?

When the fireworks ended, Jordan suggested they return to the dance. "Chelsea and Brandon must be wondering about your whereabouts."

"I don't know about Chelsea, but Brandon probably is."

"I was surprised to see him still here today."

"I thought he'd have gone home by now too," she admitted as they walked down Main Street.

"He appears to like our little town."

"Yes. But not enough to permanently locate here. I'm sure of that."

"Seemed like he enjoyed McLaughlin's . . ."

Dillon weighed his words, surprised he'd mention it again. Was he really bothered by this? Or was she just hoping?

"Can I ask you something, Dillon?" He paused beneath a streetlamp.

"Of course. Anything." She looked up at him.

"Are you sure you're really finished with that relationship? You act a little uncertain to me."

"I'm not uncertain," she insisted. "It's just that Brandon is so persistent."

"Some women enjoy being pursued like that." He studied her.

"The truth is I once wanted him to pursue me like that," she confessed.

"And now?"

"Now it's just frustrating." She sighed. "I can't wait for him to go home Friday."

"You're sure he's leaving?"

"His flight is booked."

Jordan smiled. "Well, sorry to be so nosy . . . but I've been wondering." He started to walk again. "And you have to admit, from my perspective, it looks like you guys are on-again, off-again."

"I can see how it might look like that. But, believe me, I've made myself clear to Brandon." They reentered the park where the music was playing loudly and the crowd was lively.

"Looks like the older generation and kids have cleared out," Dillon observed as they went back to the table they'd been occupying earlier. Although she was hoping he'd invite her to dance, they sat down and for a bit no one said anything. She followed Jordan's gaze out to the dance floor and, unless it was her imagination, his eyes were fixed on Vivian. She was dancing with a guy Dillon didn't recognize. And then Brandon and Chelsea came over to join them.

"Whew . . . I'm ready for a break," Chelsea announced as she sat down.

"Not me." Brandon reached for Dillon's hand. "And I believe you owe me a dance or two. Remember our agreement?"

"Agreement?" But he was pulling her to her feet and tugging her out to the dance floor. "What agreement?" She paused on the sidelines.

"You and Chelsea were supposed to take turns dancing with me. But I've only been dancing with Chelsea—where were you anyway?" He scowled in Jordan's direction.

"Just watching the fireworks from a better location."

"With Jordan?"

"Sure. Why not?"

"Come on." He wrapped an arm around her, clasping her hand. "Let's dance."

Not wanting to make a scene, she let him lead her to the floor. Fortunately the music was too loud and lively for conversation, but she was determined to excuse herself when the song ended.

She was just trying to peel herself away from Brandon when she noticed that Jordan was on the dance floor—with Vivian again. And when the next song started, feeling disappointed, she turned to Brandon. "Another?"

He grinned. "You bet."

Okay, she knew she was being juvenile, but it was like she couldn't help herself—she pretended to be having a good time with Brandon, smiling and dancing with enthusiasm. And seeing that Jordan was still dancing with Vivian—for the last song of the evening—Dillon smiled at Brandon . . . and again they were dancing. This time to a slower number.

"Thanks for giving me the last dance," Brandon said above the music. "I really appreciate it, Dillon."

She immediately recognized that look in his eyes . . . hopefulness and expectations. What had she done? As the song was ending, Brandon moved them to the sidelines of the dancers, and then, pulling her close—and holding her tight—he landed her with a kiss. A rather long and passionate kiss. And although it almost stirred some of the old feelings she used to have for him, she knew it was wrong. And she was aggravated. She pulled away as the music stopped. "Why did you do that?"

"Because I love you, Dillon."

More lights were coming on now and Dillon suddenly felt like everyone was looking at them, although most people were making their way out. "We need to talk," she said firmly and, seeing the back exit that Jordan had taken her through earlier, she led Brandon that way. Outside of the tennis court and away from curious onlookers, she told Brandon what she'd essentially told him over and over. "You're a good guy, Brandon, but you're not the guy for me. I want you to accept this. Once and for all." She looked into his eyes. "Can you, please, do that?"

He let out a disappointed sigh. "Guess I don't have much choice." He shrugged. "Can't say I didn't give it my best shot."

"You certainly did." She smiled in relief. "Now I'll bet Chelsea is looking for me. She's my ride."

"I can take you home," he said.

"No thanks." She headed back through the now nearly vacated tennis court, spying Chelsea on the other side. "Here I am," she called out. "Ready to go?"

"Yep." Chelsea studied Dillon. "You're sure into vanishing acts tonight."

"Sorry about that." Dillon linked arms with her. "But I'm here now. And I'm ready to go home." As they walked to Chelsea's car, Dillon attempted to fill her in on why she disappeared. But as she explained it, she knew it sounded flaky. Not for the first time, Dillon felt like she was messing up . . . she probably appeared fickle and inconsistent and unreliable. All characteristics she disliked. But wasn't Jordan guilty of the same? One moment, he acted like he was pursuing her . . . and then his attention would shift to Vivian. What was up with that?

CHAPTER
24

There was no denying that something was off with Margot the next morning, but when Dillon found her crying in the garden, she knew it was time to intervene. "Are you okay?" Dillon asked.

"Oh." Margot looked up from where she was sitting in the lawn swing. "I didn't even hear you come in here."

"I oiled the squeaky gate a few days ago." Dillon sat by her.

"Am I in your way? Do you want to work in here or something?" Margot blew her nose.

"Not really. I just weeded yesterday."

"I should probably be out weeding the lavender right now." Margot sighed.

"Maybe not right now," Dillon said. "It's pretty much the heat of the day out there. You don't want to get heatstroke again."

"That's true."

"So what's troubling you?" Dillon asked. "I know you've been down lately."

"I don't know exactly . . . maybe it's depression again. You know I've struggled with it before. But I was usually better in the summer months. I think I had SAD."

"I didn't actually know that. I mean, I knew you had your mood swings, but have you actually been treated for depression or SAD?"

Margot nodded. "For about ten years. But I got off antidepressants last year. I took a natural, holistic approach instead."

"And that works?"

"Yeah. But lately I've been kinda bummed. I feel sort of lost and maybe a bit useless."

"Oh." Dillon absorbed this. "Do you think it's related to breaking up with Don?"

Margot shrugged. "I don't know."

"He spoke to me at the Fourth of July dance."

Margot's brows arched. "Why?"

"He just wanted to know how you were doing."

"And what did you tell him?"

"Just what you'd been up to . . . about the lavender and things . . . and that you had seemed a little sad to me lately."

"You told him *that*?" Her eyes flashed.

"Well, it's the truth. You have seemed sad. And then I find you crying."

"Still, it's none of his business. And you have no right to go around gossiping about my emotional health like that."

"It wasn't gossip. It was my opinion. And it's not like I'd repeat that to anyone else. But Don cares about you, Margot. I don't see any reason not to be honest with him."

"Yeah, so he can gloat. He probably thinks I'm missing him."

"Aren't you?"

"I don't know. Not really. I don't think that's it. It feels like something bigger . . . or something chemical. I don't know. But I should probably make an appointment with my shrink." She frowned.

"Or with God."

"God?" She scowled. "You know I don't believe in all that."

"Maybe that's your problem." Dillon sighed. "I couldn't live without God."

"Well, I suppose that's because you're weaker than I am. Weak people need to rely on religion."

"So you think your parents were weak too?"

"I don't know if I'd say that."

"But you are saying you don't need God?"

"That's right."

Dillon considered this. It wasn't that she'd expected a different answer from her mother. Margot had always taken a hard stance against God. "So, what about this earth, the air you breathe, the water you drink, the food you eat . . . do you need those things?"

"Of course."

"Then you must need God too."

"I don't get your reasoning."

"Well, God created all those things. If you need those things, you must need God."

"Well, that's your opinion."

"That's true." Dillon tried to think. "What about when you were a baby, Margot, did you need your parents?"

"Of course."

"Do you think you knew that?"

"I don't know . . . I doubt it."

"Maybe that's like you right now. Maybe you really need God, but you just don't know it."

Margot didn't say anything.

"And, just now, you were crying and saying you were depressed . . . that doesn't exactly sound like the picture of strength to me. Yet, you say that I'm weak for believing in God. Does that make any sense to you?"

"Maybe not . . ."

"I can admit that I am weak. Even this morning, I woke up feeling a little bummed too."

"You did?" Margot looked interested. "Why?"

Dillon didn't want to admit that she'd felt bummed about Jordan, regretting the way things had gone at the dance. "That doesn't really matter. The point is that I gave that weakness to God and now I feel fine. In fact, I feel happy."

"Well, good for you." Margot's tone was sarcastic.

"I'm not trying to sound smug," Dillon clarified. "It's just that I like having a connection with my heavenly Father. You know I never knew my earthly dad."

"I know . . . and I've told you before that I'm sorry about that."

"I wasn't trying to guilt you, Margot. Just making a point. I like being able to take my troubles to God. It makes a huge difference in my life. And I just wish you could experience it too." Dillon stood. "I'm sorry if that sounded like a sermon. But it's only because I care about you."

Margot's eyes widened. "Really, Dilly, you truly care about me?"

"Of course. You're my mom."

"I know . . . but I've been a pretty lousy mom."

Dillon put a hand on Margot's shoulder. "You probably did the best you could. And you did me a big favor when you let me come live with Grandma and Grandpa."

"I know you won't believe this, Dilly, but that was a sacrifice. I really wanted you with me. I felt like such a loser to let you go."

"Well, thank you for the sacrifice." Dillon's smile felt sad. "At least we're learning to get along better now. That's something."

Margot nodded. "Yes, I hope so."

Now Dillon did something she couldn't remember ever doing before. She leaned down and hugged her mother. "Hopefully we'll get better at it too." She could see that Margot was starting to cry again, but with nothing more to say, Dillon excused herself. Whatever this was that Margot was struggling through might be good for her. And perhaps it was a trial she needed to face alone.

● ● ●

Although Dillon had thoroughly enjoyed her days off thanks to her new campsite, she was glad to get back to her weekday routine on Monday. It was fun seeing the kids again and she could tell they were happy to see her too. As her last class began—and Janelle dropped off the twins, then left— Dillon wondered if Jordan might possibly pick up his nieces. She hoped so. But before class was over, Janelle showed up. And she was just in time to see both twins performing face-floating accompanied by kicking.

"That's wonderful," Janelle told Dillon after the class ended.

"I am so impressed with their progress. Thank you for working so hard with them."

"They're doing the work," Dillon told her as she wrapped her towel around her shoulders.

"Can Dillon come to our party?" Chloe asked her mom.

"Yes, yes," Emma chimed in. "Can Dillon come?"

"Of course." Janelle smiled at Dillon. "If she wants to come."

"What kind of party?" Dillon asked the twins.

"Our birthday!" they said in unison.

"When is your birthday?" Dillon asked.

"Tomorrow," they answered.

"And the party is a barbecue at my house tomorrow night," Janelle explained. "We'd love to have you join us, if you're interested."

"I'd love to come." Dillon nodded. "Sounds like fun."

Janelle gave her the details, and Dillon assured her she'd be there. As Dillon went into the dressing room, she felt fairly sure this would be an opportunity to see Jordan, but that wasn't why she'd agreed. In fact, the idea of facing him made her a bit nervous. She'd come to the conclusion that if she was flaky and fickle, he was equally so. And under the circumstances, she'd nearly convinced herself to forget all about Jordan Atwood. She didn't need to be jerked around like that.

○ ○ ○

Dillon tried to relax as she rang Janelle's doorbell. *This is no big deal*, she told herself, *and it's not about Jordan.* To her surprise an attractive gray-haired woman answered. "Oh?" Dillon smiled nervously. "I thought this was Janelle's—"

"This is Janelle's house." The woman opened the door wider. "I'm Janelle's mom." She stuck out her hand. "Donna Atwood."

"I'm Dillon Michaels." She shook her hand.

"I guessed that already." Donna smiled, but her eyes looked serious. "You have a pair of sincere fans in my granddaughters."

"It's mutual." Dillon held up the pair of wrapped packages for the girls. "I hope they'll like these."

"Janelle and the girls are in the kitchen." Donna lowered her voice. "But I was hoping to get in a private word with you."

"Oh?"

Donna took the presents, setting them on the foyer table. "We can go in there." As Dillon was led into a den-like room, a brand-new wave of nerves hit her. What was going on? For some reason she felt like she was in trouble . . . like being called on the carpet.

"I know you probably think this is quite mysterious." Donna closed the door, standing in front of it. "But I wanted to ask you a couple of questions."

"Questions?" Dillon pursed her lips.

"It's not that I'm trying to manage my son's life, Dillon. Goodness knows, he's a grown man. But I suppose it's hard to stop being a mother . . . and I'm still somewhat protective of him."

Dillon felt her brows rising, but said nothing.

"I know that Jordan has become interested in you, Dillon. Don't ask me how I know, because as you may have guessed, Jordan is rather tight-lipped about his feelings."

Dillon simply nodded, waiting with curiosity.

"So I'm going to tip his hand a bit, Dillon. I'm sure Jordan would throw a fit if he knew, but I suppose a mother has some rights."

Dillon wasn't so sure. She resented it when Margot had attempted to influence her own love life. Still, she just waited.

"Jordan got his heart badly broken about six or seven years ago. He never speaks of it, but I know it took a toll on him. He's very careful now."

Dillon nodded. "I'd wondered if something like that had happened. But if it's been that long . . . wouldn't he have moved past it by now?"

"Most people would . . . but Jordan is the sort of fellow who—when he gives his heart—goes all out."

"That's an admirable quality."

"I agree. And although I can tell he's interested in you—and, according to my daughter and the twins, you're worthy of his interest—Janelle mentioned there's another fellow vying for your attention."

Dillon attempted to briefly explain the trouble with Brandon. "I keep telling him that it's completely over, but he just kept pressuring me. Fortunately, he's gone back to Colorado now and I assume it's the last I'll hear from him."

Donna sighed. "Well, that's a relief."

"I suspected that Jordan may have resented Brandon a little. But I wish he would've given me the opportunity to explain it to him . . . instead of jumping to conclusions."

"Well, like I said, when it comes to his heart, Jordan has a tendency to hold back."

Dillon nodded. "May I ask you a question?"

"Of course."

"Can you tell me a bit more about this heartbreak that happened to Jordan? Just a little heads-up to help me navigate."

"Sure. He met this girl in Seattle. They went together for a few years. He brought her home several times. We all liked her and thought she was the one. So did Jordan. He planned to propose at Christmas, but just a week before the holidays, she broke up and ran off to Vegas to marry Jordan's best friend."

"Ouch." Dillon frowned. "That's pretty harsh."

"Yes. It wasn't a very festive Christmas that year."

Dillon put her hand on Donna's arm. "Well, I can assure you I'd never do anything like that."

"But you just told me how you suddenly left your boyfriend in Colorado, Dillon."

"That was different." Dillon quickly explained Brandon's neglect and fear of commitment and how he took her for granted.

"But it sounds like he's changed."

"I admit he was acting like he's changed, but I wasn't convinced. Besides that, my feelings for him changed when I left Colorado."

"That's good to know." Donna checked her watch. "Well, I don't want to keep you too long, don't want to arouse suspicion."

"Right." Dillon was trying to gauge this woman. On one hand she acted sincerely concerned for her son's welfare, but the situation also felt intrusive . . . and Dillon still wasn't sure that Donna fully approved of her. To make matters worse, Dillon felt more uneasy than ever. How was she supposed to act now? They were barely in the kitchen when the twins rushed over to her. Thankful for this distraction, she allowed them to monopolize her completely, even agreeing to visit their bedroom upstairs.

In the girls' room, Dillon took her time to examine every nook and cranny. They obviously enjoyed this attention and eagerly showed her everything—from Emma's ant farm to Chloe's international doll collection.

"So have you gotten any birthday presents yet?" Dillon sat on one of the beds, still not ready to join the party downstairs.

They showed her a couple of things their mom had given them earlier, and then Dillon confided to them that she shared their birthday month.

"When's your birthday?" Emma asked.

"Oh, later this week."

"When? When?" Chloe pressed.

"Sunday." Dillon told them the actual date.

"We're birthday buddies," Emma declared.

"Speaking of birthdays . . . we should probably go downstairs for your party." They all trooped down the stairs, reaching the foyer just as Jordan entered with an armload of gifts. Naturally his nieces, like magnets, went straight to him— asking what was in the packages and if they could open them.

"You know what your mom said," he told the girls. "After we eat, and before the cake." He greeted Dillon. "I didn't expect to see you here."

"The girls invited me." She picked up the gifts she'd brought, still on the foyer table, and followed their merry processional into the kitchen. She really didn't want to overthink this evening, but after Donna's questions . . . followed by Jordan's polite but somewhat cool greeting, she wondered if she'd been wrong to come. Especially since it had been the girls who'd invited her—not the hostess. And so she decided that, as soon as the girls finished opening their gifts, she would excuse herself . . . and make a quick and hopefully graceful getaway from what was probably meant to be a family get-together.

CHAPTER

25

illon was relieved to discover that a few other non-relative friends, including Vivian Porter, were also guests at the twins' birthday party. "I'm surprised to see you here," Vivian told Dillon as the guests were ushered outside for dinner. "I didn't realize you were friends with the family."

As they sat down at a long picnic table covered in a brightly colored plastic tablecloth, Dillon explained about swimming lessons. She nodded to the nearby in-ground swimming pool. "I understand Janelle's urgency now. I'm glad the girls are becoming water-safe. And they should be swimming before long."

"That's right," Janelle told Vivian as she set a generous plate of hamburgers in the center of the table. "Dillon was our miracle worker. Emma and Chloe have made marvelous progress."

"It's about time," Jordan teased his nieces. "Seven-year-olds should know how to swim."

"We do," Emma insisted.

"Well, almost," Dillon corrected. "Your floating skills are definitely superb. And before your session ends, I'm sure you'll be nearly swimming."

"I asked the girls to do a demonstration," Janelle said as she sat down. "After dinner."

"Shouldn't they wait half an hour before going into the water?" Donna asked.

"That's an old wives' tale," Dillon explained.

Janelle asked Jordan to say a birthday blessing, and then they began to eat. There were about a dozen people at the table, and everyone was well acquainted, chattering back and forth as if they'd been friends for quite some time. Even so, Dillon tried not to feel like the odd man out. And when there was a lull, she turned to Vivian.

"My trailer is completely finished now," she told her. "Inside and out."

Vivian looked impressed. "Good for you. I'd love to see it sometime."

"Anytime you like. I think it turned out pretty cute. I love it."

"Have you taken it anywhere yet?" Vivian asked her.

"Not really, although I did move it to a better location on the farm." Dillon didn't admit how much help she'd needed from Grandpa.

"That's nice, but it's not the same as towing it on a real road," Vivian pointed out. "Anything can happen when you're traveling at sixty miles an hour. And what about your pickup—last time I saw you in it, you were broken down."

"It's running just fine now. My grandpa checked it over for me."

"Even so, your trailer could have a problem on the highway. Happens all the time with old trailers that haven't been maintained."

"I'm sure my trailer will be fine." Dillon felt defensive. "It's very sturdy and solid and—"

"Don't be so sure," Jordan chimed in. "That old Oasis sat for a long time, Dillon." He paused to tell the others that Dillon had taken possession of Uncle Jack's trailer.

"Oh, I remember that trailer," Janelle said. "I used to play house in it."

"That's sort of what I'm doing now," Dillon said. "Playing house. But it's been so much fun. I totally love it."

"And she's fixed that old trailer up real nice," Jordan told Janelle. "You should see it."

"I'd love to!"

"It's like my little dollhouse," Dillon admitted.

"I wish we had a trailer," Chloe said wistfully.

"Me too," Emma echoed. "Then we could go camping with Uncle Jordan."

"Is your vintage club taking its annual trip this year?" Janelle asked Jordan.

"It's next weekend," Vivian told her. "At Silver Lake. I can't wait. We've been planning on it for a year."

"I wanna go," Chloe said with longing.

"Me too," Emma chimed.

"Why don't you girls all come?" Jordan said to Janelle.

"For starters we don't have a trailer." Janelle passed the potato salad to her mom. "And, as you know, I've never been much of a camper and—" Before she could finish her excuses, her daughters cut her off with pleading and begging—and Janelle feigned an irritated look. "Thanks a lot, *Uncle Jordan.*"

He just laughed. "You three girls could stay with me. It might be crowded, but we could throw up a tent for overflow."

Naturally, this got the twins even more excited, and they acted as if the plan were set in stone. "You have to come too," Chloe told Dillon.

"Yes! We'll all go camping together," Emma chimed in.

"Oh, I don't know . . ." As much as Dillon would love to be included, she didn't think the decision should be up to the twins. "Sounds like this trip's been planned for a long time. They might not have room for another trailer."

"That's true," Vivian told Dillon. "We only reserved enough spots for the members of the club. And this time of year, Silver Lake Campground is always full." She made a sympathetic smile. "Maybe next year."

"But it's Dillon's birthday," Chloe declared loudly. "She has to come camping with us. Don't you, Dillon?"

"It's your birthday?" Janelle asked Dillon.

"It's on Sunday," Emma declared. "She told us so."

"Isn't there some way to squeeze in another trailer?" Janelle asked Jordan. "After all, you're president of the club."

"It's too late," Vivian answered for him—perhaps a bit too quickly and eagerly. Or else Dillon was imagining things.

"Like Vivian suggested, maybe I can come next year." Dillon wanted to be a good sport despite intense disappointment. How fun would it be to take her little trailer on a real campout—and at the lake?

"But it's her birthday, Uncle Jordan," Chloe insisted. "She *has* to come."

"As a matter of fact, the Mortensons called yesterday. Rob has to travel for business this week and Rachel said there's no way she's towing the trailer and three kids on her own," Jordan told Vivian. "No reason Dillon couldn't use their spot. I haven't canceled it yet."

"But she's not a member," Vivian reminded him.

"Well, we can easily induct her." Jordan grinned. "It's not like we have a secret handshake or some painful initiation rituals."

Vivian nodded with a smile, but she didn't look overly pleased with this new development.

Janelle looked at her brother. "I think if you're letting the girls and me come, Dillon should be welcome too."

Jordan turned to Dillon. "So how about it? Wanna go camping with a bunch of fun-loving kooks?"

"If it's really okay with everyone else, I'd love to come." Dillon was afraid to be too happy. Especially since Vivian was still resistant. What if she lobbied other members and pulled the plug?

"It's okay with me," Jordan said.

"And he's president," Chloe declared. "Uncle Jordan can make the rules."

"Well, just because you're president doesn't mean you make the rules," Janelle explained. "To do that, you'd have to be king." She grinned at Jordan. "And I don't plan to start bowing down to my big brother."

"What about Dillon's trailer?" Vivian asked. "She hasn't even taken it out yet. What if it's not road worthy?"

"That's a good point," Jordan agreed. "It hasn't been out for years. Anything could go wrong."

"And what about that old pickup? Is it really able to tow on the highway?" Vivian asked.

"I think *Jack* will do just fine." Dillon instantly regretted telling her the name.

"*Jack*?" Vivian's brows arched with amusement.

"I mean my pickup. I, uh, I named it *Jack*."

"And her trailer is *Rose*," Jordan explained. "They're a matched pair."

"Well, that's cute, and the pickup probably goes well with your trailer. That's nice for photos, but doesn't mean it's ready for the road," Vivian said with a superior tone. "There are mechanical things to consider."

"That's true." Jordan turned to Dillon. "Your bearings, axle, tires, and a few other things should all be checked by a mechanic."

"I don't think there's anything wrong with them," Dillon assured Jordan, but judging by his expression she knew he was doubtful. She wanted to say more in defense of her pickup and trailer, but the twins were so excited about the camping trip that she couldn't get a word in edgewise. She hoped she hadn't bitten off more than she could chew by agreeing to this little expedition. But she felt determined to prove herself—and *Jack* and *Rose* too. She wanted to show everyone, especially Vivian, that she and her trailer were worthy of membership in their exclusive trailer club.

After dinner, the twins eagerly opened their gifts. By the time they came to Dillon's present, she felt unsure. She'd thought her choice was perfect this afternoon, but now she was worried these snorkeling sets could be expecting too much of the girls—even worse, they might hate them. So she braced herself for the reaction. To her relief, the girls were delighted. With Jordan's help, they tugged the pieces out from the packaging and put on everything, making them resemble a pair of miniature frogmen and causing all the grown-ups to laugh.

"You'll want to save the flippers until you get used to the masks," Dillon explained as the goofy-looking girls marched around the yard. "And you'll need some help learning to use the snorkels. But a lot of kids get really good at snorkeling."

"Can we try them now?" Chloe asked her mom.

"You still have presents to unwrap." Janelle pointed to the few remaining gifts. "But afterwards. Maybe Dillon can help you with it."

"Sure," Dillon agreed.

"Will you get in the pool with us?" Chloe asked.

"Well, I don't have my swimsuit." Dillon felt relieved that her pool bag wasn't still in her car. The idea of performing snorkeling lessons with everyone else looking on was a bit unsettling. She already felt like a fish out of water. Of course, she might feel more comfortable *in* the water.

"We're about the same size. I can loan you something," Janelle offered. Before Dillon could decline, the twins were rejoicing that Dillon was going to give them snorkeling lessons. She knew she couldn't tell them no—not at their own birthday celebration, with a gift she'd given them—and so she simply smiled and agreed.

Dillon tried to repress her self-conscious feelings as she and the twins came back down in their swimsuits. Fortunately, she'd also borrowed an oversized T-shirt to use as a cover-up. Then, ignoring the onlookers and pretending she was at the community pool, she told the girls to get into the water and began helping them adjust their masks.

"To start with, you'll just hold your breath like when you're

251

doing the face-float," she explained. "But after you get the hang of it, you'll be ready for the snorkel."

To Dillon's relief it sounded as if the other party guests had returned to visiting among themselves and were not paying much heed to the pool. Then, knowing Emma was the braver of the two girls, Dillon decided to start with her.

"We'll take turns," she told Chloe. "You watch how Emma does this and then you can be next." She was about to start Emma off when, to her surprise, Jordan came to the edge of the pool, removed his shirt and flip-flops, and, wearing only his cargo shorts, eased himself down into the water. "Looks like you could use some help." He grinned at her. "How about we both take a girl?"

"Do you know how to snorkel?" she asked.

"You bet. I might be a little rusty, but I took scuba diving in college."

"So did I," she told him.

Jordan grasped Chloe's hand. "Wanna work with me or Dillon?"

Chloe opted for Dillon, so Jordan took Emma and, before long, both girls were successfully floating with their masks on. After several runs, they were both excited and exclaiming at how well they could see the bottom of the pool now.

"How about trying snorkels?" Jordan asked Dillon. "Do you think they're ready?"

"Why not?" Dillon turned to the girls. "You think you can do this?" They both eagerly agreed. "First you need to understand how a snorkel works." Dillon explained how they could use the tube to breathe. "But you breathe only through your mouth. Your nose is plugged with the mask. Do you understand?" She had them remove their masks, put the snorkel in their mouths, then use the other hand to plug their nose and practice breathing. "Now sink into the water and try it."

It wasn't long until they were pretty comfortable with breathing through the snorkel. "Now we'll get your masks on and Jordan and I will help you float while you breathe through your snorkels," Dillon told them. "We'll help make sure your snorkels stay above water." She exchanged glances with Jordan and he nodded.

"Yep, otherwise you might suck in a bunch of yucky pool water," he teased. "No one wants to drink that."

With Dillon and Jordan assisting, both girls managed to go the width of the pool. They went back and forth a few times with assistance, then Emma insisted she wanted to do it all by herself. Dillon reminded her of what to do if she accidentally sucked in a little water. "Just blow it out real hard and stand up and you'll be fine."

"And I'll walk beside you," Jordan told her. Then Dillon and Chloe watched as Emma made it the full width of the pool without his actual help. "That was fantastic!" Jordan patted her on the back as she stood up.

"I wanna try—my turn!" Chloe declared. So Dillon reminded her of how to blow out the water, then staying nearby just like Jordan had done, she walked her across the pool. After a few more trips across, and a couple of water sucking incidents, both girls were getting surprisingly good at it. Chloe called out, inviting her mom to come watch. Then Janelle and the birthday party guests came over to observe, clapping after the twins made another perfect snorkeling float without help.

"That was amazing!" Janelle told the girls.

"Bravo!" Donna called out.

"Your girls will be ready for Hawaii any day now," Jordan teased his sister.

"Yeah, I wish." Janelle wrinkled her nose. "But it's very cool they're catching on so fast."

"Well, this is just the first step," Dillon explained as she hoisted herself to the edge of the pool deck. "They've got a ways to go before they're ready for open water."

"Well, you were a good sport to get in there with them and get wet." Janelle smiled. "Thanks so much." She handed Dillon a pool towel.

"I think I'll go get dressed." Dillon stood, realizing the other guests were all gathered at the pool now. "I'll leave Uncle Jordan to finish their lesson."

Dillon hurried back to Janelle's room, and as she dressed, she considered returning to her earlier plan to make a quick getaway. She would thank Janelle for her hospitality, make an excuse, and vamoose. But as she ran her fingers through her splash-dampened hair, she remembered how Vivian had acted about the upcoming camping trip. The only way Dillon could describe it was *territorial*. Like she wanted to keep Dillon out of the trailer club. That, plus remembering the Fourth of July dance, made Dillon suspect Vivian might have her eye on Jordan. And that brought out Dillon's competitive spirit. She wasn't going to let Vivian scare her away.

As she went downstairs, Dillon felt ready to hold her ground. And if Donna's comments about Jordan's interest were true, she not only had a right to remain here, she had a responsibility. She'd acted flaky around Jordan before—she didn't want to do that tonight!

CHAPTER
26

*S*he grown-ups were still sitting around the now-empty pool, and Janelle was sticking candles into the pair of pink and purple birthday cakes. Dillon offered her help and Janelle sent her to the house to fetch a basket loaded with paper plates, napkins, and plastic forks.

Dillon had just located the basket when Jordan appeared. "Looks like you got dried off okay," she told him.

"Except my shorts, but this fabric doesn't really absorb water." He smiled. "That was a great gift you gave the girls—the snorkel sets *and* the lesson. They loved it."

"It was fun." She picked up the basket.

"Yeah. It was." He reached for the basket. "I can get that for you."

"Thanks." She placed a hand on his forearm to stop him. "Uh, can I ask you something before we go back out there?"

His brows arched. "Sure. What's up?"

"Well, I'm not quite sure how to say this, but I really don't want to be a camp crasher and—"

"Huh?" He looked confused. "Camp crasher?"

"You know, like a party crasher. I hate pushing my way into your special camping club, and Vivian didn't think I'd—"

"To be honest, I don't know why she was so resistant tonight. But our motto's always been the more the merrier. Well, unless we grow too big. But that hasn't happened yet. The real requirement is only that you own a restored vintage trailer." He grinned. "And it helps to be approved by the president."

"And you really do approve?"

He nodded. "Sure."

"So it's okay?"

"Of course. But, as the president and your friend, I'd like to come by and check out a few things first."

"Such as?"

"Like I mentioned, the Oasis could need new bearings or at the least to be repacked. And the axle needs checking, and I'm sure the tires are worn out. There's a few other things to look into as well. So if it's alright with you, I can come by sometime this week. Sooner is better just in case there's a problem. Give you time to fix it before our campout."

"How about tomorrow?" she suggested.

"I probably can't get over there until after five. Does that work?"

"Sure. I could even fix you dinner as a thank-you—I mean, if you'd like."

"I'd like." His eyes twinkled.

"And don't forget my offer to help with your trailer's inte-

256

rior," she reminded him. "That was supposed to be my thank-you for how you helped *Rose* with painting and everything."

"Do you have time this week?"

"Sure. My afternoons are free."

"Now that Janelle and the girls are staying with me, might be nice to spiff things up a little."

"And you mentioned your trailer's smaller than mine . . . so if you're too crowded, the girls or Janelle could stay with me. You know I've got those extra bunks."

"Might take you up on that." He chuckled. "When you see the size of my trailer, you'll understand."

"So how soon can I get a look at it?" she asked.

"How about tomorrow afternoon?"

"Great. That way I can do a quick inventory and have the rest of the week to pull it together."

"Sounds like a plan. It's parked at my mom's place." As he gave her the address and handed over the key, the twins rushed into the kitchen—in their dry clothes and drippy hair—announcing it was birthday cake time. They all went outside, the birthday song was sung, candles were blown out, and Dillon helped Janelle dish up cake and ice cream until the last guest was served.

"Come on," Jordan told Dillon as he picked up a plate, "I see a couple of empty chairs over there."

Dillon followed him to the far side of the pool, which Jordan explained his mother had decorated with floating candles and colored balloons. And now strings of colorful paper lanterns were glowing cheerfully in the twilight. "It looks absolutely magical out here," Dillon said as he led her to a pair of lone chairs.

"My mom and Janelle . . . they love celebrations."

Grateful for the distance from the other guests, Dillon sat down. "This has been such a fun evening," she said. "You have a lovely family."

"We're not a big family, but we're close." He gazed out over the yard with guests sprinkled about. "We got closer after losing Dad."

"I like your mom," she said. Although she still had uncertainties about Donna's opinions about her, Dillon knew it was only because Donna loved her son. And really, Dillon's first impression of Donna had been positive.

"Mom's a good egg." He chuckled. "Maybe a little nosy at times, but it's only because she cares."

Did he know what Donna had told her? Probably not. "My mom can be intrusive," she admitted. "And it's hard to take sometimes. But that's probably because she was so checked out and distant while I was growing up. I sometimes don't think she's earned the right."

"But she loves you." He smiled. "I could see that when I was there."

"Yes, in her way, she does love me." Dillon sighed. "I think I'm starting to realize that now."

"You know, I brought you over here for a specific reason," he said. "I set these chairs here so I could speak privately with you."

"Oh?" She glanced at his profile in the dim light.

"I feel like I should apologize for the Fourth of July."

"Apologize?"

"You know, for kidnapping you away like that. Taking you from your friend . . . and Brandon."

She laughed. "Believe me, I was glad to escape Brandon. And Chelsea barely noticed I was missing."

"But then you danced with Brandon," Jordan pointed out. "For the rest of the evening."

"That's true." Dillon pursed her lips, trying to determine how much to say. "And you danced with Vivian."

"Well, that's because she asked me."

"And Brandon asked me."

"So he's gone back to Colorado?"

She nodded. "Yep. Just like he said."

"And you and he . . . you're really finished with that?"

"Absolutely." She smiled. "I couldn't have been happier after he left."

"Well, I just—"

"Hey, you guys!" Vivian walked past the pool. "What're you doing way over here? The party's over there."

"There weren't enough chairs—"

"Then pick up your chairs and bring 'em," Vivian told Jordan.

Jordan handed Dillon his plate, and picking up both their chairs, they went over to join the group. Although Dillon was disappointed to lose her one-on-one time with Jordan, she consoled herself with the idea of having him over for dinner tomorrow. Already she was imagining her campsite . . . light strings and outdoor candles . . . cooking on her little stove and small barbecue. It had the potential to be a very romantic evening.

○ ○ ○

After her last swim lesson, Dillon went to Jordan's mom's house to check out his trailer. She was barely out of her car when Donna came out. "Jordan told me you'd be coming by," she said. "It's parked over there."

"Your yard is beautiful," Dillon said as they walked across the driveway. "I love your lavender."

Donna smiled. "Thank you. As you can tell, I adore lavender. And fortunately, the deer leave it alone."

Dillon explained a bit about their lavender project. "My mom started it, but Grandpa and I helped. It's fun watching the plants growing."

"I'd love to see it sometime." Donna stopped in front of a cute red-and-white trailer. "Well, there's Jordan's baby."

"Wow, that paint job looks impeccable." Dillon ran her hand over it.

"He had it professionally done."

"And those tires and hubcaps look new."

"Yes. Jordan made sure the trailer is in tip-top condition."

Dillon pulled out the key he'd given her, inserting it into the shiny aluminum door. "I can't wait to see the interior."

"Jordan gave you a key?"

"Yes. Didn't he tell you that he's allowing me to be his interior designer?"

Donna's pale brows arched. "Really? That's surprising."

"Well, he liked what I'd done with my trailer."

"Interesting." Donna waited as Dillon opened the door. "Well, as you'll see, he's restored everything in there, but it's a bit sparse."

Dillon went inside, looking around. "Wow, he did a fabulous job. Everything looks perfect." She ran a hand over the stainless steel countertop. Everything inside was color coordinated—red, white, and black mixed with the stainless. But there were very few personal touches.

"He's put a lot of money into these finishes."

Dillon opened the sleek Lucite cupboard above the sink, only to see paper plates and cups and a few utilitarian things. She continued to poke around. Jordan hadn't exaggerated when he said his trailer needed some attention. "It definitely looks like a bachelor pad," she told Donna as she opened a closet to see a sleeping bag and pillow.

"Well, a lot of people consider Jordan to be a confirmed bachelor." Donna chuckled. "Although I'm still hoping that will change. I'd like a few more grandkids."

Dillon felt her cheeks warming as she pulled out her phone to make some notes. "Well, I guess I've seen enough in here . . . for now. It gives me some ideas of what he might need." She turned to Donna. "But the truth is, I don't really know Jordan that well. I don't know what his likes and dislikes might be. I'd love to find some personal touches, you know, not just kitchen things or linens, but maybe something to put on the wall. Just to warm it up some. Does he have any hobbies or interests?"

"Well, he's always been a car guy. As a kid he used to collect those fancy car models—I can't remember their names. But they were usually sporty and red."

"Okay, that helps." Dillon looked at the black-and-white checkerboard floor. "Anything else?"

"He likes watching some pro sports. Not everything, mind you. He's not that much into football, but he's followed the Blazers since he was a kid. Well, other than the years when they were such a mess no one wanted to follow them."

"That helps too." Dillon pocketed her phone then led the way out, carefully locking the door behind them.

"Before you go," Donna paused in the driveway, "I'd like to say something."

"Sure." Dillon braced herself for another warning, but Donna smiled.

"I hope I didn't scare you off last night. It's just that, well . . ."

"You love your son," Dillon finished for her. "I understand. And I actually think it's very sweet. Jordan is lucky to have you."

"Well, thank you. But I have a feeling you didn't need me to say all that, Dillon. You appear to be a genuinely good person. I should've known that when the twins and Janelle were singing your praises. But I suppose I needed to see it for myself."

"Thanks. I appreciate you saying that. And I honestly wouldn't do anything to hurt Jordan. Not intentionally."

"I believe you." Donna nodded.

They said goodbye. As Dillon drove back toward town, she felt awkward about her conversation with Donna. Although she appreciated the kind words, they were adding even more pressure. The expectations were quickly rising. And Dillon wasn't sure if she'd be able to measure up . . . or whether Jordan would approve of these assumptions his mother was making. Maybe he really was a confirmed bachelor who wanted nothing beyond friendship and a little help with his trailer's décor.

As Dillon came into town, she knew her first stop would be the Silver Slipper, and she wasn't looking forward to it. Unfortunately, no other business could compete with Vivian's well-stocked shop—or her vintage trailer section. Hopefully the proprietress wouldn't be working right now. Dillon was about to go inside when she noticed the antique emporium across the street. Curious as to what they might have, she decided to go there first.

With her eyes peeled for anything red, white, or black, she perused the various vendor sections until she found one that screamed "Jordan's trailer." Plus everything in this section was 20 percent off. Before long, she'd collected an interesting assortment of old-fashioned Coca-Cola signs and paraphernalia, a pair of red-and-white salt-and-pepper shakers, and several other charming pieces. As she set her collection by the cash register, she asked about car-related collectibles.

"One guy has a whole section with car stuff." The woman told her where it was located and Dillon went back to look. Sure enough, there were lots of interesting pieces and plaques, and although she wasn't quite sure what kinds of cars they were, or how she'd use them, she selected several items that looked bright and fun. Hopefully Jordan would agree.

"I'm making these purchases for a friend," she explained. "If he doesn't like them, would it be a problem to return anything?"

"It's fine as long as it's within two days and you have your receipt."

Dillon thanked her, and feeling like a successful huntress, carried her bags to her car. This was a good start. She braced herself for the Silver Slipper, but before she crossed the street to go inside, she watched as a pickup carrying a load of lumber passed by. The red bandana attached to the back of the wood caught her eye. And instead of going into Vivian's chic shop, Dillon headed for Atwood's.

As she went inside, she was glad not to spy Jordan around. She didn't really want to explain why she was on the hunt for red bandanas because she wasn't even sure if her idea would work. The clerk directed her to the aisle, and she gathered up all the red bandanas they had. Then, feeling inspired, she gathered up black ones too. Next she went to the kitchen aisle, thinking she might save a few bucks by getting some of the necessities here, rather than at the Silver Slipper.

Her instincts proved right. She found a shiny teakettle, ceramic mugs, and several kitchen utensils—all in red. She also found red-and-white gingham towels and a few other cute plastic containers that looked useful. She was surprised Jordan hadn't gathered up some of these things himself. Maybe he hadn't liked them. Well, she would keep receipts, and anything he didn't like would be returned.

Getting a cart, she decided to check out their camping section. There she discovered a perfect set of unbreakable dishes in red-and-white checks. Also some acrylic glasses trimmed to match the dishes. They even had an inexpensive set of silverware with red Lucite handles that looked perfect with the dishes. She also got a couple strings of camp lights and a pair of shiny silver oil lanterns. This was fun! Even if Jordan didn't like anything she'd picked out today, she was still enjoying herself. And she would enjoy putting the whole thing together. In fact, that gave her an idea.

"Is Jordan here today?" she asked the clerk as she was checking out.

"Not right now. He's making a delivery."

"Oh." Dillon got out her phone, thinking she could just text him her idea. "By the way, these items are for Jordan's vintage trailer," she said suddenly. "I guess I should've asked if he gets a discount."

"He gets a big discount. But he has to authorize it."

"Can he do that by phone?"

"Of course."

So Dillon called his number. "Sorry to bother you," she said quickly when he answered. "But I'm getting a few things for your trailer at the hardware store. You guys have some great stuff. Anyway, I guess you can get a discount?"

"Yeah, absolutely. And they can put it on my account too."

"I'll hand you over to the clerk." Dillon gave her the phone and waited. When she got the phone back, she stepped away from the counter and continued. "And I got an idea. I thought if you could bring your trailer out to the farm, it would be easier for me to work on it. I need to do some measuring and sewing for your curtains and things."

He chuckled. "You're making me curious now."

"Would you mind bringing it out there?"

"Not at all. I'll drive it over this evening."

She thanked him and said goodbye, waiting as the cashier finished ringing up her purchases. Thanks to Jordan's discount, the total was very reasonable. Hopefully Jordan wouldn't think she was trying to be cheap. More importantly, when it was all said and done, she hoped he would approve. But there wasn't time to obsess over that now. She had a busy afternoon ahead.

CHAPTER
27

*S*till needing to get groceries for tonight's dinner with Jordan, Dillon was tempted to skip the Silver Slipper altogether. But she was parked right in front and knew it was the only store in town that sold fabric. Plus she suspected she'd find some trailer treasures inside. So once again she loaded her purchases into the back of her car, and then she braced herself. The little silver bell dinged as Dillon went into the pretty shop. But not seeing a salesperson around, Dillon picked up a shopping basket and slipped back to the vintage trailer section to peruse. Ironically, there were some things back there very similar to items Dillon had already gathered, but with much higher prices.

Dillon did find a few items, and as she set a cute plastic platter in her cart, she heard Vivian greeting her. Dillon turned to smile at her.

"I thought your trailer was all set up." Vivian studied the red-and-white plastic platter in Dillon's basket. "And that doesn't exactly look like your color scheme."

"It's not for me." Dillon picked up a stainless steel soap dispenser, then seeing the price, set it down.

"Oh?"

"No, you're right. My trailer is pretty much set. Didn't I show you photos?"

"Yes. Of the interior."

Dillon picked up a black-and-white plastic pitcher, examining it. She knew it would make an attractive and usable accent in Jordan's trailer, so despite being overpriced, she put it in her basket. "I mostly came to check out your fabric selection," she told Vivian as she headed for the fabric.

"Looking for anything special?" Vivian trailed her.

"I'm not really sure." Dillon wanted to be elusive, but it only increased Vivian's curiosity. "I need a plain white cotton fabric. Something to line curtains, you know?"

"I have some muslin. Would this work?" Vivian pulled out a bolt.

"Yes, that's good. I think I'll need, say, five yards." Dillon pointed to a bolt of black-and-white gingham—with big checks. "And I'd like . . . about three yards of that."

"Okay." Vivian removed the bolt. "I guess I'll have to cut it myself since Lilly's on her break."

"I'll keep browsing while you do that." Dillon went over to the soft goods section and was happily surprised to see a thick polar fleece throw in red-and-black buffalo check. Perfect! She continued to look around, but didn't find anything that looked worth the price on the tags. Vivian's markup had to be pretty

267

high. As Dillon waited at the register, she decided it would be worth the half-hour drive to the closest superstore to get some of the bedding Jordan would need for his sister and nieces.

Vivian's brow creased with curiosity as she carried the fabric pieces to the register. "So you didn't mention what you're working on, Dillon." Her tone was sweet as sugar. "Is this for a trailer by any chance? Are you working on another project?"

"Yes, it is for a trailer," Dillon answered pleasantly.

"Red, black, and white . . ." Vivian began to ring up the merchandise. "Whose trailer might that be?"

Dillon didn't like this cat-and-mouse game and decided to be up-front. "It's for Jordan's trailer. I'm fixing it up for him."

"Really?" Vivian blinked. "Does Jordan even know you're doing this?"

"Of course." Did Vivian really think Dillon would do this without his okay?

"Because Jordan is quite protective of his trailer. I've offered to help him before—and not that long ago—but he always makes an excuse."

"Well, I guess he wants it to be comfortable for Janelle and the girls, you know, since they're going on the camping trip."

"Maybe . . . but Jordan always claims he has a very specific plan for his trailer. Did he discuss that with you?"

Dillon shook her head. "He didn't mention anything specific."

Vivian looked skeptical. "Well, I'll be curious to see how this turns out."

"So will I." Dillon's smile was stiff. She, more than anyone, knew that her décor decisions could go sideways on her. But it was a risk she wanted to take.

"You don't sound too confident." Vivian told her the total. "To be honest, this is still new to me. But I had such fun doing my own trailer and, well, Jordan likes how it looks . . . I guess I'm hoping he'll like what I do to his too."

"If he doesn't and if you need to return your purchases, remember to save your receipt. Of course that doesn't apply to the fabric." She held up the black-checked material and then slid it into the bag. "I suppose that might go nicely in there. But if it's for curtains, I doubt you'll have enough."

Dillon shrugged. "I guess I'll find out."

"Well, I can't wait to see how it turns out." Vivian's smile looked catty and Dillon suspected she was hoping for a good laugh. But this only added to Dillon's determination to make it look good. She paid Vivian and, thanking her, made a quick exit.

◐ ◐ ◐

By five thirty, after scrambling all afternoon, Dillon was prepared for Jordan to show up. She hadn't put the steaks on her little barbecue yet, but the rest of the meal was ready to go. This would be the first time she'd entertained at her trailer, and she was excited for the evening to begin. All of today's trailer treasures were safely stashed in her car, and she didn't want to tip her hand to him in regard to her design plan. She wanted to have his trailer completely done before her big "unveiling." Hopefully by tomorrow.

Her plan for tonight was to serve dinner outside—as if they were camping. She'd even put a pretty tablecloth on her little camp table, complete with fresh flowers in a mason jar. Her string of lights was ready to plug in, and she had a couple of oil lanterns ready to light for more ambience after the sun set. Everything looked perfect and she couldn't wait for Jordan to arrive.

It was close to six when she spotted his pickup and trailer coming down the driveway. She went out to meet him, explaining that he could park in her old spot next to the barn. She watched as he expertly backed it in—without any help from her. She felt a mixture of awe and envy. Why couldn't she do it like that?

"We're going to eat at my trailer," she explained as he got a small toolbox from the back of his pickup.

As they walked over to the pond, she asked about his day—eager to get him talking so she wouldn't have to describe her whirlwind of activity in acquiring things for his trailer. Especially since Vivian's questioning had been reverberating through her mind for the last several hours. What if Vivian was right and Jordan really did have very specific expectations—and what if Dillon's design plan didn't meet them? She knew she never would've entrusted her trailer to anyone else. Why had he allowed her to help?

At her little campsite, Jordan set down his toolbox then looked around with what seemed like approval. "Very nice place you got here, Dillon. Looks like you're a serious camper."

"I've been loving my setup. There's just one more thing I'd like—I ordered a turquoise-and-white striped awning from that place you told me about." She paused to light the grill. "It's supposed to arrive this week. Hopefully in time for this weekend."

"That'll be good." He kicked a trailer tire as if testing it.

"I've got some of Grandpa's New Yorker steaks to grill," she told him. "I thought while they're cooking, you might give *Rose* her checkup. Hopefully she'll pass the exam."

"Dr. Jordan at your service." He picked up his toolbox.

And so for the next half hour, Dillon busied herself with grilling steaks and corn on the cob . . . and Jordan poked around on her trailer. When she announced dinner was ready, he went inside her trailer to wash up.

"So nice and homey in there," he said as he came back outside.

"Thanks." She wanted to say it was a relief to hear since she was still a little uncertain about how his would turn out. Instead she waved to the little table. "And dinner is served."

After they sat down, Jordan asked if he could say a blessing. "Absolutely," she told him, waiting as he said a sweet prayer, even asking traveling protection for all the campers who would be meeting at the lake this weekend. As they started to eat, she inquired about *Rose*'s checkup. "What's the prognosis, doctor?"

His brow creased. "Well, I hate to be the bearer of bad news—especially after you made this fabulous meal—but it's not good."

Dillon's heart sank. "What do you mean?"

"*Rose* needs some serious work before I'd proclaim her road ready."

"What kind of work?"

He went through a list that sounded very much like what he'd predicted at the birthday party. "That much work could take a day or two."

Dillon considered this. "Will it be ready by Friday?"

"That's your best-case scenario, but you'd have to get it into

271

the shop ASAP. And mechanics in this town usually have a waiting list."

"Oh . . . I didn't realize my trailer was in such bad shape." She let out a disappointed sigh.

"If it's any consolation, what you need fixed is pretty typical for an old trailer. And my trailer was in much worse condition when I got it."

"I suppose this means I'll miss out on this year's campout." She tried to hide how hard this was hitting her, but she honestly felt close to tears. "Maybe by next year . . ."

Jordan pursed his lips. "Not necessarily."

She brightened. "What do you mean?"

"Well, I have a good friend who's an excellent mechanic . . . and Brent just happens to owe me a favor."

"Really?" Her hopes were rising. "Do you think—"

"Do you mind if I call him right now?"

"No, of course not. Go ahead."

Jordan stood up, pulled out his phone, and stepped away from the table. Dillon waited as he spoke to Brent. He explained the situation, then listened to his friend's response.

"Sure, I can do that. Thanks, buddy." Jordan hung up the phone then grinned at her.

"Well?" She waited. "What did he say?"

"He'll look at it. He can't promise anything until he sees it for himself. He pointed out that sometimes it takes time to locate the right parts for an old trailer."

"Oh." She nodded, absorbing this. "But at least he'll try."

"He suggested you bring it over to him as soon as possible. Tonight or tomorrow morning at the latest."

"I, uh, yeah sure, I can do that." She tried to appear more

confident than she felt. Hopefully it wouldn't involve backing up.

"Or I can do it." He picked up his corncob. "It's on my way home, and I have my pickup here. Might as well let me drop it off."

"Oh, thank you!" She beamed at him. "I really, really appreciate it."

They continued to eat, visiting congenially, but Dillon felt distracted. What if her trailer was in worse shape than they thought? What if it would take weeks—and lots of money—to fix? Was she ready for that? And what about her lovely sleeping quarters? Did this mean she was relegated to the house again?

They'd barely finished dinner when Jordan stood. "You know, if we want Brent to get started on your trailer right away, I might as well get it to him before dark. That way I can show him what I already found and he'll have a head start on things." He frowned. "As much as I hate to eat and run— especially from such a nice dinner—it might be for the best."

"Yes, of course. I really appreciate you doing this, Jordan."

"You better go in there and get *Rose* ready for traveling."

She suddenly remembered towing it before and how every loose item took flight. "Yes, it'll take me a few minutes." She pointed to the table. "I'll just leave all this out here for now. I can wash up these things in the house."

She hurried inside and began tucking things snugly away. And then she hurriedly packed a bag to take into the house. Finally done, she looked longingly at her trailer. "I'll see you again soon, *Rose*." As silly as it was, she felt slightly teary to tell her beloved trailer goodbye. She patted the countertop. "I hope you get all fixed up—better than new."

Dillon went outside to see that Jordan had backed his pickup to the trailer and was already hitching up. "At least your hitch is good," he told her. "But these chains look a little dicey."

"Yeah, that's what Grandpa said too." She dropped her duffel bag on the ground. "I'll start lowering the jacks." She got down and began to work the handle on one side while Jordan got on the other one, and before long, *Rose* was ready to go.

Dillon picked up her bag. "Looks like it's back to Grandpa's saggy sofa for me."

"Hopefully it won't be for long." Jordan's eyes lit up. "Or use my trailer if you like. That bed's pretty comfy."

"Really? You wouldn't mind?"

"Not at all. After all, you'll be working in there anyway. Make yourself at home."

She thanked him and, feeling a bit less discouraged, forced a smile and waved while she watched him tow *Rose* away. Although she knew some would think she was childish, she prayed that *Rose*'s mechanical work would be finished in time for the camping trip.

Uncertain whether Margot and Grandpa would still be eating their dinner, Dillon decided to wait on doing her own dishes. Instead, she parked her car next to Jordan's trailer and began to unload today's finds. It was only a matter of time until his previously barren trailer looked like a mess with all the bags and boxes and stuff piled around. But she knew once everything was in place, it would look much better. Hopefully, it would look good!

lthough Dillon had spent several hours working on Jordan's trailer on Wednesday evening, there was still much to do. She went straight home after work the next day, and with Grandma's sewing machine whirling along, she kept at it—sewing curtains and pillow covers. Before long she heard a knock at the door. Worried it might be Jordan, and not wanting him to see his perfect little trailer looking so completely trashed by her work in progress, she cautiously cracked the door open.

"What's going on in here?" Margot asked.

"Oh." Dillon opened it wider. "I thought I already told you I'm working on the interior of Jordan's trailer."

"Yeah, but I thought you'd join us for a late lunch." Margot held up a plate. "Did you eat yet?"

"No." Dillon smiled. "Thank you! I'm actually starving, but

I didn't even realize it until now." She stepped outside to where she'd set up her camp chairs and invited Margot to join her.

"So any word on your trailer yet?" Margot asked.

Dillon shook her head as she chewed. She'd shared the sad news with Grandpa and Margot while doing her dishes in the kitchen last night. "I'd call Jordan to ask, but I don't want to sound like a nag." She forked into the salad.

"So . . . I wanted to run something by you, Dilly."

Dillon looked up. Something about Margot's tone sounded odd. "What's up?"

"Well, Don called me today." She let out a long sigh. "He says he misses me."

"And did that surprise you?"

"No, not exactly. But I guess I'm surprised at my reaction."

"What's that?"

"Well . . . I miss him too."

Dillon smiled. "I thought you did."

"As much as I love being here with you and Dad . . . I'm wondering if I made the best decision, you know, to leave Don and move back home."

Dillon just nodded.

"And I feel bad for flip-flopping like this. Not that I've made up my mind. But I realize I started that lavender project and now I'm thinking of abandoning it. And I know that's irresponsible and I hate leaving it on Dad."

"If it's any consolation, I love the lavender project," Dillon assured her. "I'd be happy to carry on for you and I'll bet Grandpa would be too."

"Really?" Margot's eyes lit up. "That's good to know."

"As far as I'm concerned, you're free, Margot. Do what you

think is best for you. Besides, just because you're not living here doesn't mean you can't remain involved."

"Yeah, that's true. And, don't get me wrong, I'm not committing to anything yet. Don really doesn't know how I feel. I played my cards pretty close to my chest."

"Uh-huh . . ."

"But I just wanted to talk it through with someone. Not Dad though. He'd just tell me we should get married—end of story."

Dillon wanted to advise the same thing but just kept eating.

"But I am thinking about going back, and I'm curious as to your thoughts, Dilly."

Dillon set down her fork. "Well, I like Don. He seems to genuinely love you, Margot. And like I told you last week, you seem unhappy to me."

"Yeah, when you told me I needed God." Margot wrinkled her nose.

"Well, I still believe that. But it's possible you need Don too."

Margot barely nodded. "Yeah, you could be right."

"And I know you won't want to hear what I'm about to say, but it's only because I love you and—"

"You love me, Dilly? Really? Or are you just saying that?"

Dillon considered her words. "I do love you. I know I don't always act like it. And we don't always see eye to eye. Plus we've had some pretty good fights over the years. But I do love you. You're my mom."

"Well, that's nice to hear." Margot tipped her head to one side. "And I hope you know that I love you too, Dilly. I'll admit I've never been the greatest at showing it."

"I guess we both could work on that."

Margot's eyes narrowed. "Now what are you going to say that I don't want to hear? Why not just get it out there?"

"Okay, then . . . I agree with Grandpa. I think if you love Don, and it's obvious he loves you, you guys should just get married."

"Why? What difference does a piece of paper make?"

"It's not just a piece of paper. It's a legal agreement that proves you're really committed to each other. And it makes it harder for you to just split because things aren't going how you want on any given day. It proves to both of you and everyone around you that your relationship is solid and real and lasting. Call me old-fashioned, but I happen to think it makes sense."

"Sounds like you've given this a lot of thought."

Dillon shrugged. "Yeah, I guess."

They talked a bit longer, and Margot even agreed to think about the marriage suggestion. Then—to Dillon's surprise— they hugged. It was like a true mother-daughter moment. Amazing!

●●●

Dillon was on pins and needles during her trailer's absence. Like an overprotective mother whose child was hospitalized, she fretted over the welfare of *Rose*. She knew it was silly—and she couldn't confess her obsession to anyone—but she was really concerned. What if *Rose* wasn't fixable? Would Dillon just have to keep her parked at the farm—never to take a real adventure?

The other thing troubling Dillon was whether or not Jordan would like his trailer's new interior design. By Thursday afternoon, Dillon was finished. She'd tried to respect the color scheme already in place and that this was a bachelor's trailer, but she'd also tried to cozy it up. And she loved how it had turned out. Even Margot gave it two thumbs up. Hopefully Jordan wouldn't be disappointed when he came to pick it up.

Dillon had considered inviting him for dinner, but worried that might be awkward if Jordan didn't like his trailer, she decided against it. When it was getting close to six, she was literally pacing back and forth outside of Jordan's trailer, checking the time on her phone and bracing herself for a humiliating rejection.

She opened the door and peeked inside. And what she saw made her smile. The curtains she'd made from red bandanas and black-and-white checks were charming. The old-fashioned Coca-Cola items were cheerful, and the Italian red sports car collectibles, which Grandpa had told her the names of but she'd already forgotten, fit in perfectly. She fluffed one of the several throw pillows she'd made, confirming to herself that these fabric items had really softened the place up. Very welcoming! At least she hoped so. She closed the door and went outside, and there, coming up the driveway, was Jordan's red pickup.

She eagerly waved him toward her, and as soon as he got out she couldn't stop herself from inquiring about her trailer.

"I haven't heard from Brent," Jordan said with a concerned expression. "I suppose I should give him a call." He reached for his phone.

"Well, maybe you should check out your trailer first," she suggested. As badly as she wanted to hear the news about *Rose*, she wanted to get this reveal over with. Bracing herself, she opened the door and, holding her breath, waited as

Jordan went inside. Instead of following him, she remained outside—she wanted to allow him the chance to take it all in without her chatter or disclaimers. But when he stayed inside for several minutes, her concerns grew. What if he was so disappointed he didn't want to come out and face her? Jordan was a nice guy—he wouldn't enjoy telling her that it was all wrong.

Finally, unable to stand another moment, Dillon went inside. "Well—what do you think? I mean, things can change if it's not what you like. I know I took a lot of personal license with it, but I tried to keep you in mind and—"

"It's perfect." He turned to look at her.

She felt a rush of relief. "Seriously? You like it?"

"I love it, Dillon. Really, it's perfect." He started pointing out all the things he liked and saying how surprised he was that she had thought of everything. "And this is going to be so great for Janelle and the girls too. They're going to love it." His eyes twinkled. "I might even win the grand prize."

"Grand prize?"

"Yes. Every year we have a contest for the most attractive trailer. All the members vote. We actually have four categories. One prize for exterior only. One for interior only. Another prize for best overall campsite. And the grand prize is for the entire trailer."

"That sounds like fun." Fun she would most likely miss out on.

"Yeah, and it's surprising how competitive it gets. Vivian takes it very seriously. She's won the grand prize the past two years. I've actually won for exterior before, but everyone teased me about my Spartan interior." He grinned. "Not this year.

Thanks, Dillon. I really do love it." He pointed to the curtains. "These are great!"

She explained how that idea had come to her and some of the other things, and Jordan just kept praising her work. "You can't believe how good it is to hear that," she confessed. "I was so worried."

"Why would you be worried?"

"Well . . . Vivian mentioned that you had specific ideas for it."

He laughed. "That's because I didn't want her to do it for me. She was chomping at the bit to do my trailer. But I didn't want it to look professional, you know? Plus, I figured her prices would be outrageous. Speaking of that, how much do I owe you?"

She handed him the envelope with the receipts with the total written on top. "I tried to be fairly frugal, but—"

"No worries. I like it so much, I don't really care." He looked at the total. "Wow, this is way less than I expected. Are you sure?"

She reminded him that a lot of items came from his own store. "You'll see that bill later."

"No problem." He looked around again. "You really could go into the rehab trailer business, Dillon. You have a natural gift."

"Thanks." She sighed.

"Speaking of trailers, why don't I give Brent a call?"

"Would you? I'm not sure I can stand much more suspense about *Rose*."

"I don't blame you." He got out his phone and she waited as he talked. "That's great," he finally said. "I'll tell her." He hung up and smiled. "As it turns out, my good buddy Brent is almost done. He said if you want, you can pick it up tonight. He thinks he'll finish up in about an hour."

"Really? *Rose* will be all done? And road worthy?"

"Sounds like it." He repeated what Brent had just told him and the cost of the work. "How about you come with me? I'll take my trailer home, we'll snag a bite to eat, and then we'll pick up your trailer and bring it back here. Sound good?"

"Yes—I'd love that! Let me grab my purse and I'm ready."

As they dropped off Jordan's trailer, Dillon tried to convince herself that this was not a date. It was only two good friends helping each other and getting something to eat. Still, she felt differently at heart. She felt certain that they were more than just friends . . . and she was eager for their relationship to take the next step.

While they ate burgers, Dillon quizzed Jordan about the upcoming weekend. She asked how many people belonged to the club, what sorts of things she should bring, and lots of other questions. "You know what," Jordan finally said, "I'll forward you all the stuff that Vivian put together several months ago. She's the secretary. Her last newsletter should answer all your questions."

"Thanks." Dillon felt dismayed to remember that Vivian was so involved in the club. She might be imagining things, but she felt pretty sure that Vivian didn't like her. And she suspected it was related to Jordan. "I tracked my awning," she told him as they were finishing up. "It's supposed to be delivered tomorrow morning." She frowned. "Probably not soon enough for me to get it up before heading to the lake."

"Just bring it along. I'll put it up for you."

"Great. Thanks!"

"I'm leaving for the lake around noon—just to make sure our spaces are ready and everything looks good. When do you think you can get away?"

"I plan to leave as soon as I finish my last lesson. Not long after that, I hope." She cringed inwardly, trying to imagine how it would go towing her trailer all that way on her own. And what about when it was time to put her trailer into place? What if she had to back it up? "Can I make a little confession?" she asked meekly.

"Of course." He set down his shake. "Something wrong?"

"Not exactly." Now she explained her backing-up challenges. "It's like I'm dyslexic or something. Grandpa tried to help me, but I just kept messing up. Do you think I'll have to back up my trailer when I get to the campground?"

"Probably." He grinned. "But don't worry, I'll be there to help. And I'll teach you some tricks."

By the time they reached Brent's shop, the sun was going down, but it was still light enough to see *Rose* parked out in front. "Oh, she looks wonderful," Dillon said. "And her new shoes are lovely."

"New shoes?" Jordan parked the truck.

"Her tires, silly." Dillon laughed as she hopped out. She ran over to *Rose*, resisting the urge to hug her as Jordan introduced her to Brent.

"You're all set to go." Brent went over all he'd repaired and replaced, and Dillon handed over her debit card.

"Thank you so much." She patted her trailer. "*Rose* thanks you too."

Brent laughed. "You trailer nuts. You really take this stuff seriously."

"Of course." Dillon nodded, watching as Jordan hooked *Rose* to his pickup.

"Well, I gotta admit that this is a cute one. Have fun with her."

Dillon assured him she would. As Jordan drove her and *Rose* home, she felt her hopes rising even higher. The upcoming weekend promised to be her best birthday ever. She'd been trying to keep it under wraps that her birthday was Sunday. And despite the twins announcing it to everyone, she suspected that with camping preparations and all, they'd have forgotten it by now. Since she'd never been big on birthdays herself, she hoped this one would slip by unnoticed. Just being able to camp by the lake in her sweet trailer was more than enough to make her a truly happy camper!

CHAPTER
29

With Grandpa's help, Dillon was able to hitch *Rose* up to *Jack*. "Looks good," he said as he gave one of the new chrome chains a jerk to check the connection. "I'm glad you got it all checked out mechanically, Dillon."

"Yes, I was silly to think it didn't need some work. I'm just glad it got done in time for this camping trip."

"You feel okay about driving up to the lake by yourself?" he asked.

"Sure."

"And what about backing it up?" He rubbed his chin.

"Jordan promised to help."

Grandpa smiled and nodded. "Like the sound of that." He removed a large envelope from his pocket. "You should have this."

"What is it?"

"The registration and temporary license stuff for the pickup and trailer. I got it all changed into your name. You better have it with you. Just in case you get stopped. And I went ahead and put you on my insurance too. The card's in there. You're covered for six months. After that, it's up to you." He grinned. "Happy birthday, sweetie."

Dillon hugged him. "Thank you so much, Grandpa! This trailer and pickup, well, they're absolutely the best birthday present ever."

"Seems meant to be."

Dillon checked her watch. "Well, I guess I should be heading out."

"Your mom asked you to wait for her." Grandpa peered toward the road. "She promised to be right back."

"Okay. I guess I'll just double-check to make sure everything's good and snug in there." She made her final inspection, then locked the door. Next she checked the back of her pickup where she'd packed all her outdoor camp gear, reminding herself to stop for ice in town. Grandpa had loaned her his old metal ice chest, which went nicely with her trailer, but she had enough ice for only an hour or two and didn't want the salads she'd prepared for the camp potlucks to go bad—and her little fridge in the trailer was already full. This was all so exciting. She was about to close her tailgate when she heard Margot's car coming up the driveway.

"Not so fast," Margot called as she pulled up beside the pickup. "I have a birthday surprise for you."

Curious as to what Margot—someone who almost always forgot Dillon's birthday—might have up her sleeve, Dillon watched as Margot opened the back of her SUV, hefting out a large verdigris pot overflowing with gorgeous red geraniums, trailing ivy, and several other pretty blooms.

"This is heavy," Margot huffed as she set the planter on Dillon's tailgate.

"It's absolutely beautiful!" Dillon was both surprised and impressed.

"Special order from the nursery."

"It's perfect."

"Happy birthday, Dilly-Dilly."

"Thank you—I love it." Dillon made room for the heavy planter in the pickup bed.

"And that's not all." Margot went back to her car. "I got a matched pair."

Dillon hopped down and went to help.

"You see, I was looking at one of those trailer books you'd left in the kitchen and I noticed that some of the trailers had pretty flowerpots outside. I thought you could put these on either side of your door."

"These are so great, Margot." Dillon carried the second pot to the tailgate, then admired it. "So thoughtful of you. Thanks!"

Margot looked uncertain. "Is it silly to take them camping with you?"

"Oh, I think it'll be fun." Dillon pushed it back, then closed the tailgate. "I bet I'll have the prettiest campsite up there." She hugged her mother. "It means so much that you remembered my birthday."

"Well, you know as well as anyone that I'm not usually good with dates. Dad jogged my memory."

"Well, I really do love my flowerpots." Dillon fished her keys out of her shorts pocket.

"And guess what?" Margot beamed at her.

"What?"

"Don is taking me out to dinner tomorrow night."

"And you're going?"

She nodded. "He said he wants to court me."

"Court you?"

"Yes, I know it sounds old-fashioned, but I sort of like it."

"I think it sounds perfect. I hope you guys have a wonderful time."

"Well, I won't keep you here. I know you're eager to hit the road. Be sure and drive safe and have a super weekend, Dilly-Dilly," Margot said, and then she broke out with the happy birthday song.

Dillon hugged her and, feeling like life could hardly get any better, she got behind the wheel of her pickup and took off. Of course, she felt a bit nervous when she pulled out onto the main road, but she'd been doing a lot of research about towing trailers, and really, there wasn't that much to it. The main rule was to give yourself more time and don't forget how much room your rig and trailer take on the road.

Dillon stopped at the grocery store, parking on the perimeter to ensure she wouldn't get blocked in and need to back up. She bought ice and a few other things, then came out to see a young couple standing beside her trailer.

"Is this yours?" the man asked.

"Yes." Dillon waited, wondering if this was a problem.

"It's very cool," the woman said. "Do you mind if we take some photos?"

"Not at all." Dillon smiled as she opened her tailgate, putting her ice and other items in the cooler.

"It's so cute," the woman said as Dillon closed the tailgate.

Dillon thanked her, and the man inquired if she ever planned on selling it.

"No, I don't think so." She patted the side of the trailer. "This is like my baby and I've worked pretty hard on her." She didn't admit that it was also her living quarters.

"Is it as cute inside as outside?" the woman asked.

"Take a look." Dillon unlocked the door, waiting as the woman poked her head inside. "It's cuter when everything is in its place, but I have to put stuff away for traveling."

"It's adorable!" They both thanked her, and Dillon locked it up. Feeling happy and excited, she started out again. This time on the highway. Going fast felt a bit challenging at first, but reminding herself that everything was road worthy, she managed to maintain the speed limit.

Her side mirrors revealed a trail of impatient drivers behind her. Naturally, they wanted to go above the speed limit. So when she got a chance to use a pull-out, she let them pass by. Then, curious as to how Rose was traveling behind her, she got out to check everything. But it all looked perfectly sound and secure, so feeling more confident, she took off again and managed to push herself a bit faster without getting overly nervous. With her window open and the pine-scented air wafting in, Dillon felt completely content. She was like a gypsy on the road, about to embrace a new adventure. What a way to live!

CHAPTER
30

*B*y the time she reached Silver Lake Campground, she felt like an old pro at trailer hauling. Why had she been so worried? Of course, there was still that whole backing-up thing . . . but Jordan would help her. She even paused by the entrance to the campground and used her phone to take some pics of her truck and trailer in front of the camp sign and trees. Maybe she would make a *Rose* scrapbook.

She followed the directions that she'd gleaned from the newsletter Jordan had forwarded her and eventually found the section of spaces reserved for the Silverdale Vintage Camp Club. It felt good to think she was a member.

Jordan had texted her to meet him at camp space #34. As she slowly drove down the narrow, tree-lined road, she spotted two trailers already parked in place. One was obviously

Jordan's, with his pickup right next to it, and a few spaces away a silver Airstream trailer gleamed in the sunshine. Next to it was a cotton-candy-pink station wagon with woody sides. Dillon slowed down, hoping that Jordan would pop out from his space, but not seeing him, she continued along to space #34, which happened to be lakeside and right next to Jordan's. Judging by the size and layout of the small campground, there was definitely no other option but to back into it.

Trying to suppress her anxiety, she pulled past the space far enough that she hoped she would be able to back into it—if she knew how to back. But worried she might smack straight into a tree on her own devices, she turned off the pickup, pulled on the emergency brake and got out to look around. Hoping that Jordan would show up to help her, she was surprised to see Vivian emerging from the shiny silver trailer. Of course, that was *The Silver Slipper* Vivian had told her about.

"What are you doing?" Vivian asked.

"Oh, hi." Dillon attempted a smile. "I just got here."

Vivian gave her a halfhearted greeting then pointed to her pickup and trailer. "You can't just park in the middle of the road. Other campers are on their way."

"I don't plan to leave it there," Dillon explained. "But Jordan was going to help me back into—"

"You don't need him. I'll help you. Just keep your eye on me."

"But I—"

"Come on," Vivian urged. "The Jacksons will be here any minute. I just got a text from Stephanie that they're—"

"But where's Jordan? He was going—"

"He's busy, Dillon. Now are you going to back up your

trailer or not?" She frowned. "To be part of this club, you have to be able to manage your own trailer. Is that too much for you?"

"No, no . . . I just don't have much backing-up experience."

"Then it's time you got some. Hurry up before the Jacksons arrive. Now it looks like you should be parked in space #47 and that's over there." She pointed down the road.

"Jordan said space #34." Dillon pointed to the camping spot next to Jordan.

"No, that's wrong." Vivian pulled out a paper and showed it to her.

Now Dillon pulled out her phone and showed her Jordan's text. "Maybe I should call him to make sure."

"No, that's okay. We'll just put you there for now and you can move it later. Hurry up before we get a traffic jam."

So Dillon got into her pickup and silently prayed for heavenly help as she started the engine. It wasn't just her pride at stake here—she didn't want to be a roadblock or aggravate Vivian more. But she sure wished it was Jordan directing her. For all she knew, Vivian might back her straight into the lake.

Taking in a deep breath, Dillon stuck her head out the open window and called out to Vivian. "Okay. I'm ready."

"Can you see me in your rearview mirror?" Vivian called back.

Dillon checked, then nodded.

"Okay then. Just follow my hand signals and turn the steering wheel when I tell you." And now Vivian motioned her to back up then pointed sharply to the right.

"No, no!" Vivian shouted, holding her hands up to tell her to stop. "The other way."

Dillon remembered how Grandpa had said it was all backward and so she attempted to turn the other way, but apparently that wasn't working either.

"Pull forward again," Vivian shouted. "We'll start over."

So Dillon pulled forward and tried again, but for the second time, it just wasn't right. And Vivian's expressions and comments were not helping a bit.

"What's wrong with you?" Vivian finally demanded. She leaned into Dillon's window with an exasperated look. "Can't you follow simple directions?"

"It's just that you keep yelling at me," Dillon told her. "You say one way and then the other. I can't figure you out." She spotted Jordan jogging down the road toward her, waving eagerly. "Oh, there he is." Dillon sighed. "Thanks, Vivian, I'll let Jordan take it from here."

Vivian rolled her eyes and stepped back. With hands folded in front of her, she watched as Jordan talked to Dillon. "I get the dyslexia thing. It's not that unusual. But just keep your eyes on me," he instructed. "I'll point in the direction you should turn the steering wheel. Okay?"

"So I shouldn't do the opposite?"

"Not this time." As he stood there, locking eyes with her, pointing this way and that, she pretended she was a robot and he had the commands, trying to do exactly as he indicated. And to her utter surprise, he held up his hands for her to stop and announced she was parked. "Good job."

"You're kidding." She got out to see, then grinned. "It looks perfect. Thanks."

"And we're neighbors." He nodded to his trailer as Vivian approached. "So we can—"

"Speaking of campsite locations—" Vivian had a suspicious expression—"this camp spot is assigned to the Millers. The Mortenson spot is over—"

"I asked the Millers to switch spaces, and they agreed. They're still lakeside and actually closer to the dock, which they wanted anyway."

"Why, may I ask, does Dillon's trailer need to be right here?" Vivian's eyes narrowed.

"Because Janelle and the girls will be staying partly with her and partly with me. This seemed more convenient."

"Oh." Vivian shrugged. "Well, I guess that makes sense."

Jordan turned back to Dillon. "Did that awning come in time?"

"It's back there." She nodded to her still-loaded pickup bed.

"Well, I'll help you unhitch, then you can park the pickup right there." He pointed to a space on the backside of her trailer.

"Doesn't she know how to unhitch by herself?" Vivian asked.

"I'm sure she does." Jordan, already cranking down the hitch, nodded to where a yellow pickup and trailer were approaching. "But that's the Jacksons there, and we need to get out of their way pronto."

Dillon unhooked the chains and did what she could to help, then hurried to park *Jack* right next to *Rose* just in time for the Jacksons to get past her. The couple smiled and waved and didn't act the least bit impatient. Nothing like Vivian.

While Dillon went inside her trailer to pull it together, Jordan went to work on her awning, which went up surprisingly easily and looked adorable. "I love it," Dillon exclaimed when she finally came out. "It's perfect. Thanks so much for putting it up." She glanced over to where Vivian was busy with her own campsite. "I hope this isn't breaking any rules. I don't want Vivian to get upset over you helping me."

He laughed. "Don't worry about her. She'll settle down after a while. I'm going to finish setting up my trailer. The formal trailer tour runs until dinnertime. And prizes are awarded at tonight's campfire, so you want to get *Rose* looking as good as possible." He winked. "Thanks to you, I plan to be your biggest competition."

"Yes, you and Vivian—and everyone else," she said. "But it sounds like fun. And I can't wait to see the inside of other people's trailers."

"I'll warn you that some campers put treats in their trailers— I'm not sure it wins any votes, but I won't say that it doesn't."

Dillon nodded. "Thanks for the heads-up. I got a bag of chocolate kisses with the twins in mind. I'll set those out. Anything else I should know?"

"Well, some of them really stage their trailers. Some will set tables and everything. It's like a show. And people like to take photos too. We've talked about doing our own calendar. So you want *Rose* to put her best foot forward."

"Great. I'll do that."

With golden oldies music playing on her fully charged phone, Dillon set to work. If you could call it work. It felt more like play. It didn't take long to get the interior set up. Everything inside was in its place—even the table was set with the flower arrangement she'd gathered from Grandma's garden and placed in a mason jar on the table.

Next she set up her outside area, which looked better than ever with her new awning and cheerful birthday planters flanking the door. She even put up her strings of camping lights, and since she'd brought extra batteries for them, she decided to turn them on during the trailer tour. She would light her lanterns too. She had no hopes of winning any prizes, but as the newcomer, she planned to pull out all the stops. When she was completely done with everything, she got out a small plaque she'd painted just the night before—WELCOME TO DESERT ROSE with a couple of coral-colored roses on each end—and hung it above the door. Perfect.

Dillon got a soda from her ice chest, then sat down in one of her outdoor chairs, put her feet on the matching footstool, and looked out over the calm blue lake. Life was good. Definitely good. And she intended to enjoy it to the fullest.

A couple of other trailers had been parked while she'd been setting up. A lime-green one and an aqua blue. It looked like their owners were busily setting up now. From where she sat, Dillon could see Vivian's campsite. It looked like she and Jordan were discussing something. And Vivian, instead of acting like Ms. Bossy Pants, like she'd done with Dillon, was all sunshine and smiles now. Well, whatever. Dillon wasn't going to let Vivian get to her. This was too nice to spoil.

She'd just finished her soda when Jordan came over. "Hey, this is looking good," he told her as he checked out her outside area. "You're turning into serious competition."

She laughed. "I did this for myself. I don't care if I get any votes, I just want to enjoy it."

"Come check out my domain." He reached for her hand. "Maybe you can give me some pointers for my exterior area. And I'm not sure I put everything back together on the inside— not like you had it yesterday."

"I doubt you need my help, but I'd like to see it."

With his trailer awning out and his camp furnishings set up, Jordan's campsite looked very inviting. "Hey, you've even hung up the lights I got you."

"You bet. Now come inside."

She went into his trailer and immediately noticed that it wasn't quite like she'd had it. "This looks good, but want me to tweak a little?" she asked.

"Of course!"

She made a few little changes and Jordan approved. "Thanks. I'm hoping to give Vivian real competition this year."

"How does her place look?" Dillon asked.

"I've only seen the outside, which is pretty slick in a girly sort of way, but she won't let me peek inside. I suspect she's made some changes."

"Well, I'm sure she feels there's a lot at stake since she's sort of the trailer décor expert in town." Dillon suspected that money was no object for Vivian's trailer.

"Yeah, like a walking—or rolling—advertisement for her shop."

Dillon checked her watch. "So when do you expect Janelle and the girls to arrive?"

"Not until dinnertime. Janelle had some loose ends to tie up on a real estate listing."

"They'll miss the trailer tour."

"Well, they don't get votes anyway. And I'm sure they can snoop around as much as they like later. Our club members love showing their trailers."

"I'm really looking forward to the tour."

"Well, that's not until later. Wanna do something fun in the meantime?"

"Sure."

"Ever been kayaking?"

She shook her head.

"Well, I reserved a couple of kayaks at the lodge. I need someone to hike over and get them with me. Then we'll have to paddle back across the lake. You up for it?"

"Absolutely!"

Before long, after putting on life vests and getting a quick lesson from Jordan, Dillon was paddling with him across the lake. "This is great," she called out to him. "I love it."

"Pretty cool." He pointed to the sky. "Bald eagle at twelve o'clock high."

Shielding her eyes, she peered upward. "Beautiful," she said.

"Nothing like being out here," Jordan said. "A weekend isn't really enough."

"Maybe not, but I plan to make the most of it."

He nodded. "Yep. Me too."

They paddled leisurely, taking in the sights . . . a family of mallard ducks, some kids with colorful floatable toys, fishermen, and the general beauty of the tree-rimmed mountain lake. By the time they were back at their section of campground, the trailer tour was in full swing.

"Where do we put the kayaks?" Dillon asked as she tugged her kayak up onto the beach area.

"Here. They're for everyone to use. Just stick the life vest and paddle inside."

She was unfastening her vest when she heard Vivian calling down to them. "Where have you guys been?" she demanded. "Don't you know it's trailer tour time?"

"No worries," Jordan called back. "We're here now."

"Yes, but your trailers should be open and ready for—"

"And they will be," Jordan assured her. "Relax."

She scowled and turned, marching away.

"I don't think she liked your suggestion," Dillon said quietly.

"Well, I think she's taking this too seriously." Jordan gave Dillon a hand as they stepped over a fallen log. "This is supposed to be fun."

"I'm having fun," she told him.

He grinned. "Me too."

He continued to hold her hand as they walked into the campground. Not that she minded—she didn't!

"Wow, the place has really filled up," she observed. "It's so colorful and cute. I can't wait to take some photos."

"Our fellow campers are already on the prowl," Jordan said as they paused by his trailer.

"Looks like the competition has begun."

He winked, then released her hand. "And may the best trailers win."

As she went over to unlock her trailer's door, she doubted that she had a real chance to win, but she was excited about having other trailer aficionados stopping by her campsite—and curious to hear their comments. She was equally curious to see their trailers.

Dillon hooked her trailer door open, leaving the screen door closed to keep the bugs out. Besides that, it was an awfully cute screen door. She was just adjusting the *Desert Rose* nameplate when she heard footsteps behind her. Turning, she felt slightly dismayed to see Vivian.

"Thought I'd start with you." Vivian's smile looked stiff. "As the newest member, I'm sure everyone will be curious." She reached for the screen door handle. "Mind if I go in?"

"Not at all." Dillon smiled. "Make yourself at home." She considered going in with her, but wasn't sure she wanted to hear Vivian's comments. She felt certain that her trailer wouldn't match up to Vivian's perfectionist expectations. And really, she didn't care. She loved *Desert Rose*, and that was enough.

After a few minutes, Vivian came out. "You've done a nice job with it, Dillon." Her smile looked more genuine as she unpeeled a chocolate kiss from the bowl Dillon had placed on the counter. "Kudos to you."

"Thanks. That means a lot coming from you. I mean, because you're an expert," Dillon said. "Mind if I go look at your trailer now?"

"Of course not. That's what this is all about. And no one needs to stick with their trailer. Everyone in our group is trustworthy." She popped the chocolate into her mouth, then headed for Jordan's trailer.

Dillon was eager to see Vivian's trailer. With the way it was parked, she still hadn't seen the exterior set up. But as soon as she stepped into Vivian's camp spot, she could see it was perfection. Like something right out of one of the vintage trailer books—only better. White wicker furnishings were stylishly arranged with soft pink cushions. And a small white table with two pink canvas chairs was completely set for what looked like a rather formal dinner. Complete with a lacy tablecloth, pink roses, candles, china, and crystal. A little over the top for Dillon's taste, but admittedly pretty.

Inside the trailer was similar to the outside, but even more elegant. A small crystal chandelier hung over the dinette table, which was set similar to the one outside. The walls were covered in embossed wallpaper that had a pale-pink-and-white treatment. The window coverings were white lace, and the countertops were white marble—the real thing. The floors were hardwood, with a couple of expensive-looking Persian rugs. This was definitely not a space to bring children or pets.

The bedding was layered and beautiful. And the small gilt framed paintings on the wall looked like originals. The bathroom had more marble and the tiny shower had a lace shower curtain. Everything looked fresh and clean and shining and expensive. Scented candles in cut-crystal containers were artfully placed, along with a couple small vases of pale pink roses. It was stunningly beautiful. But overwhelming.

"Wow," Dillon said as she exited the trailer to discover an older couple preparing to go inside.

"How was it?" the woman asked.

"Wow," Dillon said again.

The woman rolled her eyes. "That's what I figured." She stuck out her hand. "I'm Lynette Miller and this is Jim."

Dillon introduced herself as she shook their hands. "I'm new. My trailer's over there. Nothing like this."

"No one's is ever anything like Vivian's." Jim just shook his head.

"She keeps raising the bar," Lynette said.

"That doesn't mean you have to keep hopping over it," her husband told her.

Lynette laughed. "Don't worry. I'm not even trying." She pointed down the road. "We're the lime-green job in space #29." Then they went inside Vivian's trailer. As Dillon walked away she could hear them saying it was "just too much." And Dillon agreed.

As she visited the other trailers, she felt a real sense of relief. No one's trailer compared with Vivian's. And that was refreshing. Some were bare bones but handsome. Some were shabby-chic and clever. Some were completely vintage, with everything restored to its original appearance. But all were unique and interesting. And Dillon felt like her trailer fit in just fine. Maybe not with Vivian's showpiece, but she was in good company with the rest of them—and that felt great!

CHAPTER
31

*D*illon had made several new friends by the time she was helping to set up the potluck in the covered communal area. Everyone was still chatting about the trailer tour, and not surprisingly, Vivian's trailer—or *the palace*, as several women were now calling it—was the hottest topic. Fortunately Vivian wasn't around to overhear them.

"Who's she trying to impress anyway?" A no-nonsense woman named Dee stuck a spoon into a big bowl of pasta salad. Her trailer was the smallest. A cute, well-equipped blue teardrop with just enough room for Dee and her terrier, Scotty.

"I thought Viv outdid herself last year," Lynette said. "Boy, was I wrong."

"China and crystal," another woman said. "How on earth did she pack all that—and why?"

303

"And that wicker outdoor furniture," Dee added. "She couldn't have gotten all that into her station wagon."

"I'll bet she hired someone to bring it up here for her," someone said. "I heard she was the first one here. She probably needed several hours just to set everything up."

"Maybe Jordan brought it up for her," Dee suggested. "They've always been on good terms."

"Which makes no sense if you ask me. Jordan is down-to-earth and Vivian . . . well, not so much."

Dillon looked up from where she was slicing onions to see that Vivian was approaching. She quickly called out a greeting to her—partly to warn the other women, and partly because she didn't want Vivian to hear their comments. Not that the women were being mean exactly, but they were certainly being candid.

"This all looks good," Vivian announced as she set a big green salad and bag of chips on the table.

"And those burgers sure smell good." Dee nodded over to the barbecue area where the men were congregated. "I'm starved."

"Don't forget to vote," Vivian said in a cheerful tone. "Jordan plans to count right after dinner, and we don't want anyone to miss out."

The discussion returned to the trailer tour observations, only without any derogatory mention of "the palace."

"I loved that *Desert Rose*," a woman Dillon hadn't met declared. "Very fresh and fun. Whose is it, anyway?"

"It's Dillon's," Lynette told her, pointing to Dillon. "Our newest member. Dillon, this is Kate Green."

Dillon waved her knife. "Nice to meet you."

"Well, your trailer is really sweet," Kate told her. "Nicely done."

"Thanks." Dillon turned to the sound of shrill little-girl voices. "Emma and Chloe," she exclaimed. "You're here!"

They both hugged her. "Mama said to ask which one is your trailer."

Dillon laid down her knife next to the generous pile of onion slices. "Why don't I show you?" She rinsed her hands in the big cement sink, then took the girls down to her trailer. "I'm right next to your uncle. My trailer is called *Desert Rose*." She pointed to it.

"It's beautiful," Emma declared.

"Can we go inside?" Chloe asked.

"Sure. I'll go check on your mom." Dillon found Janelle with their bags out in front of Jordan's trailer. They greeted each other and Janelle complimented Dillon on Jordan's new décor.

"He told me you fixed it up, but I had no idea it would be so cool."

"He wanted it to be nice for you and the girls." Dillon explained the girls were in her trailer now. "Have you decided who's sleeping where?"

"I told the girls they could choose since it was their idea to come camping." She nodded to Jordan's trailer. "They already saw this and said they want to stay here, so it looks like I'll be bunking with you—if you don't mind."

"Not at all."

"Good. I think it'll be better than being with my brother. He snores."

Dillon laughed. "Want to see your digs?"

"You bet."

Dillon led her over to find the twins up on the front bunk. "We want to stay with Dillon," Chloe announced. "Mama can stay with Uncle Jordan."

"But you said—"

"We changed our mind," Emma told her.

"We love Dillon's trailer. And it's bigger too."

"Well, I guess this is what I get for letting the girls decide," Janelle told Dillon.

"You could stay too if you want. Might be cozy, but it's—"

"No, that might hurt Jordan's feelings." Janelle wrinkled her nose. "I'll bunk with my brother."

○ ○ ○

Dinner was a fun gathering. The twins stuck to Dillon like glue. Not that she minded. It was actually fun to have two such devoted fans. And already they were making plans with her to "swim" in the lake the next day. Dillon wasn't sure how much actual swimming they would do, but at least they could have fun in the water. And Dillon assured Janelle that she was happy to play lifeguard. Of course, when some other parents overheard this, they asked if she'd want to keep an eye on their kids too.

"Sure," Dillon told them. "I used to lifeguard at the pool as a teenager."

"She's our swimming teacher," Chloe told them. "And she's really good."

"Well, we won't have any lessons tomorrow." Dillon grinned. "Just free play."

After dinner was cleaned up, the campers drifted off in

separate ways. Some went back to their sites to visit, some took walks, some started games of horseshoes or lawn bowling. And Jordan announced he was going to go count votes.

"And I'm going with him," Jim Miller announced. "Just to make sure he doesn't cheat." He laughed as he elbowed Jordan.

"I think I'll go back to my trailer," Dillon told Janelle and the girls.

"Can we come with you?" Chloe asked.

"Sure. And I even packed a few things that might interest you girls."

"Can I come too?" Janelle asked in a little girl voice.

"Of course."

As they trekked over to Dillon's site, the girls bubbled about how cool everything was and how fun it was to go camping. And although Dillon was already thoroughly enjoying herself, their enthusiasm just enhanced it all.

At her trailer, she opened one of the banquette's bench seats to show the girls where she'd packed checkers and several other board games as well as drawing paper, felt-tip pens, and a few other fun things.

"You brought these for us?" Chloe asked incredulously.

"Sure. I hope you find something you like in there." She went outside where Janelle had already made herself comfortable. "I guess we'll see how long they can be entertained without the help of electronics."

"I love being disconnected like this." Janelle sighed. "No one can call me to work."

"Will it be a problem if you get a buyer or something?"

"I've got my girl Tessa on it. If anything really big comes up, she'll leave a message for me at the lodge or drive up here.

But I'm hoping for just a quiet, uninterrupted weekend. I'm way overdue."

For the next hour, they just visited congenially, listening to the girls as they played games and drew pictures at the table inside. Then, as it began to get dark, Jordan stopped by to announce it was campfire time. "Be sure and get something warm to wear or bring blankets," he said as he handed them sticks for roasting marshmallows. "It gets cold up here quickly, and the fire only warms your front side."

Before long, wearing sweatshirts and carrying their sticks, they joined the others around a big, crackling fire. Jim Miller had his guitar and was starting to lead them in a goofy camp song. His wife, Lynette, was managing the s'mores station. And everyone looked happy to be there.

After s'mores, Jordan stood up. "As always, we need to have our business meeting. There's not much to go over, and I'll try to wrap it up quickly." He went over some budget things, explaining that since campsite fees had gone up slightly, dues would be a bit higher for next year. Then he mentioned the plans for a vintage calendar, encouraging everyone to send him their best pictures to be considered for inclusion. "We'll set it up online for everyone to vote in a month or two. Vivian has already offered to carry the calendars in her shop. And, of course, I'll have them available at my store too. Any other businesses can contact me if they're interested." He turned to Jim. "Now, Jim has some announcements to make . . . regarding this afternoon's vote."

Jim stood and cleared his throat as he unfolded a piece of paper. "As usual, we had some close races. And I have to say that having been a member of this club for the last five years,

I'm really impressed with how great everyone's trailers look. I think we should put together a super-looking calendar and—"

"Oh, Jim," his wife said, "just get to the point!"

Others chimed in.

"Okay, okay," he said. "I'll start by announcing the winner of the Best Trailer Exterior. This goes to the camper or campers who've put the most effort into restoring their trailer. And this year's prize goes to Ben and Shelby Grant." Everyone clapped and the Grants came up to receive a small trophy with a little trailer on it. "Good work on *Suzy Q*—she's turned into a real cutie pie." He looked at the paper. "The next prize goes to the Best Campsite. This is awarded for cleverness and creativity outside of the trailer. And as we all know, some of us put in more work than others. This year's prize for the most attractive campsite goes to the Jacksons."

Again the applause was enthusiastic. And Dillon had to agree, the Jacksons' site was really great. It wasn't just attractive, it was comfortable looking and inviting, and there were various things to do. Plus they had piped sixties music out via an old drive-in-theater speaker. The next prize, Jim announced, was for Best Interior Design. Dillon wondered if this would go to Vivian, although there were a number of trailers that Dillon had liked better.

"This award goes to our newest member, Dillon Michaels, for her *Desert Rose*." Everyone clapped loudly and the twins jumped up and down while cheering. "The *Desert Rose* definitely has a unique and very attractive color scheme and a lot of fun and unexpected perks throughout. Congratulations, Dillon!"

Dillon was too stunned to say anything more than thank you as she accepted her little trophy.

"And finally, our grand prize will go to the best overall trailer. This is judged on interior, exterior, campsite, and tow vehicle. And this year's winner is our own president, Jordan Atwood. Good thing I didn't let him count the votes this year." Everyone clapped and cheered. "I gotta give it to you, Jordan, you really went all out this year. And we all thought it was about time you did something to your interior. That old sleeping bag on the sofa and using paper plates was wearing thin." They all laughed.

Dillon glanced over to Vivian, wondering how she was taking all this. Despite all the effort she'd put into her incredibly elegant trailer, she hadn't won a single prize. Hopefully she wasn't feeling too bummed about it. But then again, maybe she'd forgotten that camping was by nature meant to be more casual and friendly. Maybe this would be a good reminder.

With everyone, or almost everyone, in good spirits, they continued to sing songs and make s'mores, and Jim actually told a fairly lame "ghost story." When he finished, Janelle nudged Dillon. "I think my girls might need to call it a night."

Dillon nodded. "Why don't I take them? You stay here and enjoy the fire."

"Oh, you don't have to—"

"I want to." Dillon took both their sticky hands and led them back to her trailer. With its outdoor lights glowing, it was very welcoming. She led them inside and set their bags down. "You girls wash up in the bathroom, get all that marshmallow goop off, and then get into your PJs and brush your teeth," she told them.

To her relief, they didn't protest. After a bit of help and

instructions for using the little bathroom, they were ready for bed. She pulled down the mini ladder that doubled as a bed rail and helped them into the bunk. "You sure there's enough room up there for both of you?" she asked.

"Yeah, it's really big and roomy," Chloe told her. "We like it!"

"Do you want us to say our prayers?" Emma asked.

"Sure." Dillon sat at the banquette beneath them. "Go ahead." She smiled as the girls took turns praying, adding their own personal touches then simultaneously saying amen.

"Can you read us a bedtime story?" Chloe asked.

"A story?"

"Yeah!" Emma said. "We saw your books in the bench, Dillon."

"Hmm . . . how about if I just *tell* you a story?" Both girls agreed, so Dillon dredged her memory for one of the old fairy tales her grandma used to tell her. Grandma had been a great storyteller, but her fairy tales had always been different from the Disney versions. "How about Cindy, queen of the ash bin?" Dillon asked. The girls both cheerfully agreed, and Dillon started with "Once upon a time . . ." Sitting below them, she began to tell them a condensed version of her grandma's take on Cinderella—as well as she could remember it.

When she finished, it was quiet above, so she went outside to turn off her string lights and close the main door. She was surprised to see Jordan sitting in one of her camp chairs. "What're you doing here?" she asked.

"Just enjoying story time." He chuckled.

"Oh." She sat down in the other chair.

"And giving my sister her space to get ready for bed. It's pretty tight in there."

"It's quiet out here. Does that mean the campers have all gone to bed?"

"That's not unusual on the first night out. Folks are tired from all the preparations and getting set up. Tomorrow night is when it gets more lively."

"Congratulations on winning the grand prize."

Jordan laughed. "I think you deserve part of it."

"Well, I got my own." She remembered Vivian's face. "But I feel bad for Vivian's sake. She looked pretty disappointed. Think of all the work she must've put into her trailer and everything."

"Yeah, I felt a little sorry for her too. She's used to winning. But most everyone thought she took it too far this year. I mean, this is camping, right?"

"Yeah . . . but she's so into design . . . and there's her shop . . . I can sort of understand. Not that I'd ever be into that much glitz and glamour."

"Well, don't worry, Vivian will get over it."

"Yes, I'm sure she will. I was thinking the twins should go see her trailer tomorrow. I think they'd be impressed."

"Yeah, maybe they can have a tea party. My nieces love tea parties."

"Not a bad idea."

"Speaking of tomorrow, want to go kayaking in the morning?"

"Sure."

"I thought it'd be fun to see the sunrise over the lake, but that means getting up early. Like five thirty."

"That's okay. But what about the girls? I shouldn't leave them—"

"Don't worry, I'll let Janelle know."

"Great. Then I'd love to see the sunrise from a kayak."

"Which is why I'll tell you good night now." Jordan sat for a moment, gazing at her and almost making her wonder if he planned to kiss her . . . but then he stood. "See you in the morning. Sleep well."

She told him good night too. Then, giving him time to get back to his campsite, she turned off the lights and went inside. All was quiet, and she felt certain the girls were asleep as she quietly got ready for bed. Even though she'd been sleeping in her snug little trailer for a while now, it felt like a new experience to know she was sharing it with the little girls. Like three happy campers!

CHAPTER

he sunrise was well worth getting up for the next morning. The entire lake glowed like burnished gold. And the snow-capped mountains east of them were painted a peachy pink. "It's magical," Dillon said as they paused in the center of the serene lake to take it in.

Jordan nodded. "I thought you'd like it." The kayaks barely rocked in the placid water, the silence broken only with the occasional sounds of nearby birds. "Looks like we're going to have a great day. Nothing but blue sky and sunshine."

Dillon sighed happily. Had there ever been a better start to a day . . . a better weekend? She didn't think so. She wished it could last forever.

"Want to paddle over to the lodge for some coffee?" he asked.

"Sure." She followed his lead at first. Then, feeling she was really getting the hang of it, she paddled faster and quickly shot ahead of him. And then the race was on, both of them paddling full-out until they reached the beach next to the lodge simultaneously.

"Wow." Jordan got out of his kayak and helped her out as well. "You gave me a real run for the money there."

"That was fun." She laughed as he helped her up the shore, still holding her hand as they walked up to the lodge. She smiled up at him. "You better watch out, I might just beat you on the way back."

"I accept the challenge." Still hand in hand, he led her up to the coffee kiosk outside of the lodge and they both ordered coffee. He only released her hand to pay for their drinks. Dillon couldn't help but think this really did feel like a date. At least something more than just friendship.

They found a lakeside bench and sat to drink their coffees, talking about everything from the weekend activities to city politics. Then, realizing what time it was, Jordan reminded her that they'd both signed up to help fix breakfast this morning. He took her empty cup and she sprinted down toward the kayaks. "Catch me if you can," she yelled as she got into hers and started to paddle.

Despite her lead, Jordan soon caught up, and then, when she got tired of paddling hard, he slowed down to keep pace with her. By the time they reached camp, it was clear that the other campers were up and moving around. Dillon checked on her trailer and the girls to discover that Janelle had crawled into Dillon's bed. "I hope you don't mind," Janelle said sheepishly. "But I came to check on the girls and, well, your bed was still warm and—"

"That's okay," Dillon told her. "I don't blame you."

"It's so comfortable." Janelle sat up, stretching. "Way better than my brother's spare bunk. You know how to live."

Dillon laughed. "Well, you girls just make yourselves at home. I promised to help with breakfast. You have about half an hour before it'll be ready."

○○○

Breakfast was fun and the morning continued in a lovely, laid-back sort of way. Dillon enjoyed getting to know the other campers as well as taking a short hike with Jordan. Once again, he was attentive and, unless it was her imagination, romantic. But after their hike he had to meet with Jim Miller and a couple of others regarding "tonight's entertainment." He wouldn't go into any detail but assured her it should be amusing.

Shortly before noon, she went with Janelle and the twins to visit Vivian's palace trailer—although Dillon had no intention of calling it that. She suspected Vivian was already feeling a bit hurt. And it was a relief when Chloe and Emma both made a big fuss over how fancy everything was—exclaiming over every detail.

"It really is beautiful," Dillon told Vivian as the women went back outside. "I couldn't believe you didn't win a prize last night. No one's trailer compares to this."

"Well, I have to admit I went a little overboard." Vivian looked sheepish. "But I wanted to get photos for a couple of projects I'm working on. Shots of my trailer will be in the real glamping section."

"Glamping?" Janelle asked as they sat down in the wicker chairs.

"Glamorous camping," Dillon explained. "I even have a glamping book that I got at the Silver Slipper."

"I just love that book," Vivian admitted.

Dillon smiled at her. "To be honest, I learned a lot about trailers and camping from that book."

"So I decided to make *The Silver Slipper* a real glamping trailer," Vivian told them. "And I've already gotten some great photos to use."

"I noticed you've been taking a lot of photos during the trailer tour," Dillon said.

"Yes. I'm collecting for our club calendar as well as a book I'm putting together." She turned to Dillon. "In fact, I got some very good ones of your *Desert Rose*."

"Isn't her trailer sweet?" Janelle said. "So different."

"Yes, and if Dillon agrees, I'll feature it—not only in the calendar but for my book as well."

"Of course, I'll agree. I'd love to be part of both projects." Dillon smiled. Was it possible that Vivian was actually warming up to her? She hoped so.

As the girls came out to explore the exterior of Vivian's glamping trailer, Dillon shared Jordan's suggestion that it would make a great location for a fancy tea party. Naturally, the girls jumped—literally—at this idea and Vivian eagerly agreed to host it. "How about this afternoon," she suggested. "And since it was his idea, we'll insist that Jordan comes too."

"But we have to go swimming too," Emma told her mom. "Remember, Dillon's our lifeguard?"

"How about after swimming? Will that work?" Janelle suggested to Vivian. They agreed to come at three thirty. And, although Dillon hadn't really wanted to come for tea before, now that it looked like Jordan might come, she felt differently. If nothing else, it might be interesting to see how Vivian handled everything.

It was nearly two by the time Dillon took Emma and Chloe down to the roped-off swimming area by the dock. Naturally, the water was much colder than the pools they were used to, so the girls were hesitant to go beyond knee-depth. Until they saw the older kids bravely taking the plunge. And then with the help of their floaty toys and the heat of the sun, they began to enjoy themselves.

When Janelle came to pick up the girls for the tea party, Dillon knew she couldn't leave the other young swimmers unsupervised. Especially since it was clear a couple of them weren't swimmers. "Tell Vivian I'll have to take a rain check," she called to Janelle. "Rather, a swim check."

After they left, Dillon realized she didn't really mind missing the elegant *Silver Slipper* tea party. She was more comfortable in the role of lifeguard. And she knew the parents of these kids appreciated it. Still she was curious about the interaction between Jordan and Vivian. She wasn't too concerned about Jordan, but she had no doubts that Vivian had more than just a friendly interest. Anyone could see that.

As she sat on the dock, Dillon told herself that if Jordan's feelings toward her were as strong as she believed, she had no reason to worry. Except for that one nagging concern . . . the rumor that Jordan was a confirmed bachelor. She understood his mother's explanation . . . and it made sense that he would err on the side of caution. But she thought they'd made real progress in the past several days.

It was a little past five by the time the last of the kids left the swimming hole. On her way back to her trailer, feeling soggy and dirty but perfectly happy, Dillon took a peek at *The Silver Slipper*. To her surprise it looked like only Jordan and Vivian were sitting out in front . . . and they looked totally engrossed. Sitting head to head, in what appeared to be an intimate conversation, they didn't even see her walking by.

Pulling her beach towel more tightly around her, Dillon hurried over to her trailer to discover Janelle and the girls sitting outside. The girls were coloring and Janelle was reading a novel. The picture of contentment.

"I thought you were at the tea party?" Dillon paused by the door.

"That's all done," Chloe informed her.

Janelle looked up from her book. "You look like a drowned rat."

"I just had to jump in the lake to help Kerry Miller. He got in too deep." Dillon forced a smile. "So . . . how was the tea party?"

"Nice. Although I'm not sure Vivian is used to exuberant young guests." Janelle glanced at her girls, who were acting like perfect angels just now.

Dillon bit her tongue before mentioning that Jordan must've enjoyed himself—since he was still there! Instead, she went inside and began to clean up for dinner. Since she'd already done her KP duty, she was free to relax tonight. Still, she felt anything but relaxed as she remembered how Jordan and Vivian had looked so engrossed in each other's company just now. What was going on?

As she toweled her hair, she wondered if she'd been deluded to assume that Jordan had feelings for only her. Was she that naïve? Maybe he was that eternal bachelor. Maybe he liked having a string of girls following him around. Perhaps he wanted one for each day of the week!

She didn't believe that. Not really. But she did feel conflicted . . . and hurt. And although she'd never admit as much to anyone, she was also jealous of Vivian. Perhaps Vivian had reason to appear so confident and self-assured when it came to Jordan Atwood.

At dinnertime, Jordan sat with Janelle and the girls . . . and consequently Dillon as well. But she wasn't sure he would've joined her if it wasn't for his sister and nieces. As a result, Dillon found it hard to chat and she felt relieved when he announced that he'd be busy with a horseshoes tournament after dinner. "I'd ask you to join in, but everyone already signed up."

"Oh, that's okay. I'm not very good at horseshoes anyway." She forced a smile. "I'll be a spectator." But when she went over to watch, she realized that Jordan and Vivian were partners.

"They won last year," Lynette Miller told Dillon and Janelle. "Jim and I plan to give them a run for their money this year."

Dillon acted unconcerned as she watched for a while. There was no denying that Jordan and Vivian were good, but feeling increasingly uncomfortable, Dillon excused herself, explaining to Janelle she was tired. "I got up so early this morning. I think I need a little break." And she did need a break.

Despite feeling more than a little glum over her assumptions about Jordan . . . and Vivian, Dillon felt encouraged to be back at her trailer. It was always amazing how *Desert Rose* welcomed her—with open arms. Dillon spent a little time just straightening things up, and then, happy to be alone at her own sweet campsite, she sat down with a book and pretended to read . . . but drifted off to sleep.

When she woke, it was dusky out and the twins were urging her to hurry up and come to the campfire with them. "And you better put on something warm," Janelle told her. "You girls get on your long pants and sweatshirts."

Before long, still feeling groggy from her after-dinner nap, Dillon trudged up the hill with Janelle and the girls to the campfire area. It wasn't that she wasn't enthused about this group time, especially since it had been fun last night. It was simply that she wasn't eager to see Jordan. Especially if he was still cozying up with Vivian.

She convinced herself that she'd overblown everything between her and Jordan. That was her mistake. In Jordan's defense, he'd simply been kind and thoughtful and helpful these past several days. And that little bit of hand-holding? Good grief, she'd held hands with boys in middle school . . . and it hadn't meant they'd wanted to marry her. Really, she just needed to grow up and accept reality.

Because the log bench seats were mostly occupied, Dillon encouraged Janelle and the girls to squeeze into a spot in the front row so the girls could see better. Then she took a seat in back next to the Jacksons. Tonight, Jordan and Jim Miller were taking the lead in singing and storytelling. Then a small group of campers performed a humorous skit—naturally, the cast included Vivian. Despite Dillon's resolve to keep a stiff upper lip, she felt herself crumbling inside. What had begun as an incredibly beautiful and perfect day was fading fast . . . and so was she.

So while the merry campers were in the midst of an exuberant cowboy song that they were performing in rounds, Dillon
slipped away. Slinking into the shadows, she found her way
back to her trailer. There she put a note on the door for Janelle,
apologizing that she was so tired she'd gone to bed, but inviting
Janelle to just come in and help the twins get ready for bed.
She knew it was a coward's way out, but she didn't really care.
She wanted to shed her tears without an audience.

When she finally heard them come in, Dillon pretended
to be fast asleep, which was ridiculous because between the
lights and bumps and loud whispering, she never would've
slept through it. But she really didn't want to face them. Didn't
want them to see she'd been crying.

"Does she know?" Emma whispered loudly while they were
brushing their teeth in the tiny bathroom.

"I don't think so," Chloe answered.

"And don't you girls say a word about it," Janelle whispered.
"Just get into bed and go to sleep."

Dillon was curious as to what they were talking about, but
at the same time preferred her ignorance. For all she knew, it
was possible that Jordan had proposed marriage to Vivian tonight. Maybe in front of the whole group. Maybe that was what
she'd heard them cheering so loudly about a few minutes ago.

In that case, she certainly wouldn't want to hear about it.
Not now. For the first time, in her sweet little trailer, she did
not sleep like a log. She tossed and turned and wound up rising
before the sun. She slipped into warm clothes, and thinking
she'd take out a kayak—and clear her head—she went outside.
But both kayaks were gone. She peered out onto the lake,
spotting them at a distance. She really couldn't tell who was

in them, but for whatever reason she felt certain it was Jordan ... and Vivian. Probably celebrating their engagement with the rising of the sun.

Dillon knew she was being perfectly silly. It was highly unlikely that Jordan had proposed to Vivian last night ... or that he'd propose to anyone for that matter. But for some reason she couldn't convince herself otherwise.

Dillon strolled around the campground, finally stopping at the dock. She sat on the bench and, feeling drained and empty, just gazed out over the lake. As she watched it slowly coming to life with the morning sun, there was no denying the beauty. But it just didn't look as spectacular as it had yesterday. Her one consolation was that this camping weekend would end today. Everyone had to be out of the campground by two. Perhaps she would leave a bit earlier.

Dillon felt the lump in her throat returning and knew she needed to do something to bolster her spirits before seeing the others. She didn't want to be the one unhappy camper that dragged everyone else down. Her only recourse—a lesson she'd learned long ago, but sometimes forgot—was to give her heartache to God. She knew his ways were higher than hers. And she knew he could handle her brokenness ... and that, in time, he would restore her. She would get past this.

"Hey, there." Janelle called out as she walked out on the dock. "We were wondering what had become of you." She came over and sat down next to Dillon. "Are you okay?"

Dillon forced a smile. "Yeah, I'm fine."

"We missed you last night. I didn't realize you'd left the campfire."

"I was pretty worn out."

"What a beautiful morning." Janelle took a deep breath.

"Yes, I thought I'd take out a kayak, but someone beat me to it." Dillon pointed to the pair on the lake. "Is that Jordan and Vivian out there?" She tried to sound nonchalant.

"I don't know about Vivian, but Jordan was just getting up when I left." Janelle turned to Dillon. "Can I ask you something?"

"Sure."

"Well, Jordan is worried that something is wrong. I mean with you."

"Oh no, I'm fine." Dillon hated to lie but told herself it was for the right reason.

"Did Jordan do anything to offend you yesterday?" Janelle peered curiously at her.

"Why . . . I mean, what are you getting—"

"Jordan stayed up late last night talking to me about everything, Dillon. My brother really likes you. He really, really likes you. And he thought you felt the same. And then it felt like you suddenly turned chilly on him. The poor guy is confused. And if you don't mind me saying so, he's hurt. Jordan doesn't usually put himself out there like that. But he was doing it for you."

"What about Vivian?" Dillon asked. "It looked like he was putting himself out there for her too." Now she described seeing them cozying up at Vivian's campsite, and then horseshoes, and even the skit. "And Vivian acts like, well, you know."

"I know that Vivian has been after Jordan for a couple of years. But he only thinks of her as a friend. He's always made that clear. I also know that Vivian started talking to him about her calendar project at the tea party yesterday afternoon. She monopolized his time so much by showing him photos on her phone that the girls and I got bored and left."

"Oh . . ."

"So did you misread all that?"

Dillon nodded. "I guess so."

Janelle brightened. "Well, that's a relief. I told Jordan over and over last night that you didn't strike me as the kind of girl who would lead a guy on and then just leave him hanging like that."

"No, I would never do that. Not to anyone—especially not to Jordan."

"So you're as interested in him as he is in you?"

Dillon nodded again.

"Well, I told the twins I'd be right back. They're getting dressed. So I better go."

"I'll go with you," Dillon stood. "I haven't even brushed my teeth or anything yet." As they returned to Dillon's trailer, she was relieved not to see anyone. Especially Jordan. She suspected she looked a fright. As Janelle herded her girls out of the trailer, Dillon used the privacy to do some much-needed primping. So all her worries had been for nothing! What a silly fool she'd been. She should've known Jordan wasn't like that.

CHAPTER
33

*F*inally, feeling ready for the day and suspecting that breakfast was probably being served, Dillon emerged from her trailer and hiked up to the group area. There, to her total surprise, everyone was waiting with balloons, a birthday banner, and a sheet cake. And suddenly everyone was singing "Happy Birthday" to her.

"Blow out your candles," Jordan told her. "We didn't know how many to put on, so I insisted the girls stop at thirty."

"Thank you!" Dillon grinned at him. She took in a deep breath, and knowing that her wish was probably already coming true, she blew toward the candles. With the help of the girls, she managed to put them all out.

"Are you surprised?" Chloe asked.

"Absolutely." Dillon nodded. "I almost forgot it was my birthday."

"We didn't," Emma told her.

"This is your birthday breakfast," Chloe said. "It was my idea."

"The girls insisted you had to have your cake first thing," Janelle told her. "I wanted to wait until lunch."

"Cake for breakfast," Dillon declared. "What could be better?"

As they ate breakfast together—bacon and eggs and birthday cake—Dillon felt fairly certain that Janelle had informed Jordan that all was well with her. At least she hoped so. Since Jordan was acting fairly normal, she tried to do the same. Still, she hoped that they'd have a chance later to talk about all this stuff. It felt like they needed to clear the air . . . and get a fresh start. Perhaps even a birthday kiss?

So when they were done eating and Jordan invited her to take a walk, she gladly agreed. They were just setting out when a small rental RV pulled into their camp area. "Someone must be lost," Jordan said as the vehicle parked near the group area.

Dillon glanced at the gaudily painted RV van then suddenly felt sick. "Oh no!"

"What's wrong?" Jordan asked.

"I can't believe it," she said in a hushed tone. "It's—it's Brandon."

"What?" Jordan frowned. "Why is he here?"

"I have no idea. I haven't seen him since—"

"Dillon!" Brandon got out of the RV, extracting what looked like a giant bouquet of red roses and, wearing a confident smile that defied all common sense, he strolled over to them. "Happy birthday, honey!"

"Brandon?" She looked at him with a horrified expression.

"What on earth are you doing here? How did you even know how to find—"

"Margot told me you were here. So I rented this RV for a few days and came up to find you. The camp host said your group was over here." He grinned. "So here I am, wishing you a very happy birthday." He handed her the roses with a flourish.

"But I—"

"Now, don't say anything. Not yet." Brandon reached into his jacket pocket. "I have a very important question to ask you."

"Brandon, don't—"

"Please, let me say this without interruption, Dillon." He pulled out a small blue velvet box. "It's too important."

"I think I should excuse myself," Jordan said stiffly. "This looks like a private moment."

"But I don't want you—"

"Let him go," Brandon said abruptly to her. And before she could stop him, Jordan was gone. Then, to her complete and astonished horror, Brandon got down on one knee and, declaring his love, asked her to become his wife.

"No, Brandon." She folded her arms in front of her, firmly shaking her head. "I'm sorry you went to all this trouble. Especially after I already told you—over and over—that we were over and done with."

"But this is the real deal, Dillon." He stood, brushing off his knee. "I'm not asking you just to be my girl, or to wait a whole year. I'm asking you to marry me, Dillon. And we can do it right now if you want."

"*I don't want!*" Dillon sensed eyes on her and turned to see all her fellow campers staring down at her with way too much interest. "Come walk with me, Brandon." She grabbed his arm, tugging him away. "You have to understand this once and for all. I am not ever going to marry you. Not now. Not next year. *Never.*"

"But it was what you'd always wanted. And now that I'm really ready to do it, I can't believe you're blowing me off like this."

"I told you the last time I saw you, Brandon. No is no."

"I didn't propose to you the last time. Not like this anyway." He held out the velvet box. "You didn't even look at the ring. It's really—"

"I do not want the ring." She paused in the shadow of some trees. "You have to believe me, Brandon. I will *never* marry you. Never ever." She handed him back the roses. "Please, go."

He looked truly dismayed.

"I'm sorry if that hurts, but you can't say I didn't warn you before. I wish you'd listened." She glanced around, hoping to spot Jordan nearby . . . and desperately hoping Brandon's sudden unexpected appearance hadn't just set them back again. But she didn't see Jordan anywhere.

"But I thought we made real progress when I was here last time. Remember we had that great lunch right here at this very lake. It was a good day. Remember?" Brandon was giving her his kicked puppy look, but she wasn't buying it.

"Sure, we parted on friendly terms, Brandon. But that was all. I didn't want hard feelings between us, but I never did anything to make you believe I'd marry you."

"So I did all this for nothing?"

She nodded. "I'm sorry, but you did."

He scowled. "So there's nothing left to say."

"Not as far as I'm concerned. I just wish you'd listened before. Then you wouldn't have gone to all this trouble." She wanted to add that he was ruining her birthday, but didn't.

Brandon just shook his head and, without another word, turned and stomped away. Dillon watched as he got back into that hideous RV and drove off. It wasn't until he was out of sight with only a trail of dust left behind that she realized she was shaking and on the verge of angry tears. Why had he done this? And on her birthday too? How selfish.

Not ready to return to her camping friends, and wondering how she would ever live down this embarrassing episode, she decided to just walk it off. Hopefully she'd cross paths with Jordan. As she walked, she couldn't shake the expression in his eyes when Brandon had pulled out that stupid velvet box—it was a cross between confusion and hurt. Dillon knew she'd have to explain this to him . . . and apologize for Brandon's stupidity.

By the time she'd circled the whole campground, she felt like her breathing had stabilized and her blood pressure returned to normal. In fact, she could almost see the humor of the whole situation. She could almost imagine explaining it to Jordan and having a good laugh over the whole thing. *Almost*.

The campers had drifted away from the group area and Dillon went to her trailer in the hopes of finding Jordan. But it was only Janelle and the girls, packing up.

"What was *that* all about?" Janelle asked Dillon after they stepped outside.

Dillon sighed. "That was my delusional ex-boyfriend." She explained about Brandon and his stubborn persistence. "I really thought I set him straight the last time he was here, but apparently he didn't believe me. I honestly think he might be a narcissist. It's like he only thinks of himself and what he wants."

"Did he really propose?" Janelle asked. "With a ring and everything?"

Dillon nodded. "Unfortunately. I think he honestly thought it would turn my head, that I would forget everything and agree."

"He does sound a bit narcissistic."

"Is Jordan in his trailer?" Dillon glanced next door.

"No. I'm not sure where he went. He disappeared while your, uh, suitor was still here. The girls are getting their stuff out of your trailer."

"You're not leaving yet, are you?"

"No, we'll stick around for lunch. And I promised them they could go swimming later on."

"Oh, good." Dillon looked down to the nearby beach, noticing a kayak was missing. "I wonder if Jordan is on the lake."

"Maybe." Janelle frowned. "I don't want to worry you, Dillon, but he looked pretty upset when he walked away."

Dillon nodded. "Well, hopefully I can find him and set him straight. If he gets back before I do, tell him I'm taking out a kayak."

Before long, Dillon was on the lake, but because of the time of day, there were other boats and canoes and kayaks out as well. Trying to spot Jordan, if he was even out here, might be a challenge. But she was determined.

Finally, she thought she recognized him on the far side of the lake. Paddling full force, as if she thought he might escape her somehow, she got close enough to call out and wave.

As he paddled toward her, she prepared her statement—

starting with an apology. But before she got the words out, he was apologizing to her. "I'm sorry I took off like that," he said. "But I just couldn't stand it."

"I'm sorry Brandon did that," she told him. "The poor guy needs his head examined." She shook her head. "I don't know how I could've made myself more clear to him last time he was here. But he really thought he could persuade me otherwise today."

"But he couldn't?"

"Of course not." She held up her hands in frustration. "I very bluntly told him that I would never marry him—ever. Hopefully he got it this time. Otherwise he should be locked up."

Jordan shrugged. "Well, you can't really blame him."

"I can and do blame him," she argued. "I've told him again and—"

"No, I mean you can't blame him for loving you." Jordan smiled. "I know how he feels."

She blinked. "You do?"

He nodded, paddling closer to her kayak. "Yes, I do."

"Really?" She was afraid to get too happy . . . what if she'd heard him wrong?

"I suppose I was aggravated at Brandon because I'd planned to tell you that today. It felt like he'd cut me off at the knees."

"You'd planned to tell me . . . ?" She studied him closely.

"Yes. I'd decided that since it was your birthday, I would tell you how I really feel about you, Dillon. Then Brandon came along and . . ."

"Well, Brandon is gone now." She smiled. "And it's still my birthday."

"Okay then." He set his paddle down then reached for her hand. "I love you, Dillon. And it's about time you knew it."

She felt so happy that she could hardly contain it. "I love you too, Jordan."

He pulled her closer, bumping their kayaks together in an awkward attempt to kiss her. Not just a peck either. It was a long, sweet, passionate kiss. But then, feeling dizzy—or perhaps unbalanced—Dillon felt her kayak tilting too far toward his. She grabbed for him as it toppled over, causing his kayak to follow suit. The next thing she knew they were both plunged into the chilly lake. But Jordan simply laughed and kissed her again—soggy but sweet. And she knew they were just a pair of happy campers . . . getting ready for a brand-new adventure.

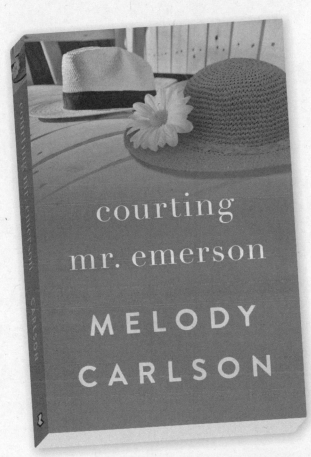

CHAPTER

1

*G*eorge Emerson didn't need anybody. Or so he told himself as he carefully shaved with his straight-edged razor, just like he always did seven days a week at exactly 7:07 each morning. George knew that most men used more modern razors, but this silver implement had been left to him by the grandfather who'd helped raise him. Wiping his razor across a soft terry towel, he stretched his neck to examine his smoothly shaved chin in the foggy mirror. He could see better with his reading glasses, but after so many years of the same routine, George felt certain the job was done right.

As he closed the bathroom window, shutting out the humming "music" of his overly friendly neighbor, George wondered if there was some polite way to avoid Lorna Atwood this morning. She'd been puttering around her yard for the last ten minutes, and George felt certain it was in the hopes of catching him on his way to work.

As he replaced the cap on his Barbasol shave cream and returned his razor to its chipped ceramic mug, a pinging in the kitchen told him that the coffee was done. The automatic-timed coffee maker was one of the few modern perks that George had been talked into a few years ago. But, as with most electronic devices, he still didn't fully trust the fancy machine. What if it got its wires crossed and decided to make coffee in the middle of the night?

George peeked out the kitchen window as he filled his stainless steel travel cup with steaming coffee, only to see that Lorna was now sitting on her front porch. He slipped two thin slices of whole wheat bread into the toaster, removed a hard-boiled egg from the fridge, and poured himself a small glass of grapefruit juice. This was his standard weekday breakfast. On weekends he'd sometimes fry or poach himself an egg or, if feeling particularly festive, he might stroll over to the Blue Goose Diner and splurge on pancakes and bacon, which he'd leisurely consume while reading the newspaper. Although it had probably been more than a year since he'd indulged in that.

But today was Friday, and by 7:27, George's breakfast was finished, his dishes washed. With his travel mug refilled and briefcase in hand, he locked his front door, checked to be sure it was secure, then checked again just in case. Lingering for a moment, he pretended to check his watch, glancing left and right to be sure Lorna wasn't lurking nearby.

The sun seemed high in the sky for late May, but that was only because he'd never fully adjusted to the late-start days that Warner High had implemented last fall. Although it had disrupted his internal time clock, George had to admit that students seemed moderately more awake with an extra hour of sleep.

"Hello, Mr. Emerson," Lorna Atwood chirped merrily.

She popped out from the shadows of her front porch like a jack-in-the-box in Lycra. "Lovely day today, isn't it?"

He peered up at the cloudless sky then nodded an affirmative. "Looks like a good one, for sure."

"Especially for this time of year in western Oregon. Last year it rained all the way through May and June." She hurried over to him with a hot pink coffee cup in hand. Had she coordinated it to match her lipstick? "Now, you didn't forget about my invitation, did you?" Lorna looked hopeful.

George feigned confusion then tapped the side of his forehead. "I'm so sorry, Mrs. Atwood, but I realized that I do have other plans for tonight. I hope you'll please excuse me."

"Oh, well." Her smile remained fixed. "Perhaps another time. With summer round the corner, we should have plenty of chances to get together. I'll just have to take a rain check from you." She peered upward. "Speaking of rain checks, I heard it's supposed to cloud up this weekend. Maybe I can collect on mine then." She winked.

George forced a polite smile as he tipped his head and continued past her small yard. Her lawn was in need of mowing again. Hopefully he wouldn't have to remind her of her rental agreement and that she was responsible for her own landscaping chores. The little yellow bungalow, owned by him, was nearly identical to the one he lived in—except his was cornflower blue. His grandparents had helped him to invest in these little neglected houses in the late eighties, back when real estate had been ridiculously low. He'd purchased the first bungalow for his own use shortly after acquiring his teaching position at the nearby high school. Since he had no interest in driving, it had made sense to live within walking distance of his work. And he'd been employed at Warner High ever since.

With the help of his grandfather's handyman expertise, George had spent weekends and evenings fixing up his little blue house. It provided a good distraction from the dreams that had not gone as planned. Perhaps that was why his grandparents had encouraged him to take on three more little houses—to divert him from his pain and to keep him occupied. Of course, they wisely called it a "good investment." Plus it proved a clever way to increase real estate values in his neighborhood. Buying derelict properties had seemed a bit reckless at the time, especially since residents were fleeing urban neighborhoods, flocking to the "safety" of the suburbs. But in the past decade, the trend had reversed. People returned to town, and rentals in his neighborhood were at an all-time high. His three rental bungalows, just one block away from downtown, never went unoccupied nowadays.

Mrs. Atwood, his most recent tenant, had been overjoyed to get in. Although she'd only been here a few months, George soon learned to exercise caution when engaging with her. The gregarious divorcée could "chat" nonstop if given the opportunity. He suspected her husband had fled in order to attain some peace and quiet, although Mrs. Atwood claimed to be the victim of her ex-husband's "midlife crisis." To be fair, she wasn't bad looking—just talked too much. And tried too hard.

George had performed some minor repairs on the bungalow shortly after she moved in. Grateful for his "improvements," she eagerly invited him for dinner. When he declined, she insisted on baking him her "famous cherry pie." He pretended to appreciate her gesture, but the overly sweet and syrupy pie wound up in the trash since George wasn't big on desserts. Just the same, he penned a polite thank-you note and taped it to the clean pie plate that he discreetly placed on her porch very early the next morning. But since then, her efforts to befriend him had only intensified—and, short of rudeness or dishonesty, he was running out of excuses to decline.

George was no stranger to feminine attempts to *befriend* him, and over the years, he'd learned to take women's flattering attentions in stride. It wasn't that he was devastatingly handsome—he might be getting older, but he wasn't delusional. Even in his prime, back in the previous millennium when his students had nicknamed him "Mr. Bean," George had been aware that he was no Cary Grant. The comparison to the quirky BBC character may have been meant as an insult, but George hadn't minded.

He actually kind of admired Mr. Bean. And George knew the kids' teasing was the result of his buttoned-up attire. His response to kids dressing like gangbangers had been to step it up by wearing nappy ties and sports coats to school—an attempt to lead by example. Not that it had worked. But it was a habit he'd continued and, despite his fellow teachers' preference for casual dress, George liked his more traditional style. Ironically, it seemed the ladies liked it too. At least they used to, and ones like Mrs. Atwood apparently still did.

Now that he was in his midfifties, George suspected that women like Mrs. Atwood weren't attracted so much by his appearance as by his availability. It had never been particularly easy being a bachelor. Sometimes he'd suspected someone had pinned a target to his back. But as the years passed, many began to refer to him as a "confirmed bachelor." Truth be told, George didn't mind the confirmed part—it sounded better than being committed.

"Good morning, Mr. Emerson." Jemma Spencer waved to him as she bounded up the front steps to the school. "Isn't it a gorgeous day!"

"It certainly is." George politely opened the door for her, waiting as the younger woman went in ahead of him. Jemma was new at Warner High. Fairly fresh out of college, she was energetic and strikingly pretty—and, like most of his fellow teachers, young enough to be his daughter. "And how are things going in the Art Department, Miss Spencer?" He paused to show his ID badge at the security check.

"The natives are restless." Her dark brown eyes sparkled as if she were restless too.

"Yes, with only six days left of school, you have to expect that. Especially on a warm, sunny day like this."

"I think I'll take my students outside today," she confided as they continued toward the main office together, "to draw trees or flowers or clouds or butterflies or whatever. Maybe they'll just stare off into space, but hopefully it'll get the ants out of their pants."

He chuckled. "You're a brave woman."

"Not really, it's just that I'm kinda antsy too." She winked as they turned down the hall by the office. "I'm counting the days until summer break."

"Any big plans?" he asked with mild interest.

"My boyfriend and I are going to Iceland," she declared.

"Interesting—"

"Iceland?" a male voice called out from the faculty room. "Did someone say Iceland? I went there for spring break and it was fabulous. Want to see my photos?"

Suddenly many of the younger teachers were talking at once, sharing phone photos, eagerly recounting travel experiences, talking about the lure of Iceland or other exotic locales, and bragging about various offbeat plans for their upcoming summer. In the past, George might've engaged in this sort of enthusiastic banter—even sharing some of his own travel stories—but since he'd made no plans for the upcoming summer . . . or the past several summers for that matter, he kept his mouth closed and simply collected papers from his mailbox and checked the staff bulletin board. Then, without looking back, he quietly exited the noisy faculty room.

As he walked toward the Language Arts Department, George felt old. Not in a stiff, sore, achy sort of way—although he knew the spring had been missing from his step for some time now. He felt old as in outdated—like the dinosaur of Warner High. It was no secret that he was the oldest teacher on staff, or that the administration had been encouraging him to retire the last couple of years. But now he was nearly fifty-five, which sounded dangerously close to sixty, and budgets had been cut once again. His principal knew she could save money by hiring a less senior language arts teacher. George had resisted her in the past. But this year, he'd caved.

After a bad bout of flu last winter, George had given in, announcing that this would be his last year to teach. And now, in less than a week, he would be officially retired after more than thirty years. Not that anyone appeared to put much value on experience nowadays . . . or even care that he would soon be gone.

More and more, George had begun to feel invisible at this school, as if each year diminished his presence. Even the students looked right through him at times. Not that it was so unusual for a teacher to be ignored. As an English instructor he was accustomed to his students' general lack of interest in academia. He tried to impress upon them the need for good writing skills—and sometimes they got it. But thanks to this electronic age, which he detested, there was a complete disregard for spelling and grammar and structure. As hard as he'd tried to make his favorite class—English literature—relevant and appealing, most of his students didn't know the difference between Chaucer and Shakespeare. Even more, they didn't care.

He sighed as he clicked the pass-code pad numbers beside his classroom door. He remembered a time when no doors were locked inside of campus. Now everyone had pass-codes for everything. Security cams and uniformed police abounded—so much so that he sometimes felt like he was teaching in a prison. And to be fair, some of his students might be better off in a prison. He flicked on the fluorescent lights then walked through the stale-smelling classroom. Not for the first time, he wished the high windows could open and get fresh air in here. He'd raised this issue before, pointing out how it might actually help to wake the students up. But thanks to budget challenges, no changes had been made.

As George punched the number code into his office door, he remembered what this school had been like back in the *dark ages*—back when he'd been a student in this very building, back when dinosaurs roamed freely. What a different world that had been. Although the building, which was new and modern back then, hadn't changed much.

But then some things never changed. Over the years he'd observed that teens from every decade bore striking similarities. Peel back the veneer of current trends and fashions and you'd usually discover a frustrated mix of rebelliousness and insecurity. To be fair, his generation had been no different. He remembered the late seventies well. His class had its share of druggies and dropouts and slackers, yet his peers, even all these years later, felt more real to him than today's youth. Of course, it was possible that his memory was impaired by his age, but when he looked back he saw an authenticity that he felt was missing from kids nowadays.

Maybe it was because his generation hadn't been plugged into all these electronic gadgets and devices . . . pads and pods and phones that were attached at the hip of all his students. Even though the school had a policy of no personal electronics during class time, most of the students managed to bend the rules. It really made him feel crazy at times. What happened to connecting with your friends by looking into their faces while conversing? Or using a phone and hearing a real voice on the other end? He didn't understand these shorthand messages they exchanged, with bad grammar and silly little pictures. And the complaints he got when he explained a letter-writing assignment to his class! You'd think he'd asked them to gouge out their eyeballs—or to destroy their mobile phones.

He'd recently looked out over a classroom only to feel that he was gazing upon a roomful of zombies. It was as if they were all dead inside—just empty shells. He knew he was old-fashioned, but he honestly believed that computer technology had stolen the very souls of this generation. Of course, this had simply confirmed what he knew—it was time to quit.

Melody Carlson is the beloved author of well over two hundred novels. She has been a finalist for or the recipient of many awards, including the *Romantic Times* Career Achievement Award. She lives in central Oregon.

No One Is Too Old to Change Their Lives—
OR FIND A NEW LOVE

George Emerson doesn't want his predictable life to change, but free-spirited ex-hippie Willow West has other plans for him. They may soon discover that no one is too old to change their lives—or find love.

"I've found my new go-to author for *rom-com with heart.*"

—CARLA LAUREANO,
RITA Award–winning author

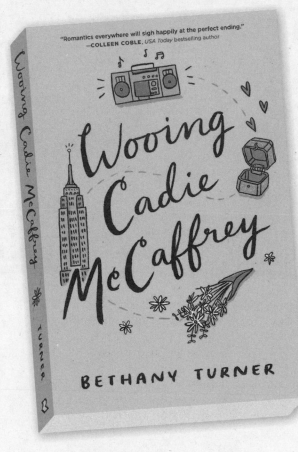

"Romantics everywhere will sigh happily at the perfect ending."
—COLLEEN COBLE, *USA Today* bestselling author

Wooing Cadie McCaffrey

BETHANY TURNER

When Cadie McCaffrey breaks up with her adorably
oblivious boyfriend, he determines to win her back by
pulling out every "foolproof" romantic comedy tactic he's
ever seen. What could go wrong?